PRAISE FOR *COLD FIRE* BY DEAN KOONTZ

"Irresistible. COLD FIRE doesn't disappoint." —*Newsweek*

"A swift, psychospiritual adventure . . . offers plenty of surging suspense and sentiment." —*Kirkus Reviews*

"[Koontz's] name has come to be recognized as a guarantee of a good, solid read. COLD FIRE is his most enjoyable book to date." —*London Times*

"Unforgettable. A stunning showdown."
—*Bowling Green Sentinel-Tribune*

"Koontz is an expert at creating believable characters."
—*Detroit News and Free Press*

"A master storyteller, sometimes humorous, sometimes shocking, but always riveting. His characters sparkle with life. And his fast-paced plots are wonderfully fiendish, taking unexpected twists and turns, yet in the end they are satisfyingly logical." —*San Diego Union*

"Suspenseful, entertaining . . . vivid storytelling [that] offers the reader an unsettling insight into deep trauma and the after-effects of unresolved sorrow." —*Sunday Cape Cod Times*

"A unique, spellbinding novel with depth, sensitivity and personality." —*Boston Herald*

"An exciting, well-conceived story . . . filled with spectacular descriptive scenes . . . creative and captivating."
—*Lansing State Journal*

DEAN KOONTZ
COLD FIRE

BERKLEY BOOKS, NEW YORK

This is a work of fiction. The characters and events described in this book are imaginary and resemblance to actual persons living or dead is purely coincidental.

This Berkley book contains the complete text of the original hardcover edition. It has been completely reset in a typeface designed for easy reading and was printed from new film.

A Berkley Book / published by arrangement with Nkui, Inc.

To Nick and Vicky Page,
who know how to be
good neighbors and friends
—if they would only *try*.
&
Dick and Pat Karlan,
who are among the few
in "Hollywood"
who own their souls
—and always will.

My life is better for
having known you all.
Weirder, but better!

Part One

THE HERO, THE FRIEND

In the real world
as in dreams,
nothing is quite
what it seems.

—THE BOOK OF COUNTED SORROWS

▲

Life without meaning
cannot be borne.
We find a mission
to which we're sworn
—or answer the call
of Death's dark horn.
Without a gleaning
of purpose in life,
we have no vision,
we live in strife,
—or let blood fall
on a suicide knife.

—THE BOOK OF COUNTED SORROWS

AUGUST 12

1

Even before the events in the supermarket, Jim Ironheart should have known trouble was coming. During the night he dreamed of being pursued across a field by a flock of large blackbirds that shrieked around him in a turbulent flapping of wings and tore at him with hooked beaks as precision-honed as surgical scalpels. When he woke and was unable to breathe, he shuffled onto the balcony in his pajama bottoms to get some fresh air. But at nine-thirty in the morning, the temperature, already ninety degrees, only contributed to the sense of suffocation with which he had awakened.

A long shower and a shave refreshed him.

The refrigerator contained only part of a moldering Sara Lee cake. It resembled a laboratory culture of some new, exquisitely virulent strain of botulinus. He could either starve or go out into the furnace heat.

The August day was so torrid that birds, beyond the boundaries of bad dreams, preferred the bowers of the trees to the sun-scorched open spaces of the southern California sky; they sat silently in their leafy shelters, chirruping rarely and without enthusiasm. Dogs padded cat-quick along sidewalks as hot as griddles. No man, woman or child paused to see if an egg would fry on the concrete, taking it as a matter of faith.

After eating a light breakfast at an umbrella-shaded

table on the patio of a seaside cafe in Laguna Beach, he was enervated again and sheathed in a dew of perspiration. It was one of those rare occasions when the Pacific could not produce even a dependable mild breeze.

From there he went to the supermarket, which at first seemed to be a sanctuary. He was wearing only white cotton slacks and a blue T-shirt, so the air-conditioning and the chill currents rising off the refrigerated display cases were refreshing.

He was in the cookie department, comparing the ingredients in fudge macaroons to those in pineapple-coconut-almond bars, trying to decide which was the lesser dietary sin, when the fit hit him. On the scale of such things, it was not much of a fit—no convulsions, no violent muscle contractions, no sudden rivers of sweat, no speaking in strange tongues. He just abruptly turned to a woman shopper next to him and said, "Life line."

She was about thirty, wearing shorts and a halter top, good-looking enough to have experienced a wearying array of come-ons from men, so perhaps she thought he was making a pass at her. She gave him a guarded look. "Excuse me?"

Flow with it, he told himself. Don't be afraid.

He began to shudder, not because of the air-conditioning but because a series of *inner* chills swam through him, like a wriggling school of eels. All the strength went out of his hands, and he dropped the packages of cookies.

Embarrassed but unable to control himself, he repeated: "Life line."

"I don't understand," the woman said.

Although this had happened to him nine times before, he said, "Neither do I."

She clutched a box of vanilla wafers as though she might throw it in his face and run if she decided he was a walking headline (BERSERK MAN SHOOTS SIX IN SUPERMARKET). Nevertheless, she was enough of a good Samaritan to hang in for another exchange: "Are you all right?"

No doubt, he was pale. He felt as if all the blood had drained out of his face. He tried to put on a reassuring smile, knew it was a ghastly grimace, and said, "Gotta go."

Turning away from his shopping cart, Jim walked out of the market, into the searing August heat. The forty-degree temperature change momentarily locked the breath in his lungs. The blacktop in the parking lot was tacky in places. Sun silvered the windshields of the cars and seemed to shatter into dazzling splinters against chrome bumpers and grilles.

He went to his Ford. It had air-conditioning, but even after he had driven across the lot and turned onto Crown Valley Parkway, the draft from the dashboard vents was refreshing only by comparison with the baking-oven atmosphere in the car. He put down his window.

Initially he did not know where he was going. Then he had a vague feeling that he should return home. Rapidly the feeling became a strong hunch, the hunch became a conviction, and the conviction became a compulsion. He absolutely *had* to get home.

He drove too fast, weaving in and out of traffic, taking chances, which was uncharacteristic of him. If a cop had stopped him, he would not have been able to explain his desperate urgency, for he did not understand it himself.

It was as if his every move was orchestrated by someone unseen, controlling him much the way that he controlled the car.

Again he told himself to flow with it, which was easy since he had no choice. He also told himself not to be afraid, but fear was his unshakable companion.

When he pulled into his driveway in Laguna Niguel, the spiky black shadows of palm fronds looked like cracks in the blazing-white stucco walls of his small house, as if the structure had dried out and split open in the heat. The red-tile roof appeared to ripple like overlapping waves of flame.

In his bedroom, sunlight acquired a coppery hue as it poured through the tinted windows. It laid a penny-colored glow in stripes across the bed and off-white carpet, alternating with bands of shade from the half-open plantation shutters.

Jim switched on a bedside lamp.

He didn't know he was going to pack for travel until he found himself taking a suitcase from his closet. He gathered up his shaving gear and toiletries first. He didn't know his destination or how long he would be gone, but he included two changes of clothes. These jobs—adventures, missions, whatever in God's name they were—usually didn't require him to be away more than two or three days.

He hesitated, worried that he had not packed enough. But these trips were dangerous; each could be his last, in which case it didn't matter whether he packed too much or too little.

He closed the suitcase and stared at it, not sure what to do next. Then he said, "Gotta fly," and he knew.

The drive to John Wayne Airport, on the southeastern edge of Santa Ana, took less than half an hour. Along the way he saw subtle reminders that southern California had been a desert before the importation of water through aqueducts. A billboard urged water conservation. Gardeners were installing low-maintenance cactus and ice plant in front of a new Southwestern-style apartment building. Between the greenbelts and the neighborhoods of lushly landscaped properties, the vegetation on undeveloped fields and hills was parched and brown, waiting for the kiss of a match in the trembling hand of one of the pyromaniacs contributing to the annual, devastating wildfire season.

In the main terminal at the airport, travelers streamed to and from the boarding gates. The multi-racial crowd belied the lingering myth that Orange County was culturally bland and populated solely by white Anglo-Saxon Protestants. On his way to the bank of TV monitors that displayed a list of arriving and departing PSA flights, Jim heard four languages besides English.

He read the destinations from top to bottom on the monitor. The next to last city—Portland, Oregon—struck a spark of inspiration in him, and he went straight to the ticket counter.

The clerk who served him was a clean-cut young man, as straight-arrow as a Disneyland employee—at first glance.

"The flight to Portland leaving in twenty minutes," Jim said. "Is it full up?"

The clerk checked the computer. "You're in luck, sir. We have three open seats."

While the clerk processed the credit card and issued the ticket, Jim noticed the guy had pierced ears. He wasn't wearing earrings on the job, but the holes in his lobes were visible enough to indicate that he wore them regularly when he was off duty and that he preferred heavy jewelry. When he returned Jim's credit card, his shirtsleeve pulled up far enough on his right wrist to reveal the snarling muzzle of what appeared to be a lavishly detailed, colorful dragon tattoo that extended up his entire arm. The knuckles of that hand were crusted with scabs, as if they had been skinned in a fight.

All the way to the boarding gate, Jim wondered what subculture the clerk swam in after he shed his uniform at the end of the work day and put on street clothes. He had a hunch the guy was nothing as mundane as a biker punk.

The plane took off to the south, with the merciless glare of the sun at the windows on Jim's side. Then it swung to the west and turned north over the ocean, and he could see the sun only as a reflection in the sea below, where its blazing image seemed to transform the water into a vast churning mass of magma erupting from beneath the planet's crust.

Jim realized he was clenching his teeth. He looked down at the armrests of his seat, where his hands were tightly hooked like the talons of an eagle to the rock of a precarious roost.

He tried to relax.

He was not afraid of flying. What he feared was Portland . . . and whatever form of death might be waiting there for him.

2

Holly Thorne was at a private elementary school on the west side of Portland to interview a teacher, Louise Tarvohl, who had sold a book of poetry to a major New York publisher, not an easy feat in an age when most people's knowledge of poetry was limited to the lyrics of pop songs and occasional rhyming television ads for dog food, underarm deodorant, or steel-belted radial tires. Only a few summer classes were under way. Another instructor assumed responsibility for Louise's kids, so she and Holly could talk.

They sat at a redwood picnic table on the playground, after Holly checked the bench to be sure there was no dirt on it that might stain her white cotton dress. A jungle gym was to their left, a swing set to their right. The day was pleasantly warm, and a breeze stirred an agreeable fragrance from some nearby Douglas firs.

"Smell the air!" Louise took a deep button-popping breath. "You can sure tell we're on the edge of five thousand acres of parkland, huh? So little stain of humanity in the air."

Holly had been given an advance copy of the book, *Soughing Cypress and Other Poems,* when Tom Corvey, the editor of the *Press*'s entertainment section, assigned her to the story. She had wanted to like it. She enjoyed seeing people succeed—perhaps because she had not achieved much in her own career as a journalist and needed to be reminded now and then that success was attainable. Unfortunately the poems were jejune, dismally sentimental celebrations of the natural world that read like something written by a Robert Frost manqué, then filtered through the sensibilities of a Hallmark editor in charge of developing saccharine cards for grandma's birthday.

Nevertheless Holly intended to write an uncritical piece. Over the years she had known far too many reporters who, because of envy or bitterness or a misguided sense of moral superiority, got a kick out of slanting and coloring a story to make their subjects look foolish. Except when dealing with exceptionally vile criminals and politicians, she had never been able to work up enough hatred to write that way—which was one reason her career spiral had spun her down through three major newspapers in three large cities to her current position in the more humble offices of the *Portland Press.* Biased journalism was often more colorful than balanced reporting, sold more papers, and was more widely commented upon and admired. But though she rapidly came to dislike Louise Tarvohl even more than the woman's bad poetry, she could work up no enthusiasm for a hatchet job.

"Only in the wilderness am I alive, far from the sights and sounds of civilization, where I can hear the voices of nature in the trees, in the brush, in the lonely ponds, in the dirt."

Voices in the dirt? Holly thought, and almost laughed.

She liked the way Louise looked: hardy, robust, vital, alive. The woman was thirty-five, Holly's senior by two years, although she appeared ten years older. The crow's-feet around her eyes and mouth, her deep laugh lines, and her leathery sun-browned skin pegged her as an outdoors woman. Her sun-bleached hair was pulled back in a ponytail, and she wore jeans and a checkered blue shirt.

"There is a purity in forest mud," Louise insisted, "that can't be matched in the most thoroughly scrubbed and sterilized hospital surgery." She tilted her face back for a moment to bask in the warm sunfall. "The purity of the natural world cleanses your soul. From that renewed purity of soul comes the sublime vapor of great poetry."

"Sublime vapor?" Holly said, as if she wanted to be sure that her tape recorder would correctly register every golden phrase.

"Sublime vapor," Louise repeated, and smiled.

The inner Louise was the Louise that offended Holly. She had cultivated an otherworldly quality, like a spectral projection, more surface than substance. Her opinions and attitudes were insubstantial, based less on facts and insights than on whims—iron whims, but whims nonetheless—and she expressed them in language that was flamboyant but imprecise, overblown but empty.

Holly was something of an environmentalist herself, and she was dismayed to discover that she and Louise fetched up on the same side of some issues. It was unnerving to have allies who struck you as goofy; it made your own opinions seem suspect.

Louise leaned forward on the picnic bench, folding her arms on the redwood table. "The earth is a living thing. It could talk to us if we were worth talking to, could just open a mouth in any rock or plant or pond and talk as easily as I'm talking to you."

"What an exciting concept," Holly said.

"Human beings are nothing more than lice."

"Lice?"

"Lice crawling over the living earth," Louise said dreamily.

Holly said, "I hadn't thought of it that way."

"God is not only *in* each butterfly—God *is* each butterfly, each bird, each rabbit, every wild thing. I would sacrifice a million human lives—ten million and more!—if it meant saving one innocent family of weasels, because God *is* each of those weasels."

As if moved by the woman's rhetoric, as if she didn't think it was eco-fascism, Holly said, "I give as much as I can every year to the Nature Conservancy, and I think of myself as an environmentalist, but I see that my consciousness hasn't been raised as far as yours."

The poet did not hear the sarcasm and reached across the table to squeeze Holly's hand. "Don't worry, dear. You'll get there. I sense an aura of great spiritual potentiality around you."

"Help me to understand. . . . God is butterflies and rabbits and every living thing, and God is rocks and dirt and water—but God isn't us?"

"No. Because of our one *unnatural* quality."

"Which is?"

"Intelligence."

Holly blinked in surprise. "Intelligence is unnatural?"

"A high degree of intelligence, yes. It exists in no other creatures in the natural world. That's why nature shuns us, and why we subconsciously hate her and seek to obliterate her. High intelligence leads to the concept of progress. Progress leads to nuclear weapons, bio-engineering, chaos, and ultimately to annihilation."

"God . . . or natural evolution didn't give us our intelligence?"

"It was an unanticipated mutation. We're mutants, that's all. Monsters."

Holly said, "Then the less intelligence a creature exhibits . . ."

". . . the more natural it is," Louise finished for her.

Holly nodded thoughtfully, as if seriously considering the bizarre proposition that a dumber world was a better world, but she was really thinking that she could not write this story after all. She found Louise Tarvohl so preposterous that she could not compose a favorable article and still hang on to her integrity. At the same time, she had no heart for making a fool of the woman in print. Holly's problem was not her deep and abiding cynicism but her soft heart; no creature on earth was more certain to suffer frustration and dissatisfaction with life than a bitter cynic with a damp wad of compassion at her core.

She put down her pen, for she would be making no notes. All she wanted to do was get away from Louise, off the playground, back into the real world—even though the real world had always struck her as just slightly less screwy than this encounter. But the least she owed Tom Corvey was sixty to ninety minutes of taped interview, which would provide another reporter with enough material to write the piece.

"Louise," she said, "in light of what you've told me, I think you're the most natural person I've ever met."

Louise didn't get it. Perceiving a compliment instead of a slight, she beamed at Holly.

"Trees are sisters to us," Louise said, eager to reveal another facet of her philosophy, evidently having forgotten that human beings were lice, not trees. "Would you cut off the limbs of your sister, cruelly section her flesh, and build your house with pieces of her corpse?"

"No, I wouldn't," Holly said sincerely. "Besides, the city probably wouldn't approve a building permit for such an unconventional structure."

Holly was safe: Louise had no sense of humor—therefore, no capacity to be offended by the wisecrack.

While the woman prattled on, Holly leaned into the picnic table, feigning interest, and did a fast-backward scan of her entire adult life. She decided that she had spent all of that precious time in the company of idiots, fools, and crooks, listening to their harebrained or sociopathic plans and dreams, searching fruitlessly for nuggets of wisdom and interest in their boobish or psychotic stories.

Increasingly miserable, she began to brood about her personal life. She had made no effort to develop close women friends in Portland, perhaps because in her heart she felt that Portland was only one more stop on her peripatetic journalistic journey. Her experiences with men were, if anything, even more disheartening than her professional experiences with interviewees of both sexes. Though she still hoped to meet the right man, get married, have children, and enjoy a fulfilling domestic life, she wondered if anyone nice, sane, intelligent, and genuinely interesting would ever enter her life.

Probably not.

And if someone like that miraculously crossed her path one day, his pleasant demeanor would no doubt prove to be a mask, and under the mask would be a leering serial killer with a chainsaw fetish.

8

3

Outside the terminal at Portland International Airport, Jim Ironheart got into a taxi operated by something called the New Rose City Cab Company, which sounded like a corporate stepchild of the long-forgotten hippie era, born in the age of love beads and flower power. But the cabbie—Frazier Tooley, according to his displayed license—explained that Portland was called the City of Roses, which bloomed there in multitudes and were meant to be symbols of renewal and growth. "The same way," he said, "that street beggars are symbols of decay and collapse in New York," displaying a curiously charming smugness that Jim sensed was shared by many Portlanders.

Tooley, who looked like an Italian operatic tenor cast from the same mold as Luciano Pavarotti, was not sure he had understood Jim's instructions. "You just want me to drive around for a while?"

"Yeah. I'd like to see some of the city before I check into the hotel. I've never been here before."

The truth was, he didn't know at which hotel he should stay or whether he would be required to do the job soon, tonight, or maybe tomorrow. He hoped that he would learn what was expected of him if he just tried to relax and waited for enlightenment.

Tooley was happy to oblige—not with enlightenment but with a tour of Portland—because a large fare would tick up on the meter, but also because he clearly enjoyed showing off his city. In fact, it was exceptionally attractive. Historic brick structures and nineteenth-century cast-iron-front buildings were carefully preserved among modern glass high rises. Parks full of fountains and trees were so numerous that it sometimes seemed the city was in a forest, and roses were everywhere, not as many blooms as earlier in the summer but radiantly colorful.

After less than half an hour, Jim suddenly was overcome by the feeling that time was running out. He sat forward on the rear seat and heard himself say: "Do you know the McAlbury School?"

"Sure," Tooley said.

"What is it?"

"The way you asked, I thought you knew. Private elementary school over on the west side."

Jim's heart was beating hard and fast. "Take me there."

Frowning at him in the rearview mirror, Tooley said, "Something wrong?"

"I have to be there."

Tooley braked at a red traffic light. He looked over his shoulder. "What's wrong?"

"I just have to be there," Jim said sharply, frustratedly.

"Sure, no sweat."

Fear had rippled through Jim ever since he had spoken the words "life line" to the woman in the supermarket more than four hours ago. Now those ripples swelled into dark waves that carried him toward McAlbury School. With an overwhelming sense of urgency that he could not explain, he said, "I have to be there *in fifteen minutes!*"

"Why didn't you mention it earlier?"

He wanted to say, I didn't *know* earlier. Instead he said, "Can you get me there in time?"

"It'll be tight."

"I'll pay triple the meter."

"Triple?"

"If you make it in time," he said, withdrawing his wallet from his pocket. He extracted a hundred-dollar bill and thrust it at Tooley. "Take this in advance."

"It's that important?"

"It's life and death."

Tooley gave him a look that said: What—are you nuts?

"The light just changed," Jim told him. "Let's move!"

Although Tooley's skeptical frown deepened, he faced front again, hung a left turn at the intersection, and tramped on the accelerator.

Jim kept glancing at his watch all the way, and they arrived at the school with only three minutes to spare. He tossed another bill at Tooley, paying even more than three times the meter, pulled open the door, and scrambled out with his suitcase.

Tooley leaned through his open window. "You want me to wait?"

Slamming the door, Jim said, "No. No, thanks. You can go."

He turned away and heard the taxi drive off as he anxiously studied the front of McAlbury School. The building was actually a rambling white Colonial house with a deep front porch, onto which had been added two single-story wings to provide more classrooms. It was shaded by Douglas firs and huge old sycamores. With its lawn and playground, it occupied the entire length of that short block.

In the house part of the structure directly in front of him, kids were coming out of the double doors, onto the porch, and down the steps. Laughing and chattering, carrying books and large drawing tablets and bright lunchboxes decorated with cartoon characters, they approached him along the school walk, passed through the open gate in the spearpoint iron fence, and turned either uphill or down, moving away from him in both directions.

Two minutes left. He didn't have to look at his watch. His heart was pounding two beats for every second, and he *knew* the time as surely as if he had been a clock.

Sunshine, filtered through the interstices of the arching trees, fell in delicate patterns across the scene and the people in it, as if everything had been draped over with an enormous piece of gossamer lacework stitched from golden thread. That netlike ornamental fabric of light seemed to shimmer in time to the rising and falling music of the children's shouts and laughter, and the moment should have been peaceful, idyllic.

But Death was coming.

Suddenly he knew that Death was coming for one of the children, not for any of the three teachers standing on the porch, just for one child. Not a big catastrophe, not an explosion or fire or a falling airplane that would wipe out a dozen of them. Just one, a small tragedy. But *which* one?

Jim refocused his attention from the scene to the players in it, studying the children as they approached him, seeking the mark of imminent death on one of their fresh young faces. But they all looked as if they would live forever.

"Which one?" he said aloud, speaking neither to himself nor to the children but to. . . . Well, he supposed he was speaking to God. "Which one?"

Some kids went uphill toward the crosswalks at that intersection, and others headed downhill toward the opposite end of the block. In both directions, women crossing guards in bright-orange safety vests, holding big red paddlelike "stop" signs, had begun to shepherd their charges across the streets in small groups. No moving cars or trucks were in sight, so even without the crossing guards there seemed to be little threat from traffic.

One and a half minutes.

Jim scrutinized two yellow vans parked at the curb downhill from him. For the most part, McAlbury seemed to be a neighborhood school, where kids walked to and from their homes, but a few were boarding the vans. The two drivers stood by the doors, smiling and joking with the ebullient, energetic passengers. None of the kids boarding the vans seemed doomed, and the cheery yellow vehicles did not strike him as morgue wagons in bright dress.

But Death was nearer.

It was almost among them.

An ominous change had stolen over the scene, not in reality but in Jim's perception of it. He was now less aware of the golden lacework of light than he was of the shadows within that bright filigree: small shadows the shape of leaves or bristling clusters of evergreen needles; larger shadows the shape of tree trunks or branches; geometric bars of shade from the iron rails of the spearpoint fence. Each blot of darkness seemed to be a potential doorway through which Death might arrive.

One minute.

Frantic, he hurried downhill several steps, among the children, drawing puzzled looks as he glanced at one then another of them, not sure what sort of sign he was searching for, the small suitcase banging against his leg.

Fifty seconds.

The shadows seemed to be growing, spreading, melting together all around Jim.

He stopped, turned, and peered uphill toward the end of the block, where the crossing guard was standing in the intersection, holding up her red "stop" sign, using her free hand to motion the kids across. Five of them were in the street. Another half dozen were approaching the corner and soon to cross.

One of the drivers at the nearby school vans said, "Mister, is something wrong?"

Forty seconds.

Jim dropped the suitcase and ran uphill toward the intersection, still uncertain about what was going to happen and which child was at risk. He was pushed in that direction by the same invisible hand that had made him pack a suitcase and fly to Portland. Startled kids moved out of his way.

At the periphery of his vision, everything had become ink-black. He was aware only of what lay directly ahead of him. From one curb to the other, the intersection appeared to be a scene revealed by a spotlight on an otherwise night-dark stage.

Half a minute.

Two women looked up in surprise and failed to get out of his way fast enough. He tried to dodge them, but he brushed against a blonde in a summery white dress, almost knocking her down. He kept going because he could feel Death among them now, a cold presence.

He reached the intersection, stepped off the curb, and stopped. Four kids in the street. One was going to be a victim. But which of the four? And a victim of what?

Twenty seconds.

The crossing guard was staring at him.

All but one of the kids were nearing the curb, and Jim sensed that the sidewalks were safe territory. The street would be the killing ground.

He moved toward the dawdler, a little red-haired girl, who turned and blinked at him in surprise.

Fifteen seconds.

Not the girl. He looked into her jade-green eyes and knew she was safe. Just *knew* it somehow.

All the other kids had reached the sidewalk.

Fourteen seconds.

Jim spun around and looked back toward the far curb. Four more children had entered the street behind him.

Thirteen seconds.

The four new kids started to arc around him, giving him wary sidelong looks. He knew he appeared to be a little deranged, standing in the street, wide-eyed, gaping at them, his face distorted by fear.

Eleven seconds.

No cars in sight. But the brow of the hill was little more than a hundred yards above the intersection, and maybe some reckless fool was rocketing up the far side with the accelerator jammed to the floorboard. As soon as that image flashed through his mind, Jim knew it was a prophetic glimpse of the instrument Death would use: a drunk driver.

Eight seconds.

He wanted to shout, tell them to run, but maybe he would only panic them and cause the marked child to bolt straight *into* danger rather than away from it.

Seven seconds.

He heard the muffled growl of an engine, which instantly changed to a loud roar, then a piston-shattering scream. A pickup truck shot over the brow of the hill. It actually took flight for an instant, afternoon sun flashing off its windshield and coruscating across its chromework, as if it were a flaming chariot descending from the heavens on judgment day. With a shrill bark of rubber against blacktop, the front tires met the pavement again, and the rear of the truck slammed down with a jarring crash.

Five seconds.

The kids in the street scattered—except for a sandy-haired boy with violet eyes the shade of faded rose petals. He just stood there, holding a lunchbox covered with brightly colored cartoon figures, one tennis shoe untied, watching the truck bear down on him, unable to move, as if he sensed that it wasn't just a truck rushing to meet him but his destiny, inescapable. He was an eight- or nine-year-old boy with nowhere to go but to the grave.

Two seconds.

Leaping directly into the path of the oncoming pickup, Jim grabbed the kid. In what felt like a dream-slow swan dive off a high cliff, he carried the boy with him in a smooth arc to the pavement, rolling toward the leaf-littered gutter, feeling nothing from his impact with the street, his nerves so numbed by terror and adrenaline that he might as well have been tumbling across a field of lush grass and soft loam.

The roar of the truck was the loudest thing he had ever heard, as if it were a thunder *within* him, and he felt something strike his left foot, hard as a hammer blow. In the same instant a terrible wrenching force seemed to wring his ankle as if it were a rag. A white-hot current of pain crackled up his leg, sizzling into his hip joint, exploding in that socket of bone like a Fourth of July bottle rocket bursting in a night sky.

▼ ▲ ▼

Holly started after the man who had collided with her, angry and intending to tell him off. But before she reached the intersection, a gray-and-red pickup erupted over the brow of the hill, as if fired out of a giant slingshot. She halted at the curb.

The scream of the truck engine was a magic incantation

that slowed the flow of time, stretching each second into what seemed to be a minute. From the curb, she saw the stranger sweep the boy out of the path of the pickup, executing the rescue with such singular agility and grace that he almost appeared to be performing a mad, slow-motion ballet in the street. She saw the bumper of the truck strike his left foot, and watched in horror as his shoe was torn off and tossed high into the air, tumbling end over end. Peripherally, she was aware of the man and boy rolling toward the gutter, the truck swerving sharply to the right, the startled crossing guard dropping the paddlelike "stop" sign, the truck ricocheting off a parked car across the street, the man and boy coming to rest against the curb, the truck tipping onto its side and sliding downhill in cascades of yellow and blue sparks—but all the while her attention was focused primarily on that shoe tumbling up, up, into the air, silhouetted against the blue sky, hanging at the apex of its flight for what seemed like an hour, then tumbling slowly, slowly down again. She couldn't look away from it, was mesmerized by it, because she had the macabre feeling that the foot was still in the shoe, torn off at the ankle, bristling with splinters of bone, trailing shorn ribbons of arteries and veins. Down it came, down, down, straight toward her, and she felt a scream swelling in the back of her throat.

Down . . . down . . .

The battered shoe—a Reebok—plopped into the gutter in front of her, and she lowered her eyes to it the way she always looked into the face of the monster in a nightmare, not wanting to see but unable to turn away, equally repelled by and attracted to the unthinkable. The shoe was empty. No severed foot. Not even any blood.

She swallowed the unreleased scream. She tasted vomit in the back of her throat, and swallowed that too.

As the pickup came to rest on its side more than half a block down the hill, Holly turned the other way and ran to the man and boy. She was the first to reach them as they started to sit up on the blacktop.

Except for a scraped palm and a small abrasion on his

chin, the child appeared to be unhurt. He was not even crying.

She dropped to her knees in front of him. "Are you okay, honey?"

Though dazed, the boy understood and nodded. "Yeah. My hand hurts a little, that's all."

The man in the white slacks and blue T-shirt was sitting up. He had rolled his sock halfway off his foot and was gingerly kneading his left ankle. Though the ankle was swollen and already enflamed, Holly was still surprised by the absence of blood.

The crossing guard, a couple of teachers, and other kids gathered around, and a babble of excited voices rose on all sides. The boy was helped up and drawn into a teacher's arms.

Wincing in pain as he continued to massage his ankle, the injured man raised his head and met Holly's gaze. His eyes were searingly blue and, for an instant, appeared as cold as if they were not human eyes at all but the visual receptors of a machine.

Then he smiled. In a blink, the initial impression of coldness was replaced by one of warmth. In fact Holly was overwhelmed by the clarity, morning-sky color, and beauty of his eyes; she felt as if she were peering through them into a gentle soul. She was a cynic who would equally distrust a nun and Mafia boss on first encounter, so her instant attraction to this man was jolting. Though words were her first love and her trade, she was at a loss for them.

"Close call," he said, and his smile elicited one from her.

4

Holly waited for Jim Ironheart in the school hallway, outside the boys' restroom. All of the children and teachers had at last gone home. The building was silent, except for the periodic muffled hum of the maintenance man's electric buffer as he polished the vinyl tile up on the second floor. The air was laced with a faint perfume of chalk dust, craft paste, and pine-scented disinfectant wax.

Outside in the street, the police probably were still overseeing a couple of towing-company employees who were righting the overturned truck in order to haul it away. The driver had been drunk. At the moment he was in the hospital, where physicians were attending to his broken leg, lacerations, abrasions, and contusions.

Holly had gotten nearly everything she required to write the story: background on the boy—Billy Jenkins—who had nearly been killed, the facts of the event, the reactions of the eye-witnesses, a response from the police, and slurred expressions of regret mixed with self-pity from the inebriated driver of the truck. She lacked only one element, but it was the most important—information about Jim Ironheart, the hero of the whole affair. Newspaper readers would want to know everything about him. But at the moment all she could have told them was the guy's name and that he was from southern California.

His brown suitcase stood against the wall beside her, and

she kept eyeing it. She had the urge to pop the latches and explore the contents of the bag, though at first she didn't know why. Then she realized it was unusual for a man to be carrying luggage through a residential neighborhood; a reporter was trained—if not genetically compelled—to be curious about anything out of the ordinary.

When Ironheart came out of the restroom, Holly was still staring at the suitcase. She twitched guiltily, as if caught pawing through the contents of the bag.

"How're you feeling?" she asked.

"Fine." He was limping. "But I told you—I'd rather not be interviewed."

He had combed his thick brown hair and blotted the worst of the dirt off his white cotton pants. He was wearing both shoes again, although the left was torn in one spot and battered.

She said, "I won't take much of your time."

"Definitely," he agreed, smiling.

"Oh, come on, be a good guy."

"Sorry, but I'd make dull copy anyway."

"You just saved a child's life!"

"Other than that, I'm boring."

Something about him belied his claim to dullness, although at first Holly could not pinpoint the reason for his strong appeal. He was about thirty-five, an inch or two under six feet, lean but well-muscled. Though he was attractive enough, he didn't have the looks that made her think of movie stars. His eyes were beautiful, yes, but she was never drawn to a man merely because of his looks and certainly not because of one exceptional feature.

He picked up his suitcase and began to limp along the corridor.

"You should see a doctor," she said, falling in at his side.

"At worst, it's sprained."

"It still should be treated."

"Well, I'll buy an Ace bandage at the airport, or when I get back home."

Maybe his manner was what she found so appealing. He spoke softly, smiled easily, rather like a Southern gentleman, though he had no accent. He also moved with unusual grace even when he was limping. She remembered how she had been reminded of ballet when, with the fluidity of a dancer, he had swept the little boy out of the path of the hurtling truck. Exceptional physical grace and an unforced gentility were appealing in a man. But neither of those qualities was what fascinated her. Something else. Something more elusive.

As they reached the front door, she said, "If you're really intent on going home again, I can give you a ride to the airport."

"Thank you. That's very kind, but I don't need a ride."

She followed him onto the porch. "It's a damned long walk."

He stopped, and frowned. "Oh. Yeah. Well . . . there's got to be a phone here. I'll call a cab."

"Come on, you don't have to be afraid of me. I'm not a serial killer. I don't keep a chainsaw in my car."

He stared at her a beat, then grinned disarmingly. "Actually, you look more like the type who favors bludgeoning with a blunt instrument."

"I'm a reporter. We use switchblades. But I haven't killed anyone this week."

"Last week?"

"Two. But they were both door-to-door salesmen."

"It's still homicide."

"Justifiable, though."

"Okay, I accept your offer."

Her blue Toyota was at the far curb, two back from the parked car into which the drunk driver had slammed. Downhill, the tow truck was just hauling away the totaled pickup, and the last of the policemen was getting into a patrol car. A few overlooked splinters of tempered glass from the truck's broken windows still glimmered on the blacktop in the late-afternoon sunshine.

They rode for a block or so in silence.

Then Holly said, "You have friends in Portland?"

"Yeah. From college."

"That's who you were staying with?"

"Yeah."

"They couldn't take you to the airport?"

"They could've if it was a morning flight, but this afternoon they were both at work."

"Ah," she said. She commented on clusters of brilliant yellow roses that hung from vines entwining a split-rail fence at a house they passed, and asked if he knew that Portland called itself the City of Roses, which he did. After another silence, she returned to the *real* conversation: "Their phone wasn't working, huh?"

"Excuse me?"

"Your friends." She shrugged. "I just wondered why you didn't call a cab from their place."

"I intended to walk."

"To the airport?"

"My ankle was fine then."

"It's still a long walk."

"Oh, but I'm a fitness nut."

"Very long walk—especially with a suitcase."

"It's not that heavy. When I'm exercising, I usually walk with handweights to get an upper-body workout."

"I'm a walker myself," she said, braking for a red light. "I used to run every morning, but my knees started hurting."

"Mine too, so I switched to walking. Gives your heart the same workout if you keep up your pace."

For a couple of miles, while she drove as slowly as she dared in order to extend the time she had with him, they chatted about physical fitness and fat-free foods. Eventually he said something that allowed her to ask, with complete naturalness, the names of his friends there in Portland.

"No," he said.

"No what?"

"No, I'm not giving you their names. They're private people, nice people, I don't want them being pestered."

"I've never been called a pest before," she said.

"No offense, Miss Thorne, but I just wouldn't want

them to have to be in the paper and everything, have their lives disrupted."

"Lots of people *like* seeing their names in the newspaper."

"Lots don't."

"They might enjoy talking about their friend, the big hero."

"Sorry," he said affably, and smiled.

She was beginning to understand why she found him so appealing: his unshakable poise was irresistible. Having worked for two years in Los Angeles, Holly had known a lot of men who styled themselves as laid-back Californians; each portrayed himself as the epitome of self-possession, Mr. Mellow—*rely on me, baby, and the world can never touch either of us; we are beyond the reach of fate*—but none actually possessed the cool nerves and unflappable temperament to which he pretended. A Bruce Willis wardrobe, perfect tan, and studied insouciance did not a Bruce Willis make. Self-confidence could be gained through experience, but real aplomb was something you were either born with or learned to imitate—and the imitation was never convincing to the observant eye. However, Jim Ironheart had been born with enough aplomb, if rationed equally to all the men in Rhode Island, to produce an entire state of cool, unflappable types. He faced hurtling trucks and a reporter's questions with the same degree of equanimity. Just being in his company was oddly relaxing and reassuring.

She said, "That's an interesting name you have."

"Jim?"

He was having fun with her.

"Ironheart," she said. "Sounds like an American Indian name."

"Wouldn't mind having a little Chippewa or Apache blood, make me less dull, a little bit exotic, mysterious. But it's just the Anglicized version of the family's original German name—Eisenherz."

By the time they were on the East Portland Freeway, rapidly approaching the Killingsworth Street exit, Holly was dismayed at the prospect of dropping him at the airline terminal. As a reporter, she still had a lot of unanswered questions. More important, as a woman, she was more intrigued by him than she had been by any man in ages. She briefly considered taking a far more circuitous route to the airport; his lack of familiarity with the city might disguise her deception. Then she realized that the freeway signs were already announcing the upcoming exit to Portland International; even if he had not been reading them, he could not have failed to notice the steady air traffic in the deep-blue eastern sky ahead of them.

She said, "What do you do down there in California?"

"Enjoy life."

"I meant—what do you do for a living?"

"What's your guess?" he asked.

"Well . . . one thing for sure: you're not a librarian."

"Why do you say that?"

"You have a sense of mystery about you."

"Can't a librarian be mysterious?"

"I've never known one who was." Reluctantly she turned onto the airport exit ramp. "Maybe you're a cop of some kind."

"What gives you that idea?"

"Really good cops are unflappable, cool."

"Gee, I think of myself as a warm sort of guy, open and easy. You think I'm cool?"

Traffic was moderately heavy on the airport approach road. She let it slow her even further.

"I mean," she said, "that you're very self-possessed."

"How long have you been a reporter?"

"Twelve years."

"All of it in Portland?"

"No. I've been here a year."

"Where'd you work before?"

"Chicago . . . Los Angeles . . . Seattle."

"You like journalism?"

Realizing that she had lost control of the conversation, Holly said, "This isn't a game of twenty questions, you know."

"Oh," he said, clearly amused, "that's exactly what I thought it was."

She was frustrated by the impenetrable wall he had erected around himself, irritated by his stubbornness. She was not used to having her will thwarted. But he had no meanness in him, as far as she could see, and no great talent for deception; he was just determined to preserve his privacy. As a reporter who had ever-increasing doubts about a journalist's right to intrude in the lives of others, Holly sympathized with his reticence. When she glanced at him, she could only laugh softly. "You're good."

"So are you."

As she stopped at the curb in front of the terminal, Holly said, "No, if I were good, by now I'd at least have found out what the hell you do for a living."

He had a charming smile. And those *eyes*. "I didn't say you were as good as I am—just that you were good." He got out and retrieved his suitcase from the back seat, then returned to the open front door. "Look, I just happened to be in the right place at the right time. By sheer chance, I was able to save that boy. It wouldn't be fair to have my whole life turned upside down by the media just because I did a good deed."

"No, it wouldn't," she agreed.

With a look of relief, he said, "Thank you."

"But I gotta say—your modesty's refreshing."

He looked at her for a long beat, fixed her with his exceptional blue eyes. "So are you, Miss Thorne."

Then he closed the door, turned away, and entered the terminal.

Their last exchange played again in her mind:

Your modesty's refreshing.

So are you, Miss Thorne.

She stared at the terminal door through which he had disappeared, and he seemed too good to have been real, as if she had given a ride to a hitchhiking spirit. A thin haze filtered flecks of color from the late-afternoon sunlight, so the air had a vague golden cast of the kind that sometimes hung for an instant in the wake of a vanishing revenant in an old movie about ghosts.

A hard, hollow rapping noise startled her.

She snapped her head around and saw an airport security guard tapping with his knuckles on the hood of her car. When he had her attention, he pointed to a sign: LOADING ZONE.

Wondering how long she had sat there, mesmerized by thoughts of Jim Ironheart, Holly released the emergency brake and slipped the car in gear. She drove away from the terminal.

Your modesty's refreshing.

So are you, Miss Thorne.

All the way back into Portland, a sense of the uncanny lay upon her, a perception that someone preternaturally special had passed through her life. She was unsettled by the discovery that a man could so affect her, and she felt uncomfortably girlish, even foolish. At the same time, she enjoyed that pleasantly eerie mood and did not want it to fade.

So are you, Miss Thorne.

5

That evening, in her third-floor apartment overlooking Council Crest Park, as she was cooking a dinner of angel-hair pasta with pesto sauce, pine nuts, fresh garlic, and chopped tomatoes, Holly suddenly wondered how Jim Ironheart could have known that young Billy Jenkins was in danger even before the drunken driver in the pickup truck had appeared over the crest of the hill.

She stopped chopping in the middle of a tomato and looked out the kitchen window. Purple-red twilight was settling over the greensward below. Among the trees, the park lamps cast pools of warm amber light on the grass-flanked walkways.

When Ironheart had charged up the sidewalk in front of McAlbury School, colliding with her and nearly knocking her down, Holly started after him, intending to tell him off. By the time she reached the intersection, he was already in the street, turning right then left, looking a little agitated . . . wild. In fact he seemed so strange, the kids moved around him in a wide arc. She had registered his panicked expression and the kids' reaction to him a second or two *before* the truck had erupted over the crest like a daredevil's car flying off the top of a stunt ramp. Only then had Ironheart focused on Billy Jenkins, scooping the boy out of the path of the truck.

Perhaps he had heard the roar of the engine, realized

something was approaching the intersection at reckless speed, and acted out of an instinctive perception of danger. Holly tried to remember if she had been aware of the racing engine as early as when Ironheart had collided with her, but she could not recall. Maybe she had heard it but had not been as alert to its meaning as he had. Or perhaps she hadn't heard it at all because she had been trying to shake off the indefatigable Louise Tarvohl, who had insisted on walking with her to her car; she had felt that she'd go stark raving mad if she were forced to listen to even another minute of the poet's chatter, and she had been distracted by the desperate need to escape.

Now, in he· kitchen, she was conscious of only one sound: the vigorously boiling water in the big pot on the stove. She should turn the gas down, put in the pasta, set the timer. . . . Instead she stood at the cutting board, tomato in one hand and knife in the other, staring out at the park but seeing the fateful intersection near the McAlbury School.

Even if Ironheart had heard the approaching engine from halfway down the block, how could he so quickly determine the direction from which the truck was approaching, that its driver was out of control, and that the children were consequently in danger? The crossing guard, initially much closer to the sound than Ironheart, had been taken by surprise, as had the kids themselves.

Okay, well, some people had sharper senses than others—which was why composers of symphonies could hear more complex harmonies and rhythms in music than could the average concertgoer, why some baseball players could see a pop fly against a glary sky sooner than others, and why a master viniculturist could appreciate subtler qualities of a rare vintage than could a stoned-blind wino who was only concerned with the effect. Likewise, some people had far quicker reflexes than others, which was part of what made Wayne Gretzky worth millions a year to a professional ice-hockey team. She had seen that Ironheart had the lightning reflexes of an athlete. No doubt he was also blessed with especially keen hearing. Most people with a notable physical advantage also had other gifts: it was all a matter of good genes. That was the explanation. Simple enough. Nothing unusual. Nothing mysterious. Certainly nothing supernatural. Just good genes.

Outside in the park, the shadows grew deeper. Except at those places where lamplight was shed upon it, the pathway disappeared into gathering darkness. The trees seemed to crowd together.

Holly put down the knife and went to the stove. She lowered the gas flame under the big pot, and the vigorously bubbling water fell to a slow boil. She put the pasta in to cook.

Back at the cutting board, as she picked up the knife, she looked out the window again. Stars began to appear in the sky as the purple light of dusk faded to black and as the crimson smear on the horizon darkened to burgundy. Below, more of the park walkway lay in shadow than in lamplight.

Suddenly she was gripped by the peculiar conviction that Jim Ironheart was going to walk out of darkness into a pool of amber light on the pathway, that he was going to raise his head and look directly up at her window, that somehow he knew where she lived and had come back for her. It was a ridiculous notion. But a chill quivered along her spine, tightening each knotted vertebra.

▼▲▼

Later, near midnight, when Holly sat on the edge of her bed and switched off the nightstand lamp, she glanced at her bedroom window, through which she also had a view of the park, and again a chill ran up her back. She started to lie down, hesitated, and got up instead. In panties and T-shirt, her usual sleeping attire, she moved through the dark room to the window, where she parted the sheers between the drapes.

He was not down there. She waited a minute, then another. He did not appear. Feeling foolish and confused, she returned to bed.

▼▲▼
▲

She woke in the dead hours of the night, shuddering. All she could remember of the dream were blue eyes, intensely blue, with a gaze that penetrated her as completely as a sharp knife slicing through soft butter.

She got up and went into the bathroom, guided only by the thin wash of moonglow that filtered through the sheers over the window. In the bathroom she did not turn on the light. After she peed, she washed her hands and stood for a while just looking at her dim, amorphous reflection in the silvery-black mirror. She washed her hands. She got a drink of cold water. She realized that she was delaying her return to the bedroom because she was afraid she would be drawn to the window again.

This is ridiculous, she told herself. What's gotten into you?

She reentered the bedroom and found herself approaching the window instead of the bed. She parted the sheers.

He was not out there.

Holly felt as much disappointment as relief. As she stared into the night-swaddled reaches of Council Crest Park, an extended chill quivered through her again, and she realized that only half of it was generated by a nameless fear. A strange excitement coursed through her, as well, a pleasant anticipation of . . .

Of what?

She didn't know.

Jim Ironheart's effect on her was profound and lingering. She had never experienced anything like it. Although she struggled to understand what she was feeling, enlightenment eluded her. Mere sexual attraction was not the explanation. She was long past puberty, and neither the tidal pull of hormones nor the girlish desire for romance could affect her like this.

At last she returned to bed. She was certain that she would lie awake for the rest of the night, but to her surprise she soon drifted off again. As she trembled on the wire of

COLD FIRE ▲ 35

consciousness, she heard herself mumble, *"those eyes,"* then fell into the yawning void.

▼▲▼

In his own bed in Laguna Niguel, Jim woke just before dawn. His heart was pounding. Though the room was cool, he was bathed in sweat. He'd been having one of his frequent nightmares, but all he could recall of it was that something relentless, powerful, and vicious had been pursuing him . . .

His sense of onrushing death was so powerful that he had to turn on the lights to be certain that something inhuman and murderous was not actually in the room with him. He was alone.

"But not for long," he said aloud.

He wondered what he meant by that.

AUGUST 20 THROUGH AUGUST 22

1

Jim Ironheart peered anxiously through the dirty windshield of the stolen Camaro. The sun was a white ball, and the light it shed was as white and bitter as powdered lime. Even with sunglasses, he had to squint. Rising off sunscorched blacktop, currents of superheated air formed into mirages of people and cars and lakes of water.

He was tired, and his eyes felt abraded. The heat illusions combined with occasional dust devils to hamper visibility. The endless vistas of the Mojave Desert made it difficult to maintain an accurate perception of speed; he didn't *feel* as if the car was streaking along at nearly a hundred miles an hour, but it was. In his condition, he should have been driving a lot slower.

But he was filled with a growing conviction that he was too late, that he was going to screw up. Someone was going to die because he had not been quick enough.

He glanced at the loaded shotgun angled in front of the other bucket seat, its butt on the floor, barrels pointed away from him. A full box of shells was on the seat.

Half sick with dread, he pressed the accelerator even closer to the floorboard. The needle on the speedometer dial shivered past the hundred mark.

He topped a long, gradual rise. Below lay a bowl-shaped valley twenty or thirty miles in diameter, so alkaline that it was mostly white, barren but for a few gray tumbleweeds and a stubble of desert scrub. It might have been formed by an asteroid impact eons ago, its outlines considerably softened by the passage of millennia but otherwise still as primeval as any place on earth.

The valley was bisected by the black highway on which mirages of water glistened. Along the shoulders, heat phantoms shimmered and writhed languorously.

He saw the car first, a station wagon. It was pulled off to the right of the roadway, approximately a mile ahead, near a drainage culvert where no water flowed except during rare storms and flash floods.

His heart began to pound harder, and in spite of the rush of cool air coming out of the dashboard vents, he broke into a sweat. *This* was the place.

Then he spotted the motor home, too, half a mile beyond the car, surfacing out of one of the deeper water mirages. It was lumbering away from him, toward the distant wall of the valley, where the highway sloped up between treeless, red-rock mountains.

Jim slowed as he approached the station wagon, not sure where his help was needed. His attention was drawn equally to the wagon and the motor home.

As the speedometer needle fell back across the gauge, he waited for a clearer understanding of his purpose. It didn't come. Usually he was compelled to act, as if by an inner voice that spoke to him only on a subconscious level, or as if he were a machine responding to a pre-programmed course of action. Not this time. Nothing.

With growing desperation, he braked hard and fishtailed to a full stop next to the Chevy station wagon. He didn't bother to pull onto the shoulder. He glanced at the shotgun beside him, but he knew somehow that he did not need it. Yet.

He got out of the Camaro and hurried toward the station wagon. Luggage was piled in the rear cargo area. When he looked through the side window, he saw a man sprawled on the front seat. He pulled open the door—and flinched. So much blood.

The guy was dying but not dead. He had been shot twice

in the chest. His head lay at an angle against the passenger-side door, reminding Jim of Christ's head tilted to one side as he hung upon the cross. His eyes cleared briefly as he struggled to focus on Jim.

In a voice as frantic as it was fragile, he said, "Lisa . . . Susie . . . My wife, daughter . . ."

Then his tortured eyes slipped out of focus. A thin wheeze of breath escaped him, his head lolled to one side, and he was gone.

Sick, stricken by an almost disabling sense of responsibility for the stranger's death, Jim stepped back from the open door of the station wagon and stood for a moment on the black pavement under the searing white sun. If he had driven faster, harder, he might have been there a few minutes sooner, might have stopped what had happened.

A sound of anguish, low and primitive, rose from him. It was almost a whisper at first, swelling into a soft moan. But when he turned away from the dead man and looked down the highway toward the dwindling motor home, his cry quickly became a shout of rage because suddenly he knew what had happened.

And he knew what he must do.

In the Camaro again, he filled the roomy pockets of his blue cotton slacks with shotgun shells. Already loaded, the short-barreled pump-action 12-gauge was within easy reach.

He checked the rearview mirror. On this Monday morning, the desert highway was empty. No help in sight. It was all up to him.

Far ahead, the motor home vanished through shimmering thermal currents like undulant curtains of glass beads.

He threw the Camaro in gear. The tires spun in place for an instant, then skidded on the clutching sun-softened blacktop, issuing a scream that echoed eerily across the desert vastness. Jim wondered how the stranger and his family had screamed when he'd been shot point-blank in the chest. Abruptly the Camaro overcame all resistance and rocketed forward.

Tramping the accelerator to the floor, he squinted ahead

to catch a glimpse of his quarry. In seconds the curtains of heat parted, and the big vehicle hove into view as if it were a sailing ship somehow making way on that dry sea.

The motor home couldn't compete with the Camaro, and Jim was soon riding its bumper. It was an old thirty-foot Roadking that had seen a lot of miles. Its white aluminum siding was caked with dirt, dented, and rust-spotted. The windows were covered with yellow curtains that had no doubt once been white. It looked like nothing more than the home of a couple of travel-loving retirees living on dwindling Social Security assets, unable to maintain it with the pride they had when it had been new.

Except for the motorcycle. A Harley was chained to a wrought-iron rack to the left of the roof-service ladder on the back of the motor home. It wasn't the biggest bike made, but it was powerful—and not something that a pair of retirees typically tooled around on.

In spite of the cycle, nothing about the Roadking was suspicious. Yet in its wake Jim Ironheart was overcome by a sense of evil so strong that it might as well have been a black tide washing over him with all the power of the sea behind it. He gagged as if he could smell the corruption of those to whom the motor home belonged.

At first he hesitated, afraid that any action he took might jeopardize the woman and child who were evidently being held captive. But the riskiest thing he could do was delay. The longer the mother and daughter were in the hands of the people in the Roadking, the less chance they had of coming out of it alive.

He swung into the passing lane. He intended to get a couple of miles ahead of them and block the road with his car.

In the Roadking's rearview mirror, the driver must have seen Jim stop at the station wagon and get out to inspect it. Now he let the Camaro pull almost even before swinging the motor home sharply left, bashing it against the side of the car.

Metal shrieked against metal, and the car shuddered.

The steering wheel spun in Jim's hands. He fought for control and kept it.

The Roadking pulled away, then swerved back and bashed him again, driving him off the blacktop and onto the unpaved shoulder. For a few hundred yards they rattled forward at high speed in those positions: the Roadking in the wrong lane, risking a head-on collision with any oncoming traffic that might be masked by the curtains of heat and sun glare; the Camaro casting up huge clouds of dust behind it, speeding precariously along the brink of the two-foot drop-off that separated the raised roadbed from the desert floor beyond.

Even a light touch of the brakes might pull the car a few inches to the left, causing it to drop and roll. He only dared to ease up on the accelerator and let his speed fall gradually.

The driver of the Roadking reacted, reducing his speed, too, hanging at Jim's side. Then the motor home moved inexorably to the left, inch by inch, edging relentlessly onto the dirt shoulder.

Being much the smaller and less powerful of the two vehicles, the Camaro could not resist the pressure. It was pushed leftward in spite of Jim's efforts to hold it steady. The front tire found the brink first, and that corner of the car dropped. He hit the brakes; it didn't matter anymore. Even as he jammed his foot down on the pedal, the rear wheel followed the front end into empty space. The Camaro tipped and rolled to the left.

Using a safety harness was a habit with him, so he was thrown sideways and forward, and his sunglasses flew off, but he didn't crack his face against the window post or shatter his breastbone against the steering wheel. Webs of cracks, like the work of a spider on Benzedrine, spread across the windshield. He squeezed his eyes shut, and gummy bits of tempered glass imploded over him. The car rolled again, then started to roll a third time but only made it halfway, coming to rest on its roof.

Hanging upside down in the harness, he was unhurt but

badly shaken. He choked on the clouds of white dust that poured in through the shattered windshield.

They'll be coming for me.

He fumbled frantically for the harness release, found it, and dropped the last few inches onto the ceiling of the overturned car. He was curled on top of the shotgun. He had been damn lucky the weapon hadn't discharged as it slammed around inside the tumbling Camaro.

Coming for me.

Disoriented, he needed a moment to find the door handle, which was over his head. He reached up, released it. At first the door would not open. Then it swung outward with a metallic popping and squeaking.

He crawled off the ceiling, out onto the floor of the desert, feeling as if he had become trapped in a surreal Daliesque world of weird perspectives. He reached back in for the shotgun.

Though the ash-fine dust was beginning to settle, he was still coughing it out of his lungs. Clenching his teeth, he tried to swallow each cough. He needed to be quiet if he were to survive.

Neither as quick nor as inconspicuous as the small desert lizards that scooted across his path, Jim stayed low and dashed to a nearby arroyo. When he arrived at the edge of that natural drainage channel, he discovered it was only about four feet deep. He slid over the lip, and his feet made a soft slapping sound as they hit the hard-packed bottom.

Crouching in that shallow declivity, he raised his head slowly to ground level and looked across the desert floor toward the overturned Camaro, around which the haze of alkaline dust had not yet entirely dissipated. On the highway, the Roadking finished reversing along the pavement and halted parallel to the wrecked car.

The door opened, and a man climbed out. Another man, having exited from the far side, hurried around the front of the motor home to join his companion. Neither of them was the kindly-retiree-on-a-budget that one might have imagined behind the wheel of that aging caravan. They appeared to be in their early thirties and as hard as heat-tempered desert rock. One of them wore his dark hair pulled back and knotted into a redoubled ponytail—the passé style that kids now called a "dork knob." The other had short spiky hair on top, but his head was shaved on the sides—as if he thought he was in one of those old Mad Max movies. Both wore sleeveless T-shirts, jeans, and cowboy boots, and both carried handguns. They headed cautiously toward the Camaro, splitting up to approach it from opposite ends.

Jim drew down below the top of the arroyo, turned right—which was approximately west—and hurried in a crouch along the shallow channel. He glanced back to see if he was leaving a trail, but the silt, baked under months of fierce sun since the last rain, did not take footprints. After about fifty feet, the arroyo abruptly angled to the south, left. Sixty feet thereafter, it disappeared into a culvert that led under the highway.

Hope swept through him but did not still the tremors of fear that had shaken him continuously since he had found the dying man in the station wagon. He felt as if he was going to puke. But he had not eaten breakfast and had nothing to toss up. No matter what the nutritionists said, sometimes it paid to skip a meal.

Full of deep shade, the concrete culvert was comparatively cool. He was tempted to stop and hide there—and hope they would give up, go away.

He couldn't do that, of course. He wasn't a coward. But even if his conscience had allowed him to buy into a little cowardice this time, the mysterious force driving him would not permit him to cut and run. To some extent, he was a marionette on strings invisible, at the mercy of a puppeteer unseen, in a puppet-theater play with a plot he could not understand and a theme that eluded him.

A few tumbleweeds had found their way into the culvert, and their brittle spines raked him as he shoved through the barrier they had formed. He came out on the other side of the highway, into another arm of the arroyo, and scrambled up the wall of that parched channel.

Lying belly-flat on the desert floor, he slithered to the

edge of the elevated roadbed and eased up to look across the pavement, east toward the motor home. Beyond the Roadking, he could see the Camaro like a dead roach on its back. The two men were standing near it, together now. Evidently, they had just checked the car and knew he was not in it.

They were talking animatedly, but they were too far away for Jim to hear what they were saying. A couple of words carried to him, but they were faded by distance and distorted by the furnace-dry air.

Sweat kept trickling into his eyes, blurring his vision. He blotted his face with his sleeve and squinted at the men again.

They were moving slowly away from the Camaro now, deeper into the desert. One of them was wary, swiveling his head from side to side, and the other studied the ground as they moved, no doubt searching for signs of Jim's passage. Just his luck, one of them would turn out to have been raised by Indian scouts, and they'd be all over him faster than an iguana on a sand beetle.

From the west came the sound of an engine, low at first but growing rapidly louder even as Jim turned his head to look in that direction. Out of a waterfall mirage came a Peterbilt. From Jim's low vantage point, the truck looked so huge that it didn't even seem like a truck but like some futuristic war machine that had traveled backward in time from the twenty-second century.

The driver of the Peterbilt would see the overturned Camaro. In the traditional Samaritan spirit that most truckers showed on the road, he would stop to offer assistance. His arrival would rattle the two killers, and while they were distracted, Jim would get the drop on them.

He had it all figured out—except it didn't work that way. The Peterbilt didn't slow as it approached, and Jim realized he was going to have to flag it down. But before he could even rise up, the big truck swept past with a dragon roar and a blast of hot wind, breaking the speed limit by a Guinness margin, as if it were a judgment wagon driven by a demon and loaded with souls that the devil wanted in hell *right now.*

Jim fought the urge to leap up and yell after it: Where's your traditional Samaritan spirit, you shithead?

Silence returned to the hot day.

On the far side of the road, the two killers looked after the Peterbilt for a moment, then continued their search for Jim.

Furious and scared, he eased back from the shoulder of the highway, flattened out again, and belly-crawled eastward toward the motor home, dragging the shotgun with him. The elevated roadbed was between him and them; they could not possibly see him, yet he more than half expected them to sprint across the blacktop and pump half a dozen rounds into him.

When he dared look up again, he was directly opposite the parked Roadking, which blocked the two men from his view. If he couldn't see them, they couldn't see him. He scrambled to his feet and crossed the pavement to the passenger side of the motor home.

The door on that flank was a third of the way from the front bumper to the rear, not opposite the driver's door. It was ajar.

He took hold of the handle. Then he realized that a third man might have stayed inside with the woman and girl. He couldn't risk going in there until he had dealt with the two outside, for he might be trapped between gunmen.

He moved to the front of the Roadking, and just as he reached the corner, he heard voices approaching. He froze, waiting for the guy with the weird haircut to come around the front bumper. But they stopped on the other side.

"—who gives a shit—"

"—but he mighta seen our license number—"

"—chances are, he's bad hurt—"

"—wasn't no blood in the car—"

Jim sank to one knee by the tire, looked under the vehicle. They were standing on the other side, near the driver's door.

"—we just take the next southbound—"

"—with cops on our tail—"

"—by the time he gets to any cops, we'll be in Arizona—"

"—you hope—"

"—I *know*—"

Rising, moving cautiously, Jim slipped around the front corner of the Roadking. He eased past the first pair of headlights and the engine hatch.

"—cut across Arizona into New Mexico—"

"—they got cops, too—"

"—into Texas, put a few states between us, drive all night if we have to—"

Jim was grateful that the shoulder of the highway was dirt rather than loose gravel. He crept silently across it to the driver's-side headlights, staying low.

"—you know what piss-poor cooperation they got across state lines—"

"—he's out there somewhere, damn it—"

"—so're a million scorpions and rattlesnakes—"

Jim stepped around to their side of the motor home, covering them with the shotgun. "Don't move!"

For an instant they gaped at him the way *he* might have stared at a three-eyed Martian with a mouth in its forehead. They were only about eight feet away, close enough to spit on, which they looked like they deserved. At a distance they had appeared as dangerous as snakes with legs, and they still looked deadlier than anything that slithered in the desert.

They were holding their handguns, pointed at the ground. Jim thrust the shotgun at them and shouted, "Drop 'em, damn it!"

Either they were the hardest of hard cases or they were nuts—probably both—because they didn't freeze at the sight of the shotgun. The guy with the redoubled ponytail flung himself to the ground and rolled. Simultaneously, the refugee from *Road Warrior* brought up his pistol, and Jim pumped a round into the guy's chest at point-blank range, blowing him backward and down and all the way to hell.

The survivor's feet vanished as he wriggled under the Roadking.

To avoid being shot in the foot and ankle, Jim grabbed the open door and jumped onto the step beside the driver's seat. Even as his feet left the ground, two shots boomed from under the motor home, and one of them punctured the tire beside which he'd been standing.

Instead of retreating into the Roadking, he dropped back to the ground, fell flat, and shoved the shotgun under the vehicle, figuring to take his adversary by surprise. But the guy was already out from under on the other side. Jim could see only the black cowboy boots hurrying toward the rear of the motor home. The guy turned the corner—and vanished.

The ladder. At the right rear corner. Next to the racked motorcycle.

The bastard was going onto the roof.

Jim hustled all the way under the Roadking before the killer could look over the edge of the roof, spot him, and fire down. It was no cooler beneath the vehicle, because the sun-scorched earthen shoulder radiated the heat it had been storing up since dawn.

Two cars roared by on the highway, one close after the other. He hadn't heard them coming, maybe because his heart was beating so hard that he felt as if he were inside a kettle drum. He cursed the motorists under his breath, then realized they couldn't be expected to stop when they saw a guy like Dork Knob prowling the top of the motor home with a handgun.

He had a better chance of winning if he continued to do the unexpected, so he immediately crawled on his belly, fast as a marine under fire, to the rear of the Roadking. He twisted onto his back, eased his head out past the rear bumper, and peered up across the Harley, at the ascending rungs that appeared to dwindle into blazing white sun.

The ladder was empty. The killer was already on the roof. He might think that he had temporarily mystified his pursuer with his vanishing act, and in any case he wouldn't expect to be followed with utter recklessness.

Jim slid all the way into the open and went up the ladder. He gripped the hot siderail with one hand, holding the compact shotgun with the other, trying to ascend as soundlessly as possible. His adversary was surprisingly quiet on the aluminum surface above, making barely enough noises of his own to cover an occasional pop and squeak from the aged rungs under Jim's feet.

At the top, Jim cautiously raised his head and squinted across the roof. The killer was two-thirds of the way toward the front of the Roadking, at the right side, looking down. He was moving along on hands and knees, which must have hurt; although the time-stained white paint reflected a lot of the sun, it had stored sufficient heat to sting even well-callused hands and to penetrate blue denim. But if the guy was in pain, he didn't show it; he was evidently as suicidally macho as his dead buddy had been.

Jim eased up another rung.

The killer actually lowered himself onto his belly, though the roof must have scorched instantly through his thin T-shirt. He was trying to maintain as low a profile as possible, waiting for Jim to appear below.

Jim eased up one more rung. The roof now met him at mid-torso. He turned sideways on the ladder and jammed one knee behind the outer upright, wedging himself in place so he would have both hands for the shotgun and so the recoil would not knock him backward to the ground.

If the guy on the roof didn't have a sixth sense, then he was just damned lucky. Jim had not made a sound, but the creep suddenly glanced back over his shoulder and spotted him.

Cursing, Jim swung the shotgun around.

The killer flung himself sideways, off the roof.

Without getting in a shot, Jim pulled his knee from behind the upright and jumped from the ladder. He hit the ground hard but kept his balance, stepped around the corner of the motor home, and squeezed off one round.

But the creep was already bolting through the side door. At worst, he caught a few pellets in one leg. Probably not even that.

He was going after the woman and child.

Hostages.

Or maybe he just wanted to slaughter them before he was cut down himself. The past couple of decades had seen the rise of the vagabond sociopath, roaming the country, looking for easy prey, racking up long lists of victims, attaining sexual release as much from brutal murder as from rape.

In his mind, Jim heard the anguished voice of the dying man in the station wagon: *Lisa . . . Susie . . . My wife, daughter . . .*

With no time for caution, his anger having grown greater than his fear, he raced after the killer, through the door, into the Roadking, entering aft of the cockpit. His sun-dazzled eyes couldn't handle the comparative gloom of the motor home's interior, but he was able to see the psychotic sonofabitch heading toward the rear of the motor home, past the lounge area and into the galley.

A shadowy figure now, with just a dark oval for a face, the killer turned and fired. The slug tore a chunk out of a wall-hung storage cabinet to the left of Jim, showering him with splinters of Formica and smoking particle board.

He didn't know where the woman and child were. He was afraid of hitting them. A shotgun wasn't a precise weapon.

The killer fired again. The second bullet passed so close to Jim's face that it left a wake of stinging-hot wind, like a kiss of fire burning across his right cheek.

He pumped out one round, and the blast shook the tinny walls. The killer screamed and was flung hard against the kitchen sink. Jim fired again, reflexively, half-deafened by the double explosion. The guy was virtually lifted off his feet, hurled backward, slammed against the rear wall, beside a closed door that separated the main living area from the bedroom. Then he dropped.

Grabbing a couple of shells from his pants pocket, reloading the shotgun magazine, Jim moved deeper into the Roadking, past a tattered and sagging sofa.

He knew the man had to be dead, but he could not see

COLD FIRE ▲ 49

well enough to be certain of anything. Though shafts of the
Mojave sun shoved in like hot branding irons through the
windshield and the open doors, the heavily draped side
windows insured that the rear of the Roadking was filled
with shadows, and there was a thin acrid haze of smoke
from all the gunfire.

When he reached the end of the narrow chamber and
looked down, he had no doubt that the man crumpled on
the floor was dead. Bloody human garbage. Garbage alive,
now garbage dead.

At the sight of the torn and battered corpse, a savage
elation gripped him, a furious righteousness that was both
thrilling and frightening. He wanted to be sickened by
what he had done, even if the dead man had deserved to
die, but although the carnage nauseated him, he was not
morally repulsed. He had encountered purest evil in
human form. Both these bastards deserved worse than he
had been able to do to them, deserved long and slow deaths
with great suffering, much terror. He felt like an avenging
angel, come to judgment, filled with a holy rage. He knew
he was teetering on the edge of a psychosis of his own,
knew that only the insane were unreservedly certain of the
virtue of even their most outrageous acts, but he could find
no doubt within him. In fact his anger swelled as if he were
God's avatar into whom flowed a direct current of the
Almighty's apocalyptic wrath.

He turned to the closed door.

The bedroom lay beyond.

The mother and child had to be in there.

Lisa . . . Susie . . .

But who else?

Sociopathic killers usually operated alone, but sometimes they paired up as these two had done. Larger al-
liances, however, were rare. Charles Manson and his
"family," of course. There were other examples. He
couldn't rule anything out, not in a world where the trendi-
est professors of philosophy taught that ethics were always
situational and that everyone's point of view was equally
right and valuable, regardless of its logic or hate quotient.

It was a world that bred monsters, and this beast might be hydra-headed.

He knew caution was called for, but the exhilarating righteous wrath that filled him also gave him a sense of invulnerability. He stepped to the bedroom door, kicked it open, and shouldered through, knowing he might be gut-shot, not giving a damn, shotgun in front of him, ready to kill and be killed.

The woman and child were alone. On the filthy bed. Bound at wrists and ankles with sturdy strapping tape. Tape across their mouths.

The woman, Lisa, was about thirty, slim, an unusually attractive blonde. But the daughter, Susie, was remarkably more beautiful than her mother, ethereally beautiful: about ten years old, with luminous green eyes, delicate features, and skin as flawless as the membranous interior surface of an eggshell. The girl seemed, to Jim, to be an embodiment of innocence, goodness, and purity—an angel cast down into a cesspool. New power informed his rage at the sight of her bound and gagged in the bedroom's squalor.

Tears streamed down the child's face, and she choked on muffled sobs of terror behind the tape that sealed her lips. The mother was not crying, though grief and fear haunted her eyes. Her sense of responsibility to her daughter—and a visible rage not unlike Jim's—seemed to keep her from falling over the brink of hysteria.

He realized they were afraid of him. As far as they knew, he was in league with the men who had abducted them.

As he propped the shotgun against the built-in dresser, he said, "It's all right. It's over now. I killed them. I killed them both."

The mother stared at him wide-eyed, disbelieving.

He didn't blame her for doubting him. His voice sounded strange: full of fury, cracking on every third or fourth word, tremulous, going from a whisper to a hard bark to a whisper again.

He looked around for something with which to cut them

free. A roll of the strapping tape and a pair of scissors lay on the dresser.

Grabbing the scissors, he noticed X-rated videotapes also stacked on the dresser. Suddenly he realized that the walls and ceiling of the small room were papered with obscene photographs torn from the pages of sex magazines, and with a jolt he saw it was filth with a twisted difference: child pornography. There were grown men in the photos, their faces always concealed, but there were no grown women, only young girls and boys, most of them as young as Susie, many of them younger, being brutalized in every way imaginable.

The men he had killed would have used the mother only briefly, would have raped and tortured and broken her only as an example to the child. Then they would have cut her throat or blown her brains out on some desolate dirt road out in the desert, leaving her body for the delectation of lizards and ants and vultures. It was the child they really wanted, and for whom they would have made the next few months or years a living hell.

His anger metastasized into something beyond mere rage, far beyond wrath. A terrible darkness rose inside of him like black crude oil gushing up from a wellhead.

He was furious that the child had seen those photographs, had been forced to lie in those stained and foul-smelling bedclothes with unspeakable obscenity on every side of her. He had the crazy urge to pick up the shotgun and empty a few more rounds into each of the dead men.

They had not touched her. Thank God for that. They hadn't had time to touch her.

But the room. Oh, Jesus, she had suffered an assault just by being in that room.

He was shaking.

He saw that the mother was shaking, too.

After a moment he realized that her tremors were not of rage, like his, but of fear. Fear of *him*. She was terrified of him, more so now than when he had come into the room.

He was glad there was no mirror. He would not have

wanted to see his own face. Right now there must be some kind of madness in it.

He had to get a grip on himself.

"It's all right," he assured her again. "I came to help you."

Eager to free them, anxious to quiet their terror, he dropped to his knees beside the bed and cut the tape that was wound around the woman's ankles, tore it away. He snipped the tape around her wrists, as well, then left her to finish freeing herself.

When he cut the bindings from Susie's wrists, she hugged herself defensively. When he freed her ankles, she kicked at him and squirmed away across the gray and mottled sheets. He didn't reach for her, but backed off instead.

Lisa peeled the tape off her lips and pulled a rag out of her mouth, choking and gagging. She spoke in a raspy voice that was somehow simultaneously frantic and resigned: "My husband, back at the car, my husband!"

Jim looked at her and said nothing, unable to put such bleak news into words in front of the child.

The woman saw the truth in his eyes, and for a moment her lovely face was wrenched into a mask of grief and agony. But for the sake of her daughter, she fought down the sob, swallowed it along with her anguish.

She said only, "Oh, my God," and each word reverberated with her loss.

"Can you carry Susie?"

Her mind was on her dead husband.

He said, "Can you carry Susie?"

She blinked in confusion. "How do you know her name?"

"Your husband told me."

"But—"

"Before," he said sharply, meaning *before he died*, not wanting to give false hope. "Can you carry her out of here?"

"Yeah, I think so, maybe."

He could have carried the girl himself, but he didn't

believe that he should touch her. Though it was irrational and emotional, he felt that what those two men had done to her—and what they *would* have done to her, given a chance—was somehow the responsibility of all men, and that at least a small stain of guilt was his as well.

Right now, the only man in the world who should touch that child was her father. And he was dead.

Jim rose from his knees and edged away from the bed. He backed into a narrow closet door that sprang open as he stepped aside of it.

On the bed, the weeping girl squirmed away from her mother, so traumatized that she did not at first recognize the benign intention of even those familiar loving hands. Then abruptly she shattered the chains of terror and flew into her mother's arms. Lisa spoke softly and reassuringly to her daughter, stroked her hair, held her tight.

The air-conditioning had been off ever since the killers had parked and gone to check the wrecked Camaro. The bedroom was growing hotter by the second, and it stank. He smelled stale beer, sweat, what might have been the lingering odor of dried blood rising from dark maroon stains on the carpet, and other foul odors that he dared not even try to identify.

"Come on, let's get out of here."

Lisa did not appear to be a strong woman, but she lifted her daughter as effortlessly as she would have lifted a pillow. With the girl cradled in her arms, she moved toward the door.

"Don't let her look to the left when you go out," he said. "One of them's dead just beside the door. It isn't pretty."

Lisa nodded once, with evident gratitude for the warning.

As he started to follow her through the doorway, he saw the contents of the narrow closet that had come open when he'd backed against it: shelves of homemade videotapes. On the spines were titles hand-printed on strips of white adhesive tape. Names. The titles were all names. CINDY. TIFFANY. JOEY. CISSY. TOMMY. KEVIN. Two were labeled SALLY. Three were labeled WENDY. More names. Maybe thirty in all. He knew what he was looking at, but he didn't want to believe it. Memories of savagery. Mementoes of perversion. Victims.

The bitter blackness welled higher in him.

He followed Lisa through the motor home to the door, and out into the blazing desert sun.

2

Lisa stood in the white-gold sunshine on the shoulder of the highway, behind the motor home. Her daughter stood at her side, clung to her. Light had an affinity for them: it slipped in scintillant currents through their flaxen hair, accented the color of their eyes much the way a jeweler's display lamp enhanced the beauty of emeralds on velvet, and lent an almost mystical luminosity to their skin. Looking at them, it was difficult to believe that the light around them was not within them, too, and that a darkness had entered their lives and filled them as completely as night filled the world in the wake of dusk.

Jim could barely endure their presence. Each time he glanced at them, he thought of the dead man in the station wagon, and sympathetic grief twisted through him, as painful as any physical illness he had ever known.

Using a key that he found on a ring with the motor home ignition key, he unlocked the iron rack that held the Harley-Davidson. It was an FXRS-SP with a 1340cc. single-carburetor, two-valve, push-rod V-twin with a five-speed transmission that powered the rear wheel through a toothed belt instead of a greasy chain. He'd ridden fancier and more powerful machines. This one was standard, about as plain as a Harley could get. But all he wanted from the bike was speed and easy handling; and if it was in good repair, the SP would provide him with both.

Lisa spoke worriedly to him as he unracked the Harley and looked it over. "Three of us can't ride out of here on that."

"No," he said. "Just me."

"Please don't leave us alone."

"Someone'll stop for you before I go."

A car approached. The three occupants gawked at them. The driver put on more speed.

"None of them stop," she said miserably.

"Someone will. I'll wait until they do."

She was silent a moment. Then: "I don't want to get into a car with strangers."

"We'll see who stops."

She shook her head violently.

He said, "I'll know if they're trustworthy."

"I don't . . ." Her voice broke. She hesitated, regained control. "I don't trust anyone."

"There are good people in the world. In fact, most of them are good. Anyway, when they stop, I'll know if they're okay."

"How? How in God's name can you know?"

"I'll know." But he could not explain the *how* of it any more than he could explain how he had known that she and her daughter needed him out here in this sere and blistered wasteland.

He straddled the Harley and pressed the starter button. The engine kicked in at once. He revved it a little, then shut it off.

The woman said, "Who are you?"

"I can't tell you that."

"But why not?"

"This one's too sensational. It'll make nationwide head-lines."

"I don't understand."

"They'd splash my picture everywhere. I like my pri-vacy."

A small utility rack was bolted to the back of the Harley. Jim used his belt to strap the shotgun to it.

With a tremor of vulnerability in her voice that broke his heart, Lisa said, "We owe you so much."

He looked at her, then at Susie. The girl had one slender arm around her mother, clinging tightly. She was not listening to their conversation. Her eyes were out of focus, blank—and her mind seemed far away. Her free hand was at her mouth, and she was chewing on her knuckle; she had actually broken the skin and drawn her own blood.

He averted his eyes and stared down at the cycle again.

"You don't owe me anything," he said.

"But you saved—"

"Not everyone," he said quickly. "Not everyone I *should* have."

The distant growl of an approaching car drew their attention to the east. They watched a souped-up black Trans Am swim out of the water mirages. With a screech of brakes, it stopped in front of them. Red flames were painted on the fender back of the front wheel, and the rims of both the wheel v. .¹¹s were protected with fancy chrome trim. Fat twin chrome tailpipes glistered like liquid mercury in the fierce desert sun.

The driver got out. He was about thirty. His thick black hair was combed away from his face, full on the sides, a ducktail in back. He was wearing jeans and a white T-shirt with the sleeves rolled up to reveal tattoos on both biceps.

"Somethin' wrong here?" he asked across the car.

Jim stared at him for a beat, then said, "These people need a ride to the nearest town."

As the man came around the Trans Am, the passenger door opened, and a woman got out. She was a couple of years younger than her companion, dressed in baggy tan shorts, a white halter top, and a white bandana. Unruly dyed-blond hair sprayed out around that piece of headgear, framing a face so heavily made up that it looked like a testing ground for Max Factor. She wore too much clunky costume jewelry, as well: big dangling silver earrings; three strands of glass beads in different shades of red; two bracelets on each wrist, a watch, and four rings. On the upper slope of her left breast was a blue and pink butterfly tattoo.

"You break down?" she asked.

Jim said, "The motor home has a flat."

"I'm Frank," the guy said. "This is Verna." He was chewing gum. "I'll help you fix the tire."

Jim shook his head. "We can't use the motor home anyway. There's a dead man in it."

"Dead man?"

"And another one over there," Jim said, gesturing beyond the Roadking.

Verna was wide-eyed.

Frank stopped chewing his gum for a beat, glanced at the shotgun on the Harley rack, then looked at Jim again. "You kill them?"

"Yeah. Because they kidnapped this woman and her child."

Frank studied him a moment, then glanced at Lisa. "That true?" he asked her.

She nodded.

"Jesus jumpin' catfish," Verna said.

Jim glanced at Susie. She was in another world, and she would need some professional help to reenter this one. He was certain she couldn't hear a thing they said.

Curiously, he felt as detached as the child looked. He was still sinking into that internal darkness, and before long it would swallow him completely. He told Frank: "These guys I killed—they wasted the husband . . . the father. His body's in a station wagon a couple of miles west of here."

"Oh, shit," Frank said, "that's a rough one."

Verna drew against Frank's side and shuddered.

"I want you to take them to the nearest town, fast as you can. Get medical attention for them. Then contact the state police, get them out here."

"Sure," Frank said.

But Lisa said, "Wait . . . no . . . I can't . . ." Jim went to her, and she whispered to him: "They look like . . . I can't. . . . I'm just afraid . . ."

Jim put a hand on her shoulder, stared directly into her eyes. "Things aren't always what they appear to be. Frank and Verna are okay. You trust me?"

"Yes. Now. Of course."

"Then believe me. You can trust them."

"But how can you know?" she asked, her voice breaking.

"I *know*," he said firmly.

She continued to meet his eyes for a few seconds, then nodded and said, "All right."

The rest was easy. As docile as if she had been drugged, Susie allowed herself to be lifted into the back seat. Her mother joined her there, cuddled her. When Frank was behind the wheel again and Verna at his side, Jim gratefully accepted a can of root beer from their ice chest. Then he closed Verna's door, leaned down to the open window, and thanked her and Frank.

"You're not waitin' here for the cops, are you?" Frank asked.

"No."

"You're not in trouble, you know. You're the hero here."

"I know. But I'm not waiting."

Frank nodded. "You got your reasons, I guess. You want us to say you was a bald guy with dark eyes, hitched a ride with a trucker going east?"

"No. Don't lie. Don't lie for me."

"Whatever you want," Frank said.

Verna said, "Don't worry. We'll take good care of them."

"I know you will," Jim said.

He drank the root beer and watched the Trans Am until it had driven out of sight.

He climbed on the Harley, thumbed the starter button, used the long heavy shift to slide the gearwheel into place, rolled in a little throttle, released the clutch, and rode across the highway. He went off the shoulder, down the slight incline, onto the floor of the desert, and headed directly south into the immense and inhospitable Mojave.

For a while he rode at over seventy miles an hour, though he had no protection from the wind because the SP had no fairing. He was badly buffeted, and his eyes filled repeatedly with tears that he tr ed to blame entirely on the raw, hot air that assaulted him.

Strangely, he did not mind the heat. In fact he didn't even feel it. He was sweating, yet he felt cool.

He lost track of time. Perhaps an hour had passed when he realized that he had left the plains and was moving across barren hills the color of rust. He reduced his speed. His route was now filled with twists and turns between rocky outcroppings, but the SP was the machine for it. It had two inches more suspension travel fore and aft than did the regular FXRS, with compatible spring and shock rates, plus twin disc brakes on the front—which meant he could corner like a stunt rider when the terrain threw surprises at him.

After a while he was no longer cool. He was *cold.*

The sun seemed to be fading, though he knew it was still early afternoon. Darkness was closing on him from within.

Eventually he stopped in the shadow of a rock monolith about a quarter of a mile long and three hundred feet high. Weathered into eerie shapes by ages of wind and sun and by the rare but torrential rains that swept the Mojave, the formation thrust out of the desert floor like the ruins of an ancient temple now half-buried in sand.

He propped the Harley on its kickstand.

He sat down on the shaded earth.

After a moment he stretched out on his side. He drew up his knees. He folded his arms across his chest.

He had stopped not a moment too soon. The darkness filled him completely, and he fell away into an abyss of despair.

3

Later, in the last hour of daylight, he found himself on the Harley again, riding across gray and rose-colored flats where clumps of mesquite bristled. Dead, sun-blackened tumbleweed chased him in a breeze that smelled like powdered iron and salt.

He vaguely remembered breaking open a cactus and sucking the moisture out of the water-heavy pulp at the core of the plant, but he was dry again. Desperately thirsty.

As he came over a gentle rise and throttled down a little, he saw a small town about two miles ahead, buildings clustered along a highway. A scattering of trees looked supernaturally lush after the desolation—physical and spiritual—through which he had traveled for the past several hours. Half convinced that the town was only an apparition, he angled toward it nevertheless.

Suddenly, silhouetted against a sky that was growing purple and red with the onset of twilight, the spire of a church appeared, a cross at its pinnacle. Though he realized that he was to some extent delirious and that his delirium was at least partly related to serious dehydration, Jim turned at once toward the church. He felt as if he needed the solace of its interior spaces more than he needed water.

Half a mile from the town, he rode the Harley into an arroyo and left it there on its side. The soft sand walls of the channel gave way easily under his hands, and he quickly covered the bike.

He had assumed he could walk the last half mile with relative ease. But he was worse off than he had realized. His vision swam in and out of focus. His lips burned, his tongue stuck to the roof of his dry mouth, and his throat was sore—as if he were in the grip of a virulent fever. The muscles in his legs began to cramp and throb, and each foot seemed to be encased in a concrete boot.

He must have blacked out on his feet, because the next thing he knew, he was on the brick steps of the white clapboard church, with no recollection of the last few hundred yards of his journey. The words OUR LADY OF THE DESERT were on a brass plaque beside the double doors.

He had been a Catholic once. In a part of his heart, he still was a Catholic. He had been many things—Methodist, Jew, Buddhist, Baptist, Moslem, Hindu, Taoist, more— and although he was no longer any of them in practice, he was still all of them in experience.

Though the door seemed to weigh more than the boulder that had covered the mouth of Christ's tomb, he managed to pull it open. He went inside.

The church was much cooler than the twilit Mojave, but not really cool. It smelled of myrrh and spikenard and the slightly sweetish odor of burning votive candles, causing memories of his Catholic days to flood back to him, making him feel at home.

At the doorway between narthex and nave, he dipped two fingers in the holy-water font and crossed himself. He cupped his hands in the cool liquid, brought them to his mouth, and drank. The water tasted like blood. He looked into the white marble basin in horror, certain that it was brimming with gore, but he saw only water and the dim, shimmering reflection of his own face.

He realized that his parched and stinging lips were split. He licked them. The blood was his own.

Then he found himself on his knees at the front of the nave, leaning against the sanctuary railing, praying, and he did not know how he had gotten there. Must have blacked out again.

The last of the day had blown away as if it were a pale skin of dust, and a hot night wind pressed at the church windows. The only illumination was from a bulb in the narthex, the flickering flames of half a dozen votive candles in red-glass containers, and a small spotlight shining down on the crucifix.

Jim saw that his own face was painted on the figure of Christ. He blinked his burning eyes and looked again. This time he saw the face of the dead man in the station wagon. The sacred countenance metamorphosed into the face of Jim's mother, his father, the child named Susie, Lisa—and then it was no face at all, just a black oval, as the killer's face had been a black oval when he had turned to shoot at Jim inside the shadow-filled Roadking.

Indeed, it wasn't Christ on the cross now, it *was* the killer. He opened his eyes, looked at Jim, and smiled. He jerked his feet free of the vertical support, a nail still bristling from one of them, a black nail hole in the other. He wrenched his hands free, too, a spike still piercing each palm, and he just *drifted* down to the floor, as if gravity had no claim on him except what he chose to allow it. He started across the altar platform toward the railing, toward Jim.

Jim's heart was racing, but he told himself that what he saw was only a delusion. The product of a fevered mind. Nothing more.

The killer reached him. Touched his face. The hand was as soft as rotting meat and as cold as a liquid gas.

Like a true believer in a tent revival, collapsing under the empowered hand of a faith healer, Jim shivered and fell away into darkness.

4

A white-walled room.

A narrow bed.

Spare and humble furnishings.

Night at the windows.

He drifted in and out of bad dreams. Each time that he regained consciousness, which was never for longer than a minute or two, he saw the same man hovering over him: about fifty, balding, slightly plump, with thick eyebrows and a squashed nose.

Sometimes the stranger gently worked an ointment into Jim's face, and sometimes he applied compresses soaked in ice water. He lifted Jim's head off the pillows and encouraged him to drink cool water through a straw. Because the man's eyes were marked by concern and kindness, Jim did not protest.

Besides, he had neither the voice nor the energy to protest. His throat felt as if he had swallowed kerosene and then a match. He did not have the strength even to lift a hand an inch off the sheets.

"Just rest," the stranger said. "You're suffering heatstroke and a bad sunburn."

Windburn. That's the worst of it, Jim thought, remembering the Harley SP, which had not been equipped with a Plexiglas fairing for weather protection.

▼▲▼

Light at the windows. A new day.

His eyes were sore.

His face felt worse than ever. Swollen.

The stranger was wearing a clerical collar.

"Priest," Jim said in a coarse and whispery voice that didn't sound like his own.

"I found you in the church, unconscious."

"Our Lady of the Desert."

Lifting Jim off the pillows again, he said, "That's right. I'm Father Geary. Leo Geary."

Jim was able to help himself a little this time. The water tasted sweet.

Father Geary said, "What were you doing in the desert?"

"Wandering."

"Why?"

Jim didn't answer.

"Where did you come from?"

Jim said nothing.

"What is your name?"

"Jim."

"You're not carrying any ID."

"Not this time, no."

"What do you mean by that?"

Jim was silent.

The priest said, "There was three thousand dollars in cash in your pockets."

"Take what you need."

The priest stared at him, then smiled. "Better be careful what you offer, son. This is a poor church. We need all we can get."

▼▲▼

Later still, Jim woke again. The priest was not there. The house was silent. Once in a while a rafter creaked and a window rattled softly as desert wind stirred fitfully outside.

When the priest returned, Jim said, "A question, Father."

"What's that?"

His voice was still raspy, but he sounded a bit more like himself. "If there's a God, why does He allow suffering?"

Alarmed, Father Geary said, "Are you feeling worse?"

"No, no. Better. I don't mean my suffering. Just . . . why does He allow suffering in general?"

"To test us," the priest said.

"Why do we have to be tested?"

"To determine if we're worthy."

"Worthy of what?"

"Worthy of heaven, of course. Salvation. Eternal life."

"Why didn't God *make* us worthy?"

"Yes, he made us perfect, without sin. But then we sinned, and fell from grace."

"How could we sin if we were perfect?"

"Because we have free will."

"I don't understand."

Father Geary frowned. "I'm not a nimble theologian. Just an ordinary priest. All I can tell you is that it's part of the divine mystery. We fell from grace, and now heaven must be earned."

"I need to pee," Jim said.

"All right."

"Not the bedpan this time. I think I can make it to the bathroom with your help."

"I think maybe you can, too. You're really coming around nicely, thank God."

"Free will," Jim said.

The priest frowned.

▼▲▼

By late afternoon, nearly twenty-four hours after Jim stumbled into the church, his fever registered only three-tenths of a degree on the thermometer. His muscles were no longer spasming, his joints did not hurt any more, he was not dizzy, and his chest did not ache when he drew a deep breath. Pain still flared across his face periodically.

When he spoke he did so without moving his facial muscles more than absolutely necessary, because the cracks in his lips and in the corners of his mouth reopened easily in spite of the prescription cortisone cream that Father Geary applied every few hours.

He could sit up in bed of his own volition and move about the room with only minimal help. When his appetite returned, as well, Father Geary gave him chicken soup, then vanilla ice cream. He ate carefully, mindful of his split lips, trying to avoid tainting the food with the taste of his own blood.

"I'm still hungry," Jim said when he finished.

"Let's see if you can keep that down first."

"I'm fine. It was only sunstroke, dehydration."

"Sunstroke can kill, son. You need more rest."

When the priest relented a while later and brought him more ice cream, Jim spoke through half-clenched teeth and frozen lips: "Why are some people killers? Not cops, I mean. Not soldiers. Not those who kill in self-defense. The other kind, the murderers. Why do they kill?"

Settling into a straight-backed rocker near the bed, the priest regarded him with one raised eyebrow. "That's a peculiar question."

"Is it? Maybe. Do you have an answer?"

"The simple one is—because there's evil in them."

They sat in mutual silence for a minute or so. Jim ate ice cream, and the stocky priest rocked in his chair. Another twilight crept across the sky beyond the windows.

Finally Jim said, "Murder, accidents, disease, old age . . . Why did God make us mortal in the first place? Why do we have to die?"

"Death's not the end. Or at least that's what I believe. Death is only our means of passage, only the train that conveys us to our reward."

"Heaven, you mean."

The priest hesitated. "Or the other."

Jim slept for a couple of hours. When he woke, he saw the priest standing at the foot of the bed, watching him intently.

"You were talking in your sleep."

Jim sat up in bed. "Was I? What'd I say?"

" 'There is an enemy.' "

"That's all I said?"

"Then you said, 'It's coming. It'll kill us all.' "

A shiver of dread passed through Jim, not because the words had any power of themselves, and not because he understood them, but because he sensed that on a subconscious level he knew all too well what he had meant.

He said, "A dream, I guess. A bad dream. That's all."

But shortly past three o'clock in the morning, during that second night in the rectory, he thrashed awake, sat straight up in bed, and heard the words escaping him again, *"It'll kill us all."*

The room was lightless.

He fumbled for the lamp, switched it on.

He was alone.

He looked at the windows. Darkness beyond.

He had the bizarre but unshakable feeling that something hideous and merciless had been hovering near, something infinitely more savage and strange than anyone in recorded history had ever seen, dreamed, or imagined. Trembling, he got out of bed. He was wearing an ill-fitting pair of the priest's pajamas. For a moment he just stood there, not sure what to do.

Then he switched off the light and, barefoot, went to one window, then the other. He was on the second floor. The night was silent, deep, and peaceful. If something had been out there, it was gone now.

5

The following morning, he dressed in his own clothes, which Father Geary had laundered for him. He spent most of the day in the living room, in a big easy chair, his feet propped on a hassock, reading magazines and dozing, while the priest tended to parish business.

Jim's sunburnt and wind-abraded face was stiffening. Like a mask.

That evening, they prepared dinner together. At the kitchen sink, Father Geary cleaned lettuce, celery, and tomatoes for a salad. Jim set the table, opened a bottle of cheap Chianti to let it breathe, then sliced canned mushrooms into a pot of spaghetti sauce on the stove.

They worked in a comfortable mutual silence, and Jim wondered about the curious relationship that had evolved between them. There had been a dreamlike quality to the past couple of days, as if he had not merely found refuge in a small desert town but in a place of peace outside the real world, a town in the Twilight Zone. The priest had stopped asking questions. In fact, it now seemed to Jim that Father Geary had never been half as probing or insistent as the circumstances warranted. And he suspected that the priest's Christian hospitality did not usually extend to the boarding of injured and suspicious strangers. Why he should receive special consideration at Geary's hands was a mystery to him, but he was grateful for it.

When he had sliced half the mushrooms in the can, he suddenly said, "Life line."

Father Geary turned from the sink, a stalk of celery in hand. "Pardon me?"

A chill swept through Jim, and he almost dropped the knife into the sauce. He put it on the counter.

"Jim?"

Shivering, he turned to the priest and said, "I've got to get to an airport."

"An airport?"

"Right away, Father."

The priest's plump face dimpled with perplexion, wrinkling his tanned forehead far past his long-vanished hairline. "But there's no airport here."

"How far to the nearest one?" Jim asked urgently.

"Well . . . two hours by car. All the way to Las Vegas."

"You've got to drive me there."

"What? Now?"

"Right now," Jim said.

"But—"

"I have to get to Boston."

"But you've been ill—"

"I'm better now."

"Your face—"

"It hurts, and it looks like hell, but it's not fatal. Father, I *have* to get to Boston."

"Why?"

He hesitated, then decided on a degree of revelation. "If I don't get to Boston, someone there is going to be killed. Someone who shouldn't die."

"Who? Who's going to die?"

Jim licked his peeling lips. "I don't know."

"You don't know?"

"But I will when I get there."

Father Geary stared at him for a long time. At last he said, "Jim, you're the strangest man I've ever known."

Jim nodded. "I'm the strangest man *I've* ever known."

▼▲▼

When they set out from the rectory in the priest's six-year-old Toyota, an hour of light remained in the long August day, although the sun was hidden behind clouds the color of fresh bruises.

They had been on the road only half an hour when lightning shattered the bleak sky and danced on jagged legs across the somber desert horizon. Flash after flash erupted, sharper and brighter in the pure Mojave air than Jim had ever seen lightning elsewhere. Ten minutes later, the sky grew darker and lower, and rain fell in silvery cataracts the equal of anything that Noah had witnessed while hurrying to complete his ark.

"Summer storms are rare here," Father Geary said, switching on the windshield wipers.

"We can't let it delay us," Jim said worriedly.

"I'll get you there," the priest assured him.

"There can't be that many flights east from Vegas at night. They'd mostly leave during the day. I can't miss out and wait till morning. I've got to be in Boston *tomorrow.*"

The parched sand soaked up the deluge. But some areas were rocky or hard-packed from months of blistering sun, and in those places the water spilled off slopes, forming rivulets in every shallow declivity. Rivulets became streams, and streams grew swiftly into rivers, until every bridged arroyo they passed over was soon filled with roiling, churning torrents on which were borne clumps of uprooted desert bunch-grass, fragments of dead tumbleweed, driftwood, and dirty white foam.

Father Geary had two favorite cassette tapes, which he kept in the car: a collection of rock-'n'-roll golden oldies, and an Elton John best-of. He put on Elton. They moved through the storm-hammered day then through the rain-swept night to the melodies of "Funeral for a Friend," "Daniel," and "Benny and the Jets."

The blacktop glimmered with quicksilver puddles. To Jim, it was eerie that the water mirages on the highway a few days ago had now become real.

He grew more tense by the minute. Boston called to him, but it was far away, and few things were darker or more treacherous than a blacktop highway through a storm-wracked desert at night. Unless, perhaps, the human heart.

The priest hunched over the wheel as he drove. He studied the highway intently while singing along softly with Elton.

After a while Jim said, "Father, wasn't there a doctor in town?"

"Yes."

"But you didn't call him."

"I got the cortisone prescription from him."

"I saw the tube. It was a prescription for you, made out three months ago."

"Well . . . I've seen sunstroke before. I knew I could treat you."

"But you seemed awfully worried there at first."

The priest was silent for a few miles. Then he said, "I don't know who you are, where you come from, or why you really need to get to Boston. But I do know you're a man in trouble, maybe deep trouble, as deep as it ever gets. And I know . . . at least, I *think* I know that you're a good man at heart. Anyway, it seemed to me that a man in trouble would want to keep a low profile."

"Thanks. I do."

A couple of miles farther, the rain came down hard enough to overwhelm the windshield wipers and force Geary to reduce speed.

The priest said, "You're the one who saved that woman and her little girl."

Jim tensed but did not respond.

"You fit the description on TV," the priest said.

They were silent for a few more miles.

Father Geary said, "I'm not a sucker for miracles."

Jim was baffled by that statement.

Father Geary switched off Elton John. The only sounds were the swish-hum of the tires on the wet pavement and the metronomic thump of the windshield wipers.

"I believe that the miracles of the Bible happened, yes, I accept all of that as real history," the priest said, keeping his eyes on the road. "But I'm reluctant to believe that some statue of the Holy Mother wept real tears in a church in Cincinnati or Peoria or Teaneck last week after the Wednesday-night bingo games, witnessed only by two teenagers and the parish cleaning lady. And I'm not ready to believe that a shadow resembling Jesus, cast on someone's garage wall by a yellow bug light, is a sign of impending apocalypse. God works in mysterious ways, but not with bug lights and garage walls."

The priest fell silent again, and Jim waited, wondering where all this was leading.

"When I found you in the church, lying by the sanctuary railing," Geary said in a voice that grew more haunted word by word, "you were marked by the stigmata of Christ. There was a nail hole in each of your hands—"

Jim looked at his hands and saw no wounds.

"—and your forehead was scratched and prickled with what might have been punctures from a crown of thorns."

His face was still such a mess from the punishment of sun and wind that it was no use searching in the rearview mirror for the minor injuries the priest had described.

Geary said, "I was . . . frightened, I guess. But fascinated, too."

They came to a forty-foot-long concrete bridge at an arroyo where the runoff had overflowed the banks. A dark lake had formed and risen above the edge of the elevated roadbed. Geary bulled forward. Plumes of water, reflecting the car's lights, unfurled on both sides like great white wings.

"I'd never seen stigmata," Geary continued when they were out of the flooded area, "though I'd heard of the phenomenon. I pulled up your shirt . . . looked at your side . . . and found the enflamed scar of what might have been a spear wound."

The events of recent months had been so filled with surprises and amazements that the threshold on Jim's sense of wonder had been raised repeatedly. But the priest's story leaped across it, got to him, and sent a chill of awe along his spine.

Geary's voice had fallen to little more than a whisper.

"By the time I got you back to the rectory and into bed, those signs were gone. But I knew I hadn't imagined them. I'd seen them, they'd been real, and I knew there was something special about you."

The lightning had fizzled out long ago; the black sky was no longer adorned by bright, jagged necklaces of electricity. Now the rain began to abate, as well, and Father Geary was able to reduce the speed of the windshield wipers even as he increased that of the aging Toyota.

For a while neither of them seemed to know what to say. Finally the priest cleared his throat. "Have you experienced this before—these stigmata?"

"No. Not that I'm aware of. But then, of course, I wasn't aware this time until you told me."

"You didn't notice the marks on your hands before you passed out at the sanctuary railing?"

"No."

"But this isn't the only unusual thing that's been happening to you lately."

Jim's soft laugh was wrenched from him less by amusement than by a sense of dark irony. "Definitely not the only unusual thing."

"Do you want to tell me?"

Jim thought about it awhile before replying. "Yes, but I can't."

"I'm a priest. I respect all confidences. Even the police have no power over me."

"Oh, I trust you, Father. And I'm not particularly worried about the police."

"Then?"

"If I tell you . . . the enemy will come," Jim said, and frowned as he heard himself speaking those words. The statement seemed to have come *through* him rather than from him.

"What enemy?"

He stared out at the vast, lightless expanse of desert. "I don't know."

"The enemy you spoke of in your sleep last night?"

"Maybe."

"You said it would kill us all."

"And it will." He went on, perhaps even more interested in what he said than the priest was, for he had no idea what words he would speak until he heard them. "If it finds out about me, if it discovers that I'm saving lives, special lives, then it'll come to stop me."

The priest glanced at him. "Special lives? Exactly what do you mean by that?"

"I don't know."

"If you tell me about yourself, I'll never repeat to another soul a word of what you say. So whatever this enemy is—how could it find out about you just because you confide in me?"

"I don't know."

"You don't know."

"That's right."

The priest sighed in frustration.

"Father, I'm really not playing games or being purposefully obscure." He shifted in his seat and adjusted the safety harness, trying to get more comfortable; however, his discomfort was less physical than spiritual, and not easily remedied. "Have you heard the term 'automatic writing'?"

Glowering at the road ahead, Geary said, "Psychics and mediums talk about it. Superstitious claptrap. A spirit supposedly seizes control of the medium's hand, while he's in a trance, and writes out messages from Beyond." He made a wordless sound of disgust. "The same people who scoff at the idea of speaking with God—or even at the mere idea of God's existence—naively embrace any con-artist's claim to be a channeler for the spirits of the dead."

"Well, nevertheless, what happens to me sometimes is that someone or something else seems to speak through me, an oral form of automatic writing. I know what I'm saying only because I listen to myself saying it."

"You're not in a trance."

"No."

"You claim to be a medium, a psychic?"

"No. I'm sure I'm not."

"You think the dead are speaking through you?"

"No. Not that."

"Then who?"

"I don't know."

"God?"

"Maybe."

"But you don't know," Geary said exasperatedly.

"I don't know."

"You're not only the strangest man I've ever met, Jim. You're also the most frustrating."

▼▲▼

They arrived at McCarran International in Las Vegas at ten o'clock that night. Only a couple of taxis were on the approach road to the airport. The rain had stopped. The palm trees stirred in a mild breeze, and everything looked as if it had been scrubbed and polished.

Jim opened the door of the Toyota even as Father Geary braked in front of the terminal. He got out, turned, and leaned back in for a last word with the priest.

"Thank you, Father. You probably saved my life."

"Nothing that dramatic."

"I'd like to give Our Lady of the Desert some of the three thousand I'm carrying, but I might need it all. I just don't know what's going to happen in Boston, what I might have to spend it for."

The priest shook his head. "I don't expect anything."

"When I get home again, I'll send some money. It'll be cash in an envelope, no return address, but it's honest money in spite of that. You can accept it in good conscience."

"It's not necessary, Jim. It was enough just to meet you. Maybe you should know . . . you brought a sense of the mystical back into the life of a weary priest who had sometimes begun to doubt his calling—but who'll never doubt again."

They regarded each other with a mutual affection that clearly surprised them both. Jim leaned into the car, Geary reached across the seat, and they shook hands. The priest had a firm, dry grip.

"Go with God," Geary said.

"I hope so."

AUGUST 24 THROUGH AUGUST 26

1

Sitting at her desk in the *Press* newsroom in the post-midnight hours of Friday morning, staring at her blank computer screen, Holly had sunk so low psychologically that she just wanted to go home, get into bed, and pull the covers over her head for a few days. She despised people who were always feeling sorry for themselves. She tried to shame herself out of her funk, but she began to pity herself for having descended to self-pity. Of course, it was impossible not to see the humor in that situation, but she was unable to manage a smile at her own expense; instead, she pitied herself for being such a silly and amusing figure.

She was glad that tomorrow morning's edition had been put to bed and that the newsroom was almost deserted, so none of her colleagues could see her in such a debased condition. The only other people in sight were Tommy Weeks—a lanky maintenance man who was emptying wastecans and sweeping up—and George Fintel.

George, who was on the city-government beat, was at his desk at the far end of the big room, slumped forward, head on his folded arms, asleep. Occasionally he snored loud enough for the sound to carry all the way to Holly. When the bars closed, George sometimes returned to the newsroom instead of to his apartment, just as an old dray horse, when left on slack reins, will haul its cart back along a familiar route to the place it thinks of as home. He would wake sometime during the night, realize where he was, and wearily weave off to bed at last. "Politicians," George often said, "are the lowest form of life, having undergone devolution from that first slimy beast that crawled out of the primordial sea." At fifty-seven, he was too burnt-out to start over, so he continued to spend his days writing about public officials whom he privately reviled, and in the process he had come to hate himself, as well, and to seek solace in a prodigious daily intake of vodka martinis.

If she'd had any tolerance for liquor, Holly would have worried about winding up like George Fintel. But one drink gave her a nice buzz, two made her tipsy, and three put her to sleep.

I hate my life, she thought.

"You self-pitying wretch," she said aloud.

Well, I do. I hate it, everything's so hopeless.

"You nauseating despair junkie," she said softly but with genuine disgust.

"You talking to me?" Tommy Weeks said, piloting a push broom along the aisle in front of her desk.

"No, Tommy. Talking to myself."

"You? Gee, what've you got to be unhappy about?"

"My life."

He stopped and leaned on his broom, crossing one long leg in front of the other. With his broad freckled face, jug ears, and mop of carroty hair, he looked sweet, innocent, kind. "Things haven't turned out like you planned?"

Holly picked up a half-empty bag of M & Ms, tossed a few pieces of candy into her mouth, and leaned back in her chair. "When I left the University of Missouri with a journalism degree, I was gonna shake up the world, break big stories, collect Pulitzers for doorstops—and now look at me. You know what I did this evening?"

"Whatever it was, I can tell you didn't enjoy it."

"I was down at the Hilton for the annual banquet of the Greater Portland Lumber Products Association, interviewing manufacturers of prefab pullmans, plyboard salesmen, and redwood-decking distributors. They gave out the Timber Trophy—that's what they call it—for the 'lumber-products man of the year.' I got to interview him, too. Rushed back here to get it all written up in time for the morning edition. Hot stuff like that, you don't want to let the bastards at *The New York Times* scoop you on it."

"I thought you were arts and leisure."

"Got sick of it. Let me tell you, Tommy, the wrong poet can turn you off the arts for maybe a decade."

She tossed more chocolate morsels in her mouth. She usually didn't eat candy because she was determined not to wind up with a weight problem like the one that had always plagued her mother, and she was gobbling M & Ms now just to make herself feel more miserable and worthless. She was in a bad downward spiral.

She said, "TV and movies, they make journalism look so glamorous and exciting. It's all lies."

"Me," Tommy said, "I haven't had the life I planned on, either. You think I figured to wind up head of maintenance for the *Press,* just a glorified janitor?"

"I guess not," she said, feeling small and self-centered for whining at him when his lot in life was not as desirable as her own.

"Hell, no. From the time I was a little kid, I *knew* I was gonna grow up to drive one of those big damn old sanitation trucks, up there in that high cab, pushin' the buttons to operate the hydraulic-ram compactor." His voice became wistful. "Ridin' above the world, all that powerful machinery at my command. It was my dream, and I went for it, but I couldn't pass the city physical. Have this kidney problem, see. Nothin' serious but enough for the city's health insurers to disqualify me."

He leaned on his broom, gazing off into the distance, smiling faintly, probably visualizing himself ensconced in the kingly driver's seat of a garbage truck.

Staring at him in disbelief, Holly decided that his broad face did not, after all, look sweet and innocent and kind. She had misread the meaning of its lines and planes. It was a *stupid* face.

She wanted to say, You idiot! I dreamed of winning Pulitzers, and now I'm a hack writing industry puff pieces about the damn Timber Trophy! *That* is tragedy. You think having to settle for being a janitor instead of a garbage collector is in any way comparable?

But she didn't say anything because she realized that they *were* comparable. An unfulfilled dream, regardless of whether it was lofty or humble, was still a tragedy to the dreamer who had given up hope. Pulitzers never won and sanitation trucks never driven were equally capable of inducing despair and insomnia. And that was the most depressing thought she'd had yet.

Tommy's eyes swam into focus again. "You gotta not dwell on it, Miss Thorne. Life . . . it's like gettin' a blueberry muffin in a coffeeshop when what you ordered was the apricot-nut. There aren't any apricots or nuts in it, and you can get tied up in knots just thinkin' about what you're missin', when the smarter thing to do is realize that blueberries have a nice taste, too."

Across the room, George Fintel farted in his sleep. It was a window-rattler. If the *Press* had been a big newspaper, with reporters hanging around who'd just returned from Beirut or some war zone, they'd have all dived for cover.

My God, Holly thought, *my life's nothing but a bad imitation of a Damon Runyon story. Sleazy newsrooms after midnight. Half-baked philosopher-janitors. Hard-drinking reporters who sleep at their desks. But it was Runyon as revised by an absurdist writer in collaboration with a bleak existentialist.*

"I feel better just having talked to you," Holly lied. "Thanks, Tommy."

"Anytime, Miss Thorne."

As Tommy set to work with his push broom again and moved on down the aisle, Holly tossed some more candy into her mouth and wondered if she would be able to pass the physical required of potential sanitation-truck drivers. On the positive side, the work would be different from journalism as she knew it—collecting garbage instead of dispensing it—and she would have the satisfaction of knowing that at least one person in Portland would desperately envy her.

She looked at the wall clock. One-thirty in the morning. She wasn't sleepy. She didn't want to go home and lie awake, staring at the ceiling, with nothing to do but indulge in more self-examination and self-pity. Well, actually, that *is* what she wanted, because she was in a wallowing mood, but she knew it wasn't a healthy thing to do. Unfortunately, she was without alternatives: weekday, wee-hour nightlife in Portland was a twenty-four-hour doughnut shop.

She was less than a day away from the start of her vacation, and she desperately needed it. She had made no plans. She was just going to relax, hang out, never once look at a newspaper. Maybe see some movies. Maybe read a few books. Maybe go to the Betty Ford Center to take the self-pity detox program.

She had reached that dangerous state in which she began to brood about her name. Holly Thorne. Cute. Real cute. What in God's name had possessed her parents to hang that one on her? Was it possible to imagine the Pulitzer committee giving that grand prize to a woman with a name more suitable to a cartoon character? Sometimes—always in the still heart of the night, of course—she was tempted to call her folks and demand to know whether this name thing had been just bad taste, a misfired joke, or conscious cruelty.

But her parents were salt-of-the-earth working-class people who had denied themselves many pleasures in order to give her a first-rate education, and they wanted nothing but the best for her. They would be devastated to hear that she loathed her name, when they no doubt thought it was clever and even sophisticated. She loved them fiercely, and she had to be in the deepest trenches of depression before she had the gall to blame them for her shortcomings.

Half afraid that she would pick up the phone and call them, she quickly turned to her computer again and accessed the current-edition file. The *Press*'s data-retrieval system made it possible for any reporter on staff to follow any story through editing, typesetting, and production. Now that tomorrow's edition had been formatted, locked down, and sent to press, she could actually call up an image of each page on her screen. Only the headlines were big enough to read, but any portion of the image could be enlarged to fill the screen. Sometimes she could cheer herself a little by reading a big story before the newspaper hit the street; it sparked in her at least a dim glimmer of the feeling of being an insider, which was one aspect of the job that attracted every dream-besotted young person to a vocation in journalism.

But as she scanned the headlines on the first few pages, looking for an interesting story to enlarge, her gloom deepened. A big fire in St. Louis, nine people dead. Presentiments of war in the Mid-East. An oil spill off Japan. A huge storm and flood in India, tens of thousands homeless. The federal government was raising taxes again. She had always known that the news industry flourished on gloom, disaster, scandal, mindless violence, and strife. But suddenly it seemed to be a singularly ghoulish business, and Holly realized that she no longer *wanted* to be an insider, among the first to know this dreadful stuff.

Then, just as she was about to close the file and switch off the computer, a headline arrested her: MYSTERIOUS STRANGER SAVES BOY. The events at McAlbury School were not quite twelve days in the past, and those four words had a special association for her. Curiosity triggered, she instructed the computer to enlarge the quadrant in which the story began.

The dateline was Boston, and the story was accompanied by a photograph. The picture was still blurry and dark, but the scale was now large enough to allow her to read the text, although not comfortably. She instructed the computer to further enlarge one of the already enlarged quadrants, pulling up the first column of the article so she could read it without strain.

The opening line made Holly sit up straighter in her chair: *A courageous bystander, who would say only that his name was Jim, saved the life of Nicholas O'Conner, 6, when a New England Power and Light Company vault exploded under a sidewalk in a Boston residential area Thursday evening.*

Softly, she said, "What the hell . . . ?"

She tapped the keys, instructing the computer to shift the field of display rightward on the page to show her the multiply enhanced photo that accompanied the piece. She went to a bigger scale, then to a still bigger one, until the face filled the screen.

Jim Ironheart.

Briefly she sat in stunned disbelief, immobilized. Then she was stricken by a need to know more—not only an intellectual but a genuinely physical need that felt not unlike a sudden and intense pang of hunger.

She returned to the text of the story and read it through, then read it again. The O'Conner boy had been sitting on the sidewalk in front of his home, directly on the two-by-three-foot concrete lid that covered the entrance to the power company's vault, which was spacious enough for four men to work together within its subterranean confines. The kid had been playing with toy trucks. His parents had been within sight of him on the front porch of their house, when a stranger had sprinted along the street. "He comes right at Nicky," the boy's father was quoted, "snatches him, so I thought sure he was a nutcase child molester going to steal my son." Carrying the screaming child, the stranger leaped over a low picket fence, onto the O'Conners' lawn, just as a 17,000-volt line in the vault exploded behind him. The blast flipped the concrete lid high into the air, as if it were a penny, and a bright ball of fire roared up in its wake. Embarrassed by the effusive praise heaped on him by Nicky's grateful parents and by the neighbors who had witnessed his heroism, the stranger claimed that he had smelled burning insulation, heard a hissing coming from the vault, and knew what was about to happen because he had "once worked for a power company." Annoyed that a witness had taken his photograph, he insisted on leaving before the media arrived because, as he put it, "I place a high value on my privacy."

That hair's-breadth rescue had occurred at 7:40 Thursday evening in Boston—or 4:40 Portland time yesterday afternoon. Holly looked at the office wall clock. It was now 2:02 Friday morning. Nicky O'Conner had been plucked off that vault cover not quite nine and a half hours ago.

The trail was still fresh.

She had questions to ask the *Globe* reporter who had written the piece. But it was only a little after five in the morning in Boston. He wouldn't be at work yet.

She closed out the *Press*'s current-edition data file. On the computer screen, the standard menu replaced the enlarged newspaper text.

Through a modem she accessed the vast network of data services to which the *Press* subscribed. She instructed the Newsweb service to scan all the stories that had been carried by the wire services and published in the major U.S. newspapers during the past three months, looking for instances in which the name "Jim" had been used within ten words of either "rescue" or the phrase "saved the life." She asked for a printout of every article, if there should be any, but asked to be spared multiples of the same incident.

While Newsweb was fulfilling her request, she snatched up the phone on her desk and called long-distance information for area code 818, then 213, then 714, and 619, seeking a listing for Jim Ironheart in Los Angeles, Orange, Riverside, San Bernardino, and San Diego counties. None of the operators was able to help her. If he actually lived in southern California, as he had told her he did, his phone was unlisted.

The laser printer that she shared with three other workstations was humming softly. The first of Newsweb's finds was sliding into the receiving tray.

She wanted to hurry to the cabinet on which the printer stood, grab the first printout, and read it at once; but she restrained herself, focusing her attention on the telephone instead, trying to think of another way to locate Jim Ironheart down there in the part of California that locals called "the Southland."

A few years ago, she simply could have accessed the

California Department of Motor Vehicles computer and, for a small fee, received the street address of anyone holding a valid driver's license in the state. But after the actress Rebecca Schaeffer had been murdered by an obsessed fan who had tracked her down in that fashion, a new law had imposed restrictions on DMV records.

If she had been an accomplished computer hacker, steeped in their arcane knowledge, she no doubt could have finessed entrance to the DMV records in spite of their new safeguards, or perhaps she could have pried into credit-agency databanks to search for a file on Ironheart. She had known reporters who honed their computer skills for just that purpose, but she had always sought her sources and information in a strictly legitimate fashion, without deception.

Which is why you're writing about such thrilling stuff as the Timber Trophy, she thought sourly.

While she puzzled over a solution to the problem, she hurried to the vending room and got a cup of coffee from the coin-operated brewer. It tasted like yak bile. She drank it anyway, because she was going to need the caffeine before the night was through. She bought another cup and returned with it to the newsroom.

The laser printer was silent. She grabbed the pages from its tray and sat down at her desk.

Newsweb had turned up a thick stack of stories from the national press in which the name "Jim" was used within ten words of "rescue" or "saved the life." She counted them quickly. Twenty-nine.

The first was a human-interest piece from the *Chicago Sun-Times,* and Holly read the opening sentence aloud: "Jim Foster, of Oak Park, has rescued over one hundred stranded cats from—"

She dropped that printout in her wastecan and looked at the next one. It was from the *Philadelphia Inquirer:* "Jim Pilsbury, pitching for the Phillies, rescued his club from a humiliating defeat—"

Throwing that one aside, as well, she looked at the third. It was a movie review, so she didn't bother searching for the mention of Jim. The fourth was a reference to Jim Harrison, the novelist. The fifth was a story about a New Jersey politician who used the Heimlich maneuver to save the life of a Mafia boss in a barroom, where they were having a couple of beers together, when the *padrone* began to choke to death on a chunk of peppery-hot Slim Jim sausage.

She was beginning to worry that she would come up empty-handed by the bottom of the stack, but the sixth article, from the *Houston Chronicle,* opened her eyes wider than the vile coffee had. WOMAN SAVED FROM VENGEFUL HUSBAND. On July 14, after winning both financial and child-custody issues in a bitter divorce suit, Amanda Cutter had nearly been shot by her enraged husband, Cosmo, outside her home in the wealthy River Oaks district of the city. After Cosmo missed her with the first two shots, she had been saved by a man who "appeared out of nowhere," wrestled her maddened spouse to the ground, and disarmed him. Her savior had identified himself only as "Jim," and had walked off into the humid Houston afternoon before the police arrived. The thirty-year-old divorcée had clearly been smitten, for she described him as "handsome, sort of muscular, like a superhero right out of a movie, with the dreamiest blue eyes."

Holly could still picture Jim Ironheart's intensely blue eyes. She was not the kind of woman who would refer to them as "dreamy," although they were certainly the clearest and most arresting eyes she'd ever . . . Oh, hell, yes, they *were* dreamy. She was reluctant to admit to the adolescent reaction that he had inspired in her, but she was not any better at deceiving herself than she was at deceiving other people. She recalled an initial eerie impression of inhuman coldness, upon first meeting his gaze, but that passed and never returned from the moment he smiled.

The seventh article was about another modest Jim who had not hung around to accept thanks and praise—or media attention—after rescuing Carmen Diaz, thirty, from a burning apartment house in Miami on the fifth of July. He had blue eyes.

Poring through the remaining twenty-two articles, Holly found two more about Ironheart, though only his first name was mentioned. On June 21, Thaddeus Johnson, twelve, had almost been pitched off the roof of an eight-story Harlem tenement by four members of a neighborhood youth gang who had not responded well to his disdainful rejection of an invitation to join their drug-peddling fraternity. He was rescued by a blue-eyed man who incapacitated the four thugs with a dazzling series of Tae Kwon Do kicks, chops, thrusts, and throws. "He was like Batman without the funny clothes," Thaddeus had told the *Daily News* reporter. Two weeks prior to that, on June 7, another blue-eyed Jim "just seemed to materialize" on the property of Louis Andretti, twenty-eight, of Corona, California, in time to warn the homeowner not to enter a crawlspace under his house to repair a plumbing leak. "He told me a family of rattlers had settled in there," Andretti told the reporter. Later, when agents from the county's Vector Control inspected the crawlspace from the perimeter, with the aid of a halogen lamp, they saw not just a nest but "something out of a nightmare," and eventually extracted forty-one snakes from beneath the structure. "What I don't understand," Andretti said, "is how that guy knew the rattlers were there, when I *live* in the house and never had a clue."

Now Holly had four linked incidents to add to the rescue of Nicky O'Conner in Boston and Billy Jenkins in Portland, all since the first of June. She typed in new instructions to Newsweb, asking for the same search to be made for the months of March, April, and May.

She needed more coffee, and when she got up to go to the vending room, she saw that George Fintel had evidently awakened and staggered home. She hadn't heard him leave. Tommy was gone, as well. She was alone.

She got another cup of coffee, and it didn't taste as bad as it had before. The brew hadn't improved; her sense of taste had just been temporarily damaged by the first two cups.

Eventually Newsweb located eleven stories in March

through May that fit her parameters. After examining the printouts, Holly found only one of them of interest.

On May 15, in Atlanta, Georgia, a blue-eyed Jim had entered a convenience store during an armed robbery. He shot and killed the perpetrator, Norman Rink, who had been about to kill two customers—Sam Newsome, twenty-five, and his five-year-old daughter Emily. Flying high on a cocaine, Ice, and methamphetamine cocktail—Rink had already killed the clerk and two other customers merely for the fun of it. After wasting Rink and assuring himself that the Newsomes were unhurt, Jim had slipped away before the police arrived.

The store security camera had provided a blurry photograph of the heroic intruder. It was only the second photo Holly had found in all the articles. The image was poor. But she immediately recognized Jim Ironheart.

Some details of the incident unnerved her. If Ironheart had an amazing ability—psychic power, whatever—to foresee fatal moments in the lives of strangers and arrive in time to thwart fate, why hadn't he gotten to that convenience store a few minutes sooner, early enough to prevent the deaths of the clerk and other customers? Why had he saved the Newsomes and let the rest die?

She was further chilled by the description of his attack on Rink. He had pumped four rounds from a 12-gauge pistol-grip shotgun into the madman. Then, although Rink was indisputably dead, Jim reloaded and fired another four rounds. "He was in such a rage," Sam Newsome said, "his face red, and he was sweating, you could see the arteries pounding in his temples, across his forehead. He was crying a little, too, but the tears . . . they didn't make him seem any less angry." When done, Jim had expressed regret for cutting Rink down so violently in front of little Emily. He'd explained that men like Rink, who killed innocent people, brought out "a little madness of my own." Newsome told the reporter, "He saved our lives, yeah, but I gotta say the guy was *scary,* almost as scary as Rink."

Realizing that Ironheart might not have revealed even his first name on some occasions, Holly instructed Newsweb to search the past six months for stories in which "rescue" and "saved the life" were within ten words of "blue." She had noticed that some witnesses were vague about his physical description, but that most remembered his singularly blue eyes.

She went to the john, got more coffee, then stood by the printer. As each find was transferred to hard copy, she snatched it up, scanned it, tossed it in the wastecan if it was of no interest or read it with excitement if it was about another nick-of-time rescue. Newsweb turned up four more cases that indisputably belonged in the Ironheart file, even though neither his first nor last name was used.

At her desk again, she instructed Newsweb to search the past six months for the name "Ironheart" in the national media.

While she waited for a response, she put the pertinent printouts in order, then made a chronological list of the people whose lives Jim Ironheart had saved, incorporating the four new cases. She included their names, ages, the location of each incident, and the type of death from which each person had been spared.

She studied that compilation, noting some patterns with interest. But she put it aside when Newsweb completed its latest task.

As she rose from her chair to go to the laser printer, she froze, surprised to discover she was no longer alone in the newsroom. Three reporters and an editor were at their desks, all guys with reputations as early birds, including Hank Hawkins, editor of the business pages, who liked to be at work when the financial markets opened on the East Coast. She hadn't been aware of them coming in. Two of them were sharing a joke, laughing loudly, and Hawkins was talking on the phone, but Holly hadn't heard them until after she'd seen them. She looked at the clock: 6:10. Opalescent early-morning light played at the windows, though she had not realized that the tide of night had been receding. She glanced down at her desk and saw two more paper coffee cups than she remembered getting from the vending machine.

She realized that she was no longer wallowing in despair. She felt better than she had felt in days. Weeks. *Years.* She was a reporter again, for real.

She went to the laser printer, emptied the receiving tray, and returned with the pages to her desk. Ironhearts evidently were not newsmakers. There were only five stories involving people with that surname in the past six months.

Kevin Ironheart—Buffalo, New York. State senator. Announced his intention to run for governor.

Anna Denise Ironheart—Boca Raton, Florida. Found a live alligator in her family room.

Lori Ironheart—Los Angeles, California. Songwriter. Nominated for the Academy Award for best song of the year.

Valerie Ironheart—Cedar Rapids, Iowa. Gave birth to healthy quadruplets.

The last of the five was James Ironheart.

She looked at the heading. The story came from the Orange County *Register,* April 10, and was one of scores of pieces on the same story that had been published statewide. Because of her instructions, the computer had printed out only this single instance, sparing her sheafs of similar articles on the same event.

She checked the dateline. Laguna Niguel. California. *Southern* California. The Southland.

The piece was not accompanied by a photograph, but the reporter's description of the man included a reference to blue eyes and thick brown hair. She was sure he was *her* James Ironheart.

She was not surprised to have found him. She had known that with determined effort she would locate him sooner or later. What surprised her was the subject of the piece in which his full name appeared at last. She expected it to be yet one more story about snatching someone out of death's grasp, and she was not prepared for the headline: LAGUNA NIGUEL MAN WINS SIX MILLION LOTTO JACKPOT.

2

Having followed the rescue of Nicholas O'Conner with his first untroubled night of sleep in the last four, Jim departed Boston on Friday afternoon, August 24. Gaining three hours on the cross-country trip, he arrived at John Wayne Airport by 3:10 P.M. and was home half an hour later.

He went straight into his den and lifted the flap of carpet that revealed the safe built into the floor of the closet. He dialed the combination, opened the lid, and removed five thousand dollars, ten percent of the cash he kept there.

At his desk, he packed the hundred-dollar bills into a padded Jiffy envelope and stapled it shut. He typed a label to Father Leo Geary at Our Lady of the Desert, and affixed sufficient postage. He would mail it first thing in the morning.

He went into the family room and switched on the TV. He tried several movies on cable, but none held his interest. He watched the news for a while, but his mind wandered. After he heated a microwave pizza and popped open a beer, he settled down with a good book—which bored him. He paged through a stack of unread magazines, but none of the articles was intriguing.

Near twilight he went outside with another beer and sat on the patio. The palm fronds rustled in a light breeze. A sweet fragrance rose from the star jasmine along the property wall. Red, purple, and pink impatiens shone with almost Day-Glo radiance in the dwindling light; and as the sun finished setting, they faded as if they were hundreds of small lightbulbs on a rheostat. Night floated down like a great tossed cape of almost weightless black silk.

Although the scene was peaceful, he was restless. Day by day, week by week, since he had saved the lives of Sam Newsome and his daughter Emily on May 15, Jim had found it increasingly difficult to involve himself in the ordinary routines and pleasures of life. He was unable to relax. He kept thinking of all the good he could do, all the lives he could save, the destinies he could alter, if only the call would come again: "Life line." Other endeavors seemed frivolous by comparison.

Having been the instrument of a higher power, he now found it difficult to settle for being anything less.

▼ ▲ ▼

After spending the day collecting what information she could find on James Madison Ironheart, with only a two-hour nap to compensate for the night of sleep she had lost, Holly launched her long-anticipated vacation with a flight to Orange County. On arrival, she drove her rental car south from the airport to the Laguna Hills Motor Inn, where she had reserved a motel room.

Laguna Hills was inland, and not a resort area. But in Laguna Beach, Laguna Niguel, and other coastal towns during the summer, rooms had been booked far in advance. She didn't intend to swim or sunbathe anyway. Ordinarily, she was as enthusiastic a pursuer of skin cancer as anyone, but this had become a working vacation.

By the time she arrived at the motel, she felt as if her eyes were full of sand. When she carried her suitcase into her room, gravity played a cruel trick, pulling her down with five times the usual force.

The room was simple and clean, with enough air-conditioning to re-create the environment of Alaska, in case it was ever occupied by an Eskimo who got homesick.

From vending machines in the breezeway, she purchased a packet of peanut-butter-and-cheese crackers and a can of diet Dr Pepper, and satisfied her hunger while sitting in bed. She was so tired that she felt numb. All of her senses were dulled by exhaustion, including her sense of taste. She might as well have been eating Styrofoam and washing it down with mule sweat.

As if the contact of head and pillow tripped a switch, she fell instantly asleep.

During the night, she began to dream. It was an odd dream, for it took place in absolute darkness, with no images, just sounds and smells and tactile sensations, perhaps the way people dreamed when they had been blind since birth. She was in a dank cool place that smelled vaguely of lime. At first she was not afraid, just confused, carefully feeling her way along the walls of the chamber. They were constructed from blocks of stone with tight mortar joints. After a little exploration she realized there was actually just one wall, a single continuous sweep of stone, because the room was circular. The only sounds were those she made—and the background hiss and tick of rain drumming on a slate roof overhead.

In the dream, she moved away from the wall, across a solid wood floor, hands held out in front of her. Although she encountered nothing, her curiosity suddenly began to turn to fear. She stopped moving, stood perfectly still, certain that she had heard something sinister.

A subtle sound. Masked by the soft but insistent rattle of the rain. It came again. A squeak.

For an instant she thought of a rat, fat and sleek, but the sound was too protracted and of too odd a character to have been made by a rat. More of a creak than a squeak, but not the creak of a floorboard underfoot, either. It faded . . . came again a few seconds later . . . faded . . . came again . . . rhythmically.

When Holly realized that she was listening to the protest of an unoiled mechanism of some kind, she should have been relieved. Instead, standing in that tenebrous room, straining to imagine what machine it might be, she felt her heartbeat accelerate. The creaking grew only slightly louder, but it speeded up a lot; instead of one creak every five or six seconds, the sound came every three or four seconds, then every two or three, then once per second.

Suddenly a strange rhythmic *whoosh, whoosh, whoosh* struck up, as well, in syncopation with the creaking. It was the sound of a wide flat object cutting the air.

Whoosh.

It was close. Yet she felt no draft.

Whoosh.

She had the crazy idea that it was a blade.

Whoosh.

A large blade. Sharp. Cutting the air. Enormous.

Whoosh.

She sensed that something terrible was approaching, an entity so strange that even light—and the full sight of the thing—would not provide understanding. Although she was aware that she was dreaming, she knew she had to get out of that dark and stony place quickly—or die. A nightmare couldn't be escaped just by running from it, so she had to wake up, but she could not, she was too tired, unable to break the bonds of sleep. Then the lightless room seemed to be spinning, she had a sense of some great structure turning around and around *(creak, whoosh)*, thrusting up into the rainy night *(creak, whoosh)* and turning *(creak, whoosh)*, cutting the air *(creak, whoosh)*, she was trying to scream *(creak, whoosh)*, but she couldn't force a sound from herself *(whoosh, whoosh, whoosh)*, couldn't awaken and couldn't scream for help. *WHOOSH!*

▼ ▲ ▼

"No!"

Jim sat up in bed as he shouted the one-word denial. He was clammy and trembling violently.

He had fallen fast asleep with the lamp on, which he frequently did, usually not by accident but by design. For more than a year, his sleep had been troubled by nightmares with a variety of plots and a panoply of boogeymen, only some of which he could recall when he woke. The nameless, formless creature that he called "the enemy," and of which he had dreamed while recuperating at Our

Lady of the Desert rectory, was the most frightening figure in his dreamscapes, though not the only monster.

This time, however, the focus of the terror had not been a person or creature. It was a *place*. The windmill.

He looked at the bedside clock. Three-forty-five in the morning.

In just his pajama bottoms, he got out of bed and padded into the kitchen.

The fluorescent light seared his eyes. Good. He wanted to evaporate what residue of sleep still clung to him.

The damn windmill.

He plugged in the coffeemaker and brewed a strong Colombian blend. He sipped half the first cup while standing at the counter, then refilled it and sat down at the breakfast table. He intended to empty the pot because he could not risk going back to bed and having that dream again.

Every nightmare detracted from the quality of rest that sleep provided, but the windmill dream actually took a real physical toll. Whenever he woke from it, his chest always ached, as though his heart had been bruised from hammering too hard against his breastbone. Sometimes the shakes took hours to fade away completely, and he often had headaches that, like now, arced across the top of his skull and throbbed with such power that it seemed as if an alien presence was trying to burst out of him. He knew that if he looked in a mirror, his face would be unnervingly pale and haggard, with blue-black circles around the eyes, like the face of a terminal cancer patient from whom disease had sucked the juice of life.

The windmill dream was not the most frequent of those that plagued him, and in fact it haunted his sleep only one or two nights a month. But it was by far the worst.

Curiously, nothing much happened in it. He was ten years old again, sitting on the dusty wooden floor of the smaller upper chamber, above the main room that held the ancient millstones, with only the flickering light of a fat yellow candle. Night pressed at the narrow windows, which were almost like castle embrasures in the limestone walls. Rain tapped against the glass. Suddenly, with a creak of unoiled and half-rusted machinery, the four great wooden sails of the mill began to turn outside, faster and faster, cutting like giant scythes through the damp air. The upright shaft, which came out of the ceiling and vanished through a bore in the center of the floor, also began to turn, briefly creating the illusion that the round floor itself were rotating in the manner of a carousel. One level below, the ancient millstones started to roll against each other, producing a soft rumble like distant thunder.

Just that. Nothing more. Yet it scared the hell out of him.

He took a long pull of his coffee.

Stranger still: in real life, the windmill had been a good place, never the scene of pain or terror. It had stood between a pond and a cornfield on his grandparents' farm. To a young boy born and raised in the city, the big mill had been an exotic and mysterious structure, a perfect place to play and fantasize, a refuge in a time of trouble. He could not understand why he was having nightmares about a place that held only good memories for him.

▼▲▼

After the frightening dream passed without waking her, Holly Thorne slept peacefully for the rest of the night, as still as a stone on the floor of the sea.

3

Saturday morning, Holly ate breakfast in a booth at the motel coffeeshop. Most of the other customers were obviously vacationers: families dressed almost as if in uniforms of shorts or white slacks and brightly colored shirts. Some of the kids wore caps and T-shirts that advertised Sea World or Disneyland or Knott's Berry Farm. Parents huddled over maps and brochures while they ate, planning routes that would take them to one of the tourist attractions that California offered in such plenitude. There were so many colorful Polo shirts or Polo-shirt knockoffs in the restaurant that a visitor from another planet might have assumed that Ralph Lauren was either the deity of a major religion or dictator of the world.

As she ate blueberry pancakes, Holly studied her list of people who had been spared from death by Jim Ironheart's timely intervention:

MAY 15
Sam (25) and Emily (5) Newsome—Atlanta, Georgia (murder)

JUNE 7
Louis Andretti (28)—Corona, California (snakebite)

JUNE 21
Thaddeus Johnson (12)—New York, New
York (murder)

JUNE 30
Rachael Steinberg (23)—San Francisco, California (murder)

JULY 5
Carmen Diaz (30)—Miami, Florida (fire)

JULY 14
Amanda Cutter (30)—Houston, Texas (murder)

JULY 20
Steven Aimes (57)—Birmingham, Alabama
(murder)

AUGUST 1
Laura Lenaskian (28)—Seattle, Washington
(drowning)

AUGUST 8
Doogie Burkette (11)—Peoria, Illinois (drowning)

AUGUST 12
Billy Jenkins (8)—Portland, Oregon (traffic fa-
tality)

AUGUST 20
Lisa (30) and Susan (10) Jawolski—Mojave
desert (murder)

AUGUST 23
Nicholas O'Conner (6)—Boston, Massachusetts (explosion)

Certain patterns were obvious. Of the fourteen people
saved, six were children. Seven others were between the

ages of twenty-three and thirty. Only one was older—Steven Aimes, who was fifty-seven. Ironheart favored the young. And there was some evidence that his activities were increasing in frequency: one episode in May; three in June; three in July; and now five already in August with a full week of the month remaining.

Holly was particularly intrigued by the number of people on the list who would have been *murdered* without Ironheart's intervention. Far more people died each year in accidents than at the hands of others. Traffic fatalities alone were more numerous than murders. Yet Jim Ironheart intervened in a considerably greater number of homicides than accidents: eight of the fourteen people on the list had been spared from the malevolent intentions of murderers, over sixty percent.

Perhaps his premonitions more often related to murder than to other forms of death because human violence generated stronger psychic vibrations than accidents . . .

Holly stopped chewing and her hand froze halfway to her mouth with another forkful of blueberry pancake, as she realized just *how* strange this story was. She had been operating at a breathless pace, driven by reportorial ambition and curiosity. Her excitement, then her exhaustion, had prevented her from fully considering all of the implications and ramifications of Ironheart's activities. She put down her fork and stared at her plate, as if she could glean answers and explanations from the crumb patterns and smears in the same way that gypsies read tea leaves and palms.

What the hell *was* Jim Ironheart? A psychic?

She'd never had much interest in extrasensory perception and strange mental powers. She knew there were people who claimed to be able to "see" a murderer just by touching the clothes his victim wore, who sometimes helped police find the bodies of missing persons, who were paid well by the *National Enquirer* to foresee world events and forthcoming developments in the lives of celebrities, who said they could channel the voices of the dead to the living. But her interest in the supernatural was so minimal that she had never really formed an opinion of the validity of such claims. She didn't necessarily believe that all those people were frauds; the whole subject had bored her too much to bother thinking about it at all.

She supposed that her dogged rationality—and cynicism—could bend far enough to encompass the idea that now and then a psychic actually possessed real power, but she wasn't sure that "psychic" was an adequate description of Jim Ironheart. This guy wasn't just going out on a limb in some cheap tabloid to predict that Steven Spielberg would make another hit picture next year (surprise!), or that Schwarzenegger would still speak English with an accent, or that Tom Cruise would dump his current girlfriend, or that Eddie Murphy would still be black for the foreseeable future. *This* guy knew the precise facts of each of those impending deaths—who, when, where, how—far enough in advance to derail fate. He wasn't bending spoons with the power of his mind, wasn't speaking in the gravelly voice of an ancient spirit named Rama-Lama-Dingdong, wasn't reading futures in entrails or wax drippings or Tarot cards. He was *saving lives,* for God's sake, altering destinies, having a profound impact not only on those he saved from death but on the lives of the friends and families who would have been left shattered and bereaved. And the reach of his power extended three thousand miles from Laguna Niguel to Boston!

In fact, maybe his heroics were not confined to the borders of the continental United States. She had not researched the international media for the past six months. Perhaps he had saved lives in Italy, France, Germany, Japan, Sweden, or in Pago Pago for all she knew.

The word "psychic" definitely was inadequate. Holly couldn't even think of a suitable one-word description of his powers.

To her surprise, a sense of wonder had possessed her, like nothing she had felt since she was a kid. Now, an element of awe stole over her as well, and she shivered.

Who was this man? *What* was he?

Little more than thirty hours ago, when she had seen the

story about young Nicholas O'Conner in Boston, Holly had known she was on to a big story. By the time she examined the material that Newsweb found for her, she felt it might be the biggest story of her career, regardless of how long she worked as a reporter. Now she had begun to suspect that it might grow into the biggest story of this decade.

"Everything okay?"

Holly said, "Everything's weird," before she realized that she had not asked the question of herself.

The waitress—Bernice, according to the name embroidered on her uniform blouse—was standing beside the table, looking concerned. Holly realized that she had been staring intently at her plate while she'd been thinking about Jim Ironheart, and she had not taken a bite in some time. Bernice had noticed and thought something was wrong.

"Weird?" Bernice said, frowning.

"Uh, yeah—it's weird that I should come into what looks like an ordinary coffeeshop and get the best blueberry pancakes I've ever eaten."

Bernice hesitated, perhaps trying to decide if Holly was putting her on. "You . . . you really like 'em?"

"Love them," Holly said, forking up a mouthful and chewing the cold, sodden pancakes with enthusiasm.

"That's nice! You want anything else?"

"Just the check," Holly said.

She continued to eat the pancakes after Bernice left, because she was hungry and they were there.

As she ate, Holly looked around the restaurant at the colorfully decked-out vacationers who were absorbed in discussions of amusements experienced and amusements yet to come, and the thrill of being an insider coursed through her for the first time in years. She knew something they did not. She was a reporter with a carefully husbanded secret. When fully researched, when written up in crystalline prose as direct and yet evocative as Hemingway's best journalism (well, she was going to *try* for that, anyway), the story would earn front-page, top-of-the-page exposure in every major newspaper in the country, in the world. And what made it so good, what made her tingle, was that her secret had nothing to do with a political scandal, toxic dumping, or the other myriad forms of terror and tragedy that fueled the engine of modern news media. Her story would be one of amazement and wonder, courage and hope, a story of tragedy avoided, lives spared, death thwarted.

Life is *so* good, she thought, unable to stop grinning at her fellow diners.

▼ ▲ ▼

First thing after breakfast, with the aid of a book of street maps called the *Thomas Guide,* Holly located Jim Ironheart's house in Laguna Niguel. She had tracked down the address via computer from Portland, by checking the public records of real-estate transactions in Orange County since the first of the year. She had assumed that anyone winning six million dollars in a lottery might spend some of it on a new house, and she had assumed correctly. He hit the jackpot—presumably thanks to his clairvoyance—in early January. On May 3, he finalized the purchase of a house on Bougainvillea Way. Since the records did not show that he had sold any property, he apparently had been renting before his windfall.

She was somewhat surprised to find him living in such a modest house. The neighborhood was new, just off Crown Valley Parkway, and in the neat, well-landscaped, precision-planned tradition of south Orange County. The streets were wide, gracefully curved, lined with young palms and melaleucas, and the houses were all of compatible Mediterranean styles with roofs in different shades of red and sand and peach tiles. But even in such a desirable south-county city as Laguna Niguel, where the per-square-foot cost of a tract home could rival that of a Manhattan penthouse, Ironheart could easily have afforded better than he had purchased: It looked like a little more than two thousand square feet, the smallest model in the neighborhood; creamy-white stucco; large-pane French windows but no other apparent custom features; a lush green lawn, but small, with azaleas and impatiens and a pair of willowy queen palms that cast lacy shadows on the walls in the temperate morning sun.

She drove by slowly, giving the house a thorough looking over. No car stood in the driveway. The drapes were drawn at the windows. She had no way of knowing if Ironheart was home—short of going up to his front door and ringing the bell. Eventually, she would do just that. But not yet.

At the end of the block, she turned around and drove past the house again. The place was attractive, pleasant, but so *ordinary*. It was hard to believe that an exceptional man, with astonishing secrets, lived behind those walls.

▼ ▲ ▼

Viola Moreno's townhouse in Irvine was in one of those parklike communities the Irvine Company had built in the sixties and seventies, where the plum-thorn hedges had entered woody maturity and the red-gum eucalyptuses and Indian laurels towered high enough to spread a wealth of shade on even the brightest and most cloudless of summer days. It was furnished with an eye to comfort rather than style: an overstuffed sofa, commodious armchairs, and plump footstools, everything in earth tones, with traditional landscape paintings meant to soothe rather than challenge the eye and mind. Stacks of magazines and shelves of books were everywhere at hand. Holly felt at home the moment she crossed the threshold.

Viola was as welcoming and easy to like as her home. She was about fifty, Mexican-American, with flawless skin the shade of lightly tarnished copper and eyes that were merry in spite of being as liquid-black as squid ink. Though she was on the short side and had broadened a little with age, it was easy to see that her looks would once have turned men's heads hard enough to crack vertebrae; she was still a lovely woman. She took Holly's hand at the door, then linked arms with her to lead her through the small house and out to the patio, as if they were old friends and had not just spoken for the first time on the phone the previous day.

On the patio, which overlooked a common greensward, a pitcher of icy lemonade and two glasses stood on a glass-topped table. The rattan chairs were padded with thick yellow cushions.

"I spend a lot of my summer out here," Viola said as they settled into chairs. The day was not too hot, the air dry and clean. "It's a beautiful little corner of the world, isn't it?"

The broad but shallow green vale separated this row of townhouses from the next, shaded by tall trees and decorated with a couple of circular beds of red and purple impatiens. Two squirrels scampered down a gentle slope and across a meandering walkway.

"Quite beautiful," Holly agreed as Viola poured lemonade into their glasses.

"My husband and I bought it when the trees were just sticks and the Hydroseeded greenbelt was still patchy. But we could visualize what it would be like one day, and we were patient people, even when we were young." She sighed. "Sometimes I have bad moments, I get bitter about his dying so young and never having a chance to see what this all grew up into. But mostly I just enjoy it, knowing Joe is somewhere better than this world and that somehow he takes pleasure in my enjoyment."

"I'm sorry," Holly said, "I didn't know you'd been widowed."

"Of course you didn't, dear. How could you know? Anyway, it was a long time ago, back in 1969, when I was just thirty and he was thirty-two. My husband was a career Marine, proud of it, and so was I. So *am* I, still, though he died in Vietnam."

Holly was startled to realize that many of the early victims of that conflict would now have been past middle-age. The wives they left behind had now lived far more years without them than with them. How long until Vietnam seemed as ancient as the crusades of Richard the Lionheart or the Peloponnesian Wars?

"Such a waste," Viola said with an edge to her voice. But the edge was gone an instant later when she said, "So long ago . . ."

The life Holly had imagined for this woman—a calm and peaceful journey of small pleasures, warm and cozy, with perhaps more than its share of laughter—was clearly less than half the story. The firm and loving tone Viola used when she referred to Joe as "my husband" made it clear that no amount of time elapsed could fade his memory in her mind, and that there had been no other man since him. Her life had been profoundly changed and constricted by his death. Although she was obviously an optimistic soul and outgoing by nature, there was a shadow of tragedy on her heart.

One basic lesson that every good journalist learned early in his career was that people were seldom only what they seemed to be—and never less complex than the mystery of life itself.

Viola sipped her lemonade. "Too sweet. I always add too much sugar. Sorry." She put her glass down. "Now tell me about this brother you're searching for. You have me quite intrigued."

"As I told you when I called from Portland, I was an adopted child. The people who took me in were wonderful parents, I have no less love for them than I would for my real parents, but . . . well . . ."

"Naturally, you have a desire to know your real parents."

"It's as if . . . there's an emptiness in me, a dark place in my heart," Holly said, trying not to trowel it on too thick.

She was not surprised by the ease with which she lied, but by how well she did it. Deception was a handy tool with which to elicit information from a source who might otherwise be reluctant to talk. Journalists as highly praised as Joe McGinniss, Joseph Wambaugh, Bob Woodward, and Carl Bernstein had at one time or another argued the necessity of this ingenuity in dealing with interviewees, all in the service of getting at the truth. But Holly had never been this skillful at it. At least she had the good grace to

bè dismayed and embarrassed by her lies—two feelings
that she hid well from Viola Moreno.

"Though the adoption agency's records were barely adequate, I've learned that my real parents, my biological
parents, died twenty-five years ago, when I was only
eight." Actually, it was Jim Ironheart's parents who had
died twenty-five years ago, when he was ten, a fact she had
turned up in stories about his lottery win. "So I'll never
have a chance to know them."

"What a terrible thing. Now it's *my* turn to be sorry for
you," Viola said with a note of genuine sympathy in her
soft voice.

Holly felt like a heel. By concocting this false personal
tragedy, she seemed to be mocking Viola's very real loss.
She went on anyway: "But it's not as bleak as it might've
been, because I've discovered I have a brother, as I told
you on the phone."

Leaning forward with her arms on the table, Viola was
eager to hear the details and learn how she could help.
"And there's something I can do to help you find your
brother?"

"Not exactly. You see, I've already found him."

"How wonderful!"

"But . . . I'm afraid to approach him."

"Afraid? But why?"

Holly looked out at the greensward and swallowed hard
a couple of times, as if choking on emotion and struggling
to maintain control of herself. She was good. Academy
Award stuff. She loathed herself for it. When she spoke,
she managed to get a subtle and convincing tremor in her
voice: "As far as I know, he's the only blood relative I have
in the world, and my only link to the mother and father I'll
never know. He's my brother, Mrs. Moreno, and I love
him. Even though I've never met him, I love him. But what
if I approach him, open my heart to him . . . and he wishes
I'd never shown up, doesn't like me or something?"

"Good heavens, of course he'll like you! Why wouldn't
he like a nice young woman like you? Why wouldn't he be
delighted to have someone as sweet as you for a sister?"

I'm going to rot in hell for this, Holly thought miserably.

She said, "Well, it may sound silly to you, but I'm worried about it. I've never made good first impressions with people—"

"You've made an excellent one with me, dear."

Grind my face under your heel, why don't you? Holly thought.

She said, "I want to be careful. I want to know as much as possible about him before I knock on his door. I want to know what he likes, what he doesn't like, how he feels about . . . oh, about all sorts of things. God, Mrs. Moreno, I don't want to blow this."

Viola nodded. "I assume you've come to me because I know your brother, probably had him years ago in one of my classes?"

"You do teach history at a junior high school here in Irvine—"

"That's right. I've worked there since before Joe died."

"Well, my brother wasn't one of your students. He was an English instructor in the same school. I traced him there, and learned you'd taught in the room next to his for ten years, you knew him well."

Viola's face brightened into a smile. "You mean Jim Ironheart!"

"That's right. My brother."

"This is lovely, wonderful, this is *perfect!*" Viola enthused.

The woman's reaction was so excessive that Holly blinked in surprise and didn't know quite what to say next.

"He's a good man," Viola said with genuine affection. "I'd have liked nothing better than to've had a son like him. He comes around now and then for dinner, not as often as he used to, and I cook for him, mother him. I can't tell you how much pleasure that gives me." A wistful expression had settled on her, and she was silent a moment. "Anyway . . . you couldn't have asked for a better brother, dear. He's one of the nicest people I've ever known, a dedicated teacher, so gentle and kind and patient."

Holly thought of Norman Rink, the psychopath who

had killed a clerk and two customers in that Atlanta convenience store last May, and who had been killed in turn by gentle, kind Jim Ironheart. Eight rounds from a shotgun at point-blank range. Four rounds fired into the corpse after Rink was obviously dead. Viola Moreno might know the man well, but she clearly had no concept of the rage that he could tap when he needed it.

"I've known good teachers in my time, but none as concerned about his students as Jim Ironheart was. He sincerely cared about them, as if they were his own kids." She leaned back in her chair and shook her head, remembering. "He gave so much to them, wanted so much to make their lives better, and all but the worst-case misfits responded to him. He had a rapport with his students that other teachers would sell their souls for, yet he didn't have to surrender a proper student-teacher relationship to get it. So many of them try to be pals with their students, you see, and that never really works."

"Why did he quit teaching?"

Viola hesitated, smile fading. "Partly, it was the lottery."

"What lottery?"

"You don't know about that?"

Holly frowned and shook her head.

Viola said, "He won six million dollars in January."

"Holysmoke!"

"The first time he ever bought a ticket."

Allowing her initial surprise to metamorphose into a look of worry, Holly said, "Oh, God, now he's going to think I only came around because he's suddenly rich."

"No, no," Viola hastened to assure her. "Jim would never think the worst of anyone."

"I've done well myself," Holly lied. "I don't need his money, I wouldn't take it if he tried to give it to me. My adoptive parents are doctors, not wealthy but well-to-do, and I'm an attorney with a nice practice."

Okay, okay, you really *don't* want his money, Holly thought with self-disgust as caustic as acid, but you're still a mean little lying bitch with a frightening talent for invented detail, and you'll spend eternity standing hip-deep in dung, polishing Satan's boots.

Her mood changing, Viola pushed her chair back from the table, got up, and stepped to the edge of the patio. She plucked a weed from a large terra-cotta pot full of begonias, baby's breath, and copper-yellow marigolds. Absentmindedly rolling the slender weed into a ball between the thumb and forefinger of her right hand, she stared thoughtfully out at the parklike grounds.

The woman was silent for a long time.

Holly worried that she had said something wrong, unwittingly revealing her duplicity. Second by second, she became more nervous, and she found herself wanting to blurt out an apology for all the lies she'd told.

Squirrels capered on the grass. A butterfly swooped under the patio cover, perched on the edge of the lemonade pitcher for a moment, then flew away.

Finally, with a tremor in her voice that was real this time, Holly said, "Mrs. Moreno? Is something wrong?"

Viola flicked the balled-up weed out onto the grass. "I'm just having trouble deciding how to put this."

"Put what?" Holly asked nervously.

Turning to her again, approaching the table, Viola said, "You asked me why Jim . . . why your brother quit teaching. I said it was because he won the lottery, but that really isn't true. If he'd still loved teaching as much as he did a few years ago or even *one* year ago, he would've kept working even if he'd won a hundred million."

Holly almost breathed a sigh of relief that her cover had not been penetrated. "What soured him on it?"

"He lost a student."

"Lost?"

"An eighth-grader named Larry Kakonis. A very bright boy with a good heart—but disturbed. From a troubled family. His father beat his mother, had been beating her as long as Larry could remember, and Larry felt as if he should be able to stop it, but he couldn't. He felt responsible, though he shouldn't have. That was the kind of kid he was, a real strong sense of responsibility."

Viola picked up her glass of lemonade, returned to the edge of the patio, and stared out at the greensward again. She was silent once more.

Holly waited.

Eventually the woman said, "The mother was a co-dependent type, a victim of the father but a collaborator in her own victimization. As troubled in her own way as the father. Larry couldn't reconcile his love for his mother and his respect for her with his growing understanding that, on some level, she liked and *needed* to be beaten."

Suddenly Holly knew where this was going, and she did not want to hear the rest of it. However, she had no choice but to listen.

"Jim had worked so hard with the boy. I don't mean just on his English lessons, not just academically. Larry had opened up to him in a way he'd never been able to open to anyone else, and Jim had been counseling him with the help of Dr. Lansing, a psychologist who works part-time for the school district. Larry seemed to be coming around, struggling to understand his mother and himself—and to some extent succeeding. Then one night, May fifteenth of last year—over fifteen months ago, though it's hard to believe it's been that long—Larry Kakonis took a gun from his father's collection, loaded it, put the barrel in his mouth . . . and fired one bullet up into his brain."

Holly flinched as if struck. In fact she *had* been struck, though the blows—two of them—were not physical. She was jolted, first, by the thought of a thirteen-year-old committing suicide when the best of life lay ahead of him. A small problem could seem like a large one at that age, and a genuinely serious problem could seem catastrophic and hopeless. Holly felt a pang of grief for Larry Kakonis, and an undirected anger because the kid had not been given time enough to learn that all horrors can be dealt with and that, on balance, life offered far more joy than despair. But she was equally rattled by the date on which the boy had killed himself: May 15.

One year later, this past May 15, Jim Ironheart had performed his first miraculous rescue. Sam and Emily

Newsome. Atlanta, Georgia. Saved from murder at the hands of a sociopathic holdup man named Norman Rink.

Holly could sit still no longer. She got up and joined Viola at the edge of the patio. They watched the squirrels.

"Jim blamed himself," Viola said.

"For Larry Kakonis? But he wasn't responsible."

"He blamed himself anyway. That's how he is. But his reaction seemed excessive, even for Jim. After Larry's death, he lost interest in teaching. He stopped believing he could make a difference. He'd had so many successes, more than any teacher I've ever known, but that one failure was too much for him."

Holly remembered the boldness with which Ironheart had scooped Billy Jenkins out of the path of the hurtling pickup truck. *That* certainly had not been a failure.

"He just sort of spiraled down into gloom," Viola said, "couldn't pull himself out of it."

The man Holly had met in Portland had not seemed depressive. Mysterious, yes, and self-contained. But he'd had a good sense of humor, and he'd been quick to smile.

Viola took a sip of her lemonade. "Funny, it tastes too sour now." She set the glass down on the concrete near her feet and wiped her damp hand on her slacks. She started to speak again, hesitated, but finally said, "Then . . . he got a little strange."

"Strange? In what way?"

"Withdrawn. Quiet. He started taking martial-arts training. Tae Kwon Do. Lots of people are interested in that sort of thing, I guess, but it seemed so out of character for Jim."

It didn't seem out of character for the Jim Ironheart that Holly knew.

Viola said, "It wasn't casual with him, either. Every day after school he went for a lesson at a place in Newport Beach. He became obsessive. I worried about him. So in January, when he won the lottery, I was happy. Six million dollars! That's such a good thing, such *big* luck, it seemed like it would have to turn his life around, bring him out of his depression."

"But it didn't?"

"No. He didn't seem all that surprised or pleased by it. He quit teaching, moved out of his apartment into a house . . . and pulled back even further from his friends." She turned to Holly and smiled. It was the first smile she had managed for a while. "That's why I was so excited when you told me you were his sister, a sister he doesn't even know he has. Because maybe *you* can do for him what winning six million dollars couldn't do."

Guilt over her deception suffused Holly again, bringing a hot blush to her face. She hoped Viola would mistake it for a blush of pleasure or excitement. "It would be wonderful if I could."

"You can, I'm sure. He's alone, or feels that he is. That's part of his problem. With a sister, he won't be alone any more. Go see him today, right now."

Holly shook her head. "Soon. But not yet. I need to . . . build my confidence. You won't tell him about me, will you?"

"Of course not, dear. You should have all the fun of telling him, and what a wonderful moment that'll be."

Holly's smile felt like a pair of rigid plastic lips glued to her face, as false as part of a Halloween costume.

A few minutes later, at the front door, as Holly was leaving, Viola put a hand on her arm and said, "I don't want to give you the wrong idea. It won't be *easy* lifting his spirits, getting him back on track. As long as I've known Jim, I've felt there's a sadness deep down in him, like a stain that won't come out, which isn't such a surprise, really, when you consider what happened to his parents— his being orphaned when he was only ten, all of that."

Holly nodded. "Thanks. You've been a real help."

Viola impulsively hugged her, planted a kiss on her cheek, and said, "I want to have both you and Jim to dinner as soon as possible. Homemade green-corn tamales, black beans, and jalapeño rice so hot it'll melt your dental fillings!"

Holly was simultaneously pleased and dismayed: pleased to have met this woman, who so quickly seemed to be a favorite aunt of long acquaintance; dismayed because she had met her and been accepted by her under false pretenses.

All the way back to her rental car, Holly fiercely berated herself under her breath. She was at no loss for ugly words and clever damning phrases. Twelve years in newsrooms, in the company of reporters, had acquainted her with enough obscene language to insure her the trophy in a cursing contest with even the most foul-mouthed victim of Tourette's syndrome.

▼ ▲ ▼

The Yellow Pages listed only one Tae Kwon Do school in Newport Beach. It was in a shopping center off Newport Boulevard, between a custom window-covering store and a bakery.

The place was called Dojo, the Japanese word for a martial-arts practice hall, which was like naming a restaurant "Restaurant" or a dress shop "Dress Shop." Holly was surprised by the generic name, because Asian businessmen often brought a poetic sensibility to the titling of their enterprises.

Three people were standing on the sidewalk in front of Dojo's big window, eating éclairs and awash in the delicious aromas wafting from the adjacent bakery, watching a class of six students go through their routines with a squat but exceptionally limber Korean instructor in black pajamas. When the teacher threw a pupil to the mat inside, the plate-glass window vibrated.

Entering, Holly passed out of the chocolate-, cinnamon-, sugar-, yeast-scented air into an acidic environment of stale incense laced with a vague perspiration odor. Because of a story she'd written about a Portland teenager who won a medal in a national competition, she knew Tae Kwon Do was an aggressive Korean form of karate, using fierce punches, lightning-quick jabs, chops, blocks, chokeholds, and devastatingly powerful, leaping kicks. The teacher was pulling his blows, but there were still a lot of grunts, wheezes, guttural exclamations, and jarring thuds as students slammed to the mat.

In the far right corner of the room, a brunette sat on a stool behind a counter, doing paperwork. Every aspect and detail of her dress and grooming were advertisements for her sexuality. Her tight red T-shirt emphasized her ample chest and outlined nipples as large as cherries. With a touseled mane of chestnut hair given luster by artfully applied blond highlights, eyes subtly but exotically shadowed, mouth too lushly painted with deep-coral lipstick, a just-right tan, disablingly long fingernails painted to match the lipstick, and enough silvery costume jewelry to stock a display case, she would have been the perfect advertisement if women had been a product for sale in every local market.

"Does this thudding and grunting go on all day?" Holly asked.

"Most of the day, yeah."

"Doesn't it get to you?"

"Oh, yeah," the brunette said with a lascivious wink, "I know what you mean. They're like a bunch of bulls ramming at each other. I'm not here an hour every day till I'm so horny I can't stand it."

That was not what Holly had meant. She was suggesting that the noise was headache-inducing, not arousing. But she winked back, girl-to-girl, and said, "The boss in?"

"Eddie? He's doing a couple hundred flights of stairs," the woman said cryptically. "What'd you want?"

Holly explained that she was a reporter, working on a story that had a connection with Dojo.

The receptionist, if that's what she was, brightened at this news instead of glowering, as was often the case. Eddie, she said, was always looking to get publicity for the business. She rose from her stool and stepped to a door behind the counter, revealing that she was wearing high-heeled sandals and tight white shorts that clung to her butt as snugly as a coat of paint.

Holly was beginning to feel like a boy.

As the brunette had indicated, Eddie was delighted to

hear that Dojo would be mentioned in a newspaper piece, even if tangentially, but he wanted her to interview him while he continued to do stairs. He was not an Asian, which perhaps explained the unimaginative generic name of his business. Tall, blond, shaggy-haired, blue-eyed, he was dressed only in muscles and a pair of black spandex cyclist's shorts. He was on a StairMaster exercise machine, climbing briskly to nowhere.

"It's great," he said, pumping his exquisitely developed legs. "Six more flights, and I'll be at the top of the Washington monument."

He was breathing hard but not as hard as Holly would have been breathing after running up six flights to her third-floor apartment in Portland.

She sat in a chair he had indicated, which put the Stair-Master directly in front of her, giving her a full side view of him. His sun-bronzed skin glistened with sweat, which also darkened the hair at the nape of his thick neck. The spandex embraced him as intimately as the white shorts had clung to the receptionist. It almost seemed as if he had known Holly was coming and had carefully arranged the StairMaster and her chair to display himself to his best advantage.

Although she was plunging into deception again, Holly did not feel as bad about lying to Eddie as she had felt when lying to Viola Moreno. For one thing, her cover story this time was somewhat less fanciful: that she was doing a multipart, in-depth piece about James Ironheart (the truth), focusing on the effect that winning a lottery had upon his life (a lie), all with his approval (a lie). A veracity percentage as high as thirty-three percent was enough to salve her guilt, which she supposed didn't say much for the quality of her conscience.

"Just so you spell Dojo right," Eddie said. Looking back and down at his right leg, he added happily, "Look at that calf, hard as rock."

As if she hadn't been looking at it all along.

"The fat layer between my skin and the muscle underneath, it's hardly there, burned it all away."

Another reason she didn't mind lying to Eddie was because he was a vain, self-involved jerk.

"Three more flights to the top of the monument," he said. The rhythm of his speech was tied to the pattern of his breathing, the words rising and falling with each inhalation and exhalation.

"Just three? Then I'll wait."

"No, no. Ask your questions. I won't stop at the top. I'm gonna see how much of the Empire State Building I can climb next."

"Ironheart was a student of yours."

"Yeah. Taught him myself."

"He came to you long before he won the lottery."

"Yeah. More than a year ago."

"May of last year, I think."

"Mighta been."

"Did he tell you why he wanted to learn Tae Kwon Do?"

"Nope. But he had a passion." He almost shouted his next words, as if he'd triumphantly completed a real climb: "Top of the monument!" He increased his pace instead of slacking off.

"Did you think it was odd?"

"Why?"

"Him being a schoolteacher, I mean."

"We get schoolteachers. We get all kinds. Everyone wants to kick ass." He sucked in a very deep breath, blew it out, and said, "In the Empire State now, going up."

"Was Ironheart good?"

"Excellent! Coulda been a competitor."

"Could've been? You mean he dropped out?"

Breathing a little harder than before, the words coming in a quicker though similar rhythm, he said: "Hung in there seven or eight months. Every day. He was a real glutton for punishment. Pumping iron and doing aerobics *plus* martial arts. Ate his way through the pain. Man was getting tough enough to fuck a rock. Sorry. But he was. Then he quit. Two weeks after he won the bucks."

"Ah, I see."

"Don't get me wrong. Wasn't the money that made him quit."

"Then what?"

"He said I'd given him what he needed, he didn't want any more."

"What he needed?" she asked.

"Enough Tae Kwon Do for what he wanted to do."

"Did he say what he wanted to do?"

"Nope. Kick someone's ass, I guess."

Eddie was really pushing himself now, ramming his feet down on the StairMaster, pumping and pumping, so much sweat on his body that he appeared to be coated in oil, droplets spraying off his hair when he shook his head, the muscles in his arms and across his broad back bulging almost as fiercely as those in his thighs and calves.

Sitting in the chair about eight feet from the man, Holly felt as if she were ringside at some sleazy strip club where the gender roles had been reversed. She got up.

Eddie was staring straight ahead at the wall. His face was creased by lines of strain, but he had a dreamy, far-away look in his eyes. Maybe, instead of the wall, he saw the endless stairwell in the Empire State Building.

"Anything else he ever told you that seemed . . . interesting, unusual?" she asked.

Eddie didn't answer. He was concentrating on the climb. The arteries in his neck had swelled and were throbbing as if evenly spaced, small, fat fish were schooling through his bloodstream.

As Holly reached the door, Eddie said, "Three things."

She turned to him again. "Yeah?"

Without looking at her, his eyes still out of focus, not for an instant slackening his pace, speaking to her from the stairwell of that skyscraper in distant Manhattan, he said, "Ironheart's the only guy I ever met who can obsess better than I can."

Frowning, Holly thought about that. "What else?"

"The only lessons he missed were two weeks in September. Went up north, Marin County somewhere, to take a course in aggressive driving."

"What's that?"

"Mostly they teach chauffeurs for politicians, diplomats, rich businessmen how to handle a car like James Bond, escape terrorist traps, kidnappers, shit like that."

"He talk about why he needed that kind of training?"

"Just said it sounded like fun."

"That's two things."

He shook his head. Sweat flew, spattered the surrounding carpet and furniture. Holly was just out of range. He still didn't look at her. "Number three—after he figured he had enough Tae Kwon Do, the next thing he wanted was to learn guns."

"Learn guns?"

"Asked me if I knew anyone could teach him marksmanship, all about weapons. Revolver, pistols, rifles, shotguns . . ."

"Who'd you send him to?"

He was panting now but still able to speak clearly between each gasping breath: "Nobody. Guns aren't my thing. But you know what I think? I think he was one of these guys reads *Soldier of Fortune.* Gets caught up in the fantasy. Wants to be a mercenary. He sure was preparing for a war."

"Didn't it worry you to be helping someone like that?"

"Not as long as he paid for his lessons."

She opened the door, hesitated, watching him. "You have a counter on that contraption?"

"Yeah."

"What floor are you on?"

"Tenth," Eddie said, the word distorted as he spoke it on a deep exhalation. The next time he breathed out, he also issued a whoop of pleasure along with his wind. "Jesus, I have legs of stone, fuckin' granite, I think I could get a man in a scissor hold, crack him in half with my legs. You put that in your article, okay? I could crack a guy clean in half."

Holly left, closing the door softly behind her.

In the main room, the martial-arts class was even more active than when she had entered. The current exercise involved a group attempt to gang up on their Korean instructor, but he was blocking and throwing and whirling and leaping like a dervish, dealing with them as fast as they came at him.

The brunette had removed her silvery jewelry. She had changed into Reeboks, looser shorts, a different T-shirt, and a bra. Now she was doing stretching exercises in front of the reception counter.

"One o'clock," she explained to Holly. "My lunch hour. I always run four or five miles instead of eating. Bye." She jogged to the door, pushed through it into the warm August day, and sprinted out of sight along the front of the shopping center.

Holly went outside, too, and stood for a moment in the lovely sunshine, newly aware of how many of the shoppers, coming to and going from their cars, were in good physical shape. Having moved to the northwest almost a year and a half ago, she had forgotten how health conscious many southern Californians were—and how aware of their appearance. Per capita, Orange County had a lot fewer jowls, love handles, spare tires, pot guts, and pear-shaped bottoms than Portland.

Looking good and feeling good were imperatives of the southern-California lifestyle. It was one of the things she loved about the place. It was also one of the things she hated about it.

She went nextdoor to the bakery for lunch. From the display cases, she selected a chocolate éclair, a crème brulée tart with kiwi on top, a piece of white-chocolate macadamia-nut cheesecake with Oreo-crumb crust, a cinnamon wheel, and a slice of orange roulade. "And a diet Coke," she told the clerk.

She carried her tray to a table near a window, where she could watch the passing parade of taut, tanned bodies in summer gear. The pastries were wonderful. She ate a little of this, now a little of that, savoring each bite, intending to polish off every crumb.

After a while she realized someone was watching her. Two tables away, a heavyset woman, about thirty-five, was staring with a mixture of disbelief and envy; she only had one miserable fruit tart, a bakery junkie's equivalent of a Nutri/System multi-grain cracker.

Feeling both a need to explain herself and a certain sympathy, Holly said, "I wish I wasn't doing this, but I can't help it. If I can't do anything else, then I always binge when I'm horny."

The heavyset woman nodded. "Me, too."

▼▲▼

She drove to Ironheart's place on Bougainvillea Way. She knew enough about him now to risk approaching him, and that was what she intended to do. But instead of pulling into his driveway, she cruised slowly past the house again.

Instinct told her that the time was not right. The portrait of him that she had constructed only *seemed* to be complete. There was a hole in it somewhere. She sensed that it would be dangerous to proceed before that hole had been painted in.

She returned to the motel and spent the rest of the afternoon and early evening sitting by the window in her room, drinking Alka-Seltzer, then diet 7-Up, staring out at the jewel-blue pool in the middle of the lushly landscaped courtyard, and thinking. Thinking.

Okay, she told herself, the story to date. Ironheart is a man with a sadness at his core, probably because of being orphaned when he was only ten. Let's say he's spent a lot of his life brooding about death, especially about the injustice of premature death. He dedicates his life to teaching and helping kids, maybe because no one was there for *him* when he was a boy and had to cope with the deaths of his mother and father. Then Larry Kakonis commits suicide. Ironheart is shattered, feels he should have been able to prevent it. The boy's death brings to the surface all of Ironheart's buried rage: rage at fate, destiny, the biological fragility of the human species—rage at God. In a state of severe mental distress bordering on outright imbalance, he decides to make himself over into Rambo and *do* something to fight back at fate, which is a weird response at best, absolutely nuts at worst. With weight lifting, aerobic endurance training, and Tae Kwon Do, he turns himself into a fighting machine. He learns to drive like a stuntman. He becomes knowledgeable in the use of all manner of guns. He's ready. Just one more thing. He teaches himself to be a clairvoyant, so he can win the lottery and be independently wealthy, making it possible to devote himself to his crusade—and so he can know just *when* a premature death is about to occur.

That was where it all fell apart. You could go to a place like Dojo to learn martial arts, but the Yellow Pages had no listing for schools of clairvoyance. Where the hell had he gotten his psychic power?

She considered the question from every imaginable angle. She wasn't trying to brainstorm an answer, only figure out an approach to researching possible explanations. But magic was magic. There was no way to research it.

She began to feel as though she was employed by a sleazy tabloid, not as a reporter but as a concocter of pieces about space aliens living under Cleveland, half-gorilla and half-human babies born to amoral female zookeepers, and inexplicable rains of frogs and chickens in Tajikistan. But, damn it, the hard facts were that Jim Ironheart had saved fourteen people from death, in every corner of the country, always at the penultimate moment, with miraculous foresight.

By eight o'clock, she had the urge to pound her head against the table, the wall, the concrete decking around the pool outside, against anything hard enough to crack her mental block and drive understanding into her. She decided that it was time to stop thinking, and go to dinner.

She ate in the motel coffeeshop again—just broiled chicken and a salad to atone for lunch at the bakery. She tried to be interested in the other customers, do a little people-watching. But she could not stop thinking about Ironheart and his sorcery.

He dominated her thoughts later, as well, when she was

lying in bed, trying to sleep. Staring at the shadows on the ceiling, cast by the landscape lighting outside and the half-open Levolor blinds on the window, she was honest enough with herself to admit he fascinated her on other than professional levels. He was the most important story of her career, yes, true. And, yes, he was so mysterious that he would have intrigued anyone, reporter or not. But she was also drawn to him because she had been alone a long time, loneliness had carved an emptiness in her, and Jim Ironheart was the most appealing man she had met in ages.

Which was insane.

Because maybe *he* was insane.

She was not one of those women who chased after men who were all wrong for her, subconsciously seeking to be used, hurt, and abandoned. She was picky when it came to men. That was why she was alone, for God's sake. Few men measured up to her standards.

Sure. Picky, she thought sarcastically. That's why you've got this lech for a guy who has delusions of being Superman without the tights and cape. Get real, Thorne. Jesus.

Entertaining romantic fantasies about James Ironheart was short-sighted, irresponsible, futile, and just plain stupid.

But those *eyes.*

Holly fell asleep with an image of his face drifting in her mind, watching over her as if it were a portrait on a giant banner, rippling gently against a cerulean sky. His eyes were even bluer than that celestial backdrop.

In time she found herself in the dream of blindness again. The circular room. Wooden floor. Scent of damp limestone. Rain drumming on the roof. Rhythmic creaking. *Whoosh.* Something was coming for her, a part of the darkness that had somehow come alive, a monstrous presence that she could neither hear nor see but could feel. The Enemy. *Whoosh.* It was closing in relentlessly, hostile and savage, radiating cold the way a furnace radiated heat. *Whoosh.* She was grateful that she was blind, because she knew the thing's appearance was so alien, so terrifying, that just the sight of it would kill her. *Whoosh.* Something touched her. A moist, icy tendril. At the base of her neck. A pencil-thin tentacle. She cried out, and the tip of the probe bored into her neck, pierced the base of her skull—

Whoosh.

With a soft cry of terror, she woke. No disorientation. She knew immediately where she was: the motel, Laguna Hills.

Whoosh.

The sound of the dream was still with her. A great blade slicing through the air. But it was not a dream sound. It was real. And the room was as cold as the pitch-black place in the nightmare. As if weighted down by a heart swollen with terror, she tried to move, could not. She smelled damp limestone. From below her, as if there were vast rooms under the motel, came a soft rumbling sound of—she somehow knew—large stone wheels grinding against each other.

Whoosh.

Something unspeakable was still squirming along the back of her neck, writhing sinuously within her skull, a hideous parasite that had chosen her for a host, worming its way into her, going to lay its eggs in her brain. But she could not move.

Whoosh.

She could see nothing but bars of pale, pale light against part of the black ceiling, where the moonsoft glow of landscape lighting projected the image of the windowblind slats. She desperately wanted more light.

Whoosh.

She was making pathetic whimpers of terror, and she so thoroughly despised herself for her weakness that she was finally able to shatter her paralysis. Gasping, she sat up. Clawed at the back of her neck, trying to tear off the oily, frigid, wormlike probe. Nothing there. Nothing. Swung her legs over the edge of the bed. Fumbled for the lamp. Almost knocked it over. Found the switch. Light.

Whoosh.

She sprang off the bed. Felt the back of her head again.

Her neck. Between her shoulderblades. Nothing. Nothing there. Yet she *felt* it.

Whoosh.

She was over the edge of hysteria and unable to return, making queer little animal sounds of fear and desperation. Out of the corner of her eye, she saw movement. Swung around. The wall behind the bed. Sweating. Glistening. The entire wall bulged toward her, as if it were a membrane against which a great and terrible mass was pressing insistently. It throbbed repulsively, like an enormous internal organ in the exposed and steaming guts of a prehistoric behemoth.

Whoosh.

She backed away from the wet, malignantly animated wall. Turned. Ran. Had to get out. Fast. The Enemy. It was coming. Had followed her. Out of the dream. The door. Locked. Deadbolt. Disengaged it. Hands shaking. The Enemy. Coming. Brass security chain. Rattled it free. Door. Jerked it open. Something was on the threshold, filling the doorway, bigger than she was, something beyond human experience, simultaneously insectile and arachnoid and reptilian, squirming and jittering, a tangled mass of spider legs and antennae and serpentine coils and roachlike mandibles and multifaceted eyes and rattlesnake fangs and claws, a thousand nightmares rolled into one, but she was *awake.* It burst through the door, seized her, pain exploding from her sides where its talons tore at her, and she screamed—

—a night breeze.

That was the only thing coming through the open door. A soft, summery night breeze.

Holly stood in the doorway, shuddering and gasping for breath, looking out in astonishment at the concrete promenade of the motel. Lacy queen palms, Australian tree ferns, and other greenery swayed sensuously under the caress of the tropical zephyr. The surface of the swimming pool rippled gently, creating countless ever-changing facets, refracting the pool-bottom lights, so it seemed as if there was not a body of water in the middle of the courtyard but a hole filled with a pirate's treasure of polished sapphires.

The creature that had attacked her was gone as if it had never existed. It had not scuttled away or scurried up some web; it had simply evaporated in an instant.

She no longer felt the icy, squirming tendril on the back of her neck or inside her skull.

A couple of other guests had come out of rooms farther along the promenade, evidently to investigate her scream.

Holly stepped back from the threshold. She did not want to attract their attention now.

She glanced over her shoulder. The wall behind the bed was only a wall again.

The clock built into the nightstand showed 5:08 A.M.

She eased the door shut, and suddenly she had to lean against it, because all the strength went out of her legs.

Instead of being relieved that the strange ordeal had ended, she was shattered. She hugged herself and shivered so hard, her teeth chattered. She began to cry softly, not from fear of the experience, concern for her current safety, or concern about her sanity, but from a profound sense of having been totally violated. Briefly but for too long, she had been helpless, victimized, enslaved by terror, controlled by an entity beyond her understanding. She'd been psychologically raped. Something needful had overpowered her, forced its way into her, denying her free will; though gone now, it had left traces of itself within her, a residue that stained her mind, her soul.

Just a dream, she told herself encouragingly.

But it had not been a dream when she sat up in bed and snapped on the lamp. The nightmare had followed her into the waking world.

Just a dream, don't make so much of it, get control of yourself, she thought, struggling to regain her equanimity. You dreamed you were in that lightless place, then you *dreamed* that you sat up in bed and turned on the light, then in your *dream* you saw the wall bulging and ran for the door. But you were only sleepwalking, you were still asleep when you pulled the door open, still asleep when you saw the boogeyman and screamed, which was when you finally woke up for real, screamed yourself awake.

She wanted to believe that explanation, but it was too pat to be credible. No nightmare she'd ever known had been that elaborate in its texture and detail. Besides, she never sleepwalked.

Something real had been reaching for her. Maybe not the insect-reptile-spider thing in the doorway. Maybe that was only an image in which another entity clad itself to frighten her. But something had been pushing through to this world from . . .

From where?

It didn't matter where. From out there. From beyond. And it almost got her.

No. That was ridiculous. Tabloid stuff. Even the *National Enquirer* didn't publish trash that trashy anymore. I WAS MIND-RAPED BY A BEAST FROM BEYOND. Crap like that was three steps below CHER ADMITS BEING SPACE ALIEN, two steps below JESUS SPEAKS TO NUN FROM INSIDE A MICRO-WAVE, and even a full step below ELVIS HAD BRAIN TRANS-PLANTED, LIVES NOW AS ROSEANNE BARR.

The more foolish she felt for entertaining such thoughts, the calmer she became. Dealing with the experience was easier if she could believe that it was all a product of her overactive imagination, which had been unreasonably stimulated by the admittedly fantastic Ironheart case.

Finally she was able to stand on her own, without leaning on the door. She relocked the deadbolt, reengaged the security chain.

As she stepped away from the door, she became aware of a hot, stinging pain in her left side. It wasn't serious, but it made her wince, and she realized that a similar but lesser pain sizzled in her right side as well.

She took hold of her T-shirt to lift it and look at herself—and discovered that the fabric was slashed. Three places on the left side. Two on the right. It was spotted with blood.

With renewed dread, Holly went into the bathroom and switched on the harsh fluorescent light. She stood in front of the mirror, hesitated, then pulled the torn T-shirt over her head.

A thin flow of blood seeped down her left flank from three shallow gashes. The first laceration was just under her breast, and the others were spaced at two-inch intervals. Two scratches blazed on her right side, though they were not as deep as those on the left and were not bleeding freely.

The claws.

▼▲▼

Jim threw up in the toilet, flushed, then rinsed his mouth twice with mint-flavored Listerine.

The face in the mirror was the most troubled he had ever seen. He had to look away from the reflection of his own eyes.

He leaned against the sink. For at least the thousandth time in the past year, he wondered what in God's name was happening to him.

In his sleep he had gone to the windmill again. Never before had the same nightmare troubled him two nights in a row. Usually, weeks passed between reccurrences.

Worse, there had been an unsettling new element—more than just the rain on the narrow windows, the lambent flame of the candle and the dancing shadows it produced, the sound of the big sails turning outside, the low rumble of the millstones below, and an inexplicable pall of fear. This time he'd been aware of a malevolent presence, out of sight but drawing nearer by the second, something so evil and alien that he could not even imagine its form or full intentions. He had expected it to burst out of the limestone wall, erupt through the plank floor, or explode in upon him from the heavy timbered door at the head of the mill stairs. He had been unable to decide which way to run. Finally he had yanked open the door—and awakened with a scream. If anything had been there, he could not remember what it had looked like.

Regardless of the appearance it might have had, Jim knew what to call it: the enemy. Except that now he thought of it with a capital "T" and a capital "E." The Enemy. The amorphous beast that haunted many of his other nightmares had found its way into the windmill dream, where it had never terrorized him before.

Crazy as it seemed, he sensed that the creature was not merely a fantasy spawned by his subconscious while he slept. It was as real as he was himself. Sooner or later it would cross the barrier between the world of dreams and the waking world as easily as it had crossed the barrier between different nightmares.

4

Holly never considered going back to bed. She knew she would not sleep again for many hours, until she was so exhausted that she would be unable to keep her eyes open no matter how much strong black coffee she drank. Sleep had ceased to be a sanctuary. It was, instead, a source of danger, a highway to hell or somewhere worse, along which she might encounter an inhuman traveler.

That made her angry. Everyone needed and deserved the refuge of sleep.

As dawn came, she took a long shower, carefully but diligently scrubbing the shallow lacerations on her sides, although the soap and hot water stung the open flesh. She worried that she would develop an infection as strange as the briefly glimpsed monstrosity that had inflicted her wounds.

That sharpened her anger.

By nature, she was a good Girl Scout, always prepared for any eventuality. When traveling, she carried a few first-aid supplies in the same kit with her Lady Remington shaver: iodine, gauze pads, adhesive tape, Band-Aids, a small aerosol can of Bactine, and a tube of ointment that was useful for soothing minor burns. After toweling off from the shower, she sat naked on the edge of the bed, sprayed Bactine on her wounds, then daubed at them with iodine.

She had become a reporter, in part, because as a younger woman she had believed that journalism had the power to explain the world, to make sense of events that sometimes seemed chaotic and meaningless. More than a decade of newspaper employment had shaken her conviction that the human experience *could* be explained all or even most of the time. But she still kept a well-ordered desk, meticulously arranged files, and neat story notes. In her closets at home, her clothes were arranged according to season, then according to the occasion (formal, semi-formal, informal), then by color. If life insisted on being chaotic, and if journalism had failed her as a tool for bringing order to the world, at least she could depend on routine and habit to create a personal pocket universe of stability, however fragile, beyond which the disorder and tumult of life were kept at bay.

The iodine stung.

She was angrier. Seething.

The shower disturbed the clots that had coagulated in the deeper scratches on her left side. She was bleeding slightly again. She sat quietly on the edge of the bed for a while, holding a wad of Kleenex against the wounds, until the lacerations were no longer oozing.

By the time Holly had dressed in tan jeans and an emerald-green blouse, it was seven-thirty.

She already knew how she was going to start the day, and nothing could distract her from her plans. She had no appetite whatsoever for breakfast. When she stepped outside, she discovered that the morning was cloudless and unusually temperate even for Orange County, but the sublime weather had no mellowing influence on her and did not tempt her to pause even for a moment to relish the early sun on her face. She drove the rental car across the parking lot, out to the street, and headed toward Laguna Niguel. She was going to ring James Ironheart's doorbell and demand a lot of answers.

She wanted his full story, the explanation of how he could know when people were about to die and why he took such extreme risks to save total strangers. But she also wanted to know why last night's bad dream had become real, how and why her bedroom wall had begun to glisten and throb like flesh, and what manner of creature had popped out of her nightmare and seized her in talons formed of something more substantial than dreamstuff.

She was convinced that he would have the answers. Last night, for only the second time in her thirty-three years, she'd encountered the unknown, been sideswiped by the supernatural. The first time had been on August 12, when Ironheart had miraculously saved Billy Jenkins from being mowed down by a truck in front of the McAlbury School—although she hadn't realized until later that he had stepped right out of the Twilight Zone. Though she was willing to cop to a lot of faults, stupidity was not one of them. Anyone but a fool could see that both collisions with the paranormal, Ironheart and the nightmare-made-real, were related.

She was more than merely angry. She was pissed.

As she cruised down Crown Valley Parkway, she realized that her anger sprang, in part, from the discovery that her big, career-making story was turning out not to be strictly about amazement and wonder and courage and hope and triumph, as she had anticipated. Like the vast majority of articles that had appeared on the front pages of newspapers since the invention of the printing press, this story had a dark side.

▼▲▼

Jim had showered and dressed for church. He did not regularly attend Sunday Mass anymore, or the services of any other of the religions to which he had been sporadically committed over the years. But having been in the control of a higher power since at least last May, when he had flown to Georgia to save the lives of Sam and Emily Newsome, he was disposed to think about God more than usual. And since Father Geary had told him about the stigmata that had marked his body while he lay unconscious on the floor of Our Lady of the Desert, less than a week ago, he had felt the tidal pull of Catholicism for the first time in a couple of years. He didn't actually expect that the mystery of recent events would be cleared up by answers he would find in church—but he could hope.

As he plucked his car keys off the pegboard on the kitchen wall beside the door to the garage, he heard himself say, "Life line." Immediately, his plans for the day were changed. He froze, not sure what to do. Then the familiar feeling of being a marionette overcame him, and he hung the keys back on the pegboard.

He returned to the bedroom and stripped out of his loafers, gray slacks, dark-blue sportcoat, and white shirt. He dressed in chinos and a blousy Hawaiian shirt, which he wore over his pants in order to be as unhampered as possible by his clothing.

He needed to stay loose, flexible. He had no idea *why* looseness and flexibility were desirable for what lay ahead, but he felt the need just the same.

Sitting on the floor in front of the closet, he selected a pair of shoes—the most comfortable, broken-in pair of Rockports that he owned. He tied them securely but not too tightly. He stood up and tested the fit. Good.

He reached for the suitcase on the top shelf, then hesitated. He was not sure that he would require luggage. A few seconds later, he *knew* that he would be traveling light. He slid the closet door shut without taking down the bag.

No luggage usually meant that his destination would be within driving distance and that the round-trip, including the time needed to perform whatever work was expected of him, would take no more than twenty-four hours. But as he turned away from the closet, he surprised himself by saying, "Airport." Of course, there were a lot of places to which he could fly round-trip in a single day.

He picked his wallet off the dresser, waited to see if he felt compelled to put it down again, and finally slipped it into his hip pocket. Evidently he would need not only money but ID—or at least he would not risk exposure by carrying it.

As he walked to the kitchen again and took the car keys off the pegboard, fear played through him, although not as strongly as it had the last time he had left his house on a mission. That day he had been "told" to steal a car so it could not be traced to him, and to drive into the Mojave Desert. This time he might encounter adversaries even more formidable than the two men in the Roadking, but he was not as worried as he'd been before. He knew he could die. Being the instrument of a higher power came with no guarantees of immortality; he was still only a man whose flesh could be torn, whose bones could be broken, and whose heart could be stopped instantly with a well-placed bullet. The amelioration of his fear was attributable solely to his somewhat mystical journey on the Harley, two days with Father Geary, the report of the stigmata that had appeared on him, and the resulting conviction that a divine hand was at work in all of this.

▼▲▼

Holly was on Bougainvillea Way, a block from Iron-heart's house, when a dark-green Ford backed out of his driveway. She did not know what kind of car he drove, but since he lived alone, she assumed the Ford had to be his.

She speeded up, half intending to swing around him, angle across his bow, force him to stop, and confront him right in the street. Then she slowed down again, figuring discretion was seldom a fatal error. She might as well see where he was going, what he was up to.

As she passed his house, the automatic garage door was rolling down. Just before it closed, she was able to see that no other car was in there. The man in the Ford had to be Ironheart.

Because she had never been assigned to stories about paranoid drug lords or bent politicians or corrupt businessmen, Holly was not expert at tailing a surveillance subject through traffic. The skills and techniques of clandestine operations were not necessary when you wrote exclusively about Timber Trophies, performance artists in radiation suits who juggled live mice on the steps of city hall and called it "art," and pie-eating contests. She was also mindful of the fact that Ironheart had taken a two-week course in aggressive driving at a special school in Marin County; if he knew how to handle a car well enough to shake off pursuing terrorists, he would leave her in the dust about thirty seconds after he realized she was following him.

She hung as far back as she dared. Fortunately, the Sunday-morning traffic was heavy enough to allow her to hide behind other cars. But it was light enough so she didn't have to worry that the lanes would suddenly clog up between her and Ironheart, cutting her off until he disappeared from sight.

He drove east on Crown Valley Parkway to Interstate 5, then north toward Los Angeles on 405.

By the time they had passed the clustered high rises around South Coast Plaza, the primary shopping and office center for the two million people in the Orange County metroplex, Holly's mood was better than it had been. She was proving to be adept at mobile surveillance, staying from two to six cars in back of Ironheart but always close enough to follow if he abruptly swung onto an exit ramp. Her anger was tempered by the pleasure she took in her skillful pursuit. Now and then she even found herself admiring the clarity of the blue sky and the profusely flowering pink and white oleanders that flanked the freeway at some places.

Passing Long Beach, however, she began to worry that she was going to spend the whole day on the road with him, only to discover that wherever he was going had nothing to do with the enigma that concerned her. Even a self-appointed superhero with clairvoyant powers might just spend a day taking in a theater matinee, doing nothing more dangerous than eating Szechuan Chinese with the chef's hottest mustard.

She began to wonder, as well, if he might become aware of her through his psychic powers. Sensing her a few cars back seemed a lot easier than foreseeing the approaching death of a small boy in Boston. On the other hand, maybe clairvoyance was an inconstant power, something he could not turn on and off at will, and maybe it only worked on the big things, zapping him with either visions of danger and destruction and death—or no visions at all. Which made sense in a way. It would probably drive you insane to have psychic visions that told you in advance whether you were going to enjoy a particular movie, have a good dinner, or get a bad case of gas and the bloats from that garlicky angel-hair pasta that you were enjoying so much. Nevertheless, she dropped back a little farther, putting one more car between them.

When Ironheart left the freeway at the exit for Los Angeles International Airport, Holly became excited. Perhaps he was only meeting someone on an incoming flight. But it was more likely that he was catching a plane out, embarking on one of his timely rescue missions, just as he had flown to Portland on August 12, nearly two weeks ago. Holly was not prepared to travel; she didn't even have a change of clothes. However, she had cash and credit cards to handle expenses, and she could buy a fresh blouse anywhere. The prospect of tailing him all the way to the scene of the action tantalized her. Ultimately, when she wrote about him, she would be able to do so with more authority if she had been an eye-witness at *two* of his rescues.

She almost lost her nerve when he swung off the airport service loop into a parking garage, because there was no longer a convenient car between them to mask her presence. But the alternative was to drive on, park in another garage, and lose him. She hung back only as far as she dared and took a ticket from the dispenser seconds after he did.

Ironheart found an empty slot halfway along a row on the third level, and Holly pulled in ten spaces past him. She slumped down in her seat a little and remained in her car, giving him a headstart so there was less of a chance of him glancing back and seeing her.

She almost waited too long. When she got out of her car, she was barely in time to glimpse him as he turned right and disappeared around a wall at the bottom of the ramp.

She hurried after him. The soft, flat *slap-slap* of her footsteps echoed hollowly off the low concrete ceiling. At the base of the ramp, when she turned the corner, she saw him enter a stairwell. By the time she passed through that door after him, she heard him descend the final flight and open the door below.

Thanks to his colorful Hawaiian shirt, she was able to stay well behind him, mingling with other travelers, as he crossed the service road and entered the United Airlines terminal. She hoped they weren't going to Hawaii. Researching a story without the financial backing of the newspaper was expensive enough. If Ironheart was going to save someone's life today, she hoped he would do it in San Diego instead of Honolulu.

In the terminal, she hung back behind a group of tall Swedes, using them for cover, while Ironheart stood for a while at a bank of monitors, studying the schedule of upcoming departures. Judging by the frown on his face, he didn't see the flight he wanted. Or maybe he simply didn't yet *know* which flight he wanted. Perhaps his premonitions did not come to him full-blown; he might have to work at them, nurse them along, and he might not know exactly where he was going or whose life he would be saving until he got there.

After a few minutes, he turned from the monitors and strode along the concourse to the ticket counter. Holly continued to stay well back of him, watching from a distance, until she realized that she would not know his destination unless she was close enough to hear him give it to the clerk. Reluctantly she closed the gap.

She could wait until he had bought the ticket, of course, follow him to see which gate he waited at, then book herself on the same flight. But what if the plane took off while she was dashing through the endless hallways of the terminal? She could also try to cajole the clerk into telling her what flight Ironheart had taken by claiming to have picked up a credit card he'd dropped. But the airline might offer to return it to him; or if they found her story suspicious, they might even call security guards.

In the line at the ticket counter, she dared to close within one person of Ironheart. The only traveler between them was a burly, big-bellied man who looked like an NFL linebacker gone to seed; he had mildly offensive body odor, but he provided considerable cover, for which she was grateful.

The short line moved quickly. When Ironheart stepped up to the counter, Holly eased out around the fat man and strained forward to hear whatever destination was mentioned.

The public-address system inconveniently brought forth a woman's soft, sensuous, yet zombielike voice, announcing the discovery of a lost child. At the same time, a noisy group of New Yorkers went past, complaining about the perceived phoniness of California's have-a-nice-day service ethic, apparently homesick for hostility. Ironheart's words were drowned out.

Holly inched nearer to him.

The fat man frowned down at her, evidently suspecting her of attempted line-jumping. She smiled at him in such a way as to assure him that she had no evil intentions and that she knew he was large enough to squash her like a bug.

If Ironheart glanced back now, he would look directly into her face. She held her breath, heard the clerk say, ". . . O'Hare Airport in Chicago, leaving in twenty minutes . . . ," and slipped back behind the fat man, who looked over his shoulder to frown down at her again.

She wondered why they had come to LAX for a flight to Chicago. She was pretty sure there were plenty of connections to O'Hare from John Wayne in Orange County. Well . . . though Chicago was farther than San Diego, it was preferable to—and cheaper than—Hawaii.

Ironheart paid for his ticket and hurried off in search of his gate without glancing in Holly's direction.

Some psychic, she thought.

She was pleased with herself.

When she reached the counter, she presented a credit card and asked for a seat on the same flight to Chicago. For a moment she had the terrible feeling that the clerk would say the plane was fully booked. But there were seats left, and she got her ticket.

The departure lounge at the gate was nearly empty. Boarding of the flight had virtually been completed. Ironheart was nowhere in sight.

On the way along the tunnel-like boarding gate to the door of the aircraft, she began to worry that he would see her when she had to walk back the aisle to her seat. She could pretend not to notice him, or pretend not to recognize him if he approached her. But she doubted that he would believe her presence on his flight was sheer coincidence. An hour and a half ago, she'd been in a rush to confront him. Now she wanted nothing more than to *avoid* confrontation. If he saw her, he would abort his trip; she might never get another chance to be present at one of his last-minute rescues.

The plane was a wide-body DC-10 with two aisles. Each row of nine seats was divided into three sections: two by the window on the port side, five down the center, two by the window on the starboard side. Holly was assigned to row twenty-three, seat H, which was on the starboard flank, one seat removed from the window. As she headed back the aisle, she scanned the faces of her fellow passengers, hoping she wouldn't lock eyes with Jim Ironheart. In fact, she would rather not see him at all during the flight, and worry about catching sight of him again at O'Hare. The DC-10 was an immense aircraft. Though a number of seats were empty, more than two hundred and fifty people were onboard. She and Ironheart might very well fly around the world together without bumping into each other; getting through the few hours to Chicago should be a cinch.

Then she saw him. He was sitting in the five-wide middle section of row sixteen, the port-aisle seat, on the other side of the plane. He was paging through an issue of the airline's magazine, and she prayed that he would not look up until she was past him. Though she had to step aside for a flight attendant escorting a small boy who was flying alone, her prayer was answered. Ironheart's head remained bowed over the publication until she was past him. She reached 23-H and sat down, sighing with relief. Even if he went to the restroom, or just got up to stretch his legs, he would probably never have any reason to come around to the starboard aisle. Perfect.

She glanced at the man in the window seat beside her. He was in his early thirties, tanned, fit, and intense. He was wearing a dark-blue business suit, white shirt, and tie even on a Sunday flight. His brow was as furrowed as his suit was well-pressed, and he was working on a laptop computer. He was wearing headphones, listening to music or pretending to, in order to discourage conversation, and he gave her a cool smile calculated to do the same.

That was fine with her. Like a lot of reporters, she was not garrulous by nature. Her job required her to be a good listener, not necessarily a good talker. She was content to pass the trip with the airline's magazine and her own Byzantine thoughts.

▼▲▼

Two hours into the flight, Jim still had no idea where he was expected to go when he got off the plane at O'Hare. He was not concerned about it, however, because he had learned to be patient. The revelation always came, sooner or later.

Nothing in the airline's magazine was of interest to him, and the in-flight movie sounded as if it were about as much fun as a vacation in a Soviet prison. The two seats to the right of him were empty, so he was not required to make nice with a stranger. He tilted his seat slightly, folded his hands on his stomach, closed his eyes, and passed the time—between the flight attendants' inquiries about his appetite and comfort—by brooding about the windmill dream, puzzling out what significance it had, if any.

That was what he *tried* to brood about, anyway. But for some curious reason, his mind wandered to Holly Thorne, the reporter.

Hell, now he was being disingenuous, because he knew perfectly well why she had been drifting in and out of his thoughts ever since he had met her. She was a treat for the eyes. She was intelligent, too; one look at her, and you knew about a million gears were spinning in her head, all meshing perfectly, well-oiled, quiet and productive.

And she had a sense of humor. He would give anything to share his days and his long, dream-troubled nights with a woman like that. Laughter was usually a function of sharing—an observation, a joke, a moment. You didn't laugh a lot when you were always alone; and if you did, that probably meant you should make arrangements for a long stay in a resort with padded walls.

He had never been smooth with women, so he had often been without them. And he had to admit, even before this recent strangeness had begun, he was sometimes difficult to live with. Not depressive exactly but too aware that death was life's companion. Too inclined to brood about the coming darkness. Too slow to seize the moment and succumb to pleasure. If—

He opened his eyes and sat up straighter in his seat, because suddenly he received the revelation that he had been expecting. Or part of it, at least. He still did not know what was going to happen in Chicago, but he knew the names of the people whose lives he was expected to save: Christine and Casey Dubrovek.

To his surprise, he realized they were on this plane with him—which led him to suspect that the trouble might come in the terminal at O'Hare, or at least soon after touchdown. Otherwise he would not have crossed their path so early. Usually, he encountered the people he saved only minutes before their lives were thrown into jeopardy.

Compelled by those forces that had been guiding him periodically since last May, he got up, headed to the front of the plane, crossed over to the starboard side, and started back that aisle. He had no idea what he was doing until he stopped at row twenty-two and looked down at the mother and child in seats H and I. The woman was in her late twenties; she had a sweet face, not beautiful but gentle and pretty. The child was five or six years old.

The woman looked up at him curiously, and Jim heard himself say, "Mrs. Dubrovek?"

She blinked in surprise. "I'm sorry . . . do I know you?"

"No, but Ed told me you were taking this flight and asked me to look you up." When he spoke that name, he knew Ed was her husband, though he had no idea where that knowledge had come from. He squatted down beside her seat and gave her his best smile. "I'm Steve Harkman. Ed's in sales, I'm in advertising, so we drive each other nuts in about a dozen meetings a week."

Christine Dubrovek's madonna face brightened. "Oh, yes, he's spoken about you. You only joined the company, what, a month ago?"

"Six weeks now," Jim said, flowing with it, confident the right answers would pour out of him even if he didn't know what in the hell they were. "And this must be Casey."

The little girl was in the seat by the window. She raised her head, shifting her attention from a pop-up storybook. "I'm gonna be six tomorrow, it's my birthday, and we're gonna visit grandpop and grandma. They're real old, but they're nice."

He laughed and said, "I'll bet they're sure proud to have a granddaughter cute as you."

▼ ▲ ▼

When Holly saw him coming along the starboard aisle, she was so startled that she almost popped out of her seat. At first she thought he was looking straight at her. She had the urge to start blurting out a confession—"Yes, all right, I've been following you, checking up on you, invading your privacy with a vengeance"—even before he reached her. She knew precious few other reporters who would have felt guilty about probing into his life, but she couldn't seem to eliminate that streak of decency that had interfered with her career advancement ever since she'd gotten her journalism degree. It almost wrecked everything for her again—until she realized he was looking not at her but at the brunette immediately in front of her. Holly swallowed hard, and slid down a few inches in her seat instead of leaping up in a frenzy of confession. She picked up the airline's magazine, which she'd previously discarded; slowly, deliberately she opened it to cover her face, afraid that too quick a move would draw his attention before she had concealed herself behind those glossy pages.

The magazine blocked her view of him, but she could hear every word he was saying and most of the woman's responses. She listened to him identify himself as Steve Harkman, a company ad executive, and wondered what his charade was all about.

She dared to tilt her head far enough to peek around the magazine with one eye. Ironheart was hunkered down in the aisle beside the woman's seat, so close that Holly could have spit on him, although she was no more practiced at target-spitting than she was at clandestine surveillance.

She realized her hands were trembling, making the magazine rattle softly. She untilted her head, stared at the pages in front of her, and concentrated on being calm.

▼▲▼

"How on earth did you recognize me?" Christine Dubrovek asked.

"Well, Ed doesn't *quite* paper his office with pictures of you two," Jim said.

"Oh, that's right," she said.

"Listen, Mrs. Dubrovek—"

"Call me Christine."

"Thank you. Christine . . . I've got an ulterior motive for coming over here and pestering you like this. According to Ed, you've got a knack for matchmaking."

That must have been the right thing to say. Already aglow, her sweet face brightened further. "Well, I do like getting people together if I think they're right for each other, and I've got to admit I've had more than a little success at it."

"You make matches, Mommy?" Casey Dubrovek asked.

Uncannily in synch with the workings of her six-year-old's mind, Christine said, "Not the cigarette kind, honey."

"Oh. Good," Casey said, then returned to her pop-up storybook.

"The thing is," Jim said, "I'm new in Los Angeles, been there only eight weeks, and I'm your classic, original lonely guy. I don't like singles' bars, don't want to buy a gym membership just to meet women, and figure anybody I'd connect with through a computer service has to be as desperate and messed up as I am."

She laughed. "You don't look desperate or messed up to me."

"Excuse me, sir," a stewardess said with friendly firmness, touching Jim's shoulder, "but I can't allow you to block the aisle."

"Oh, sure, yeah," he said, standing up. "Just give me a minute." Then to Christine: "Listen, this is embarrassing, but I'd really like to talk to you, tell you about myself, what I'm looking for in a woman, and see if maybe you know someone . . . ?"

"Sure, I'd love that," Christine said with such enthusiasm that she was surely the reincarnation of either some hillbilly woman who had been a much sought-after troth-finder or a successful *schatchen* from Brooklyn.

"Hey, you know, the two seats next to mine are empty," he said. "Maybe you could sit with me the rest of the way. . . ."

He expected her to be reluctant to give up window seats, and an inexplicable twist of anxiety knotted his stomach while he waited for her response.

But she hesitated for only a second or two. "Yes, why not."

The stewardess, still hovering near them, nodded her approval.

To Jim, Christine said, "I thought Casey would like the scenery from way up here, but she doesn't seem to care much. Besides, we're almost at the back of the wing, and it blocks a lot of our view."

Jim did not understand the reason for the wave of relief that swept through him when he secured her agreement to move, but a lot of things mystified him these days. "Good, great. Thank you, Christine."

As he stepped back to let Christine Dubrovek get up, he

noticed the passenger in the seat behind her. The poor woman was evidently terrified of flying. She was holding a copy of *Vis à Vis* in front of her face, trying to take her mind off her fears with a little reading, but her hands were shaking so badly that the magazine rattled continuously.

"Where are you sitting?" Christine asked.

"The other aisle, row sixteen. Come on, I'll show you."

He lifted her single piece of carry-on luggage while she and Casey gathered up a few other small items, then he led them to the front of the plane and around to the port aisle. Casey entered row sixteen, and her mother followed.

Before Jim settled down himself, something impelled him to look back across the wide-bodied plane to the aerophobic woman whom they had left behind in row twenty-three. She had lowered the magazine. She was watching him. He knew her.

Holly Thorne.

He was stunned.

Christine Dubrovek said, "Steve?"

Across the plane, the reporter realized that Jim had seen her. She was wide-eyed, frozen. Like a deer caught in car headlights.

"Steve?"

He looked down at Christine and said, "Uh, excuse me a minute, Christine. Just a minute. I'll be right back. Wait here. Okay? Wait right here."

He went forward and across to the starboard aisle again.

His heart was hammering. His throat was tight with fear. But he didn't know why. He was not afraid of Holly Thorne. He knew at once that her presence was no coincidence, that she had tumbled to his secret and had been following him. But right now he didn't care. Discovery, being unmasked—that was not what frightened him. He had no idea what *was* cranking up his anxiety, but it was escalating to a level at which adrenaline would soon start to squirt out his ears.

As he made his way back the aisle toward the reporter, she started to get up. Then a look of resignation slid across her face, and she sat down again. She was as easy to look at as he remembered, though the skin around her eyes was slightly dark, as if from lack of sleep.

When he arrived at row twenty-three, he said, "Come on." He reached for her hand.

She did not give it to him.

"We've got to talk," he said.

"We can talk here."

"No, we can't."

The stewardess who had warned him about blocking the aisle was approaching again.

When Holly would not take his hand, he gripped her by the arm and urged her to get up, hoping she would not force him to yank her out of the seat. The stewardess probably already thought he was some pervert Svengali who was herding up the best-looking women on the flight to surround himself with a harem over there on the port side. Happily, the reporter rose without further protest.

He led her back through the plane to a restroom. It was not occupied, so he pushed her inside. He glanced back, expecting to see the stewardess watching him, but she was attending to another passenger. He followed Holly into the tiny cubicle and pulled the door shut.

She squeezed into the corner, trying to stay as far away from him as possible, but they were still virtually nose to nose.

"I'm not afraid of you," she said.

"Good. There's no reason to be."

Vibrations were conducted well by the burnished-steel walls of the lavatory. The deep drone of the engines was somewhat louder there than in the main cabin.

She said, "What do you want?"

"You've got to do exactly what I tell you."

She frowned. "Listen, I—"

"*Exactly* what I tell you, and no arguments, there's no time for arguments," he said sharply, wondering what the hell he was talking about.

"I know all about your—"

"I don't care what you know. That's not important now."

She frowned. "You're shaking like a leaf."

He was not only shaking but sweating. The lavatory was cool enough, but he could feel beads of sweat forming across his forehead. A thin trickle coursed down his right temple and past the corner of his eye.

Speaking rapidly, he said, "I want you to come forward in the plane, sit farther front near me, there're a couple of empty seats in that area."

"But I—"

"You can't stay where you are, back there in row twenty-three, no way."

She was not a docile woman. She knew her own mind, and she was not used to being told what to do. "That's my seat. Twenty-three H. You can't strongarm me—"

Impatiently, he said, "If you sit there, you're going to die."

She looked no more surprised than he felt—which was plenty damn surprised. "Die? What do you mean?"

"I don't know." But then unwanted knowledge came to him. "Oh, Jesus. Oh, my God. We're going down."

"What?"

"The plane." Now his heart was racing faster than the turbine blades in the great engines that were keeping them aloft. "Down. All the way down."

He saw her incomprehension give way to a dreadful understanding. "Crash?"

"Yes."

"When?"

"I don't know. Soon. Beyond row twenty, almost nobody's going to survive." He did not know what he was going to say until he said it, and as he listened to his own words he was horrified by them. "There'll be a better survival rate in the first nine rows, but not good, not good at all. You've got to move into my section."

The aircraft shuddered.

Holly stiffened and looked around fearfully, as if she expected the lavatory walls to crumple in on them.

"Turbulence," he said. "Just turbulence. We've got . . . a few minutes yet."

Evidently she had learned enough about him to have faith in his prediction. She did not express any doubt. "I don't want to die."

With an increasing sense of urgency, Jim gripped her by the shoulders. "That's why you've got to come forward, sit near me. Nobody's going to be killed in rows ten through twenty. There'll be injuries, a few of them serious, but nobody's going to die in that section, and a lot of them are going to walk out of it unhurt. Now, for God's sake, come on."

He reached for the door handle.

"Wait. You've got to tell the pilot."

He shook his head. "It wouldn't help."

"But maybe there's something he can do, stop it from happening."

"He wouldn't believe me, and even if he did . . . I don't know what to tell him. We're going down, yeah, but I don't know why. Maybe a mid-air collision, maybe structural failure, maybe there's a bomb aboard—it could be anything."

"But you're a psychic, you must be able to see more details if you try."

"If you believe I'm a psychic, you know less about me than you think you do."

"You've got to try."

"Oh, lady, I'd try, I'd try like a sonofbitch if it would do any good. But it won't."

Terror and curiosity fought for control of her face. "If you're not a psychic—what are you?"

"A tool."

"Tool?"

"Someone or something uses me."

The DC-10 shuddered again. They froze, but the aircraft did not take a sudden plunge. It went on as before, its three big engines droning. Just more turbulence.

She grabbed his arm. "You can't let all those people die!"

A rope of guilt constricted his chest and knotted his

stomach at the implication that the deaths of the others aboard would somehow be his fault.

He said, "I'm here to save the woman and the girl, no one else."

"That's horrible."

Opening the lavatory door, he said, "I don't like it any more than you do, but that's the way it is."

She did not let go of his arm but jerked at it angrily. Her green eyes were haunted, probably with her own visions of battered bodies strewn across the earth among smoking chunks of wreckage. She repeated herself, whispering fiercely this time: "You can't let all those people die."

Impatiently, he said, "Either come with me, or die with the rest of them."

He stepped out of the lavatory, and she followed him, but he did not know whether she was going to accompany him back to his section. He hoped to God she would. He really could not be held responsible for all the other people who would perish, because they would have died even if he had not come aboard; that was their fate, and he had not been sent to alter *their* destinies. He could not save the whole world, and he had to rely on the wisdom of whatever higher power was guiding him. But he most definitely would be responsible for Holly Thorne's death, because she would never have taken the flight if, unwittingly, he had not led her onto it.

As he moved forward along the port aisle, he glanced to his left at the portholes and clear blue sky beyond. He had a too vivid sense of the yawning void under his feet, and his stomach flopped.

When he reached his seat in row sixteen, he dared to look back. Relief flooded through him at the sight of Holly trailing close.

He pointed to a pair of empty seats immediately behind his and Christine's.

Holly shook her head. "Only if you'll sit down with me. We have to talk."

He glanced down at Christine, then at Holly. He was acutely aware of time slipping away like water swirling down a drain. The awful moment of impact was drawing closer. He wanted to pick the reporter up, stuff her into the seat, engage her seatbelt, and lock her in place. But seatbelts didn't have locks.

Unable to conceal his extreme frustration, he spoke to her through gritted teeth. "My place is with them," he said, meaning with Christine and Casey Dubrovek.

He had spoken quietly, as had Holly, but other passengers were beginning to look at them.

Christine frowned up at him, craned her neck to look back at Holly, and said, "Is something wrong, Steve?"

"No. Everything's fine," he lied.

He glanced at the portholes again. Blue sky. Vast. Empty. How many miles to the earth below?

"You don't look well," Christine said.

He realized that his face was still sheathed in a greasy film of sweat. "Just a little warm. Uh, look, I ran into an old friend. Gimme five minutes?"

Christine smiled. "Sure, sure. I'm still going over a mental list of the most-eligible."

For a moment he had no idea what the hell she was talking about. Then he remembered that he had asked her to play matchmaker for him. "Good," he said. "Great. I'll be right back, we'll talk."

He ushered Holly into row seventeen. He took the aisle seat next to her.

On the other side of Holly was a grandmotherly tub of a woman in a flower-print dress, with blue-tinted gray hair in a mass of tight curls. She was sound asleep, snoring softly. A pair of gold-framed eyeglasses, suspended around her neck on a bead chain, rested on her matronly bosom, rising and falling with her steady breathing.

Leaning close to him, keeping her voice so low it could not even carry across the narrow aisle, but speaking with the conviction of an impassioned political orator, Holly said, "You can't let all those people die."

"We've been through this," he said restively, matching her nearly inaudible pitch.

"It's your responsibility—"

"I'm just one man!"

"But one very special man."

"I'm not God," he said plaintively.

"Talk to the pilot."

"Jesus, you're relentless."

"Warn the pilot," she whispered.

"He won't believe me."

"Then warn the passengers."

"There aren't enough empty seats in this section for all of them to move here."

She was furious with him, quiet but so intense that he could not look away from her or dismiss what she was saying. She put a hand on his arm, gripping him so tightly that it hurt. "Damn it, maybe they could do *something* to save themselves."

"I'd only cause a panic."

"If you can save more, but you let them die, it's murder," she whispered insistently, anger flashing in her eyes.

That accusation hit him hard and had something of the effect of a hammer blow to the chest. For a moment he could not draw his breath. When he could speak, his voice broke repeatedly: "I hate death, people dying, I *hate* it. I want to save people, stop all the suffering, be on the side of life, but I can only do what I can do."

"Murder," she repeated.

What she was doing to him was outrageous. He could not carry the load of responsibility she wanted to pile on his shoulders. If he could save the Dubrovcks, he would be working two miracles, mother and child spared from the early graves that had been their destinies. But Holly Thorne, in her ignorance about his abilities, was not satisfied with two miracles; she wanted three, four, five, ten, a hundred. He felt as if an enormous weight was bearing down on him, the weight of the whole damned airplane, crushing him into the ground. It was not right of her to put the blame on him; it wasn't fair. If she wanted to blame someone, she should cast her accusations at God, who worked in such mysterious ways that He had ordained the necessity of the plane crash in the first place.

·"Murder." She dug her fingers into his arm even harder.

He could feel anger radiating from her like the heat of the sun reflected off a metal surface. Reflected. Suddenly, he realized that image was too apt to be anything less than Freudian. Her anger over his unwillingness to save everyone on the plane was no greater than his own anger over his inability to do so; her rage was a reflection of his own.

"Murder," she repeated, evidently aware of the profound effect that accusation had on him.

He looked into her beautiful eyes, and he wanted to hit her, punch her in the face, smash her with all of his strength, knock her unconscious, so she wouldn't put his own thoughts into words. She was too perceptive. He hated her for being *right*.

Instead of hitting her, he got up.

"Where are you going?" she demanded.

"To talk to a flight attendant."

"About what?"

"You win, okay? You win."

Making his way toward the back of the plane, Jim looked at the people he passed, chilled by the knowledge that many of them would be dead soon. As his desperation intensified, so did his imagination, and he saw skulls beneath their skin, the glowing images of bones shining through their flesh, for they were the living dead. He was nauseous with fear, not for himself but for them.

The plane bucked and shimmied as if it had driven over a pothole in the sky. He grabbed at the back of a seat to steady himself. But this was not the big one.

The flight attendants were gathered farther back in the plane, in their work area, preparing to serve the lunch trays that had just come up from the galley. They were a mixed group, men and women, a couple in their twenties and the others as old as fifty-something.

Jim approached the oldest of them. According to the tag she wore, her name was Evelyn.

"I've got to talk to the pilot," he said, keeping his voice low, although the nearest passengers were well forward of them.

If Evelyn was surprised by his request, she didn't show it. She smiled just as she had been trained to smile. "I'm sorry, sir, but that isn't possible. Whatever the problem is, I'm sure I can help—"

"Listen, I was in the lavatory, and I heard something, a *wrong* sound," he lied, "not the right kind of engine noise."

Her smile became a little wider but less sincere, and she went into her reassure-the-nervous-traveler mode. "Well, you see, during flight it's perfectly normal for the pitch of the engines to change as the pilot alters airspeed and—"

"I know that." He tried to sound like a reasonable man to whom she ought to listen. "I've flown a lot. This was different." He lied again: "I know aircraft engines, I work for McDonnell Douglas. We designed and built the DC-10. I *know* this plane, and what I heard in the lav was *wrong.*"

Her smile faltered, most likely not because she was starting to take his warning seriously but merely because she considered him to be a more inventive aerophobe than most who panicked in mid-flight.

The other flight attendants had paused in their lunch-service preparations and were staring at him, no doubt wondering if he was going to be a problem.

Evelyn said carefully, "Well, really, everything's functioning well. Aside from some turbulence—"

"It's the tail engine," he said. That was not another lie. He was receiving a revelation, and he was letting the unknown source of that revelation speak through him. "The fan assembly is starting to break apart. If the blades tear loose, that's one thing, the pieces can be contained, but if the entire fan-blade assembly shatters, God knows what could happen."

Because of the specificity of his fear, he did not sound like a typical aerophobic passenger, and all of the flight attendants were staring at him with, if not respect, at least a wary thoughtfulness.

"Everything's fine," Evelyn said, per training. "But even if we lost an engine, we can fly on two."

Jim was excited that the higher power guiding him had

evidently decided to give him what he needed to convince these people. Maybe something *could* be done to save everyone on the flight.

Striving to remain calm and impressive, he heard himself saying, "That engine has forty thousand pounds of thrust, it's a real monster, and if it blows up, it's like a bomb going off. The compressors can back-vent, and those thirty-eight titanium blades, the fan assembly, even pieces of the rotor can explode outward like shrapnel, punching holes in the tail, screwing up the rudders and elevators . . . The whole tail of the plane could disintegrate."

One of the flight attendants said, "Maybe somebody should just mention this to Captain Delbaugh."

Evelyn did not instantly object.

"I know these engines," Jim said. "I can explain it to him. You don't have to take me on the flight deck, just let me speak to him on the intercom."

Evelyn said, "McDonnell Douglas?"

"Yeah. I've been an engineer there for twelve years," he lied.

She was now full of doubt about the wisdom of the standard response she had learned in training. She was almost won over.

With hope blossoming, Jim said, "Your captain's got to shut down engine number two. If he shuts it down and goes the rest of the way on one and three, we'll make it, all of us, we'll make it alive."

Evelyn looked at the other flight attendants, and a couple of them nodded. "I guess it wouldn't hurt if . . ."

"Come on," Jim said urgently. "We might not have much time."

He followed Evelyn out of the attendants' work area and into the starboard aisle in the economy-class section, heading forward.

The plane was rocked by an explosion.

Evelyn was thrown hard to the deck. Jim pitched forward, too, grabbed at a seat to avoid falling atop the woman, overcompensated and fell to one side instead, against a passenger, then to the floor, as the plane started to shimmy. He heard lunch trays still crashing to the deck behind him, people crying out in surprise and alarm, and one thin short scream. As he tried to scramble to his feet, the aircraft nosed down, and they started to lose altitude.

▼ ▲ ▼

Holly moved forward from row seventeen, sat beside Christine Dubrovek, introduced herself as a friend of Steve Harkman's, and was nearly thrown out of her seat when a sickening shockwave pumped through the aircraft. It was followed a fraction of a second later by a solid *thump,* as if they had been struck by something.

"Mommy!" Casey had been belted in her seat, even though the seatbelt signs were not on. She was not thrown forward, but the storybooks on her lap clattered to the deck. Her eyes were huge with fear.

The plane started to lose altitude.

"Mommy?"

"It's okay," Christine said, obviously struggling to conceal her own fear from her daughter. "Just turbulence, an air pocket."

They were dropping fast.

"You're gonna be okay," Holly told them, leaning past Christine to make sure the little girl heard her reassurances. "Both of you are going to be okay if you just stay here, don't move, stay right in these seats."

Knifing down . . . a thousand feet . . . two thousand . . .

Holly frantically belted herself in her seat.

. . . three thousand . . . four thousand . . .

An initial wave of horror and panic gripped the passengers. But that was followed quickly by a breathless silence, as they all clung to the arms of their seats and waited to see if the damaged aircraft was going to pull up in time—or tip downward at an even more severe angle.

To Holly's surprise, the nose slowly came up. The plane leveled off again.

A communal sigh of relief and a smattering of applause swept through the cabin.

She turned and grinned at Christine and Casey. "We're going to be all right. We're all going to make it."

The captain came on the loudspeaker and explained that they had lost one of their engines. They could still fly just fine on the remaining two, he assured them, though he suggested they might need to divert to a suitable airfield closer than O'Hare, only to be safe. He sounded calm and confident, and he thanked the passengers for their patience, implying that the worst they would suffer was inconvenience.

A moment later Jim Ironheart appeared in the aisle, and squatted beside Holly. A spot of blood glimmered at the corner of his mouth; he had evidently been tossed around a little.

She was so exhilarated, she wanted to kiss him, but she just said, "You did it, you changed it, you made a difference somehow."

He looked grim. "No." He leaned close to her, put his face almost against hers, so they could talk in whispers as before, though she thought Christine Dubrovek must be hearing some of it. He said, "It's too late."

Holly felt as if he had punched her in the stomach. "But we leveled off."

"Pieces of the exploding engine tore holes in the tail. Severed most of the hydraulic lines. Punctured the others. Soon they won't be able to steer the airplane."

Her fear had melted. Now it came back like ice crystals forming and linking together across the gray surface of a winter pond.

They were going down.

She said, "You know *exactly* what happened, you should be with the captain, not here."

"It's over. I was too late."

"No. Never——"

"Nothing I can do now."

"But——"

A flight attendant appeared, looking shaken but sounding calm. "Sir, please return to your seat."

"All right, I will," Jim said. He took Holly's hand first,

and squeezed it. "Don't be afraid." He looked past her at
Christine, then at Casey. "You'll be all right."

He moved back to row seventeen, the seat immediately
behind Holly. She was loath to lose sight of him. He helped
her confidence just by being within view.

▼▲▼

For twenty-six years, Captain Sleighton Delbaugh had
earned his living in the cockpits of commercial airliners,
the last eighteen as a pilot. He had encountered and successfully dealt with a daunting variety of problems, a few
of them serious enough to be called crises, and he had
benefited from United's rigorous program of continuous
instruction and periodic recertification. He felt he was prepared for anything that could happen in a modern aircraft,
but he found it difficult to believe what *had* happened to
Flight 246.

After engine number two failed, the bird went into an
unplanned descent, and the controls stiffened. They
managed to correct its attitude, however, and dramatically
slow its descent. But losing eleven thousand feet of altitude
was the least of their problems.

"We're turning right," Bob Anilov said. He was Delbaugh's first officer, forty-three, and an excellent pilot.
"Still turning right. It's locking up, Slay."

"We've got partial hydraulic failure," said Chris Lodden, their flight engineer. He was the youngest of the three
and a favorite of virtually every female flight attendant
who met him, partly because he was good-looking in a
fresh-faced farmboy way, but largely because he was a
little shy, which made him a novelty among the cocksure
men on most flight crews. Chris was seated behind Anilov
and in charge of monitoring the mechanical systems.

"It's going harder right," Anilov said.

Already Delbaugh was pulling the yoke full aft, left
wheel. "Damn."

Anilov said, "No response."

"It's worse than a partial loss," Chris Lodden said, tapping and adjusting his instruments as if he was having

trouble believing what they were telling him. "How can this be right?"

The DC-10 had three hydraulic systems, well-designed backup. They couldn't have lost everything. But they had.

Pete Yankowski—a balding, red-mustached flight instructor from the company's training facility in Denver—was riding with the crew on his way to visit his brother in Chicago. As an OMC—observing member of crew—he was in the fold-down jumpseat immediately behind Delbaugh, virtually peering over the captain's shoulder. He said, "I'll go have a look at the tail, assess the damage."

As Yankowski left, Lodden said, "The only control we've got is engine thrust."

Captain Delbaugh had already begun to use it, cutting the power to the engine on the right, increasing it to the other—the port—engine in order to pull them to the left and out of their unwanted turn. When they began to swing too far to the left, he would have to increase the power to the starboard engine again and bring them around that way a little.

With the flight engineer's assistance, Delbaugh determined that the outboard and inboard elevators on the tail were gone, dead, useless. The inboard ailerons on the wings were dead. The outboard ailerons were dead. Same for the flaps and spoilers.

The DC-10 had a wingspan of over one hundred and fifty-five feet. Its fuselage was a hundred and seventy feet long. It was more than just an airplane. It was literally a ship that sailed the sky, the very definition of a "jumbo jet," and virtually the only way they now had to steer it was with the two General Electric/Pratt & Whitney engines. Which was only a little better than a driver trying to steer a runaway automobile by leaning to one side and then to the other, desperately struggling to influence its course with his shifting weight.

▼▲▼

A few minutes had passed since the tail engine exploded, and they were still aloft.

Holly believed in a god, not due to any life-altering spiritual experience, but largely because the alternative to belief was simply too grim. Although she had been raised a Methodist and for a while toyed with the idea of conversion to Catholicism, she had never made up her mind what sort of god she preferred, whether one of the gray-suited Protestant varieties or the more passionate Catholic divinity or something else altogether. In her daily life she did not turn to heaven for help with her problems, and she only said grace before meals when she was visiting her parents in Philadelphia. She would have felt like a hypocrite if she had fallen into prayer now, but she nevertheless hoped that God was in a merciful mood and watching over the DC-10, whatever His or Her gender might be and regardless of His or Her preference in worshipers.

Christine was reading one of the pop-up storybooks with Casey, adding her own amusing commentary to the adventures of the animal characters, trying to distract her daughter from the memory of the muffled explosion and subsequent plunge. The intensity of her focus on the child was a giveaway of her true inner feelings: she was scared, and she knew that the worst had not yet passed.

Minute by minute, Holly slipped deeper into a state of denial, unwilling to accept what Jim Ironheart had told her. It was not her own survival, or his, or that of the Dubroveks that she doubted. He had proven himself to be singularly successful when he entered combat with fate; and she was reasonably confident that their lives were secure in the forward section of the economy-class seats, as he had promised. What she wanted to deny, *had* to deny, was that so many others on the flight were going to die. It was intolerable to think that the old and young, men and women, innocent and guilty, moral and immoral, the kind and the mean-spirited were going to die in the same event, compacted together against some rocky escarpment or on a field of wildflowers set afire by burning jet fuel, with no favor given to those who had led their lives with dignity and respect for others.

▼ ▼
▲

Over Iowa, Flight 246 passed out of Minneapolis Center, the air-traffic-control jurisdiction after Denver Center, and now responded only to Chicago Center. Unable to regain hydraulics, Captain Delbaugh requested and received permission from United's dispatcher and from Chicago to divert from O'Haie to the nearest major airport, which was Dubuque, Iowa. He relinquished control of the plane to Anilov, so he and Chris Lodden would be able to concentrate on finding a way through their crisis.

As a first step, Delbaugh radioed System Aircraft Maintenance (SAM) at San Francisco International Airport. SAM was United's central maintenance base, an enormous state-of-the-art complex with a staff of over ten thousand.

"We have a situation here," Delbaugh told them calmly. "Complete hydraulic failure. We can stay up awhile, but we can't maneuver."

At SAM, in addition to United's own employees, experts were also on duty twenty-four hours a day from suppliers of every model of aircraft currently in operation by the airline—including a man from General Electric, where the CF-6 engines had been built, and another from McDonnell Douglas, which had designed and manufactured the DC-10. Manuals, books, and a massive amount of computer-accessible data about each airplane type was available to staff at SAM, in addition to an exhaustively detailed maintenance history of every craft in the United fleet. They could tell Delbaugh and Lodden about every mechanical problem their particular plane had experienced during its lifetime, exactly what had been done to it during its most recently scheduled maintenance, and even when upholstery damage had been repaired—virtually everything except how much loose change had fallen into its seats from passengers' pockets and been left behind during the past twelve months.

Delbaugh also hoped they could tell him how the hell he was supposed to fly an aircraft as large as an apartment building without the aid of elevators, rudders, ailerons, and other equipment that allowed him to maneuver. Even the best flight training programs were structured under the assumption that a pilot would retain *some* degree of control in a catastrophic incident, thanks to redundant systems provided by the designers. Initially, the people at SAM had trouble accepting that he had lost all hydraulics, assuming he meant he'd had a fractional loss. He finally had to snap at them to make them understand, which he deeply regretted not only because he wanted to uphold the tradition of quiet professionalism that pilots before him had established in dire circumstances, but also because he was seriously spooked by the sound of his own angry voice and thereafter found it more difficult to deceive himself that he actually felt as calm as he was pretending to be.

Pete Yankowski, the flight instructor from Denver, returned from his trip to the rear of the plane and reported that through a window he had spotted an eighteen-inch hole in the horizontal part of the tail. "There's probably more damage I couldn't see. Figure shrapnel ripped up the rear section behind the aft bulkhead, where all the hydraulic systems pass through. At least we didn't depressurize."

Dismayed at the rippling sensation that quivered through his bowels, achingly aware that two hundred and fifty-three passengers and ten other crew members were depending on him to bring them home alive, Delbaugh conveyed Yankowski's information to SAM. Then he asked for assistance in determining how to fly the severely disabled aircraft. He was not surprised when, after an urgent consultation, the experts in San Francisco could come up with no recommendations. He was asking them to do the impossible, tell him how to remain the master of this behemoth with no substantial controls other than the throttles—the same unfair request that God was making of him.

He stayed in touch with United's dispatcher office, as well, which tracked the progress of all the company's hardware in the air. In addition, both channels—the dispatcher and SAM—were patched in to United's headquarters near O'Hare International in Chicago. A lot of interested and anxious people were tied to Delbaugh by radio, but they were all as much at a loss for good suggestions as were the experts in San Francisco.

To Yankowski, Delbaugh said, "Ask Evelyn to find that guy from McDonnell Douglas she told us about. Get him up here quick."

As Pete left the flight deck again, and as Anilov struggled with his control wheel in a determined if vain attempt to get at least some response from the craft, Delbaugh told the shift manager at SAM that a McDonnell Douglas engineer was aboard. "He warned us something was wrong with the tail engine just before it exploded. He could tell from the sound of it, I guess, so we'll get him in here, see if he can help."

At SAM, the General Electric expert on CF-6 turbofan engines came back at him: "What do you mean, he could tell by the sound? How could he tell by the sound? What did it sound like?"

"I don't know," Delbaugh replied. "We didn't notice any unusual noises or unexpected changes in pitch, and neither did the flight attendants."

The voice in Delbaugh's headset crackled in response: "That doesn't make sense."

McDonnell Douglas's DC-10 specialist at SAM sounded equally baffled: "What's this guy's name?"

"We'll find out. All we know right now is his first name," Sleighton Delbaugh said. "It's Jim."

▼▲▼

As the captain announced to the passengers that they would be landing in Dubuque as a result of mechanical problems, Jim watched Evelyn approach him along the port aisle, weaving because the plane was no longer as steady as it had been. He wished she would not ask him what he knew she had to ask.

". . . and it might be a little rough," the captain concluded.

As the pilots reduced power to one engine and increased it to the other, the wings wobbled, and the plane wallowed like a boat in a swelling sea. Each time it happened, they recovered quickly, but between those desperate course corrections, when they were unlucky enough to hit air turbulence, the DC-10 did not ride through it as confidently as it had done all the way out from LAX.

"Captain Delbaugh would like you to come forward if you could," Evelyn said when she reached him, soft-voiced and smiling as if delivering an invitation to a pleasant little luncheon of tea and finger sandwiches.

He wanted to refuse. He was not entirely sure that Christine and Casey—or Holly, for that matter—would live through the crash and its immediate aftermath without him at their side. He knew that on impact a ten-row chunk of the fuselage aft of first-class would crack loose from the rest of the plane, and that less damage would be done to it than to the forward and rear sections. Before he had intervened in the fate of Flight 246, all of the passengers in those favored seats had been destined to come out of the crash with comparatively minor injuries or no injuries at all. He was sure that all of those marked for life were still going to live, but he was not certain that merely moving the Dubroveks into the middle of the safety zone was sufficient to alter their fate and insure their survival. Perhaps, after impact, he would have to be there to get them through the fire and out of the wreckage—which he could not do if he was with the flight crew.

Besides, he had no idea whether the crew was going to survive. If he was with them in the cockpit on impact . . .

He went with Evelyn anyway. He had no choice—at least not since Holly Thorne had insisted that he might be able to do more than save one woman and one child, might thwart fate on a large scale instead of a small one. He remembered too clearly the dying man in the station wagon out on the Mojave Desert and the three murdered innocents in the Atlanta convenience store last May, people who could have been spared along with others if he had been allowed to arrive in time to save them.

As he went by row sixteen, he checked out the Dubroveks, who were huddled over a storybook, then he met Holly's eyes. Her anxiety was palpable.

Following Evelyn forward, Jim was aware of the passengers looking at him speculatively. He was one of their own, elevated to special status by their predicament, which they were beginning to suspect was worse than they were being told. They were clearly wondering what special knowledge he possessed that made his presence in the cockpit desirable. If only they knew.

The plane was wallowing again.

Jim picked up a trick from Evelyn. She did not just weave where the tilting deck forced her to go, but attempted to anticipate its movement and lean in the opposite direction, shifting her point of gravity to maintain her balance.

A couple of the passengers were discreetly puking into air-sickness bags. Many others, though able to control their nausea, were gray-faced.

When Jim entered the cramped, instrument-packed cockpit, he was appalled by what he saw. The flight engineer was paging through a manual, a look of quiet desperation on his face. The two pilots—Delbaugh and First Officer Anilov, according to the flight attendant who had not entered with Jim—were struggling with the controls, trying to wrench the right-tending jumbo jet back onto course. To free them to concentrate on that task, a red-haired balding man was on his knees between the two pilots, operating the throttles at the captain's direction, using the thrust of the remaining two engines to provide what steering they had.

Anilov said, "We're losing altitude again."

"Not serious," Delbaugh said. Aware that someone had entered, Delbaugh glanced back at Jim. In the captain's position, Jim would have been sweating like a race-lathered horse, but Delbaugh's face glistened with only a fine sheen of perspiration, as if someone had spritzed him with a plant mister. His voice was steady: "You're him?"

"Yeah," Jim said.

Delbaugh looked forward again. "We're coming

around," he said to Anilov, and the co-pilot nodded. Delbaugh ordered a throttle change, and the man on the floor complied. Then, speaking to Jim without looking at him, the captain said, "You knew it was going to happen."

"Yeah."

"So what else can you tell me?"

Bracing himself against a bulkhead as the plane shuddered and wallowed again, Jim said, "Total hydraulic failure."

"I mean, something I don't know," Delbaugh replied with cool sarcasm. It justifiably could have been an angry snarl, but he was admirably in command of himself. Then he spoke to approach control, obtaining new instructions.

Listening, Jim realized that the Dubuque tower was going to bring in Flight 246 by way of a series of 360-degree turns, in an attempt to line it up with one of the runways. The pilots could not easily guide the plane into a straight approach, as usual, because they had no real control. The disabled craft's maddening tendency to turn endlessly to the right was now to be incorporated into a breathtakingly conceived plan that would let it find its way into the barn like a stubborn bull determined to resist the herder and follow its own route home. If the radius of each turn was carefully calculated and matched to an equally precise rate of descent, they might eventually be able to bring 246 head-on to a runway and all the way in.

Impact in five minutes.

Jim twitched in shock and almost spoke those four words aloud when they came to him.

Instead, when the captain finished talking to the tower, Jim said, "Is your landing gear operable?"

"We got it down and locked," Delbaugh confirmed.

"Then we might make it."

"We *will* make it," Delbaugh said. "Unless there's another surprise waiting for us."

"There is," Jim said.

The captain glanced worriedly at him again. "What?"

Impact in four minutes.

"For one thing, there'll be a sudden windshear as you're

going in, oblique to you, so it won't drive you into the ground. But the reflected updraft from it will give you a couple bad moments. It'll be like you're flying over a washboard."

"What're you talking about?" Anilov demanded.

"When you're making your final approach, a few hundred feet from the end of the runway, you'll still be at an angle," Jim said, once more allowing some omniscient higher power to speak through him, "but you'll have to go for it anyway, no other choice."

"How can you know that?" the flight engineer demanded.

Ignoring the question, Jim went on, and the words came in a rush: "The plane'll suddenly drop to the right, the wing'll hit the ground, and you'll cartwheel down the runway, end over end, off it, into a field. The whole damn plane'll come apart and burn."

The red-haired man in civilian clothes, operating the throttles, looked back at Jim in disbelief. "What crock of shit is this, who the hell do you think you are?"

"He knew about engine number two before it blew up," Delbaugh said coolly.

Aware that they were entering the second of the trio of planned 360-degree turns and that time was swiftly running out, Jim said, "None of you in the cockpit will die, but you'll lose a hundred and forty-seven passengers, plus four flight attendants."

"Oh my God," Delbaugh said softly.

"He can't *know* this," Anilov objected.

Impact in three minutes.

Delbaugh gave additional instructions to the red-haired man, who manipulated the throttles. One engine grew louder, the other softer, and the big craft began its second turn, shedding some altitude as it went.

Jim said, "But there's a warning, just before the plane tips to the right."

"What?" Delbaugh said, still unable to look at him, straining to get what response he could from the wheel.

"You won't recognize what it means, it's a strange

sound, like nothing you've heard before, because it's a structural failure in the wing coupling, where it's fixed to the fuselage. A sharp twang, like a giant steel-guitar string. When you hear it, if you increase power to the port engine immediately, compensating to the left, you'll keep her from cartwheeling."

Anilov had lost his patience. "This is nuts. Slay, I can't *think* with this guy here."

Jim knew Anilov was right. Both System Aircraft Maintenance in San Francisco and the dispatcher had been silent for a while, hesitant to interfere with the crew's concentration. If he stayed there, even without saying another word, he might unintentionally distract them at a crucial moment. Besides, he sensed that there was nothing more of value that he would be given to tell them.

He left the flight deck and moved as quickly as possible toward row sixteen.

Impact in two minutes.

▼▲▼

Holly kept watching for Jim Ironheart, hoping he would rejoin them. She wanted him nearby when the worst happened. She had not forgotten the bizarre dream from last night, the monstrous creature that had seemed to come out of her nightmare and into her motel room; neither had she forgotten how many people he had killed in his quest to protect the lives of the innocent, nor how savagely he slaughtered Norman Rink in that Atlanta convenience store. But the dark side of him was outweighed by the light. Though an aura of danger surrounded him, she also felt curiously safe in his company, as if within the protective nimbus of a guardian angel.

Through the public-address system, one of the flight attendants was instructing them on emergency procedures. Other attendants were positioned throughout the plane, making sure everyone was following directions.

The DC-10 was wallowing and shimmying again. Worse, although without a wooden timber anywhere in its structure, it was creaking like a sailing ship on a storm-tossed sea. The sky was blue beyond the portholes, but evidently the air was more than blustery; it was raging, tumultuous.

None of the passengers had any illusions now. They knew they were going in for a landing under the worst conditions, and that it would be rough. Maybe fatal. Throughout the enormous plane, people were surprisingly quiet, as if they were in a cathedral during a solemn service. Perhaps, in their minds' eyes, they were experiencing their own funerals.

Jim appeared out of the first-class section and approached along the port aisle. Holly was immensely relieved to see him. He paused only to smile encouragingly at the Dubroveks, and to put his hand on Holly's shoulder and give her a gentle squeeze of reassurance. Then he settled into the seat behind her.

The plane hit a patch of turbulence worse than anything before. She was half convinced that they were no longer flying but sledding across corrugated steel.

Christine took Holly's hand and held it briefly, as if they were old friends—which, in a curious way, they were, thanks to the imminence of death, which had a bonding effect on people.

"Good luck, Holly."

"You, too," Holly said.

Beyond her mother, little Casey looked so small.

Even the flight attendants were seated now, and in the position they had instructed the passengers to take. Finally Holly followed their example and assumed the posture that contributed to the best chance of survival in a crash: belted securely in the seat, bent forward, head tucked between her knees, gripping her ankles with her hands.

The plane came out of the shattered air, slipping down glass-smooth for a moment. But before Holly had time to feel any relief, the whole sky seemed to be shaking as though gremlins were standing at the four corners and snapping it like a blanket.

Overhead storage compartments popped open. Traincases, valises, jackets, and personal items flew out and rained down on the seats. Something struck the center of Holly's bowed back, bouncing off her. It was not heavy, hardly hurt at all, but she suddenly worried that a train-case, laden with some woman's makeup and jars of face cream, would drop at precisely the right angle to crack her spine.

▼ ▲ ▼

Captain Sleighton Delbaugh called out instructions to Yankowski, who continued to kneel between the pilots, operating the throttles while they were preoccupied with maintaining what little control they had left. He was braced, but a hard landing was not going to be kind to him.

They were coming out of the third and final 360-degree turn. The runway was ahead of them, but not straight-on, just as Jim—damn, he'd never gotten the guy's last name—had predicted.

Also as the stranger had foreseen, they were descending through exceptional turbulence, bucking and shuddering as if they were in a big old bus with a couple of bent axles, thundering down a steep and rugged mountain road. Delbaugh had never seen anything like it; even if the plane had been intact, he'd have been concerned about landing in those treacherous crosswinds and powerful rising thermals.

But he could not pull up and go on, hoping for better conditions at another airport or on another pass at this one. They had kept the jumbo jet in the air for thirty-three minutes since the tail-engine explosion. That was a feat of which they could be proud, but skill and cleverness and intelligence and nerve were not enough to carry them much farther. Minute by minute, and now second by second, keeping the stricken DC-10 in the air was increasingly like trying to fly a massive rock.

They were about two thousand meters from the end of the runway and closing fast.

Delbaugh thought of his wife and seventeen-year-old son at home in Westlake Village, north of Los Angeles, and he thought of his other son, Tom, who was already on his way to Willamette to get ready for his junior year. He longed to touch their faces and hold them close.

He was not afraid for himself. Well, not much. His relatively mild concern for his own safety was not a result of the stranger's prediction that the flight crew would survive, because he didn't know if the guy's premonitions were always correct. In part, it was just that he didn't have *time* to be concerned about himself.

Fifteen hundred meters.

Mainly, he was worried about his passengers and crew, who trusted him with their lives. If any part of the crash was his fault, due to a lack of resolve or nerve or quickness, all the good he had done and tried to do in his life would not compensate for this one catastrophic failure. Perhaps that attitude proved that he was, as some friends suggested, too hard on himself, but he knew that many pilots worked under no less heavy a sense of responsibility.

He remembered what the stranger had said: "*. . . you'll lose a hundred and forty-seven passengers . . .*"

His hands throbbed with pain as he kept a tight grip on the yoke, which vibrated violently.

"*. . . plus four flight attendants . . .*"

Twelve hundred meters.

"She wants to come right," Delbaugh said.

"Hold her!" Anilov said, for at this low altitude and on an approach, it was all in Delbaugh's hands.

One hundred and fifty-one dead, all those families bereaved, countless other lives altered by a single tragedy.

Eleven hundred meters.

But how the hell could that guy know how many would die? Not possible. Was he trying to say he was clairvoyant or what? It was all a crock, as Yankowski had said. Yeah, but he knew about the engine before it exploded, he knew about the washboard turbulence, and only an idiot would discount all of that.

A thousand meters.

"Here we go," Delbaugh heard himself say.

▼ ▲ ▼

Bent forward in his seat, head between his knees, gripping his ankles, Jim Ironheart thought of the punchline to an old joke: kiss your ass goodbye.

He prayed that by his own actions he had not disrupted the river of fate to such an extent that he would wash away not only himself and the Dubroveks but other people on Flight 246 who had never been meant to die in the crash. Because of what he had told the pilot, he had potentially altered the future, and now what happened might be worse, not better, than what had been *meant* to happen.

The higher power working through him had seemed, ultimately, to approve of his attempt to save more lives than just those of Christine and Casey. On the other hand, the nature and identity of that power was so enigmatic that only a fool would presume to understand its motives or intentions.

The plane shivered and shook. The scream of the engines seemed to grow ever more shrill.

He stared at the deck beneath his feet, expecting it to burst open in his face.

More than anything, he was afraid for Holly Thorne. Her presence on the flight was a profound deviation from the script that fate had originally written. He was eaten by a fear that he might save the lives of more people on the plane than he'd at first intended—but that Holly would be broken in half by the impact.

▼▲▼

As the DC-10 quaked and rattled its way toward the earth, Holly squeezed herself into as tight a package as she could, and closed her eyes. In her private darkness, faces swam through her mind: her mom and dad, which was to be expected; Lenny Callaway, the first boy she had ever loved, which was not expected, because she had not seen him since they were both sixteen; Mrs. Rooney, a high-school teacher who had taken a special interest in her; Lori Clugar, her best friend all through high school and half of college, before life had carried them to different corners of the country and out of touch; and more than a dozen others, all of whom she had loved and still loved. No one person could have occupied her thoughts for more than a fraction of a second, yet the nearness of death seemed to distort time, so she felt as if she were lingering with each beloved face. What flashed before her was not her life, but the special people in it—though in a way that was the same thing.

Even above the creak-rumble-shriek of the jet, and in spite of her focus on the faces in her mind, she heard Christine Dubrovek speak to her daughter in the last moments of their shaky descent: "I love you, Casey."

Holly began to cry.

▼ ▲ ▼

Three hundred meters.

Delbaugh had the nose up.

Everything looked good. As good as it *could* look under the circumstances.

They were at a slight angle to the runway, but he might be able to realign the aircraft once they were on the ground. If he couldn't bring it around to any useful degree, they would roll three thousand or maybe even four thousand feet before their angle of approach carried them off the edge of the pavement and into a field where it appeared that a crop of some kind had been harvested recently. That was not a desirable termination point, but at least by then a lot of their momentum would have been lost; the plane might still break up, depending on the nature of the bare earth under its wheels, but there was little chance that it would disintegrate catastrophically.

Two hundred meters.

Turbulence gone.

Floating. Like a feather.

"All right," Anilov said, just as Delbaugh said, "Easy, easy," and they both meant the same thing: it looked good, they were going to make it.

One hundred meters.

Nose still up.

Perfect, perfect.

Touchdown and—

TWANG!

—the tires barked on the blacktop simultaneously with the queer sound. Delbaugh remembered the stranger's warning, so he said, "Power number one!" and pulled hard to the left. Yankowski remembered as well, though he had said it was all a crock, and he responded to Delbaugh's throttle command even as it was being given. The right wing dipped, just as they had been told it would, but their quick action pulled the plane left, and the right wing came back up. There was a danger of overcompensation, so Delbaugh issued a new throttle command while still trying to hold the craft to the left. They were rolling along, rolling along, the plane shaking, and he gave the order to reverse engines because they couldn't, for God's sake, continue to accelerate, they were in mortal danger as long as they were moving at high speed, rolling, rolling, moving inexorably at an angle on the runway, rolling and slowing now, but rolling. And the right wing was tipping down again, accompanied by hellish popping and metallic tearing noises as age-fatigued steel—trouble in the joining of wing and fuselage, Jim had said—succumbed to the stress of their wildly erratic flight and once-in-a-century crosswinds. Rolling, rolling, but Delbaugh couldn't do a damn thing about a structural failure, couldn't get out there and reweld the joints or hold the damn rivets in place. Rolling, rolling, their momentum dropping, but the right wing still going down, none of his countermeasures working any longer, the wing down, and down, oh God, the wing—

▼▲▼

Holly felt the plane tipping farther to the right than before. She held her breath—or thought she did, but at the same time she heard herself gasping frantically.

The creaks and squeals of tortured metal, which had been echoing eerily through the fuselage for a couple of minutes, suddenly grew much louder. The aircraft tipped farther to the right. A sound like a cannonshot boomed through the passenger compartment, and the plane bounced up, came down hard. The landing gear collapsed.

They were sliding along the runway, rocking and jolting, then the plane began to turn as it slid, making Holly's heart clutch up and her stomach knot. It was the biggest carnival ride in the world, except it wasn't any fun at all; her seatbelt was like a blade against her midriff, cutting her in half, and if there had been a carny ticket-taker, she knew he would have had the ghastly face of a rotting corpse and a rictus for a smile.

The noise was intolerable, though the passengers' screaming was not the worst of it. For the most part their voices were drowned out by the scream of the aircraft itself as its belly dissolved against the pavement and other pieces of it were torn loose. Maybe dinosaurs, sinking into Mesozoic pits of tar, had equaled the volume of that dying cry, but nothing on the face of the earth since that era had protested its demise at such a piercing pitch and thunderous volume. It wasn't purely a machine sound; it was metallic but somehow alive, and it was so eerie and chilling that it might have been the combined, tortured cries of all the denizens of hell, hundreds of millions of despairing souls wailing at once. She was sure her eardrums would burst.

Disregarding the instructions she had been given, she raised her head and looked quickly around. Cascades of white, yellow, and turquoise sparks foamed past the portholes, as if the airplane was passing through an extravagant fireworks display. Six or seven rows ahead, the fuselage cracked open like an eggshell rapped against the edge of a ceramic bowl.

She had seen enough, too much. She tucked her head between her knees again.

She heard herself chanting at the deck in front of her, but she was caught in such a whirlpool of horror that the only way she could discover what she was saying was to strain to hear herself above the cacophony of the crash: "Don't, don't, don't, don't, don't, don't . . ."

Maybe she passed out for a few seconds, or maybe her senses shut down briefly due to extreme overload, but in a wink everything was still. The air was filled with acrid odors that her recovering senses could not identify. The ordeal was over, but she could not recall the plane coming to rest.

She was alive.

Intense joy swept through her. She raised her head, sat up, ready to whoop with the uncontainable thrill of survival—and saw the fire.

▼ ▲ ▼

The DC-10 had not cartwheeled. The warning to Captain Delbaugh had paid off.

But as Jim had feared, the chaotic aftermath of the crash held as many dangers as the impact itself.

Along the entire starboard side of the plane, where jet fuel had spilled, orange flames churned at the windows. It appeared as if he was voyaging aboard a submarine in a sea of fire on an alien world. Some of the windows had shattered on impact, and flames were spouting through those apertures, as well as through the ragged tear in the fuselage that now separated economy class from the forward section of the airliner.

Even as Jim uncoupled his seatbelt and got shakily to his feet, he saw seats catching afire on the starboard side. Passengers over there were crouching or dropping down on their hands and knees to scramble under the spreading flames.

He stepped into the aisle, grabbed Holly, and hugged her as she struggled to her feet. He looked past her at the Dubroveks. Mother and child were uninjured, though Casey was crying.

Holding Holly by the hand, searching for the quickest way out, Jim turned toward the back of the aircraft and for a moment could not understand what he was seeing. Like a voracious blob out of an old horror movie, an amorphous mass churned toward them from the hideously gouged and crumpled rear of the DC-10, black and billowy, devouring everything over which it rolled. Smoke. He hadn't instantly realized it was smoke because it was so thick that it appeared to have the substance of a wall of oil or mud.

Death by suffocation, or worse, lay behind them. They would have to go forward in spite of the fire ahead. Flames licked around the torn edge of fuselage on the starboard side, reaching well into the cabin, fanning across more than half the diameter of the sliced-open aircraft. But they should be able to exit toward the port side, where no fire was yet visible.

"Quick," he said, turning to Christine and Casey as they came out of row sixteen. "Forward, fast as you can, go, go!"

However, other passengers from the first six rows of the economy section were in the aisle ahead of them. Everyone was trying to get out fast. A valiant young flight attendant was doing what she could to help, but progress was not easy. The aisle was littered with carry-on luggage, purses, paperback books, and other items that had fallen out of the overhead storage compartments, and within a few shuffling steps, Jim's feet had become entangled in debris.

The churning smoke reached them from behind, enfolded them, so pungent that his eyes teared at once. He not only choked on the first whiff of fumes but gagged with revulsion, and he did not want to think about what might be burning behind him in addition to upholstery, foam seat cushions, carpet, and other elements of the aircraft's interior decor.

As the thick oily cloud poured past him and engulfed the forward section, the passengers ahead began to vanish. They appeared to be stepping through the folds of a black velvet curtain.

Before visibility dropped to a couple of inches, Jim let go of Holly and touched Christine's shoulder. "Let me take her," he said, and scooped Casey into his arms.

A paper bag from an LAX giftshop was in the aisle at his feet. It had burst open as people tramped across it. He saw a white T-shirt—I LOVE L.A.—with pink and peach and pale-green palm trees.

He snatched up the shirt and pushed it into Casey's

small hands. Coughing, as was everyone around him, he said, "Hold it over your face, honey, breathe through it!"

Then he was blind. The foul cloud around him was so dark that he could not even see the child he was carrying. Indeed, he could not actually perceive the churning currents of the cloud itself. The blackness was deeper than what he saw when he closed his eyes, for behind his lids, pinpoint bursts of color formed ghostly patterns that lit his inner world.

They were maybe twenty feet from the open end of crash-severed fuselage. He was not in danger of getting lost, for the aisle was the only route he could follow.

He tried not to breathe. He could hold his breath for a minute, anyway, which ought to be long enough. The only problem was that he had already inhaled some of the bitter smoke, and it was caustic, burning his throat as if he had swallowed acid. His lungs heaved and his esophagus spasmed, forcing him to cough, and every cough ended in an involuntary though thankfully shallow inhalation.

Probably less than fifteen feet to go.

He wanted to scream at the people in front of him: *move, damn you, move!* He knew they were stumbling forward as fast as they could, every bit as eager to get out as he was, but he wanted to shout at them anyway, felt a shriek of rage building in him, and he realized he was teetering on the brink of hysteria.

He stepped on several small, cylindrical objects, floundering like a man walking on marbles. But he kept his balance.

Casey was wracked by violent coughs. He could not hear her, but holding her against his chest, he could feel each twitch and flex and contraction of her small body as she struggled desperately to draw half-filtered breaths through the I LOVE L.A. shirt.

Less than a minute had passed since he had started forward, maybe only thirty seconds since he had scooped up the girl. But it seemed like a long journey down an endless tunnel.

Although fear and fury had thrown his mind into a

turmoil, he was thinking clearly enough to remember reading somewhere that smoke rose in a burning room and hung near the ceiling. If they didn't reach safety within a few seconds, he would have to drop to the deck and crawl in the hope that he would escape the toxic gases and find at least marginally cleaner air down there.

Sudden heat coalesced around him.

He imagined himself stepping into a furnace, his skin peeling off in an instant, flesh blistering and smoking. His heart already thudded like a wild thing throwing itself against the bars of a cage, but it began to beat harder, faster.

Certain that they had to be within a few steps of the hole in the fuselage that he had glimpsed earlier, Jim opened his eyes, which stung and watered copiously. Perfect blackness had given way to a charcoal-gray swirl of fumes through which throbbed blood-red pulses of light. The pulses were flames shrouded by smoke and seen only as reflections bouncing off millions of swirling particles of ash. At any moment the fire could burst upon him from out of the smoke and sear him to the bone.

He was not going to make it.

No breathable air.

Fire seeking him on all sides.

He was going to ignite. Burn like a living tallow candle. In a vision sparked by terror rather than by a higher power, he saw himself dropping to his knees in defeat. The child in his arms. Fusing with her in a steel-melting inferno . . .

A sudden wind pulled at him. The smoke was sucked away toward his left.

He saw daylight, cool and gray and easily differentiated from the deadly glow of burning jet fuel.

Propelled by a gruesome image of himself and the child fried by a flash fire on the very brink of safety, he threw himself toward the grayness and fell out of the airliner. No portable stairs were waiting, of course, no emergency chute, just bare earth. Fortunately a crop had recently been harvested, and the stubble had been plowed under for mulch. The newly tilled earth was hard enough to knock the wind out of him but far too soft to break his bones.

He clung fiercely to Casey, gasping for breath. He rolled onto his knees, got up, still holding her in his arms, and staggered out of the corona of heat that radiated from the blazing plane.

Some of the survivors were running away, as if they thought the DC-10 had been loaded with dynamite and was going to blow half the state of Iowa to smithereens any second now. Others were wandering aimlessly in shock. Still others were lying on the ground: some too stunned to go another inch; some injured; and perhaps some of them were dead.

Grateful for the clean air, coughing out sour fumes from his soiled lungs, Jim looked for Christine Dubrovek among the people in the field. He turned this way and that, calling her name, but he couldn't see her. He began to think that she had perished in the airplane, that he might not have been treading over only passengers' possessions in the port aisle but also over a couple of the passengers themselves.

Perhaps sensing what Jim was thinking, Casey let the palm tree–decorated T-shirt fall from her grasp. Clinging to him, coughing out the last of the smoke, she began to ask for her mother in a fearful tone of voice that indicated she expected the worst.

A burgeoning sense of triumph had taken hold of him. But now a new fear rattled in him like ice cubes in a tall glass. Suddenly the warm August sun over the Iowa field and the waves of heat pouring off the DC-10 did not touch him, and he felt as though he was standing on an arctic plain.

"Steve?"

At first he did not react to the name.

"Steve?"

Then he remembered that he had been Steve Harkman to her—which she and her husband and the *real* Steve Harkman would probably puzzle about for the rest of their lives—and he turned toward the voice. Christine was there, stumbling through the freshly tilled earth, her face and clothes stained from the oily smoke, shoeless, arms out to receive her little girl.

Jim gave the child to her.

Mother and daughter hugged each other fiercely.

Weeping, looking across Casey's shoulder at Jim, Christine said, "Thank you, thank you for getting her out of there, my God, Steve, I can't ever thank you enough."

He did not want thanks. All he wanted was Holly Thorne, alive and uninjured.

"Have you seen Holly?" he asked worriedly.

"Yes. She heard a child crying for help, she thought maybe it was Casey." Christine was shaking and frantic, as if she was not in the least convinced their ordeal was over, as if she thought the earth might crack open and hot lava spew out, beginning a new chapter of the nightmare. "How did we get separated? We were behind one another, then we were outside, and in the turmoil, somehow you and Casey just weren't there."

"Holly," he said impatiently. "Where'd she go?"

"She wanted to go back inside for Casey, but then she realized the cry was coming from the forward section." Christine held up a purse and chattered on: "She carried her purse out of there without realizing she did it, so she gave it to me and went back, she knew it couldn't be Casey, but she went anyway."

Christine pointed, and for the first time Jim saw that the front of the DC-10, all the way back through the first-class section, had completely torn free from the portion in which they had been riding. It was two hundred feet farther along the field. Though it was burning less vigorously than the larger mid-section, it was considerably more mangled than the rest of the craft, including the badly battered rear quarter.

He was appalled to hear that Holly had reentered *any* part of the smouldering wreckage. The cockpit and forward section rested in that Iowa field like a monolith in an alien graveyard on a faraway world, wildly out of place here, and therefore infinitely strange, huge and looming, thoroughly ominous.

He ran toward it, calling Holly's name.

▼ ▲ ▼

Though she knew it was the very plane in which she had departed Los Angeles a few hours ago, Holly could barely believe that the forward section of the DC-10 had actually once been part of a whole and functioning aircraft. It seemed more like a deeply disturbed sculptor's interpretation of a DC-10, welded together from parts of real airliners but also from junk of every description, from pie pans and cake tins and garbage cans and old lengths of pipe, from auto fenders and scrap wire and aluminum siding and pieces of a wrought-iron fence. Rivets had popped; glass had dissolved; seats had torn loose and piled up like broken and unwanted armchairs in the corner of an auction barn; metal had bent and twisted, and in places it had shattered as completely as crystal met by a hammer. Interior fuselage panels had peeled back, and heavy structural beams had burst inward. The floor had erupted upward in places, either from the impact or from an explosion below. Everywhere jagged, gnarled metal objects bristled in profusion, and it looked like nothing so much as a junkyard for old machines just after a tornado had passed through.

Trying to track down what sounded like the cries of a frightened child, Holly could not always proceed crect. She had to crouch and squirm through pinched spaces, pushing things aside when she could, going over or around or under whenever an obstacle proved to be immovable. The neat rows and aisles of the plane had been pulled and hammered into a maze.

She was shaken when she spotted yellow and red flickers of flame along the perimeter of the deck and in the starboard front corner by the bulkhead that separated the passenger cabin from the cockpit. But the fire was fitful, unlike the blistering conflagration that she had fled moments ago. It might abruptly flare up, of course, consuming everything in its path, although currently it seemed unable to find sufficiently combustible material or oxygen to do more than barely sustain itself.

Smoke curled around her in sinuous tendrils, but it was more annoying than threatening. Breathable air was in good supply, and she didn't even cough much.

More than anything, the corpses were what unnerved her. Though the crash apparently had been somewhat less severe than it would have been without Jim Ironheart's intervention, not everyone had survived, and a number of fatalities had occurred in the first-class section. She saw a man pinned to his seat by a foot-long, inch-diameter steel tube that had pierced his throat; his sightless eyes were wide open in a final expression of surprise. A woman, nearly decapitated, was on her side, still belted into her seat, which had torn free of the deck plates to which it had been bolted. Where other seats had broken free and slammed together, she saw injured passengers and cadavers heaped on one another, and the only way to tell the quick from the dead was to listen closely to determine which of them was groaning.

She blanked out the horror. She was aware of the blood, but she looked through it rather than at it. She averted her eyes from the most grievous wounds, refused to dwell on the nightmare images of the shattered passengers whom she kept confronting. Human bodies became abstract forms to her, as if they were not real but only blocks of shape and color put down on canvas by a cubist imitating Picasso. If she allowed herself to think about what she was seeing, she would either have to retrace the route she had taken and get out, or curl into a fetal ball and weep.

She encountered a dozen people who needed to be extracted from the wreckage and given immediate medical treatment, but they were all either too large or too tightly wedged in the rubble for her to be of any assistance. Besides, she was drawn forward by the haunting cries of the child, driven by that instinctive understanding that children were always to be saved first: one of the major clauses of nature's genetically programmed triage policy.

Sirens rose in the distance. She had never paused to think that professional rescuers would be on their way. It didn't matter. She couldn't go back and wait for them to handle this. What if reaching the child a minute or two sooner made all the difference between death and survival?

As Holly inched forward, now and then glimpsing anemic but worrisome flames through gaps in the web of destruction, she heard Jim Ironheart behind her, calling her name at the opening where the forward part of the plane had been amputated from the rest of it. In the chaos after falling from the midsection of the DC-10, they had apparently emerged from the smoke at different places, heading in opposite directions, for she had not been able to find him even though he should have been right behind her. She had been pretty sure that he and Casey had survived, if only because he obviously had a talent for survival; but it was good to hear his voice.

"In here!" she shouted, although the tangle of devastation prevented her from seeing him.

"What're you doing?"

"Looking for a little boy," she called back. "I hear him, I'm getting closer, but I can't see him yet."

"Get out of there!" he shouted above the increasingly loud wail of approaching emergency vehicles. "Paramedics are on the way, they're trained for this."

"Come on," she said, pushing forward. "There're other people in here who need help *now!*"

Holly was nearing the front of the first-class section, where the steel ribs of the fuselage had broken inward but not in such profusion as in the area behind her. Detached seats, carry-on luggage, and other detritus had flown forward on impact, however, piling up deeper there than anywhere else. More people had wound up in that pile, too, both dead and alive.

When she shoved a broken and empty seat out of her way and paused to get her breath, she heard Jim clawing into the wreckage behind her.

Lying on her side, she squirmed through a narrow passage and into a pocket of open space, coming face to face with the boy whose cries she had been following. He was about five years old, with enormous dark eyes. He blinked at her in amazement and swallowed a sob, as if he had never really expected anyone to reach him.

He was under an inverted bank of five seats, in a peaked space formed by the seats themselves, as if in a tent. He was lying on his belly, looking out, and it seemed as if he ought to be able to slither into the open easy enough.

"Something's got my foot," he said. He was still afraid, but manageably so. He had cast off the greater part of his terror the moment he had seen her. Whether you were five years old or fifty, the worst thing always was being alone. "Got my foot, won't let go."

Coughing, she said, "I'll get you out, honey. You'll be okay."

Holly looked up and saw another row of seats piled atop the lower bank. Both were wedged in by a mass of twisted steel pressing down from the caved-in ceiling, and she wondered if the forward section had rolled once before coming to rest right-side up.

With her fingertips she wiped the tears off his cheeks. "What's your name, honey?"

"Norwood. Kids call me Norby. It don't hurt. My foot, I mean."

She was glad to hear that.

But then, as she studied the wreckage around him and tried to figure out what to do, he said, "I can't feel it."

"Feel what, Norby?"

"My foot. It's funny, like something's holding it, 'cause I can't get loose, but then I can't *feel* my foot—you know?—like it maybe isn't there."

Her stomach twisted at the image his words conjured in her mind. Maybe it wasn't that bad. Maybe his foot was only pinched between two surfaces, just numb, but she had to think fast and move fast because he might be losing blood at an alarming rate.

The space in which he lay was too cramped for her to squeeze in past him, find his foot, and disentangle it. Instead, she rolled onto her back, bent her legs, and braced the soles of her shoes against the seats that peaked over him.

"Okay, honey, I'm going to straighten my legs, try to shove this up a little, just a couple inches. When it starts lifting, try to pull your foot out of there."

As a snake of thin gray smoke slipped from the dark space behind Norby and coiled in front of his face, he wheezed and said, "There's d-d-dead people in here with me."

"That's okay, baby," she said, tensing her legs, flexing them a little to test the weight she was trying to lever off him. "You won't be there for long, not for long."

"My seat, then an empty seat, then dead people," Norby said shakily.

She wondered how long the trauma of this experience would shape his nightmares and bend the course of his life.

"Here goes," she said.

She pressed upward with both feet. The pile of seats and junk and bodies was heavy enough, but the half-collapsed section of the ceiling, pushing down on everything else, did not seem to have any give in it. Holly strained harder until the steel deck, covered with only a thin carpet, pressed painfully into her back. She let out an involuntary sob of agony. Then she strained even harder, harder, angry that she could not move it, *furious,* and—

—it moved.

Only a fraction of an inch.

But it moved.

Holly put even more into it, found reserves she did not know she possessed, forced her feet upward until the pain throbbing in her legs was markedly worse than that in her back. The intruding tangle of ceiling plates and struts creaked and bent back an inch, two inches; the seats shoved up just that far.

"It's still got me," the boy said.

More smoke was oozing out of the lightless space around him. It was not pale-gray but darker than before, sootier, oilier, and with a new foul stench. She hoped to God the desultory flames had not, at last, ignited the upholstery and foam padding that formed the cocoon from which the boy was struggling to emerge.

The muscles in her legs were quivering. The pain in her back had seeped all the way through to her chest; each heartbeat was an aching thud, each inhalation was a torment.

She did not think she could hold the weight any longer, let alone lift it higher. But abruptly it jolted up another inch, then slightly more.

Norby issued a cry of pain and excitement. He wriggled forward. "I got away, it let go of me."

Relaxing her legs and easing the load back into place, Holly realized that the boy had thought what she, too, might have thought if she'd been a five-year-old in that hellish position: that his ankle had been clenched in the cold and iron-strong hand of one of the dead people in there with him.

She slid aside, giving Norby room to pull himself out of the hollow under the seats. He joined her in the pocket of empty space amidst the rubble and snuggled against her for comforting.

From farther back in the plane, Jim shouted: "Holly!"

"I found him!"

"I've got a woman here, I'm getting her out."

"Great!" she shouted.

Outside, the pitch of the sirens spiraled lower and finally down into silence as the rescue teams arrived.

Although more blackish smoke was drifting out of the dark space from which Norby had escaped, Holly took the time to examine his foot. It flopped to one side, sickeningly loose, like the foot of an old rag doll. It was broken at the ankle. She tore his sneaker off his rapidly swelling foot. Blood darkened his white sock, but when she looked at the flesh beneath, she discovered that it was only abraded and scored by a few shallow cuts. He was not going to bleed to death, but soon he was going to become aware of the excruciating pain of the broken ankle.

"Let's go, let's get out," she said.

She intended to take him back the way she had come,

but when she glanced to her left, she saw another crack in the fuselage. This one was immediately aft of the cockpit bulkhead, only a few feet away. It extended up the entire curve of the wall but did not continue onto the ceiling. A section of interior paneling, the insulation beneath it, structural beamwork, and exterior plating had either blown inward among the other debris or been wrenched out into the field. The resultant hole was not large, but it was plenty big enough for her to squeeze through with the boy.

As they balanced on the rim of the ravaged hull, a rescue worker appeared in the plowed field about twelve feet below them. He held his arms out for the boy.

Norby jumped. The man caught him, moved back.

Holly jumped, landed on her feet.

"You his mother?" the man asked.

"No. I just heard him crying, went in after him. He's got a broken ankle there."

"I was with my Uncle Frank," Norby said.

"Okay," the rescue worker said, trying to strike a cheerful note, "then let's find Uncle Frank."

Norby said flatly, "Uncle Frank's dead."

The man looked at Holly, as if she might know what to say.

Holly was mute and shaken, filled with despair that a boy of five should have to experience such an ordeal. She wanted to hold him, rock him in her arms, and tell him that everything would be right with the world.

But nothing is right with the world, she thought, because Death is part of it. Adam disobeyed and ate the apple, gobbled up the fruit of knowledge, so God decided to let him know all sorts of things, both light and dark. Adam's children learned to hunt, to farm, to thwart the winter and cook their food with fire, make tools, build shelters. And God, wanting to give them a *well-rounded* education, let them learn, oh, maybe a million ways to suffer and die. He encouraged them to learn language, reading and writing, biology, chemistry, physics, the secrets of the genetic code. And He taught them the exquisite horrors of brain tumors, muscular dystrophy, bubonic plague, cancer run amok in their bodies—and not least of all airplane crashes. You wanted knowledge, God was happy to oblige, He was an enthusiastic teacher, a *demon* for knowledge, piling it on in such weight and exotic detail that sometimes you felt you were going to be crushed under it.

By the time the rescue worker turned away and carried Norby across the field toward a white ambulance parked on the edge of the runway, Holly had gone from despair to anger. It was a useless rage, for there was no one but God against whom she could direct it, and the expression of it could change nothing. God would not free the human race from the curse of death just because Holly Thorne thought it was a gross injustice.

She realized that she was in the grip of a fury not unlike that which seemed to motivate Jim Ironheart. She remembered what he had said during their whispered conversation in row seventeen, when she had tried to bully him into saving not just the Dubroveks but everyone aboard Flight 246: *"I hate death, people dying, I hate it!"* Some of the people he saved had quoted him making similar remarks, and Holly remembered what Viola Moreno had said about the deep and quiet sadness in him that perhaps grew out of being an orphan at the age of ten. He quit teaching, walked away from his career, because Larry Kakonis's suicide had made all his effort and concern seem pointless. That reaction at first appeared extreme to Holly, but now she understood it perfectly. She felt the same urge to cast aside a mundane life and do something more meaningful, to crack the rule of fate, to wrench the very fabric of the universe into a shape other than what God seemed to prefer for it.

For a fragile moment, standing in that Iowa field with the wind blowing the stink of death to her, watching the rescue worker walk away with the little boy who had almost died, Holly felt closer to Jim Ironheart than she had ever been to another human being.

She went looking for him.

The scene around the broken DC-10 had become more chaotic than it had been immediately after the crash. Fire trucks had driven onto the plowed field. Streams of rich white foam arced over the broken plane, frosted the fuselage in whipped-cream-like gobs, and damped the flames on the surrounding fuel-soaked earth. Smoke still churned out of the midsection, plumed from every rent and shattered window; shifting to the whims of the wind, a black canopy spread over them and cast eerie, constantly changing shadows as it filtered the afternoon sunshine, raising in her mind the image of a grim kaleidoscope in which all the pieces of glass were either black or gray. Rescue workers and paramedics swarmed over the wreckage, searching for survivors, and their numbers were so unequal to the awesome task that some of the more fortunate passengers pitched in to help. Other passengers—some so untouched by the experience that they appeared freshly showered and dressed, others filthy and disheveled—stood alone or in small groups, waiting for the minibuses that would take them to the Dubuque terminal, chattering nervously or stunned into silence. The only things threading the crash scene together and providing it with some coherence were the static-filled voices crackling on shortwave radios and walkie-talkies.

Though Holly was searching for Jim Ironheart, she found instead a young woman in a yellow shirtwaist dress. The stranger was in her early twenties, slender, auburn-haired, with a porcelain face; and though uninjured she badly needed help. She was standing back from the still-smoking rear section of the airliner, shouting a name over and over again: "Kenny! Kenny! Kenny!" She had shouted it so often that her voice was hoarse.

Holly put a hand on the woman's shoulder and said, "Who is he?"

The stranger's eyes were the precise blue of wisteria—and glazed. "Have you seen Kenny?"

"Who is he, dear?"

"My husband."

"What does he look like?"

Dazed, she said, "We were on our honeymoon."

"I'll help you look for him."

"No."

"Come on, kid, it'll be all right."

"I don't want to look for him," the woman said, allowing Holly to turn her away from the plane and lead her toward the ambulances. "I don't want to see him. Not the way he'll be. All dead. All broken up and burned and dead."

They walked together through the soft, tilled earth, where a new crop would be planted in late winter and sprout up green and tender in the spring, by which time all signs of death would have been eradicated and nature's illusion of life-everlasting restored.

5

Something was happening to Holly. A fundamental change was taking place in her. She didn't understand what it was yet, didn't know what it would mean or how different a person she would be when it was complete, but she was aware of profound movement in the bedrock of her heart, her mind.

Because her inner world was in such turmoil, she had no spare energy to cope with the outer world, so she placidly followed the standard post-crash program with her fellow passengers.

She was impressed by the web of emotional, psychological, and practical support provided to survivors of Flight 246. Dubuque's medical and civil-defense community—which obviously had planned for such an emergency—responded swiftly and effectively. In addition psychologists, counselors, ministers, priests, and a rabbi were available to the uninjured passengers within minutes of their arrival at the terminal. A large VIP lounge—with mahogany tables and comfortable chairs upholstered in nubby blue fabric—had been set aside for their use, ten or twelve telephone lines sequestered from normal airport operations, and nurses provided to monitor them for signs of delayed shock.

United's employees were especially solicitous, assisting with local overnight accommodations and new travel arrangements, as quickly as possible reuniting the uninjured with friends or relatives who had been transported to various hospitals, and compassionately conveying word of loved ones' deaths. Their horror and grief seemed as deep as that of the passengers, and they were shaken and remorseful that such a thing could happen with one of their planes. Holly saw a young woman in a United jacket turn suddenly and leave the room in tears, and all the others, men and women alike, were pale and shaky. She found herself wanting to console *them,* put an arm around them and tell them that even the best-built and best-maintained machines were doomed to fail sooner or later because human knowledge was imperfect and darkness was loose in the world.

Courage, dignity, and compassion were so universally in evidence under such trying circumstances that Holly was dismayed by the full-scale arrival of the media. She knew that dignity, at least, would be an early victim of their assault. To be fair, they were only doing their job, the problems and pressures of which she knew too well. But the percentage of reporters who could perform their work properly was no greater than the percentage of plumbers who were competent or the percentage of carpenters who could miter a doorframe perfectly every time. The difference was that unfeeling, inept, or downright hostile reporters could cause their subjects considerable embarrassment and, in some cases, malign the innocent and permanently damage reputations, which was a lot worse than a backed-up drain or mismatched pieces of wood molding.

The whole spectrum of TV, radio, and print journalists swarmed into the airport and soon penetrated even those areas where their presence was officially restricted. Some were respectful of the survivors' emotional and mental condition, but most of them badgered the United employees about "responsibility" and "moral obligation," or hounded the survivors to reveal their innermost fears and relive the recent horror for the delectation of news consumers. Though Holly knew the drill and was expert at fending them off, she was asked the same question half a dozen times by four different reporters within fifteen minutes: "How did you feel?" How did you feel when you heard it might be a crash landing? How did you *feel* when you thought you were going to die? How did you feel when you saw that some of those around you *had* died?

Finally, cornered near a large observation window that looked out on arriving and departing flights, she blew up at an eager and expensively coiffured CNN reporter named Anlock, who simply could not understand that she was unflattered by his attentions. "Ask me what I saw, or ask me what I think," she told him. "Ask me who, what, where, why, and how, but for God's sake don't ask me how I feel, because if you're a hu..nan being you've got to *know* how I feel. If you have any empathy at all for the human condition, you've got to know."

Anlock and his cameraman tried to back off, move on to other prey. She was aware that most of the people in the crowded room had turned to see what the commotion was about, but she didn't care. She was not going to let Anlock off that easily. She stayed with him:

"You don't want facts, you just want drama, you want blood and thunder, you want people to bare their souls to you, then you edit what they say, change it, misreport it, get it all wrong most of the time, and that's a kind of rape, damn it."

She realized that she was in the grip of the same rage she had experienced at the crash site, and that she was not half as angry at Anlock as she was at God, futile as that might be. The reporter was just a more convenient target than the Almighty, who could stay hidden in some shadowy corner of His heaven. She'd thought her anger had subsided; she was disconcerted to find that same black fury welling high within her again.

She was over the top, out of control, and she didn't care—until she realized CNN was on the air live. A predatory glint in Anlock's eyes and a twist of irony in his expression alerted her that he was not entirely dismayed by her outburst. She was giving him good color, first-rate drama, and he could not resist using it even if he was the object of her abuse. Later, of course, he would magnanimously excuse her behavior to viewers, insincerely sympathizing with the emotional trauma she had endured, thus coming off as a fearless reporter *and* a compassionate guy.

Furious with herself for playing into his game when she should have known that only the reporter ever wins, Holly turned from the camera. Even as she walked away, she heard Anlock saying, ". . . quite understandable, of course, given what the poor woman has just been through . . ."

She wanted to go back and smash him in the face. And wouldn't *that* please him!

What's wrong with you, Thorne? she demanded of herself. You never lose it. Not like this. You never lose it, but now you're definitely, absolutely losing it.

Trying to ignore the reporters and suppress her sudden interest in self-analysis, she went looking for Jim Ironheart again but still had no luck locating him. He was not among the latest group arriving from the crash site. None of the United employees could find his name on the passenger roster, which did not exactly surprise Holly.

She figured he was still in the field, assisting the search-and-rescue team in whatever way he could. She was eager to speak with him, but she would have to be patient.

Although some of the reporters were wary of her after the way she verbally assaulted Anlock, she knew how to manipulate her own kind. Sipping from a Styrofoam cup of bitter black coffee—as if she needed caffeine to improve her edge—she drifted around the room and into the hall outside, pumping them without revealing that she was one of them, and she was able to obtain bits of interesting information. Among other things, she discovered that two hundred survivors were already accounted for, and that the death toll was unlikely to exceed fifty, a miraculously low number of fatalities, considering the breakup of the plane and the subsequent fire. She should have been exhilarated by that good news, for it meant Jim's intervention had permitted the captain to save many more lives than fate had intended; but instead of rejoicing, she brooded about those who, in spite of everything, had been lost.

She also learned that members of the flight crew, all of whom survived, were hoping to find a passenger who had been a great help to them, a man described as "Jim Something, sort-of-a-Kevin-Costner-lookalike with very blue eyes." Because the first federal officials to arrive on the scene were also eager to talk to Jim Something, the media began looking for him as well.

Gradually Holly realized that Jim would not be putting in an appearance. He would fade, just as he always did after one of his exploits, moving quickly beyond the reach of reporters and officialdom of all stripes. Jim was the only name for him that they would ever have.

Holly was the first person, at the site of one of his rescues, to whom he had given his full name. She frowned, wondering why he had chosen to reveal more to her than to anyone else.

Outside the door of the nearest women's restroom, she encountered Christine Dubrovek, who returned her purse and asked about Steve Harkman, never realizing that he was the mysterious Jim after whom everyone else was inquiring.

"He had to be in Chicago this evening, no matter what, so he's already rented a car and left," Holly lied.

"I wanted to thank him again," Christine said. "But I guess I'll have to wait until we're both back in Los Angeles. He works in the same company as my husband, you know."

Casey, close at her mother's side, had scrubbed the soot off her face and combed her hair. She was eating a chocolate bar, but she did not appear to be enjoying it.

As soon as she could, Holly excused herself and returned to the emergency-assistance center that United had established in a corner of the VIP lounge. She tried to arrange for a flight that, regardless of the number of connections, would return her to Los Angeles that night. But Dubuque was not exactly the hub of the universe, and all seats to anywhere in southern California were already booked. The best she could do was a flight to Denver in the morning, followed by a noon flight from Denver to LAX.

United arranged overnight lodging for her, and at six o'clock, Holly found herself alone in a clean but cheerless room at the Best Western Midway Motor Lodge. Maybe it was not really so cheerless; in her current state of mind, she would not have been capable of appreciating a suite at the Ritz.

She called her parents in Philadelphia to let them know she was safe, in case they had seen her on CNN or spotted her name among a list of Flight 246 survivors in tomorrow's newspaper. They were happily unaware of her close call, but they insisted on whipping up a prime case of retrospective fright. She found herself consoling them, instead of the other way around, which was touching because it confirmed how much they loved her. "I don't care how important this story is you're working on," her mother said, "you can take a bus the rest of the way, and a bus home."

Knowing she was loved did not improve Holly's mood.

Though her hair was a tangled mess and she smelled of smoke, she walked to a nearby shopping center, where she used her Visa card to purchase a change of clothes: socks, underwear, blue jeans, a white blouse, and a lightweight denim jacket. She bought new Reeboks, too, because she could not shake the suspicion that the discolorations on her old pair were bloodstains.

In her room again, she took the longest shower of her life, lathering and relathering herself until one entire complimentary motel-size bar of soap had been reduced to a crumbling sliver. She still did not feel clean, but she finally turned the water off when she realized that she was trying to scrub away something that was inside of her.

She ordered a sandwich, salad, and fruit from room service. When it came, she could not eat it.

She sat for a while, just staring at the wall.

She dared not turn on the television. She didn't want to risk catching a news report about the crash of Flight 246.

If she could have called Jim Ironheart, she would have

done so at once. She would have called him every ten minutes, hour after hour, until he arrived home and answered. But she already knew that his number was not listed.

Eventually she went down to the cocktail lounge, sat at the bar, and ordered a beer—a dangerous move for someone with her pathetic tolerance for alcohol. Without food to accompany it, one bottle of Beck's would probably knock her unconscious for the rest of the night.

A traveling salesman from Omaha tried to strike up a conversation with her. He was in his mid-forties, not unattractive, and seemed nice enough, but she didn't want to lead him on. She told him, as nicely as she could, that she was not looking to get picked up.

"Me neither," he said, and smiled. "All I want is someone to talk to."

She believed him, and her instincts proved reliable. They sat at the bar together for a couple of hours, chatting about movies and television shows, comedians and singers, weather and food, never touching on politics, plane crashes, or the cares of the world. To her surprise, she drank three beers and felt nothing but a light buzz.

"Howie," she said quite seriously when she left him, "I'll be grateful to you for the rest of my life."

She returned to her room alone, undressed, slid under the sheets, and felt sleep stealing over her even as she put her head on the pillow. Pulling the covers around her to ward off the chill of the air conditioner, she spoke in a voice slurred more by exhaustion than by beer: "Snuggle down in my cocoon, be a butterfly soon." Wondering where *that* had come from and what she meant by it, she fell asleep.

Whoosh, whoosh, whoosh, whoosh, whoosh . . . .

Though she was in the stone-walled room again, the dream was different in many ways from what it had been previously. For one thing, she was not blind. A fat yellow candle stood in a blue dish, and its dancing orange flame revealed stone walls, windows as narrow as embrasures, a wooden floor, a turning shaft that came through the ceiling above and disappeared through a hole into the room below, and a heavy door of iron-bound timbers. Somehow she knew that she was in the upper chamber of an old windmill, that the sound—*whoosh, whoosh, whoosh*—was produced by the mill's giant sails cutting the turbulent night wind, and that beyond the door lay curved limestone steps that led down to the milling room. Though she was standing when the dream began, circumstances changed with a ripple, and she was suddenly sitting, though not in an ordinary chair. She was in an airline seat, belted in place, and when she turned her head to the left, she saw Jim Ironheart seated beside her. "This old mill won't make it to Chicago," he said solemnly. And it seemed quite logical that they were flying in that stone structure, lifted by its four giant wood-slat sails the way an airliner was kept aloft by its jets or propellers. "We'll survive, though—won't we?" she asked. Before her eyes, Jim faded and was replaced by a ten-year-old boy. She marveled at this magic. Then she decided that the boy's thick brown hair and electric-blue eyes meant he was Jim from another time. According to the liberal rules of dreams, that made his transformation less magical and, in fact, altogether logical. The boy said, "We'll survive if *it* doesn't come." And she said, "What is *it?*" And he said, "The Enemy." Around them the mill seemed to respond to his last two words, flexing and contracting, pulsing like flesh, just as her motel-room wall in Laguna Hills had bulged with malevolent life last night. She thought she glimpsed a monstrous face and form taking its substance from the very limestone. "We'll die here," the boy said, "we'll all die here," and he seemed almost to welcome the creature that was trying to come out of the wall. *WHOOSH!*

Holly came awake with a start, as she had at some point during each of the past three nights. But this time no element of the dream followed her into the real world, and she was not terrified as she had been before. Afraid, yes. But it was a low-grade fear, more akin to disquiet than to hysteria.

More important, she rose from the dream with a buoyant sense of liberation. Instantly awake, she sat up in bed, leaned back against the headboard, and folded her arms across her bare breasts. She was shivering neither with fear nor because of a chill, but with excitement.

Earlier in the night, tongue lubricated by beer, she had spoken a truth as she had slipped off the precipice of sleep: *"Snuggle down in my cocoon, be a butterfly soon."* Now she knew what she had meant, and she understood the changes that she had been going through ever since she had tumbled to Ironheart's secret, changes that she had only begun to realize were under way when she had been in the VIP lounge at the airport after the crash.

She was never going back to the *Portland Press.*

She was never going to work on a newspaper again.

She was finished as a reporter.

That was why she had overreacted to Anlock, the CNN reporter at the airport. Loathing him, she was nevertheless eaten by guilt on a subconscious level because he was chasing a major story that she was ignoring even though she was a *part* of it. If she was a reporter, she should have been interviewing her fellow survivors and rushing to write it up for the *Press.* No such desire touched her, however, not even for a fleeting moment, so she took the raw cloth of her subconscious self-disgust and tailored a suit of rage with enormous shoulders and wide, wide lapels; then she dressed herself in it and strutted and seethed for the CNN camera, all in a frantic attempt to deny that she didn't care about journalism anymore and that she was going to walk away from a career and a commitment that she had once thought would last all her life.

Now she got out of bed and paced, too excited to sit still.

She was finished as a reporter.

Finished.

She was free. As a working-class kid from a powerless family, she had been obsessed by a lifelong need to feel important, included, a real insider. As a bright child who grew into a brighter woman, she had been puzzled by the apparent disorderliness of life, and she had been compelled to explain it as best she could with the inadequate tools of journalism. Ironically, the dual quest for acceptance and explanations—which had driven her to work and study seventy- and eighty-hour weeks for as long as she could remember—had left her rootless, with no significant lover, no children, no real friends, and no more answers to the difficult questions of life than those with which she had started. Now she was suddenly free of those needs and obsessions, no longer concerned about belonging to any elite club or explaining human behavior.

She had thought she hated journalism. She didn't. What she hated was her failure at it; and she had failed because journalism had never been the right thing for her.

To understand herself and break the bonds of habit, all she had needed was to meet a man who could work miracles, and survive a devastating airline tragedy.

"Such a *flexible* woman, Thorne," she said aloud, mocking herself. "So insightful."

Why, good heavens, if meeting Jim Ironheart and walking away from a plane crash hadn't made her see the light, then surely she'd have figured it out just as soon as Jiminy Cricket rang her doorbell and sang a cleverly rhymed lesson-teaching song about the differences between wise and stupid choices in life.

She laughed. She pulled a blanket off the bed, wound it around her nude body, sat in one of the two armchairs, drew her legs up under her, and laughed as she had not laughed since she had been a giddy teenager.

No, that was where the problem began: she had *never* been giddy. She had been a serious-minded teenager, already hooked on current events, worried about World War III because they told her she was likely to die in a nuclear holocaust before she graduated from high school; worried about overpopulation because they told her that famine would claim one and a half billion lives by 1990, cutting the world population in half, decimating even the United States; worried because man-made pollution was causing the planet to cool down drastically, insuring another ice age that would destroy civilization *within her own lifetime!!!!,* which was front-page news in the late seventies, before the Greenhouse Effect and worries about planetary warming. She had spent her adolescence and early adulthood worrying too much and enjoying too little. Without joy, she had lost perspective and had allowed every news sensation—some based on genuine problems, some entirely fraudulent—to consume her.

Now she laughed like a kid. Until they hit puberty and a tide of hormones washed them into a new existence, kids knew that life was scary, yeah, dark and strange, but they also knew that it was silly, that it was meant to be fun, that it was an adventurous journey down a long road of time to an unknown destination in a far and wondrous place.

Holly Thorne, who suddenly liked her name, knew where she was going and why.

She knew what she hoped to get from Jim Ironheart— and it was not a good story, journalistic accolades, a Pulitzer. What she wanted from him was better than that, more rewarding and enduring, and she was eager to confront him with her request.

The funny thing was, if he agreed and gave her what she wanted, she might be buying into more than excitement, joy, and a meaningful existence. She knew there was danger in it, as well. If she got what she asked from him, she might be dead a year from now, a month from now—or next week. But for the moment, at least, she focused on the prospect of joy and was not deterred by the possibility of early death and endless darkness.

Part Two

THE WINDMILL

*Nowhere can a secret keep
always secret, dark and deep,
half so well as in the past,
buried deep to last, to last.*

*Keep it in your own dark heart,
otherwise the rumors start.*

*After many years have buried
secrets over which you worried,
no confidant can then betray
all the words you didn't say.*

*Only you can then exhume
secrets safe within the tomb
of memory, of memory,
within the tomb of memory.*

—THE BOOK OF COUNTED SORROWS

▲

*In the real world
as in dreams,
nothing is quite
what it seems.*

—THE BOOK OF COUNTED SORROWS

AUGUST 27 INTO AUGUST 29

1

Holly changed planes in Denver, gained two time zones traveling west, and arrived at Los Angeles International at eleven o'clock Monday morning. Unencumbered by luggage, she retrieved her rental car from the parking garage, drove south along the coast to Laguna Niguel, and reached Jim Ironheart's house by twelve-thirty.

She parked in front of his garage, followed the tile-trimmed walkway directly to his front door, and rang the bell. He did not answer. She rang it again. He still did not answer. She rang it repeatedly, until a reddish impression of the button marked the pad of her right thumb.

Stepping back, she studied the first- and second-floor windows. Plantation shutters were closed over all of them. She could see the wide slats through the glass.

"I know you're in there," she said quietly.

She returned to her car, put the windows down, and sat behind the steering wheel, waiting for him to come out. Sooner or later he would need food, or laundry detergent, or medical attention, or toilet paper, *something,* and then she would have him.

Unfortunately, the weather was not conducive to a long stakeout. The past few days had been warm but mild. Now the August heat had returned like a bad dragon in a storybook: scorching the land with its fiery breath. The palm trees drooped and the flowers began to wilt in the blistering sùn. Behind all of the elaborate watering systems that maintained the lush landscaping, the dispossessed desert waited to reassert itself.

Baking as swiftly and evenly as a muffin in a convection oven, Holly finally put up the windows, started the car, and switched on the air conditioner. The cold draft was heavenly, but before long the car began to overheat; the needle rose swiftly toward the red section of the arc on the temperature gauge.

At one-fifteen, just three-quarters of an hour after she had arrived, Holly threw the car in reverse, backed out of the driveway, and returned to the Laguna Hills Motor Inn. She changed into tan shorts and a canary-yellow calypso blouse that left her belly bare. She put on her new running shoes, but without socks this time. At a nearby Sav-On drugstore, she bought a vinyl-strap folding lounge chair, beach towel, tube of tanning cream, picnic cooler, bag of ice, six-pack of diet soda, and a Travis McGee paperback by John D. MacDonald. She already had sunglasses.

She was back at Ironheart's house on Bougainvillea Way before two-thirty. She tried the doorbell again. He refused to answer.

Somehow she knew he was in there. Maybe *she* was a little psychic.

She carried the ice chest, folding lounger, and other items around the side of the house to the lawn in back. She set up the chair on the grass, just beyond the redwood-covered patio. In a few minutes, she was comfy.

In the MacDonald novel, Travis McGee was sweltering down there in Fort Lauderdale, where they were having a heatwave so intense it even took the bounce out of the beach bunnies. Holly had read the book before; she chose to reread it now because she had remembered that the plot unfolded against a background of tropical heat and humidity. Steamy Florida, rendered in MacDonald's vivid prose, made the dry air of Laguna Niguel seem less torrid by comparison, even though it had to be well over ninety degrees.

After about half an hour, she glanced at the house and

saw Jim Ironheart standing at the big kitchen window. He was watching her.

She waved.

He did not wave back at her.

He walked away from the window but did not come outside.

Opening a diet soda, returning to the novel, she relished the feel of the sun on her bare legs. She was not worried about a burn. She already had a little tan. Besides, though blond and fair-skinned, she had a tanning gene that insured against a burn as long as she didn't indulge in marathon sunbathing.

After a while, when she got up to readjust the lounger so she could lie on her stomach, she saw Jim Ironheart standing on the patio, just outside the sliding glass door of his family room. He was in rumpled slacks and a wrinkled T-shirt, unshaven. His hair was lank and oily. He didn't look well.

He was about fifteen feet away, so his voice carried easily to her: "What do you think you're doing?"

"Bronzing up a little."

"Please leave, Miss Thorne."

"I need to talk to you."

"We have nothing to talk about."

"Hah!"

He went back inside and slid the door shut. She heard the latch click.

After lying on her stomach for almost an hour, dozing instead of reading, she decided she'd had enough sun. Besides, at three-thirty in the afternoon, the best tanning rays were past.

She moved the lounger, cooler, and the rest of her paraphernalia onto the shaded patio. She opened a second diet soda and picked up the MacDonald novel again.

At four o'clock she heard the family-room door sliding open again. His footsteps approached and stopped behind her. He stood there for a while, evidently looking down at her. Neither of them spoke, and she pretended to keep reading.

His continued silence was eerie. She began to think about his dark side—the eight shotgun rounds he had pumped into Norman Rink in Atlanta, for one thing—and she grew increasingly nervous until she decided that he was *trying* to spook her.

When Holly picked up her can of soda from the top of the cooler, took a sip, sighed with pleasure at the taste, and put the can down again all without letting her hand tremble even once, Ironheart at last came around the lounge chair and stood where she could see him. He was still slovenly and unshaven. Dark circles ringed his eyes. He had an unhealthy pallor.

"What do you want from me?" he asked.

"That'll take a while to explain."

"I don't have a while."

"How long do you have?"

"One minute," he said.

She hesitated, then shook her head. "Can't do it in a minute. I'll just wait here till you've got more time."

He stared at her intimidatingly.

She found her place in the novel.

He said, "I could call the police, have you put off my property."

"Why don't you do that?" she said.

He stood there a few seconds longer, impatient and uncertain, then reentered the house. Slid the door shut. Locked it.

"Don't take forever," Holly muttered. "In about another hour, I'm gonna have to use your bathroom."

Around her, two hummingbirds drew nectar from the flowers, the shadows lengthened, and exploding bubbles made hollow ticking sounds inside her open can of soda.

Down in Florida, there were also hummingbirds and cool shadows, icy bottles of Dos Equis instead of diet cola, and Travis McGee was getting into deeper trouble by the paragraph.

Her stomach began to grumble. She had eaten breakfast at the airport in Dubuque, surprised that her appetite had not been suppressed forever by the macabre images burned into her mind at the crash scene. She had missed lunch, thanks to the stakeout; now she was famished. Life goes on.

Fifteen minutes ahead of Holly's bathroom deadline, Ironheart returned. He had showered and shaved. He was dressed in a blue boatneck shirt, white cotton slacks, and white canvas Top-Siders.

She was flattered by his desire to make a better appearance.

"Okay," he said, "what do you want?"

"I need to use your facilities first."

A long-suffering look lengthened his face. "Okay, okay, but then we talk, get it over with, and you go."

She followed him into the family room, which was adjacent to an open breakfast area, which was adjacent to an open kitchen. The mismatched furniture appeared to have been purchased on the cheap at a warehouse clearance sale immediately after he had graduated from college and taken his first teaching job. It was clean but well worn. Hundreds of paperback books filled free-standing cases. But there was no artwork of any kind on the walls, and no decor pieces such as vases or bowls or sculptures or potted plants lent warmth to the room.

He showed her the powder room off the main entrance foyer. No wallpaper, white paint. No designer soaps shaped like rosebuds, just a bar of Ivory. No colorful or embroidered handtowels, just a roll of Bounty standing on the counter.

As she closed the door, she looked back at him and said, "Maybe we could talk over an early supper. I'm starved."

When she finished in the bathroom, she peeked in his living room. It was decorated—to use the word as loosely as the language police would allow—in a style best described as Early Garage Sale, though it was even more Spartan than the family room. His house was surprisingly modest for a man who had won six million in the state lottery, but his furniture made the house seem Rockcfcllerian by comparison.

She went out to the kitchen and found him waiting at the round breakfast table.

"I thought you'd be cooking something," she said, pulling out a chair and sitting opposite him.

He was not amused. "What do you want?"

"Let me start by telling you what I *don't* want," she said. "I don't want to write about you, I've given up reporting, I've had it with journalism. Now, you believe that or not, but it's true. The good work you're doing can only be hampered if you're being hounded by media types, and lives will be lost that you might otherwise save. I see that now."

"Good."

"And I don't want to blackmail you. Anyway, judging by the unconscionably lavish style in which you live, I doubt you've got more than eighteen bucks left."

He did not smile. He just stared at her with those gas flame–blue eyes.

She said, "I don't want to inhibit your work or compromise it in any way. I don't want to venerate you as the Second Coming, marry you, bear your children, or extract from you the meaning of life. Anyway, only Elvis Presley knows the meaning of life, and he's in a state of suspended animation in an alien vault in a cave on Mars."

His face remained as immobile as stone. He was *tough*.

"What I want," Holly said, "is to satisfy my curiosity, learn how you do what you do, and why you do it." She hesitated. She took a deep breath. Here came the big one: "And I want to be part of it all."

"What do you mean?"

She spoke fast, running sentences together, afraid he would interrupt her before she got it all out, and never give her another chance to explain herself. "I want to work with you, help you, contribute to your mission, or whatever you call it, however you think of it, I want to save people, at least help *you* save them."

"There's nothing you could do."

"There must be something," she insisted.

"You'd only be in the way."

"Listen, I'm intelligent—"

"So what?"

"—well-educated—"

"So am I."

"—gutsy—"

"But I don't need you."

"—competent, efficient—"

"Sorry."

"Damn it!" she said, more frustrated than angry. "Let me be your secretary, even if you don't need one. Let me be your girl Friday, your good right hand—at least your *friend.*"

He seemed unmoved by her plea. He stared at her for so long that she became uncomfortable, but she would not look away from him. She sensed that he used his singularly penetrating gaze as an instrument of control and intimidation, but she was not easily manipulated. She was determined not to let him shape this encounter before it had begun.

At last he said, "So you want to be my Lois Lane."

For a moment she had no idea what he was talking about. Then she remembered: Metropolis, the *Daily Planet,* Jimmy Olsen, Perry White, Lois Lane, Clark Kent, Superman.

Holly knew he was trying to irritate her. Making her angry was another way of manipulating her; if she became abrasive, he would have an excuse to turn her away. She was determined to remain calm and reasonably congenial in order to keep the door open between them.

But she could not sit still and control her temper at the same time. She needed to work off some of the energy of anger that was overcharging her batteries. She pushed her chair back, got up, and paced as she responded to him: "No, that's exactly what I *don't* want to be. I don't want to be your chronicler, intrepid girl reporter. I'm sick of journalism." Succinctly, she told him why. "I don't want to be your swooning admirer, either, or that well-meaning but bumbling gal who gets herself in trouble all the time and has to rely on you to save her from the evil clutches of

Lex Luthor. Something amazing is happening here, and I want to be part of it. It's also dangerous, yeah, but I still want to be a part of it, because what you're doing is so . . . so meaningful. I want to contribute any way I can, do something more worthwhile with my life than I've done so far."

"Do-gooders are usually so full of themselves, so unconsciously arrogant, they do more damage than good," he said.

"I'm not a do-gooder. That's not how I see myself. I'm not at all interested in being praised for my generosity and self-sacrifice. I don't need to feel morally superior. Just *useful*."

"The world is full of do-gooders," he said, refusing to relent. "If I needed an assistant, which I don't, why would I choose you over all the *other* do-gooders out there?"

He was an impossible man. She wanted to smack him.

Instead she kept moving back and forth as she said, "Yesterday, when I crawled back into the plane for that little boy, for Norby, I just . . . well, I amazed myself. I didn't know I had anything like that in me. I wasn't brave, I was scared to death the whole time, but I got him out of there, and I never felt better about myself."

"You like the way people look at you when they know you're a hero," he said flatly.

She shook her head. "No, that's not it. Aside from one rescue worker, no one *knew* I'd pulled Norby out of there. I liked the way *I* looked at me after I'd done it, that's all."

"So you're hooked on risk, heroism, you're a courage junkie."

Now she wanted to smack him twice. In the face. *Crack, crack.* Hard enough to set his eyes spinning. It would make her feel so good.

She restrained herself. "Okay, fine, if that's the way you want to see it, then I'm a courage junkie."

He did not apologize. He just stared at her.

She said, "But that's better than inhaling a pound of cocaine up my nose every day, don't you think?"

He did not respond.

Getting desperate but trying not to show it, Holly said, "When it was all over yesterday, after I handed Norby to that rescue worker, you know what I felt? More than anything else? Not elation at saving him—that too, but not mainly that. And not pride or the thrill of defeating death myself. Mostly I felt *rage*. It surprised me, even scared me. I was so furious that a little boy almost died, that his uncle had died beside him, that he'd been trapped under those seats with corpses, that all of his innocence had been blown away and that he couldn't ever again just enjoy life the way a kid ought to be able to. I wanted to punch somebody, wanted to make somebody apologize to him for what he'd been through. But fate isn't a sleazeball in a cheap suit, you can't put the arm on fate and make it say it's sorry, all you can do is stew in your anger."

Her voice was not rising, but it was increasingly intense. She paced faster, more agitatedly. She was getting passionate instead of angry, which was even more certain to reveal the degree of her desperation. But she couldn't stop herself:

"Just stew in anger. Unless you're Jim Ironheart. *You* can do something about it, make a difference in a way nobody ever made a difference before. And now that I know about you, I can't just get on with my life, can't just shrug my shoulders and walk away, because you've given me a chance to find a strength in myself I didn't know I had, you've given me hope when I didn't even realize I was longing for it, you've shown me a way to satisfy a need that, until yesterday, I didn't even know I had, a need to fight back, to spit in Death's face. Damn it, you can't just close the door now and leave me standing out in the cold!"

He stared at her.

Congratulations, Thorne, she told herself scornfully. You were a monument to composure and restraint, a towering example of self-control.

He just stared at her.

She had met his cool demeanor with heat, had answered his highly effective silences with an ever greater cascade of words. One chance, that was all she'd had, and she'd blown it.

Miserable, suddenly drained of energy instead of over-flowing with it, she sat down again. She propped her elbows on the table and put her face in her hands, not sure if she was going to cry or scream. She didn't do either. She just sighed wearily.

"Want a beer?" he asked.

"God, yes."

▼▲▼

Like a brush of flame, the westering sun slanted through the tilted plantation shutters on the breakfast-nook window, slathering bands of copper-gold fire on the ceiling. Holly slumped in her chair, and Jim leaned forward in his. She stared at him while he stared at his half-finished bottle of Corona.

"Like I told you on the plane, I'm not a psychic," he insisted. "I can't foresee things just because I want to. I don't have visions. It's a higher power working through me."

"You want to define that a little?"

He shrugged. "God."

"God's talking to you?"

"Not talking. I don't hear voices, His or anybody else's. Now and then I'm compelled to be in a certain place at a certain time . . ."

As best he could, he tried to explain how he had ended up at the McAlbury School in Portland and at the sites of the other miraculous rescues he had performed. He also told her about Father Geary finding him on the floor of the church, by the sanctuary railing, with the stigmata of Christ marking his brow, hands, and side.

It was off-the-wall stuff, a weird brand of mysticism that might have been concocted by an heretical Catholic and peyote-inspired Indian medicine man in association with a no-nonsense, Clint Eastwood–style cop. Holly was fascinated. But she said, "I can't honestly tell you I see God's big hand in this."

"I do," he said quietly, making it clear that his conviction was solid and in no need of her approval.

Nevertheless she said, "Sometimes you've had to be pretty damned violent, like with those guys who kidnapped Susie and her mother in the desert."

"They got what they deserved," he said flatly. "There's too much darkness in some people, corruption that could never be cleaned out in five lifetimes of rehabilitation. Evil is real, it walks the earth. Sometimes the devil works by persuasion. Sometimes he just sets loose these sociopaths who don't have a gene for empathy or one for compassion."

"I'm not saying you didn't *have* to be violent in some of these situations. Far as I can see, you had no choice. I just meant—it's hard to see God encouraging his messenger to pick up a shotgun."

He drank some beer. "You ever read the Bible?"

"Sure."

"Says in there that God wiped out the evil people in Sodom and Gomorrah with volcanoes, earthquakes, rains of fire. Flooded the whole world once, didn't He? Made the Red Sea wash over the pharaoh's soldiers, drowned them all. I don't think He's going to be skittish about a little old shotgun."

"I guess I was thinking about the God of the New Testament. Maybe you heard about Him—understanding, compassionate, merciful."

He fixed her with those eyes again, which could be so appealing that they made her knees weak or so cold they made her shiver. A moment ago they had been warm; now they were icy. If she'd had any doubt, she knew from his frigid response that he had not yet decided to welcome her into his life. "I've met up with some people who're such walking scum, it'd be an insult to animals to call them animals. If I thought God always dealt mercifully with their kind, I wouldn't want anything to do with God."

▼▲▼

Holly stood at the kitchen sink, cleaning mushrooms and slicing tomatoes, while Jim separated egg whites from

yolks to make a pair of comparatively low-calorie omelettes.

"All the time, people are dying conveniently, right in
your own backyard. But often you go clear across the
country to save them."

"Once to France," he said, confirming her suspicion that
he had ventured out of the country on his missions. "Once
to Germany, twice to Japan, once to England."

"Why doesn't this higher power give you only local
work?"

"I don't know."

"Have you ever wondered what's so special about the
people you save? I mean—why them and not others?"

"Yeah. I've wondered about it. I see stories on the news
every week about innocent people being murdered or
dying in accidents right here in southern California, and I
wonder why He didn't choose to save them instead of some
boy in Boston. I just figure the boy in Boston—the devil
was conspiring to take him before his time, and God used
me to prevent that."

"So many of them are young."

"I've noticed that."

"But you don't know why?"

"Not a clue."

▼▲▼

The kitchen was redolent of cooking eggs, onions, mushrooms, and green peppers. Jim made one big omelette in a
single pan, planning to cut it in half when it was done.

While Holly monitored the progress of the whole-wheat
bread in the toaster, she said, "Why would God want you
to save Susie and her mother out there in the desert—but
not the girl's father?"

"I don't know."

"The father wasn't a bad man, was he?"

"No. Didn't seem to be."

"So why not save them all?"

"If He wants me to know, He'll tell me."

Jim's certainty about being in God's good grace and

under His guidance, and his easy acceptance that God *wanted* some people to die and not others, made Holly uneasy.

On the other hand, how could he react to his extraordinary experience in any other way? No point in arguing with God.

She recalled an old saying, a real chestnut that had become a cliché in the hands of the pop psych crowd: God grant me the courage to change those things I can't accept, to accept those things I can't change, and the wisdom to know the difference. Cliché or not, that was an eminently sane attitude.

When the two pieces of bread popped up, she plucked them from the toaster. As she toasted two more, she said, "If God wanted to save Nicholas O'Conner from being fried when that power-company vault went up, why didn't He just prevent it from exploding in the first place?"

"I don't know."

"Doesn't it seem odd to you that God has to use you, run you clear across the country, throw you at the O'Conner boy an instant before that 17,000-volt line blows up? Why couldn't He just . . . oh, I don't know . . . just spit on the cable or something, fix it up with a little divine saliva before it went blooey? Or instead of sending you all the way to Atlanta to kill Norman Rink in that convenience store, why didn't God just tweak Norman's brain a little, give him a timely stroke?"

Jim artfully tilted the pan to turn over the omelette. "Why did He make mice to torment people and cats to kill the mice? Why did He create aphids that kill plants, then ladybugs to eat the aphids? And why didn't He give us eyes in the back of our head—when He gave us so many reasons to need them there?"

She finished lightly buttering the first two slices of toast. "I see what you're saying. God works in mysterious ways."

"Very."

▼▲▼

They ate at the breakfast table. In addition to toast, they had sliced tomatoes and cold bottles of Corona with the omelettes.

The purple cloth of twilight slid across the world outside, and the undraped form of night began to reveal itself.

Holly said, "You aren't entirely a puppet in these situations."

"Yes, I am."

"You have some power to determine the outcome."

"None."

"Well, God sent you on Flight Two forty-six to save just the Dubroveks."

"That's right."

"But then you took matters into your own hands and saved more than just Christine and Casey. How many were supposed to die?"

"A hundred and fifty-one."

"And how many actually died?"

"Forty-seven."

"Okay, so you saved a hundred and two more lives than He sent you to save."

"A hundred and three, counting yours—but only because He allowed me to do it, helped me to do it."

"What—you're saying God wanted you to save just the Dubroveks, but then He changed His mind?"

"I guess so."

"God isn't sure what He wants?"

"I don't know."

"God is sometimes confused?"

"I don't know."

"God is a waffler?"

"Holly, I just don't know."

"Good omelette."

"Thank you."

"I have trouble understanding why God would ever change His mind about anything. After all, He's infallible, right? So He can't have made the wrong decision the first time."

"I don't concern myself with questions like that. I just don't think about it."

"Obviously," she said.

He glared at her, and she felt the full effect of his eyes in their arctic mode. Then focusing on his food and beer, he refused to respond to Holly's next few conversational gambits.

She realized that she was no closer to winning his trust than she had been when he had reluctantly invited her in from the patio. He was still judging her, and on points she was probably losing. What she needed was a solid knockout punch, and she thought she knew what it was, but she didn't want to use it until the right moment.

When Jim finished eating, he looked up from his empty plate and said, "Okay, I've listened to your pitch, I've fed you, and now I want you to go."

"No, you don't."

He blinked. "Miss Thorne—"

"You called me Holly before."

"Miss Thorne, please don't make me *throw* you out."

"You don't want me to go," Holly said, striving to sound more confident than she felt. "At all the scenes of these rescues, you've given only your first name. No one's learned anything more about you. Except me. You told me you lived in southern California. You told me your last name was Ironheart."

"I never said you were a bad reporter. You're good at prying information—"

"I didn't pry. You gave it. And if it wasn't something you wanted to give, a grizzly bear with an engineering degree and crowbar couldn't pry it out of you. I want another beer."

"I asked you to go."

"Don't stir yourself. I know where you keep the suds."

She got up, stepped to the refrigerator, and withdrew another bottle of Corona. She was walking on the wild side now, at least for her, but a third beer gave her an excuse—even if a flimsy one—to stay and argue with him. She had downed three bottles last night, at the motel cocktail lounge in Dubuque. But then she had still been saturated with adrenaline, as superalert and edgy as a Siamese cat on Benzedrine, which canceled out the alcohol as fast as it entered her bloodstream. Even so, she had hit the bed as hard as a lumberjack who'd downed a dozen boilermakers. If she passed out on Ironheart, she'd no doubt wake up in her car, out in the street, and she would never get inside his house again. She opened the beer and returned to the table with it.

"You *wanted* me to find you," she said as she sat down.

He regarded her with all the warmth of a dead penguin frozen to an ice floe. "I did, huh?"

"Absolutely. That's why you told me your last name and where I could find you."

He said nothing.

"And you remember your last words to me at the airport in Portland?"

"No."

"It was the best come-on line any guy's ever dropped on me."

He waited.

She made him wait a little longer while she took a sip of beer straight from the bottle. "Just before you closed the car door and went into the terminal, you said, 'So are you, Miss Thorne.' "

"Doesn't sound like much of a come-on line to me."

"It was romantic as hell."

" 'So are you, Miss Thorne.' And what had you just said to me. 'You're an asshole, Mr. Ironheart'?"

"Ho, ho, ho," she said. "Try to spoil it, go ahead, but you can't. I'd told you that your modesty was refreshing, and you said, 'So are you, Miss Thorne.' My heart just now went pitty-pat-pitty-pat again, remembering it. Oh, you knew just what you were doing, you smoothie. Told me your name, told me where you lived, gave me a lot of those eyes, those damned eyes, played coy, then hit me with 'So are you, Miss Thorne,' and walked away like Bogart."

"I don't think you should have any more of that beer."

"Yeah? Well, I think I'll sit here all night, drinking one of 'em after another."

He sighed. "In that case, I'd better have another one myself."

He got another beer and sat down again.

Holly figured she was making progress.

Or maybe he was setting her up. Maybe getting cozy over Corona was a trick of some kind. He was clever, all right. Maybe he was going to try to drink her under the table. Well, he'd lose *that* one, because she'd be under the table long before him!

"You wanted me to find you," she told him.

He said nothing.

"You know why you wanted me to find you?"

He said nothing.

"You wanted me to find you because you really did think I was refreshing, and you're the loneliest, sorriest guy between here and Hardrock, Missouri."

He said nothing. He was good at that. He was the best guy in the world at saying nothing at just the right time.

She said, "You make me want to smack you."

He said nothing.

Whatever confidence the Corona had given her suddenly began to drain away. She sensed that she was losing again. For a couple of rounds, there, she had definitely been winning on points, but now she was being beaten back by his silence.

"Why are all these boxing metaphors running through my head?" she asked him. "I hate boxing."

He slugged down some of his Corona and, with a nod, indicated her bottle, from which she had drunk only a third. "You really insist on finishing that?"

"Hell, yes." She was aware that the brewski was beginning to affect her, perhaps dangerously, but she was still plenty sober enough to recognize that the moment had come for her knockout punch. "If you don't tell me about that place, I'm going to sit here and drink myself into a fat, slovenly, alcoholic old crone. I'm going to die here at the age of eighty-two, with a liver the size of Vermont."

"Place?" He looked baffled. "What place?"

Now. She chose a soft but clear whisper in which to deliver the punch: "The windmill."

He didn't exactly fall to the canvas, and no cartoon stars swarmed around his head, but Holly could see that he had been rocked.

"You've been to the windmill?" he asked.

"No. You mean it's a real place?"

"If you don't know that much, then how could you know about it at all?"

"Dreams. Windmill dreams. Each of the last three nights."

He paled. The overhead light was not on. They were sitting in shadows, illuminated only by the secondhand glow of the rangehood and sink lights in the kitchen and by a table lamp in the adjacent family room, but Holly saw him go pale under his tan. His face seemed to hover before her in the gloom like the face-shaped wing configuration of a big snow-white moth.

The extraordinary vividness and unusual nature of the nightmare—and the fact that the effects of the dream had continued after she had awakened in her motel room—had encouraged her to believe that it was somehow connected with Jim Ironheart. Two encounters with the paranormal in such close succession *had* to be linked. But she was relieved, all the same, when his stunned reaction confirmed her suspicion.

"Limestone walls," she said. "Wooden floor. A heavy wooden door, banded in iron, that opens on some limestone steps. A yellow candle in a blue dish."

"I've dreamed about it for years," he said softly. "Once or twice a month. Never more often than that. Until the last three nights. But how can we be having the same dream?"

"Where's the real windmill?"

"On my grandparents' farm. North of Santa Barbara. In the Santa Ynez Valley."

"Did something terrible happen to you there, or what?"

He shook his head. "No. Not at all. I loved that place. It was . . . a sanctuary."

"Then why did you go pale when I mentioned it?"

"Did I?"

"Picture an albino cat chasing a mouse around a corner and running into a Doberman. That pale."

"Well, when I dream of the mill, it's always frightening—"

"Don't I know it. But if it was a good place in your life, a sanctuary like you say, then why does it feature in nightmares?"

"I don't know."

"Here we go again."

"I really don't," he insisted. "Why did *you* dream about it, if you've never even been there?"

She drank more beer, which did not clarify her thinking. "Maybe because you're projecting your dream at me. As a way to sort of make a connection between us, draw me to you."

"Why would I want to draw you to me?"

"Thanks a lot."

"Anyway, like I told you before, I'm no psychic, I don't have abilities like that. I'm just an instrument."

"Then it's this higher power of yours," she said. "It's sending me the same dream because it wants us to connect."

He wiped one hand down his face. "This is too much for me right now. I'm so damned tired."

"Me, too. But it's only nine-thirty, and we've still got a lot to talk about."

"I only slept about an hour last night," he said.

He really did look exhausted. A shave and a shower had made him presentable, but the bruise-dark rings around his eyes were getting darker; and he had not regained color in his face after turning pale at the mention of her windmill dreams.

He said, "We can pick this up in the morning."

She frowned. "No way. I'll come back in the morning, and you won't let me in."

"I'll let you in."

"That's what you say now."

"If you're having that dream, then you're part of this whether I like it or not."

His tone of voice had gone from cool to cold again, and it was clear that what he meant by "whether I like it or not" was really "even though I don't like it."

He was a loner, evidently always had been. Viola Moreno, who had great affection for him, claimed he was well-liked by his students and colleagues. She'd spoken of a fundamental sadness in him, however, that separated him from other people, and since quitting his teaching position, he had seen little of Viola or his other friends from that life. Though intrigued by the news that he and Holly were sharing a dream, though he had called her "refreshing," though he was to some degree attracted to her, he obviously resented her intrusion into his solitude.

Holly said, "No good. You'll be gone when I get here in the morning, I won't know where you went, maybe you'll never come back."

He had no energy for resistance. "Then stay the night."

"You have a spare bedroom?"

"Yeah. But there's no spare bed. You can sleep on the family-room couch, I guess, but it's damned old and not too comfortable."

She carried her half-empty beer into the adjacent family room, and tested the sagging, brown sofa. "It'll be good enough."

"Whatever you want." He seemed indifferent, but she sensed that his indifference was a pretense.

"You have any spare pajamas?"

"Jesus."

"Well, I'm sorry, but I didn't bring any."

"Mine'll be too big for you."

"Just makes them more comfortable. I'd like to shower, too. I'm sticky from tanning lotion and being in the sun all afternoon."

With the put-upon air of a man who had found his least favorite relative standing on his doorstep unannounced, he took her upstairs, showed her the guest bath, and got a pair of pajamas and a set of towels for her.

"Try to be quiet," he said. "I plan to be sound asleep in five minutes."

▼ ▲ ▼

Luxuriating in the fall of hot water and clouds of steam, Holly was pleased that the shower did not take the edge off her beer buzz. Though she had slept better last night than Ironheart claimed to have, she had not gotten a solid eight hours in the past few days, and she was looking forward to a Corona-induced sleep even on the worn and lumpy sofa.

At the same time, she was uneasy about the continued fuzziness of her mind. She needed to keep her wits about her. After all, she was in the house of an undeniably strange man who was largely a cipher to her, a walking mystery. She understood little of what was in his heart, which pumped secrets and shadows in greater quantity than blood. For all his coolness toward her, he seemed basically a good man with benign intentions, and it was difficult to believe that he was a threat to her. On the other hand, it was not unusual to see a news story about a berserk mass murderer who—after brutally slaying his friends, family, and coworkers—was described by his astonished neighbors as "a really nice guy." For all she knew, in spite of his claim to be the avatar of God, by day Jim Ironheart heroically risked his own life to save the lives of strangers—and, by night, tortured kittens with maniacal glee.

Nevertheless, after she dried off on the clean-smelling, fluffy bath towel, she took another long swallow of her Corona. She decided that a full night of deep and dreamless sleep was worth the risk of being butchered in her bed.

She put on his pajamas, rolled up the cuffs of the pants and the sleeves.

Carrying her bottle of Corona, which still contained a swallow or two, she quietly opened the bathroom door and stepped into the second-floor hallway. The house was eerily silent.

Heading toward the stairs, she passed the open door of the master bedroom and glanced inside. Extension-arm brass reading lamps were mounted on the wall on both sides of the bed, and one of them cast a narrow wedge of amber light on the rumpled sheets. Jim was lying on his back in bed, his arms folded on the two pillows under his head, and he seemed to be awake.

She hesitated, then stepped into the open doorway. "Thanks," she said, speaking softly in case he was asleep, "I feel a lot better."

"Good for you."

Holly entered the room and moved close enough to the bed to see his blue eyes shining in the backsplash of the lamp. The covers were pulled up past his navel, but he was not wearing pajama tops. His chest and arms were lean but well-muscled.

She said, "Thought you'd be asleep by now."

"Want to be, need to be, but I can't shut my mind off."

Looking down at him, she said, "Viola Moreno says there's a deep sadness in you."

"Been busy, haven't you?"

She took a small swallow of Corona. One left. She sat down on the edge of the bed. "Do your grandparents still have the farm with the windmill?"

"They're dead."

"I'm sorry."

"Grandma died five years ago, Grandpa eight months later—as if he really didn't want to go on without her. They had good, full lives. But I miss them."

"You have anybody?"

"Two cousins in Akron," he said.

"You stay in touch?"

"Haven't seen them in twenty years."

She drank the last of the Corona. She put the empty bottle on the nightstand.

For a few minutes neither of them spoke. The silence was not awkward. Indeed, it was comfortable.

She got up and went around to the other side of the bed.

She pulled back the covers, stretched out beside him, and put her head on the other two pillows.

Apparently, he was not surprised. Neither was she.

After a while, they held hands, lying side by side, staring at the ceiling.

She said, "Must've been hard, losing your parents when you were just ten."

"Real bad."

"What happened to them?"

He hesitated. "A traffic accident."

"And you went to live with your grandparents?"

"Yeah. The first year was the hardest. I was . . . in bad shape. I spent a lot of time in the windmill. It was my special place, where I went to play . . . to be alone."

"I wish we'd been kids together," she said.

"Why?"

She thought of Norby, the boy she had pulled from the sarcophagus under the DC-10's overturned seats. "So I could've known you before your parents died, what you were like then, untouched."

Another stretch of time passed in silence.

When he spoke, his voice was so low that Holly could barely hear it above the thumping of her own heart: "Viola has a sadness in her, too. She looks like the happiest lady in the world, but she lost her husband in Vietnam, never got over it. Father Geary, the priest I told you about, he looks like every devout parish rector from every old sentimental Catholic movie ever made in the thirties and forties, but when I met him he was weary and unsure of his calling. And you . . . well, you're pretty and amusing, and you have an air of efficiency about you, but I'd never have guessed that you could be as relentless as you are. You give the impression of a woman who moves easy through life, interested in life and in her work, but never moving against a current, always with it, easy. Yet you're really like a bulldog when you get your teeth in something."

Staring at the dapple of light and shadow on the ceiling, holding his strong hand, Holly considered his statement for a while. Finally she said, "What's your point?"

"People are always more . . . complex than you figure."

"Is that just an observation . . . or a warning?"

He seemed surprised by her question. "Warning?"

"Maybe you're warning me that you're not what you seem to be."

After another long pause, he said, "Maybe."

She matched his silence. Then she said, "I guess I don't care."

He turned toward her. She moved against him with a shyness that she had not felt in many years. His first kiss was gentle, and more intoxicating than three bottles or three cases of Corona.

Holly realized she'd been deceiving herself. She had needed the beer not to soothe her nerves, not to insure an uninterrupted night of sleep, but to give her the courage to seduce him—or to be seduced. She had sensed that he was abysmally lonely, and she had told him so. Now she understood that her loneliness had exceeded his, and that only the smallest part of her desolation of spirit had resulted from her disenchantment with journalism; most of it was simply the result of being alone, for the most part, all of her adult life.

Two pajama bottoms and one top seemed to dissolve between them like clothes sometimes evaporate in erotic dreams. She moved her hands over him with increasing excitement, marveling that the sense of touch could convey such intricacies of shape and texture, or give rise to such exquisite longings.

She had a ridiculously romantic idea of what it would be like to make love to him, a dreamy-eyed girl's fantasy of unmatched passion, of sweet tenderness and pure hot sex in perfect balance, every muscle in both of them flexing and contracting in sublime harmony or, at times, in breathless counterpoint, each invasive stroke a testament to mutual surrender, two becoming one, the outer world of reason overwhelmed by the inner world of feeling, no wrong word spoken, no sigh mistimed, bodies moving and meshing in precisely the same mysterious rhythms by which the great invisible tidal forces of the universe ebbed and flowed, elevating the act above mere biology and making of it a mystical experience. Her expectations proved, of course, to be ridiculous. In reality, it was more tender, more fierce, and far better than her fantasy.

▼▲▼

They fell asleep like spoons in a drawer, her belly against his back, her loins against his warm bottom. Hours later, in those reaches of the night that were usually—but no longer—the loneliest of all, they woke to the same quiet alarm of renewed desire. He turned to her, she welcomed him, and this time they moved together with an even greater urgency, as if the first time had not taken the edge off their need but had sharpened it the way one dose of heroin only increases the addict's desire for the next.

At first, looking up into Jim's beautiful eyes, Holly felt as if she were gazing into the pure fire of his soul. Then he gripped her by the sides, half lifting her off the mattress as he eased deep into her, and she felt the scratches burning in her flanks and remembered the claws of the thing that had stepped magically out of a dream. For an instant, with pain flashing in her shallow wounds, her perception shifted, and she had the queer feeling that it was a cold blue fire into which she gazed, burning without heat. But that was only a reaction to the stinging scratches and the pain-engendered memory of the nightmare. When he slid his hands off her sides and under her, lifting, she rose to meet him, and he was all warmth now, not the faintest chill about him. Together they generated enough heat to sear away that brief image of a soul on ice.

▼▲▼

The frost-pale glow of the unseen moon backlit banks of coaly clouds that churned across the night sky.

Unlike in other recent dreams, Holly was standing outside on a graveled path that led between a pond and a cornfield toward the door in the base of the old windmill. The limestone structure rose above her at a severe angle, recognizably a mill but nonetheless an alien place, unearthly.

The huge sails, ragged with scores of broken or missing vanes, were silhouetted against the foreboding sky and angled like a tilted cross. Although a blustery wind sent moon-silvered ripples across the ink-dark pond and rattled the nearby cornstalks, the sails were still. The mill obviously had been inoperable for many years, and the mechanisms were most likely too rusted to allow the sails to turn.

A spectral muddy-yellow light flickered at the narrow windows of the upper room. Beyond the glass, strange shadows moved across the interior limestone walls of that high chamber.

She didn't want to get any closer to the building, had never been more frightened of a place in her life, but she was unable to halt herself. She was drawn forward as if she were the spellbound thrall of some powerful sorcerer.

In the pond to her left, something was wrong with the moon-cast reflection of the windmill, and she turned to look at it. The pattern of light and shade on the water was reversed from what it should have been. The mill shadow was not a dark geometric form imposed on the water over the filigree of moonlight; instead, the image of the mill was brighter than the surface of the pond around it, as if the mill were luminous, the brightest object in the night, when in fact its stones rose in an ebony and forbidding pile. Where the high windows were filled with lambent light in the real mill, black rectangles floated in the impossible reflection, like the empty eyeholes in a fleshless skull.

Creak . . . creak . . . creak . . .

She looked up.

The massive sails were trembling in the wind and beginning to move. They forced the corroded gears that drove the windshaft and, in turn, the grinding stones in the millroom at its base.

Wanting only to wake up or, failing that, to flee back along the gravel path over which she had come, Holly drifted inexorably forward. The giant sails began to turn clockwise, gaining speed, producing less creaking as the gears unfroze. It seemed to her that they were like the fingers of a monstrous hand, and the jagged end of every broken vane was a claw.

She reached the door.

She did not want to go inside. She knew that within lay a hell of some kind, as bad as the pits of torture described by any fire-and-brimstone preacher who had ever thundered a sermon in old Salem. If she went in there, she would never come out alive.

The sails swooped down at her, passing just a couple of feet over her head, the splintered wood reaching for her: *Whoosh, whoosh, whoosh, whoosh.*

In the grip of a trance even more commanding than her terror, she opened the door. She stepped across the threshold. With the malevolent animation that objects possessed only in dreams, the door pulled out of her hand, slammed shut behind her.

Ahead lay the lightless lower room of the mill, in which the worn stone wheels ground against each other.

To her left, barely visible in the gloom, stairs led up. Ululant squeals and haunting cries echoed from above, like the night concert performed by the wildlife in a jungle, except none of these voices was quite that of a panther or monkey or bird or hyena. Electronic sounds were part of the mix, and what seemed to be the brittle shrieks of insects passed through a stereo amplifier. Underlying the cacophony was a monotonous, throbbing, three-note bass refrain that reverberated in the stone walls of the stairwell and, before she had climbed halfway to the second floor, in Holly's bones as well.

She passed a narrow window on her left. An extended series of lightning bolts crackled across the vault of the night, and at the foot of the mill, like a trick mirror in a funhouse, the dark pond turned transparent. Its depths were revealed, as though the lightning came from under the water, and Holly saw an infinitely strange shape resting on the bottom. She squinted, trying to get a better look at the object, but the lightning sputtered out.

The merest glimpse of the thing, however, sent a cold wind through the hollows of her bones.

She waited, hoping for more lightning, but the night remained as opaque as tar, and black rain suddenly spattered against the window. Because she was halfway to the second floor of the mill, more muddy-orange and yellow light flickered around her than had reached her at the foot of the stairs. The window glass, backed by utter darkness now and painted with sufficient luminescence to serve as a dim mirror, presented her reflection.

But the face she possessed in this dream was not her own. It belonged to a woman twenty years older than Holly, to whom she bore no resemblance.

She'd never before had a dream in which she occupied the body of another person. But now she understood why she had been unable to turn back from the mill when she'd been outside, and why she was unable to stop herself from climbing to the high room even though, on one level, she knew she was dreaming. Her lack of control was not the usual helplessness that transformed dreams into nightmares, but the result of sharing the body of a stranger.

The woman turned from the window and continued upward toward the unearthly shrieks, cries, and whispers that echoed down to her with the fluctuant light. Around her the limestone walls pounded with the tripartite bass beat, as if the mill were alive and had a massive three-chambered heart.

Stop, turn back, you're going to die up there, Holly shouted, but the woman could not hear her. Holly was only an observer in her own dream, not an active participant, unable to influence events.

Step by step. Higher.

The iron-bound timber door stood open.

She crossed the threshold. Into the high room.

The first thing she saw was the boy. He was standing in the middle of the room, terrified. His small hands, curled in fists, were at his sides. A three-inch-diameter decorative candle stood in a blue dish at his feet. A hardcover book lay beside the dish, and she glimpsed the word "mill" on the colorful dustjacket.

Turning to look at her, his beautiful blue eyes darkened by terror, the boy said, "I'm scared, help me, the walls, the *walls!*"

She realized that the single candle was not producing all of the peculiar glow suffusing the room. Other light glimmered in the walls, as if they were not made of solid limestone but of semitransparent and magically radiant quartz in shades of amber. At once she saw that something was alive *within* the stone, something luminous which could move through solid matter as easily as a swimmer could move through water.

The wall swelled and throbbed.

"It's coming," the boy said with evident fear but also with what might have been a perverse excitement, "and nobody can stop it!"

Suddenly it was born out of the wall. The curve of mortared blocks split like the spongy membrane of an insect's egg. And taking shape from a core of foul muck where limestone should have been—

"No!"

Choking on a scream, Holly woke.

She sat up in bed, something touched her, and she wrenched away from it. Because the room was awash in morning light, she saw that it was only Jim.

A dream. Just a dream.

As had happened two nights ago in the Laguna Hills Motor Inn, however, the creature of the dream was trying to force its way into the waking world. It was not coming through a wall this time. The ceiling. Directly over the bed. The white-painted drywall was no longer white or dry, but mottled amber and brown, semitransparent and luminous as the stone in the dream had been, oozing a noxious mucus, bulging as some shadowy entity struggled to be born into the bedroom.

The dream-thing's thunderous three-part heartbeat— *lub-dub-DUB, lub-dub-DUB*—shuddered through the house.

Jim rolled off the bed and onto his feet. He had slipped into his pajama bottoms again during the night, just as Holly had slipped into the roomy top which hung halfway to her knees. She scrambled to his side. They stared up in horror at the pulsing birth sac which the ceiling had become, and at the shadowy writhing form struggling to breach that containing membrane.

Most frightening of all—this apparition was in daylight. The plantation shutters had not been completely closed over the windows, and slats of morning sunshine banded the room. When something from Beyond found you in the dead hours of the night, you half expected it. But sunshine was supposed to banish all monsters.

Jim put a hand against Holly's back, pushed her toward the open door to the hallway. "Go, get out!"

She took only two steps in that direction before the door slammed shut of its own accord. As if an exceptionally powerful poltergeist were at work, a mahogany highboy, as old and well-used as everything in the house, erupted away from the wall beside her, almost knocking her down. It flew across the bedroom, slammed into the door. A dresser and a chair followed that tall chest of drawers, effectively barricading the only exit.

The windows in the far wall presented an avenue of escape, but they would have to crouch to slip under the increasingly distended central portion of the ceiling. Having accepted the illogic of the waking nightmare, Holly was now loath to press past that greasy and obscenely throbbing pouch, for fear that it would split open as she moved under it, and that the creature within would seize her.

Jim pulled her back with him into the adjoining bathroom. He kicked the door shut.

Holly swung around, searching. The only window was set high and was too small to provide a way out.

The bathroom walls were untainted by the organic transformation that had overcome the bedroom, but they still shook with the triple bass thud of the inhuman heartbeat.

"What the hell is that?" he demanded.

"The Enemy," she said at once, surprised that he didn't know. "The Enemy, from the dream."

Above them, starting from the partition that the bath shared with the bedroom, the white ceiling began to discolor as if abruptly saturated with red blood, brown bile. The sheen of semigloss paint on drywall metamorphosed into a biological surface and began to throb in time with the thunderous heartbeat.

Jim pulled her into a corner by the vanity, and she huddled helplessly against him. Beyond the pregnant droop of the lowering ceiling, she saw repulsive movement like the frenzied squirming of a million maggots.

The thudding heartbeat increased in volume, booming around them.

She heard a wet, tearing sound. None of this could be happening, yet it was, and that sound made it more real than the things she was seeing with her own eyes, because it was such a filthy sound and so hideously intimate, too *real* for a delusion or a dream.

The door crashed open, and the ceiling burst overhead, showering them with debris.

But with that implosion, the power of the lingering nightmare was exhausted, and reality finally, fully reasserted itself. Nothing monstrous surged through the open door; only the sun-filled bedroom lay beyond. Although the ceiling had looked entirely organic when it had burst in upon them, no trace of its transformed state remained; it was only a ceiling again. The rain of debris included chunks of wallboard, flaked and powdered drywall paste, splinters of wood, and wads of fluffy Fiberglas insulation—but nothing alive.

The hole itself was astonishing enough to Holly.

Two nights ago, in the motel, though the wall had bulged and rippled as if alive, it had returned to its true composition without a crack. No evidence of the dream-creature's intrusion had been left behind except the scratches in her sides, which a psychologist might have said were self-inflicted. When the dust settled, everything might have been just a fantastically detailed delusion.

But the mess in which they were now standing was no delusion. The pall of white dust in the air was real.

In a state of shock, Jim took her hand and led her out of the bathroom. The bedroom ceiling had not crashed down. It was as it had been last night: smooth, white. But the furniture was piled up against the door as if washed there by a flood.

Madness favored darkness, but light was the kingdom of reason. If the waking world provided no sanctuary from nightmares, if daylight offered no sanctuary from unreason, then there was no sanctuary anywhere, anytime, for anyone.

2

The attic light, a single sixty-watt bulb dangling from a beam, did not illuminate every corner of that cramped and dusty space. Jim probed into the many recesses with a flashlight, edged around heating ducts, peered behind each of the two fireplace chimneys, searching for . . . whatever had torn apart the bathroom ceiling. He had no idea what he expected to find. Besides the flashlight, he carried a loaded revolver. The thing that destroyed the ceiling had not descended into the bathroom, so it had to be in the attic above. However, because he lived with a minimum of possessions, Jim had nothing to store up there under the roof, which left few possible hiding places. He was soon satisfied that those high reaches of his house were untenanted except by spiders and by a small colony of wasps that had constructed a nest in a junction of rafters.

Nothing could have escaped those confines, either. Aside from the trapdoor by which he had entered, the only exits from the attic were the ventilation cut-outs in opposing eaves. Each was about two feet long and twelve inches high, covered with tightly fitted screens that could be removed only with a screwdriver. Both screens were secure.

Part of that space had plank flooring, but in some places nothing but insulation lay between the exposed floor studs, which were also the ceiling studs of the rooms below. Duck-walking on those parallel supports, Jim cautiously approached the rupture above the master bathroom. He peered down at the debris-strewn floor where he and Holly had been standing.

What in the hell had happened?

At last conceding that he would find no answers up there, he returned to the open access and climbed down into the second-floor linen closet. He folded up the accordion ladder into the closet ceiling, which neatly closed off the attic entrance.

Holly was waiting for him in the hallway. "Well?"

"Nothing," he said.

"I knew there wouldn't be."

"What happened here?"

"It's like in the dream."

"What dream?" he demanded.

"You said you've had the windmill dreams, too."

"I do."

"Then you know about the heartbeat in the walls."

"No."

"And the way the walls change."

"No, none of that, for Christ's sake! In my dream, I'm in the high room of the windmill, there's a candle, rain at the windows."

She remembered how surprised he had been at the sight of the bedroom ceiling distended and strange above them.

He said, "In the dream, I have a sense that something's coming, something frightening and terrible—"

"The Enemy," she said.

"Yes! Whatever that might be. But it never comes, not in *my* dreams. I always wake up before it comes."

He stalked down the hall and into the master bedroom, and she followed him. Standing beside the battered furniture that he had shoved away from the door, he stared up in consternation at the undamaged ceiling.

"I saw it," he said, as if she had called him a liar.

"I know you did," she said. "I saw it, too."

He turned to her, looking more desperate than she had seen him even aboard the doomed DC-10. "Tell me about your dreams, I want to hear all of them, every detail."

"Later, I'll tell you everything. First let's shower and get dressed. I want out of this place."

"Yeah, okay, me too."

"I guess you realize where we've got to go."

He hesitated.

She answered for him, "The windmill."

He nodded.

They showered together in the guest bathroom, only to save time—and because both of them were too edgy to be alone at the moment. She supposed that, in a different mood, she would have found the experience pleasantly erotic. But it was surprisingly platonic, considering the fierce passion of the night just passed.

He touched her only when they had stepped out of the shower and were hurriedly toweling dry. He leaned close, kissed the corner of her mouth, and said, "What have I gotten you into, Holly Thorne?"

▼ ▲ ▼

Later, while Jim hurriedly packed a suitcase, Holly wandered only as far as the upstairs study, which was next to his bedroom. The place had a disused look. A thin layer of dust covered the top of the desk.

Like the rest of the house, his study was humble. The cheap desk had probably been purchased at a cut-rate office-supplies warehouse. The other furniture included just two lamps, an armchair on a wheel-and-swivel base, two free-standing bookcases overflowing with worn volumes, and a worktable as bare as the long-unused desk.

All of the two hundred or more books were about religion: fat histories of Islam, Judaism, Buddhism, Zen Buddhism, Christianity, Hinduism, Taoism, Shintoism, and others; the collected works of St. Thomas Aquinas, Martin Luther; *Scientists and Their Gods;* the Bible in several versions—Douay, King James, American Standard; the Koran; the Torah, including the Old Testament and the Talmud; the Tripitaka of Buddhism, the Agama of Hinduism, the Zend-Avesta of Zoroastrianism, and the Veda of Brahmanism.

In spite of the curious completeness of that part of his personal library, the most interesting thing in the room was the gallery of photographs that occupied two walls. Of the thirty-some 8 × 10 prints, a few were in color but most were black and white. The same three people featured in all of them: a strikingly lovely brunette, a good-looking man with bold features and thinning hair, and a child who could be no one but Jim Ironheart. Those eyes. One photograph showed Jim with the couple—obviously his parents—when he was only an infant swaddled in a blanket, but in the others he was not much younger than four and never older than about ten.

When he'd been ten, of course, his parents had died.

Some photos showed young Jim with his dad, some with his mom, and Holly assumed the missing parent had always been the one with the camera. A handful included all three Ironhearts. Over the years, the mother only grew more striking; the father's hair continued to thin, but he appeared to be happier as time passed; and Jim, taking a lesson from his mother, became steadily better looking.

Often the backdrop of the picture was a famous landmark or the sign for one. Jim and both parents in front of Radio City Music Hall when he'd been about six. Jim and his father on the boardwalk at Atlantic City when Jim was four or five. Jim and his mother at a sign for Grand Canyon National Park, with a panoramic vista behind them. All three Ironhearts in front of Sleeping Beauty Castle in the heart of Disneyland, when Jim was only seven or eight. Beale Street in Memphis. The sun-splashed Fontainebleau Hotel in Miami Beach. An observation deck overlooking the faces of Mount Rushmore. Buckingham Palace in London. The Eiffel Tower. The Tropicana Hotel, Las Vegas. Niagara Falls. They seemed to have been everywhere.

In every case, no matter who was holding the camera or where they were, those in the shot looked genuinely happy. Not one face in one print was frozen in an insincere smile, or caught with one of those snap-the-damn-picture expressions of impatience that could be found in abundance in most family photo albums. Often, they were laughing instead of merely smiling, and in several instances they were caught in the middle of horseplay of one kind or another. All three were touchers, too, not simply standing side by side or in brittle poses. They were usually shown with their arms around one another, sometimes hugging, occasionally kissing one another on the cheek or casually expressing affection in some fashion.

The boy in the photographs revealed no hint of the sometimes moody adult he would become, and Holly could see that the untimely death of his parents had changed him profoundly. The carefree, grinning boy in the photographs had been lost forever.

One black-and-white particularly arrested her. It showed Mr. Ironheart sitting on a straight-backed chair. Jim, maybe seven years old, was on his father's lap. They were in tuxedos. Mrs. Ironheart stood behind her husband, her hand on his shoulder, wearing a slinky sequined cocktail dress that emphasized her wonderful figure. They faced the camera directly. Unlike the other shots, this one was carefully posed, with nothing but a piece of artfully draped cloth as a backdrop, obviously set up by a professional photographer.

"They were wonderful," Jim said from the doorway. She had not heard him approaching. "No kid ever had better folks than them."

"You traveled a lot."

"Yeah. They were always going somewhere. They loved to show me new places, teach me things firsthand. They would've made wonderful schoolteachers, let me tell you."

"What work did they do?"

"My dad was an accountant at Warner Brothers."

"The movie studio?"

"Yeah." Jim smiled. "We lived in L.A. Mom—she wanted to be an actress, but she never got a lot of jobs. So mostly she was a hostess at a restaurant on Melrose Avenue, not far from the Paramount lot."

"You were happy, weren't you?"

"Always."

She pointed to the photo in which the three of them were dressed with glittery formality. "Special occasion?"

"Times just the two of them should have celebrated, like wedding anniversaries, they insisted on including me. They always made me feel special, wanted, loved. I was seven years old when that photo was taken, and I remember them making big plans that night. They were going to be married a hundred years, they said, and be happier each year than the one before, have lots more children, own a big house, see every corner of the world before they died together in their sleep. But just three years later they were . . . gone."

"I'm sorry, Jim."

He shrugged. "It's a long time ago. Twenty-five years." He looked at his wristwatch. "Come on, let's go. It'll take us four hours to reach the farm, and it's already nine o'clock."

▼▲▼

At the Laguna Hills Motor Inn, Holly quickly changed into jeans and a blue-checkered blouse, then packed the rest of her belongings. Jim put her suitcase in the trunk of his car.

While she returned her room key and paid her bill at the front desk in the motel office, she was aware of him watching her from behind the wheel of his Ford. She would have been disappointed, of course, if he had not liked to watch her. But every time she looked through the plate-glass window at him, he was so motionless, so cool and expressionless behind his heavily tinted sunglasses, that his undivided attention was disconcerting.

She wondered if she was doing the right thing by going with him to the Santa Ynez Valley. When she walked out of the office and got in the car with him, he would be the only person in the world who knew where she was. All of her notes about him were in her suitcase; they could disappear with her. Then she would be just a woman, alone, who had vanished while on vacation.

As the clerk finished filling out the credit-card form,

Holly considered phoning her parents in Philadelphia to let them know where she was going and with whom. But she would only alarm them and be on the phone half an hour trying to reassure them that she was going to be just fine.

Besides, she had already decided that the darkness in Jim was less important than the light, and she had made a commitment to him. If he occasionally made her uneasy . . . well, that was part of what had drawn her to him in the first place. A sense of danger sharpened the edge of his appeal. At heart, he was a good man.

It was foolish to worry about her safety after she had already made love to him. For a woman, in a way that could never be true for a man, the first night of sexual surrender involved one of the moments of greatest vulnerability in a relationship. Assuming, of course, that she had surrendered not solely because of physical need but because she loved him. And Holly loved him.

"I'm in love with him," she said aloud, surprised because she had convinced herself that his appeal was largely the result of his exceptional male grace, animal magnetism, and mystery.

The clerk, ten years younger than Holly and therefore more inclined to think that love was everywhere and inevitable, grinned at her. "It's great, isn't it?"

Signing the charge slip, Holly said, "Do you believe in love at first sight?"

"Why not?"

"Well, it's not first sight, really. I've known the guy since August twelfth, which is . . . sixteen days."

"And you're not married yet?" the clerk joked.

When Holly went out to the Ford and got in beside Jim, she said, "When we get where we're going, you won't carve me up with a chainsaw and bury me under the windmill, will you?"

Apparently he understood her sense of vulnerability and took no offense, for he said with mock solemnity, "Oh, no. It's full-up under the mill. I'll have to bury pieces of you all over the farm."

She laughed. She was an idiot for fearing him.

He leaned over and kissed her. It was a lovely, lingering kiss.

When they parted, he said, "I'm taking as big a risk as you are."

"Let me assure you, I've never hacked anyone to bits with an ax."

"I mean it. I haven't been lucky in love."

"Me neither."

"This time will be different for both of us."

He gave her another kiss, shorter and sweeter than the first one, then started the car and backed out of the parking space.

In a determined attempt to keep the dying cynic in her alive, Holly reminded herself that he had not actually said he loved her. His commitment had been carefully and indirectly phrased. He might be no more reliable than other men she had trusted over the years.

On the other hand, she had not actually said that she loved him, either. Her commitment had been no more effusively stated than his. Perhaps because she still felt the need to protect herself to some extent, she had found it easier to reveal her heart to the motel clerk than to Jim.

▼▲▼

Washing down blueberry muffins with black coffee, for which they had stopped at a convenience store, they traveled north on the San Diego Freeway. The Tuesday-morning rush hour had passed, but at some places traffic still clogged all lanes and moved like a snail herd being driven toward a gourmet restaurant.

Comfortably ensconced in the passenger seat, Holly told Jim about her four nightmares, as promised. She started with the initial dream of blindness on Friday night, concluding with last night's spookshow, which had been the most bizarre and fearful of all.

He was clearly fascinated that she had dreamed about the mill without even knowing of its existence. And on Sunday night, after surviving the crash of Flight 246, she had dreamed of him at the mill *as a ten-year-old boy,* when she could not yet have known either that the mill was a familiar place to him or that he had spent a lot of time there when he was ten.

But the majority of his questions related to her most recent nightmare. Keeping his eyes on the traffic ahead, he said, "Who was the woman in the dream if she wasn't you?"

"I don't know," Holly said, finishing the final bite of the last muffin. "I had no sense of her identity."

"Can you describe her?"

"I only saw her reflection in that window, so I can't tell you much, I'm afraid." She drank the last of the coffee from her big Styrofoam cup, and thought a moment. It was easier to visualize the scenes of that dream than it should have been, for dreams were usually quick to fade from memory. Images from that one returned to her quite vividly, however, as if she had not dreamed them but experienced them in real life. "She had a broad clear face, more handsome in a womanly way than pretty. Wide-set eyes, full mouth. A beauty mark high on her right cheek, I don't think it could've been a spot on the glass, just a little round dot. Curly hair. Do you recognize her?"

"No," he replied. "Can't say that I do. Tell me what you saw at the bottom of the pond when the lightning flashed."

"I'm not sure what it was."

"Describe it as best you can."

She pondered for a moment, then shook her head. "I can't. The woman's face was fairly easy to recall because when I saw it in the dream I knew what it was, a face, a human face. But whatever was lying at the bottom of the pond . . . that was strange, like nothing I'd ever seen before. I didn't know what I was looking at, and I had such a brief glimpse of it and . . . well, now it's just gone. Is there really something peculiar under that pond?"

"Not that I know of," he said. "Could it've been a sunken boat, a rowboat, anything like that?"

"No," she said. "Nothing at all like that. Much bigger. Did a boat sink in the pond once?"

"I never heard of it, if one did. It's a deceptive-looking

bit of water, though. You expect a millpond to be shallow, but this one is deep, forty or fifty feet toward the center. It never dries out, and it doesn't shrink during dry years, either, because it's formed over an artesian well, not just an aquifer."

"What's the difference?"

"An aquifer is what you drill into when you're sinking a well, it's sort of a reservoir or stream of underground water. Artesian wells are rarer. You don't drill into one to find water, 'cause the water is already coming to the surface under pressure. You'd have the devil's own time trying to *stop* the stuff from percolating up."

The snarl of traffic began to loosen, but Jim did not take full advantage of opportunities to change lanes and swing around slower-moving vehicles. He was more interested in her answers than in making better time.

He said, "And in the dream, when you got to the top of the stairs—or when this woman got to the top of the stairs—you saw a ten-year-old boy standing there, and somehow you knew he was me."

"Yes."

"I don't look much like I looked when I was ten, so how'd you recognize me?"

"Mostly it was your eyes," Holly said. "They haven't changed much in all these years. They're unmistakable."

"Lots of people have blue eyes."

"Are you serious? Honey, your blue eyes are to other blue eyes what Sinatra's voice is to Donald Duck's."

"You're prejudiced. What did you see in the wall?"

She described it again.

"Alive in the stone? This just gets stranger and stranger."

"I haven't been bored in days," she agreed.

Beyond the junction with Interstate 10, traffic on the San Diego Freeway became even lighter, and finally Jim began to put some of his driving skills to use. He handled the car the way a first-rate jockey handled a thoroughbred horse, finessing from it that extra degree of performance that won races. The Ford was only a stock model with no modification, but it responded to him as if it wanted to be a Porsche.

After a while Holly began to ask questions of her own. "How come you're a millionaire but you live relatively cheap?"

"Bought a house, moved out of my apartment. Quit my job."

"Yeah, but a modest house. And your furniture's falling apart."

"I needed the privacy of my own house to meditate and rest between . . . assignments. But I didn't need fancy furniture."

Following a few minutes of mutual silence, she said, "Did I catch your eye the way you caught mine, right off the bat, up in Portland?"

He smiled but didn't look away from the highway. " 'So are you, Miss Thorne.' "

"So you admit it!" Holly said, pleased. "It *was* a come-on line."

They made excellent time from the west side of Los Angeles all the way to Ventura, but then Jim began to slack off again. Mile by mile, he drove with less aggression.

Initially Holly thought he was lulled by the view. Past Ventura, Route 101 hugged beautiful stretches of coastline. They passed Pitas Point, then Rincon Point, and the beaches of Carpinteria. The blue sea rose, the blue sky fell, the golden land wedged itself between them, and the only visible turbulence in the serene summer day was the white-capped surf, which slipped to the shore in low combers and broke with a light, foamy spray.

But there was a turbulence in Jim Ironheart, too, and Holly only became aware of his new edginess when she realized that he was not paying any attention to the scenery. He had slowed down not to enjoy the view but, she suspected, to delay their arrival at the farm.

By the time they left the superhighway, turned inland at Santa Barbara, crossed the city, and headed into the Santa Ynez Mountains, Jim's mood was undeniably darker. His responses to her conversational sallies grew shorter, more distracted.

State Route 154 led out of the mountains into an appealing land of low hills and fields painted gold by dry summer grass, clusters of California live oaks, and horse ranches with neat white fencing. This was not the farming-intense, agribusiness atmosphere of the San Joaquin and certain other valleys; there were serious vineyards here and there, but the occasional farms appeared to be, as often as not, gentlemen's operations maintained as getaways for rich men in Los Angeles, more concerned with cultivating a picturesque alternate lifestyle than with real crops.

"We'll need to stop in New Svenborg to get a few things before we head out to the farm," Jim said.

"What things?"

"I don't know. But when we stop . . . I'll know what we need."

Lake Cachuma came and went to the east. They passed the road to Solvang on the west, then skirted Santa Ynez itself. Before Los Olivos, they headed east on another state route, and finally into New Svenborg, the closest town to Ironheart Farm.

In the early nineteen hundreds, groups of Danish-Americans from the Midwest had settled in the Santa Ynez Valley, many of them with the intention of establishing communities that would preserve Danish folk arts and customs and, in general, the ways of Danish life. The most successful of these settlements was Solvang, about which Holly had once written a story; it had become a major tourist attraction because of its quaint Danish architecture, shops, and restaurants.

New Svenborg, with a population of fewer than two thousand, was not as elaborately, thoroughly, authentically, *insistently* Danish as Solvang. Depressing desert-style stucco buildings with white-rock roofs, weathered clapboard buildings with unpainted front porches that reminded Holly of parts of rural Texas, Craftsman bungalows, and white Victorian houses with lots of gingerbread and wide front porches stood beside structures that were distinctly Danish with half-timbered walls and thatched roofs and leaded-glass windows. Half a dozen windmills dotted the town, their vanes silhouetted against the August sky. All in all, it was one of those singular California mixes that sometimes resulted in delightful and unexpected harmonies; but in New Svenborg, the mix did not work, and the mood was discordancy.

"I spent the end of my childhood and my entire adolescence here," Jim said as he drove slowly down the quiet, shadowy main street.

She figured that his moodiness could be attributed as much to New Svenborg as to his tragic family history.

To an extent, that was unfair. The streets were lined with big trees, the charming streetlamps appeared to have been imported from the Old Country, and most of the sidewalks were gracefully curved and time-hoved ribbons of well-worn brick. About twenty percent of the town came straight from the nostalgic Midwest of a Bradbury novel, but the rest of it still belonged in a David Lynch film.

"Let's take a little tour of the old place," he said.

"We should be getting to the farm."

"It's only two miles north of town, just a few minutes away."

That was all the more reason to get there, as far as Holly was concerned. She was tired of being on the road.

But she sensed that for some reason he wanted to show her the town—and not merely to delay their arrival at Ironheart Farm. Holly acquiesced. In fact she listened with interest to what he had to tell her. She had learned that he found it difficult to talk about himself and that he sometimes made personal revelations in an indirect or even casual manner.

He drove past Handahl's Pharmacy on the east end of Main Street, where locals went to get a prescription filled, unless they preferred to drive twenty miles to Solvang. Handahl's was also one of only two restaurants in town, with (according to Jim) "the best soda fountain this side of 1955." It was also the post office and only newsstand. With its multiply peaked roof, verdigris-copper cupola, and beveled-glass windows, it was an appealing enterprise.

Without shutting the engine off, Jim parked across the street from the library on Copenhagen Lane, which was quartered in one of the smaller Victorian houses with considerably less gingerbread than most. The building was freshly painted, with well-tended shrubbery, and both the United States and California flags fluttered softly on a tall brass pole along the front walkway. It looked like a small and sorry library nonetheless.

"A town this size, it's amazing to find a library at all," Jim said. "And thank God for it. I rode my bike to the library so often . . . if you added up all the miles, I probably pedaled halfway around the world. After my folks died, books were my friends, counselors, psychiatrists. Books kept me sane. Mrs. Glynn, the librarian, was a great lady, she knew just how to talk to a shy, mixed-up kid without talking *down* to him. She was my guide to the most exotic regions of the world and distant times—all without leaving her aisles of books."

Holly had never heard him speak so lovingly or half so lyrically of anything before. The Svenborg library and Mrs. Glynn had clearly been lasting and favorable influences on his life.

"Why don't we go in and say hello to her?" Holly suggested.

Jim frowned. "Oh, I'm sure she's not the librarian any more, most likely not even alive. That was twenty-five years ago when I started coming here, eighteen years ago when I left town to go to college. Never saw her after that."

"How old was she?"

He hesitated. "Quite old," he said, and put an end to the talk of a nostalgic visit by slipping the Ford into gear and driving away from there.

They cruised by Tivoli Gardens, a small park at the corner of Main and Copenhagen, which fell laughably short of its namesake. No fountains, no musicians, no dancing, no games, no beer gardens. There were just some roses, a few beds of late-summer flowers, patchy grass, two park benches, and a well-maintained windmill in the far corner.

"Why aren't the sails moving?" she asked. "There's some wind."

"None of the mills actually pumps water or grinds grain any more," he explained. "And since they're largely decorative, no sense in having to live with the noise they make. Brakes were put on the mechanisms long ago." As they turned the corner at the end of the park, he added: "They made a movie here once."

"Who did?"

"One of the studios."

"Hollywood studio?"

"I forget which."

"What was it called?"

"Don't remember."

"Who starred in it?"

"Nobody famous."

Holly made a mental note about the movie, suspecting that it was more important to Jim and to the town than he had said. Something in the offhanded way he'd mentioned it, and his terse responses to her subsequent questions, alerted her to an unspoken subtext.

Last of all, at the southeast corner of Svenborg, he drove slowly past Zacca's Garage, a large corrugated-steel Quonset hut perched on a cement-block foundation, in front of which stood two dusty cars. Though the building had been painted several times during its history, no brush had touched it in many years. Its numerous coats of paint were worn in a random patchwork and marked by liberal encrustations of rust, which created an unintended camouflage finish. The cracked blacktop in front of the place was pitted with potholes that had been filled with loose gravel, and the surrounding lot bristled with dry grass and weeds.

"I went to school with Ned Zacca," Jim said. "His dad, Vernon, had the garage then. It was never a business to make a man rich, but it looked better than it does now."

The big airplane hangar–style roll-aside doors were open, and the interior was clotted with shadows. The rear bumper of an old Chevy gleamed dully in the gloom. Although the garage was seedy, nothing about it suggested danger. Yet the queerest chill came over Holly as she peered through the hangar doors into the murky depths of the place.

"Ned was one mean sonofabitch, the school bully," Jim said. "He could sure make a kid's life hell when he wanted to. I lived in fear of him."

"Too bad you didn't know Tae Kwon Do then, you could've kicked his ass."

He did not smile, just stared past her at the garage. His expression was odd and unsettling. "Yeah. Too bad."

When she glanced at the building again, she saw a man in jeans and a T-shirt step out of the deepest darkness into gray half-light, moving slowly past the back of the Chevy, wiping his hands on a rag. He was just beyond the infall of sunshine, so she could not see what he looked like. In a few steps he rounded the car, fading into the gloom again, hardly more material than a specter glimpsed in a moonlit graveyard.

Somehow, she knew the ghostly presence in the Quonset was Ned Zacca. Curiously, though he had been a menacing figure to Jim, not to her, Holly felt her stomach twist and her palms turn damp.

Then Jim touched the accelerator, and they were past the garage, heading back into town.

"What did Zacca do to you exactly?"

"Anything he could think of. He was a regular little sadist. He's been in prison a couple of times since those days. But I figured he was back."

"Figured? How?"

He shrugged. "I just sensed it. Besides, he's one of those guys who never gets caught at the big stuff. Devil's luck. He might do a fall every great once in a while, but always for something small-time. He's dumb but he's clever."

"Why'd you want to go there?"

"Memories."

"Most people, when they want a little nostalgia, they're only interested in good memories."

Jim did not reply to that. Even before they arrived in Svenborg, he had settled into himself like a turtle gradually withdrawing into its shell. Now he was almost back into that brooding, distant mood in which she had found him yesterday afternoon.

The brief tour had given her not a comfortable feeling of small-town security and friendliness, but a sense of being cut off at the back end of nowhere. She was still in California, the most populous state in the union, not much farther than sixty miles from the city of Santa Barbara. Svenborg had almost two thousand people of its own, which made it bigger than a lot of gas-and-graze stops along the interstate highways. The sense of isolation was more psychological than real, but it hovered over her.

Jim stopped at The Central, a prospering operation that included a service station selling generic gasoline, a small sporting-goods outlet peddling supplies to fishermen and campers, and a well-stocked convenience store with groceries, beer, and wine. Holly filled the Ford's tank at the self-service pump, then joined Jim in the sporting-goods shop.

The store was cluttered with merchandise, which overflowed the shelves, hung from the ceiling, and was stacked on the linoleum floor. Wall-eyed fishing lures dangled on a rack near the door. The air smelled of rubber boots.

At the check-out counter, Jim already had piled up a pair of high-quality summerweight sleeping bags with air-mattress liners, a Coleman lantern with a can of fuel, a sizable Thermos ice chest, two big flashlights, packages of batteries for the flashes, and a few other items. At the cash register, farther along the counter from Jim, a bearded man in spectacles as thick as bottle glass was ringing up the sale, and Jim was waiting with an open wallet.

"I thought we were going to the mill," Holly said.

"We are," Jim said. "But unless you want to sleep on a wooden floor without benefit of *any* conveniences, we need this stuff."

"I didn't realize we were staying overnight."

"Neither did I. Until I walked in here and heard myself asking for these things."

"Couldn't we stay at a motel?"

"Nearest one's clear over to Santa Ynez."

"It's a pretty drive," she said, much preferring the commute to spending a night in the mill.

Her reluctance arose only in part from the fact that the old mill promised to be uncomfortable. The place was, after all, the locus of both their nightmares. Besides, since arriving in Svenborg, she had felt vaguely . . . threatened.

"But something's going to happen," he said. "I don't know what. Just . . . something. At the mill. I feel it. We're going to . . . get some answers. But it might take a little time. We've got to be ready to wait, be patient."

Though Holly was the one who had suggested going to the mill, she suddenly didn't *want* answers. In a dim premonition of her own, she perceived an undefined but oncoming tragedy, blood, death, and darkness.

Jim, on the other hand, seemed to shed the lead weight of his previous apprehension and take on a new buoyancy. "It's good—what we're doing, where we're going. I *sense* that, Holly. You know what I mean? I'm being told we made the right move in coming here, that there's something frightening ahead of us, yes, something that's going to shock the hell out of us, maybe very real danger, but there's also something that's going to lift us up." His eyes were shining and he was excited. She had never seen him like this, not even when they had been making love. In whatever obscure way it touched him, this higher power of his was in contact with him now. She could see his quiet rapture. "I feel a . . . a strange sort of jubilation coming, a wonderful discovery, revelations . . ."

The bespectacled clerk had stepped away from the cash register to show them the total on the tape. Grinning, he said, "Newlyweds?"

At the convenience store next door, they bought ice for the chest, then orange juice, diet soda, bread, mustard, bologna-olive loaf, and pre-packaged cheese slices.

"Olive loaf," Holly said wonderingly. "I haven't eaten

this stuff since I was maybe fourteen and I learned I had arteries."

"And how about these," he said, snatching a box of chocolate-covered doughnuts off a shelf, adding it to the market basket that he was carrying. "Bologna sandwiches, chocolate doughnuts . . . and potato chips, of course. Wouldn't be a picnic without chips. The crinkled kind, okay? Some cheese twists, too. Chips and cheese twists, they go together."

Holly had never seen him like this: almost boyish, with no apparent weight on his shoulders. He might have been setting out on a camping trip with friends, a little adventure.

She wondered if her own apprehension was justified. Jim was, after all, the one whose presentiments had proven to be accurate. Maybe they *were* going to discover something wonderful at the mill, unravel the mystery behind the last-minute rescues he had performed, maybe even encounter this higher power to which he referred. Perhaps The Enemy, in spite of its ability to reach out of a dream into the real world, was not as formidable as it seemed.

At the cash register, after the clerk finished bagging their purchases and was making change, Jim said, "Wait a minute, one more thing," and hurried to the rear of the store. When he returned, he was carrying two lined yellow tablets and one black, fine-point felt-tip pen. To Holly, he said, "We'll be needing these tonight."

When they had loaded the car and pulled out of the parking lot at The Central, heading for the Ironheart Farm, Holly indicated the pen and tablets, which she was holding in a separate bag. "What'll we be needing these for?"

"I haven't the slightest idea. I just suddenly knew we have to have them."

"That's just like God," she said, "always being mysterious and obscure."

After a silence, he said, "I'm not so sure any more that it's God talking to me."

"Oh? What changed your mind?"

"Well, the issues you raised last evening, for one thing. If God didn't want little Nick O'Conner to die up there in Boston, why didn't He just stop that vault from exploding? Why chase me clear across the country and 'throw' me at the boy, as you put it? And why would He up and change His mind about the people on the airliner, let more of them live, just because I decided they should? They were all questions I'd asked myself, but you weren't willing to settle for the easy answers that satisfied me." He looked away from the street for a moment as they reached the edge of town, smiled at her, and repeated one of the questions she had asked him yesterday when she had been needling him: "Is God a waffler?"

"I would've expected . . ."

"What?"

"Well, you were so sure you could see a divine hand in this, it must be a bit of a letdown to consider less exalted possibilities. I'd expect you to be a little bummed out."

He shook his head. "I'm not. You know, I always had trouble accepting that it was God working through me, it seemed like such a crazy idea, but I lived with it just because there wasn't any better explanation. There still *isn't* a better explanation, I guess, but another possibility has occurred to me, and it's something so strange and wonderful in its way that I don't mind losing God from the team."

"What other possibility?"

"I don't want to talk about it just yet," he said as sunlight and tree shadows dappled the dusty windshield and played across his face. "I want to think it through, be sure it makes sense, before I lay it out for you, 'cause I know now you're a hard judge to convince."

He seemed happy. Really happy. Holly had liked him pretty much since she had first seen him, regardless of his moodiness. She had perceived a hopefulness beneath his glower, a tenderness beneath his gruffness, a better man beneath the exterior of a lesser one, but in his current buoyant mood, she found him easier than ever to like.

She playfully pinched his cheek.

"What?" he said.

"You're cute."

As they drove out of Svenborg, it occurred to Holly that the distribution pattern of the houses and other buildings was more like a pioneer settlement than like a modern community. In most towns, buildings were concentrated more densely in the center, with larger lots and increasing open space toward the perimeter, until finally the last structures gave way to rural precincts. But when they came to the city limits of Svenborg, the delineation between town and country was almost ruler-straight and unmistakable. Houses stopped and brushland began, with only an intervening firebreak, and Holly could not help but think of pioneers in the Old West constructing their outposts with a wary eye toward the threats that might arise out of the lawless badlands all around them.

Inside its boundaries, the town seemed ominous and full of dark secrets. Seen from the outside—and Holly turned to stare back at it as the road rose toward the brow of a gentle hill—it looked not threatening but threatened, as if its residents knew, in their bones, that something frightful in the golden land around them was waiting to claim them all.

Perhaps fire was all they feared. Like much of California, the land was parched where human endeavor had not brought water to it.

Nestled between the Santa Ynez Mountains to the west and the San Rafael Mountains to the east, the valley was so broad and deep that it contained more geographical variety than some entire states back East—though at this time of year, untouched by rain since early spring, most of it was brown and crisp. They traveled across rounded golden hills, brown meadows. The better vantage points on their two-mile route revealed vistas of higher hills overgrown with chaparral, valleys within the valley where groves of California live oaks flourished, and small green vineyards encircled by vast sere fields.

"It's beautiful," Holly said, taking in the pale hills, shining-gold meadows, and oily chaparral. Even the oaks, whose clusters indicated areas with a comparatively high water table, were not lush but a half-parched silver-green. "Beautiful, but a tinderbox. How would they cope with a fire out here?"

Even as she posed that question, they came around a bend in the road and saw a stretch of blackened land to the right of the two-lane county road. Brush and grass had been reduced to veins of gray-white ash in coal-black soot. The fire had taken place within the past couple of days, for it was still recent enough to lend a burnt odor to the August air.

"That one didn't get far," he said. "Looks like ten acres burned at most. They're quick around here, they jump at the first sign of smoke. There's a good volunteer group in town, plus a Department of Forestry station in the valley, lookout posts. If you live here, you don't forget the threat—you just realize after a while that it can be dealt with."

Jim sounded confident enough, and he had lived there for seven or eight years, so Holly tried to suppress her pyrophobia. Nevertheless, even after they had passed the charred land and could no longer smell the scorched brush, Holly had an image in her mind of the huge valley at night, aflame from end to end, vortexes of red-orange-white fire whirling like tornadoes and consuming everything that lay between the ramparts of the two mountain ranges.

"Ironheart Farm," he said, startling her.

As Jim slowed the Ford, Holly looked to the left of the blacktop county route.

A farmhouse stood a hundred feet back from the road, behind a withered lawn. It was of no particular architectural style, just a plain but cozy-looking two-story farmhouse with white aluminum siding, a red-shingle roof, and a commodious front porch. It might have been lifted off its foundation anywhere in the Midwest and plunked down on new footings here, for there were thousands like it in those cornbelt states.

Maybe a hundred yards to the left of the house, a red barn rose to a tarnished horse-and-carriage weather vane at the pinnacle of its peaked roof. It was not huge, only half again as large as the unimposing house.

Behind the house and barn, visible between them, was the pond, and the structure at its far side was the most arresting sight on the farm. The windmill.

3

Jim stopped in the driveway turnaround between house and barn, and got out of the Ford. He *had* to get out because the sight of the old place hit him harder than he had expected, simultaneously bringing a chill to the pit of his stomach and a flush of heat to his face. In spite of the cool draft from the dashboard vents, the air in the car seemed warm and stale, too low in oxygen content to sustain him. He stood in the fresh summer air, drawing deep breaths, and tried not to lose control of himself.

The blank-windowed house held little power over him. When he looked at it, he felt only a sweet melancholy that might, given time, deepen into a more disturbing sadness or even despair. But he could stare at it, draw his breath normally, and turn away from it without being seized by a powerful urge to look at it again.

The barn exerted no emotional pull on him whatsoever, but the windmill was another story. When he turned his gaze on that cone of limestone beyond the wide pond, he felt as though he were being transformed into stone himself, as had been the luckless victims of the mythological serpent-haired Medusa when they had seen her snake-ringed face.

He'd read about Medusa years ago. In one of Mrs. Glynn's books. That was in the days when he wished with all his heart that he, too, could see the snake-haired woman and be transformed into unfeeling rock. . . .

"Jim?" Holly said from the other side of the car. "You okay?"

With its high-ceilinged rooms—highest on the first floor—the two-story mill was actually four stories in height. But to Jim, at that moment, it looked far taller, as imposing as a twenty-story tower. Its once-pale stones had been darkened by a century of grime. Climbing ivy, roots nurtured by the pond that abutted one flank of the mill, twined up the rough stone face, finding easy purchase in deep-mortared joints. With no one to perform needed maintenance, the plant had covered half the structure, and had grown entirely over a narrow first-floor window near the timbered door. The wooden sails looked rotten. Each of those four arms was about thirty feet in length, making a sixty-foot spread across adjoining spans, and each was five feet wide with three rows of vanes. Since he had last seen the mill, more vanes had cracked or fallen away altogether. The time-frozen sails were stopped not in a cruciform but in an X, two arms reaching toward the pond and two toward the heavens. Even in hot bright daylight, the windmill struck Jim as menacing and seemed like a monstrous, ragged-armed scarecrow clawing at the sky with skeletal hands.

"Jim?" Holly said, touching his arm.

He jumped as if he had not known who she was. In fact, for an instant, as he looked down at her, he saw not only Holly but a long-dead face, the face of . . .

But the moment of disorientation passed. She was only Holly now, her identity no longer entwined with that of another woman as it had been in her dream last night.

"You okay?" she asked again.

"Yeah, sure, just . . . memories."

Jim was grateful when Holly directed his attention from the mill to the farmhouse. She said, "Were you happy with your grandparents?"

"Lena and Henry Ironheart. Wonderful people. They took me in. They suffered so much for me."

"Suffered?" she said.

He realized that it was too strong a word, and he wondered why he had used it. "Sacrificed, I mean. In lots of ways, little things, but they added up."

"Taking on the support of a ten-year-old boy isn't something anyone does lightly," Holly said. "But unless you demanded caviar and champagne, I wouldn't think you'd have been much of a hardship to them."

"After what happened to my folks, I was . . . withdrawn, in bad shape, uncommunicative. They put in a lot of time with me, a lot of love, trying to bring me back . . . from the edge."

"Who lives here these days?"

"Nobody."

"But didn't you say your grandparents died five years ago?"

"The place wasn't sold. No buyers."

"Who owns it now?"

"I do. I inherited it."

She surveyed the property with evident bewilderment. "But it's lovely here. If the lawn was being watered and kept green, the weeds cut down, it would be charming. Why would it be so hard to sell?"

"Well, for one thing, it's a damned quiet life out here, and even most of the back-to-nature types who dream of living on a farm really mean a farm close to a choice of movie theaters, bookstores, good restaurants, and dependable European-car mechanics."

She laughed at that. "Baby, there's an amusing little cynic lurking in you."

"Besides, it's hardscrabble all the way, trying to earn a living on a place like this. It's just a little old hundred-acre farm, not big enough to make it with milk cows or a beef herd—or any one crop. My grandpa and grandma kept chickens, sold the eggs. And thanks to the mild weather, they could get two crops. Strawberries came into fruit in February and all the way into May. That was the money crop—berries. Then came corn, tomatoes—*real* tomatoes, not the plastic ones they sell in the markets."

He saw that Holly was still enamored of the place. She stood with her hands on her hips, looking around as if she might buy it herself.

She said, "But aren't there people who work at other things, not farmers, would just like to live here for the peace and quiet?"

"This isn't a real affluent area, not like Newport Beach, Beverly Hills. Locals around here don't have extra money just to spend on lifestyle. The best hope of selling a property like this is to find some rich movie producer or recording executive in L.A. who wants to buy it for the land, tear it down, and put up a showplace, so he can say he has a getaway in the Santa Ynez Valley, which is the trendy thing to have these days."

As they talked, he grew increasingly uneasy. It was three o'clock. Plenty of daylight left. But suddenly he dreaded nightfall.

Holly kicked at some wiry weeds that had pushed up through one of the many cracks in the blacktop driveway. "It needs a little cleanup, but everything looks pretty good. Five years since they died? But the house and barn are in decent shape, like they were painted only a year or two ago."

"They were."

"Keep the place marketable, huh?"

"Sure. Why not?"

The high mountains to the west would eat the sun sooner than the ocean swallowed it down in Laguna Niguel. Twilight would come earlier here than there, although it would be prolonged. Jim found himself studying the lengthening purple shadows with the fearfulness of a man in a vampire movie hastening toward shelter before the coffin lids banged open.

What's wrong with me? he wondered.

Holly said, "You think you'd ever want to live here yourself?"

"Never!" he said so sharply and explosively that he startled not only Holly but himself. As if overcome by a dark magnetic attraction, he looked at the windmill again. A shudder swept through him.

He was aware that she was staring at him.

"Jim," she said softly, "what happened to you here? What in the name of God happened twenty-five years ago in that mill?"

"I don't know," he said shakily. He wiped one hand down his face. His hand felt warm, his face cold. "I can't remember anything special, anything odd. It was where I played. It was . . . cool and quiet . . . a nice place. Nothing happened there. Nothing."

"Something," she insisted. "Something happened."

▼▲▼

Holly had not been close to him long enough to know if he was frequently on an emotional roller coaster as he had been since they had left Orange County, or if his recent rapid swings in mood were abnormal. In The Central, buying food for a picnic, he'd soared out of the gloom that had settled over him when they crossed the Santa Ynez Mountains, and he'd been almost jubilant. Then the sight of the farm was like a plunge into cold water for him, and the windmill was the equivalent of a drop into an ice chasm.

He seemed as troubled as he was gifted, and she wished that she could do something to ease his mind. She wondered if urging him to come to the farm had been wise. Even a failed career in journalism had taught her to leap into the middle of unfolding events, seize the moment, and run with it. But perhaps this situation demanded greater caution, restraint, thought, and planning.

They got back into the Ford and drove between the house and barn, around the big pond. The graveled path, which she remembered from last night's dream, had been made wide enough for horses and wagons in another era. It easily accommodated the Ford, allowing them to park at the base of the windmill.

When she stepped from the car again, she was beside a cornfield. Only a few parched wild stalks thrust up from that abandoned plot of earth beyond the split-rail fence. She walked around the back of the car, across the gravel, and joined Jim where he stood on the bank of the pond.

Mottled blue-green-gray, the water resembled a slab of slate two hundred feet in diameter. It was almost as still as a piece of slate, as well. Dragonflies and other insects, alighting briefly on the surface, caused occasional dimples. Languid currents, far too subtle to produce ripples, made the water shimmer almost imperceptibly near the shore, where green weeds and a few clusters of white-plumed pampas grass thrived.

"Still can't remember quite what you saw in that dream?" Jim asked.

"No. It probably doesn't matter anyway. Not everything in a dream is significant."

In a low voice, almost as if speaking to himself, he said, "It was significant."

Without turbulence to stir up sediment, the water was not muddy, but neither was it clear. Holly figured she could see only a few feet below the surface. If it actually was fifty or sixty feet deep at the center, as Jim had said, that left a lot of volume in which something could remain hidden.

"Let's have a look in the mill," she said.

Jim got one of the new flashlights from the car and put batteries in it. "Even in daylight, it can be kind of dark in there."

The door was in an antechamber appended to the base of the conical main structure of the mill, much like the entrance to an Eskimo igloo. Although unlocked, the door was warped, and the hinges were rusted. For a moment it resisted Jim, then swung inward with a screech and a brittle splintering sound.

The short, arched antechamber opened onto the main room of the mill, which was approximately forty feet in diameter. Four windows, evenly spaced around the circumference, filtered sunlight through filthy panes, leeching the summer-yellow cheer from it and imparting a wintry gray tint that did little to alleviate the gloom. Jim's big flashlight revealed dust- and cobweb-shrouded machinery that could not have appeared more exotic to Holly if it had been the turbine room of a nuclear submarine. It was the cumbersome low technology of another century—massive wooden gears, cogs, shafts, grinding stones, pulleys, old rotting lengths of rope—so oversized and complicated that it all seemed like the work not merely of human beings from another age but of a different and less evolved species altogether.

Because he had grown up around mills, even though they had not been in use since before his birth, Jim knew the names of everything. Pointing with the flashlight beam, he tried to explain how the mill had functioned, talking about the spurwheel and the quant, the mace and the rynd, the runner stone and the bed stone. "Ordinarily you couldn't look up through the mechanisms quite like this. But, see, the floor of the spurwheel loft is rotted out, not much of it left, and the bridge floor gave way when those huge stones broke loose and fell."

Though he had regarded the mill with fear when they had stood outside, his mood had begun to change after they entered it. To Holly's surprise, as Jim tried to explain the millworks to her, he began to exhibit some of that boyish enthusiasm that she had first seen when they had been grocery shopping at The Central in Svenborg. He was pleased by his knowledge, and he wanted to show it off a little, the way a bookish kid was always happy to demonstrate what he had learned at the library while others his age were out playing baseball.

He turned to the limestone stairs on their left and climbed without hesitation, running one hand lightly along the curved wall as he went. There was a half-smile on his face as he looked around, as if only the good memories were flooding in on him now.

Puzzled by his extremely mercurial mood, trying to imagine how the mill could frighten and delight him simultaneously, Holly somewhat reluctantly followed him up toward what he had called "the high room." She had no good memories to associate with the mill, only the fearful images of her nightmares, and those returned to her as she ascended behind Jim. Thanks to her dream, the narrow twist of stairs was familiar to her, though she was climbing it for the first time—which was an uncanny feeling, far eerier than mere *déjà vu.*

Halfway up the stairs, she stopped at the window that overlooked the pond. The glass was frosted with dust. She used her hand to wipe one pane, and squinted at the water below. For an instant she thought she saw something strange beneath the placid surface—then realized she was seeing only the reflection of a cloud drifting across the sky.

"What is it?" Jim asked with boyish eagerness. He had stopped a few steps above her.

"Nothing. A shadow."

They continued all the way to the upper chamber, which proved to be an unremarkable room, about twelve or fourteen feet in diameter, less than fifteen feet high at its apex. The curved limestone wall wrapped around to meet itself, and curved up to form the ceiling, so it seemed as if they were standing inside the domed nose cone of a rocket. The stone was not semitransparent as it had been in her dream, and no strange amber lights played within it. An arcane mechanism was offset in the dome, through which the motion of the wind-turned sails outside was translated into horizontal movement to crank a vertical wood shaft. The thick shaft disappeared through a hole in the center of the floor.

Remembering how they had stood downstairs and looked up through the buckled and broken decks within the multi-level millworks, Holly gingerly tested the wood floor. No rot was visible. The planks and the joists under them seemed sturdy.

"Lots of dust," Jim said, as their feet stirred up little clouds with each step.

"And spiders," Holly noted.

Wrinkling her face in disgust, she peered up at the husks of sucked-dry insects dangling in the elaborate webs that had been spun around the long-stilled mechanism overhead. She didn't fear spiders, but she didn't like them either.

"We need to do some cleaning before we set up camp," he said.

"Should've bought a broom and a few other things while we were in town."

"There're cleaning materials at the house. I'll bring them here while you start unloading the car."

"The house!" Holly was exhilarated by a lovely inspiration. "When we set out for the mill, I didn't realize this property was still yours, no one living here. We can put the sleeping bags in the house, stay there, and visit this room as often as we need to."

"Nice thought," Jim said, "but it's not that easy. Something's going to happen here, Holly, something that'll give us answers or put us on the road to finding them. I feel it. I know it . . . well, just the way I know these things. But we can't pick the time for the revelation. It doesn't work that way. We can't ask God—or whatever is behind this—to punch a time clock and deliver revelations only between regular business hours. We have to stay here and be patient."

She sighed. "Okay, yeah, if you—"

Bells interrupted her.

It was a sweet silvery ringing, neither heavy nor clangorous, lasting only two or three seconds, pleasingly musical. It was so light and gay, in fact, that it should have seemed a frivolous sound against the backdrop of that ponderous stone structure. It was not in the least frivolous, however, because inexplicably it triggered in Holly serious associations—thoughts of sin and penitence and redemption.

The trilling faded even as she turned in search of the source. But before she could ask Jim what it had been, it came again.

This time, Holly understood why she associated the sound with issues of spirituality. It was the precise tone of the bells that an altarboy rang during Mass. The sweet ringing brought back to her the smell of spikenard and myrrh from her college days when she had toyed with the idea of converting to Catholicism.

The bells faded again.

She turned to Jim and saw him grinning.

"What is it?" she asked.

"I forgot all about this," he said wonderingly. "How could I have forgotten all about this?"

The bells tinkled again, silvery and pure.

"Forgot what?" she asked. "What're those bells?"

"Not bells," he said as they faded. He hesitated, and as the sound returned a fourth time, he finally said, "The ringing is in the stone."

"Ringing stone?" she said in bewilderment.

As the bells sounded twice again, she circled the room, cocking her head this way and that, until it seemed to her that the music did, indeed, originate from the limestone wall, pealing out not from any single location but equally from every block of that curved surface, no louder at one point than another.

She told herself that stone could not ring, certainly not in such a dulcet voice. A windmill was an unusual structure and could have tricky acoustics. From a high-school class trip to Washington, she remembered a tourguide showing them a spot in the Capitol's rotunda from which even a whispered conversation was picked up and, by a quirk of architecture, transmitted across the huge dome to the far side of that great space, where eavesdroppers could hear it with perfect clarity. Perhaps something similar was at work here. If bells were rung or other sounds made at a particular place in a far corner of the first floor of the mill, a peculiarity of acoustics might transmit it in equal volume along all the walls on every floor. That explanation was more logical than the concept of magical, ringing stone— until she tried to imagine who would be secretly ringing the bell, and why.

She put one hand against the wall.

The limestone was cool. She detected faint vibrations in it.

The bell fell silent.

The vibrations in the wall subsided.

They waited.

When it was clear that the ringing would not resume, Holly said, "When did you hear it before?"

"When I was ten."

"And what happened after the ringing, what did it signify?"

"I don't know."

"But you said you just remembered it."

His eyes were shining with excitement. "Yeah. I remember the ringing. But not what caused it or what followed it. Though I think . . . it's a good sign, Holly." A note of rapture entered his voice. "It means something very fine is going to happen, something . . . wonderful."

Holly was frustrated. In spite of the mystical aspect of Jim's life-saving missions—and in spite her own paranormal experiences with dreams and the creatures in them—she had come to the farm with the hope of finding logical answers to all that had transpired. She had no idea what those answers could be. But she'd had an unspoken faith in the scientific method. Rigorous investigative procedures combined with careful thought, the use of deductive and inductive reasoning as needed, would lead to solutions. But now it seemed that logic was out the window. She was perturbed by Jim's taste for mysticism, though she had to admit that he had embraced illogic from the start, with all his talk of God, and had taken no pains to conceal it.

She said, "But, Jim, how could you have forgotten anything as weird as ringing stones or any of the rest of whatever happened to you here?"

"I don't think I just forgot. I think I was *made* to forget."

"By whom?"

"By whomever or whatever just made the stone ring again, by whatever's behind all these recent events." He moved toward the open door. "Come on, let's get this place cleaned up, move in. We want to be ready for whatever's going to happen next."

She followed him to the head of the steps but stopped

there and watched him descend two at a time, with the air of a kid excited by the prospect of adventure. All of his misgivings about the mill and his fear of The Enemy seemed to have evaporated like a few beads of water on a red-hot griddle. His emotional roller coaster was cresting the highest point on the track thus far.

Sensing something above her head, Holly looked up. A large web had been spun above the door, across the curve where the wall became the ceiling. A fat spider, its body as big around as her thumbnail and its spindly legs almost as long as her little finger, greasy as a dollop of wax and dark as a drop of blood, was feeding greedily on the pale quivering body of a snared moth.

4

With a broom, dustpan, bucket of water, mop, and a few rags, they made the small upper chamber livable in short order. Jim even brought some Windex and paper towels from the store of cleaning supplies at the house, so they could scrub the grime off the windows, letting in a lot more light. Holly chased down and killed not only the spider above the door but seven others, checking darker corners with one of the flashlights until she was sure she had found them all.

Of course the mill below them was surely crawling with countless other spiders. She decided not to think about that.

By six o'clock, the day was waning but the room was bright enough without the Coleman lantern. They were sitting Indian fashion on their inflatable-mattress sleeping bags, with the big cooler between them. Using the closed lid as a table, they made thick sandwiches, opened the potato chips and cheese twists, and popped the tops off cans of root beer. Though she had missed lunch, Holly had not thought about food until they'd begun to prepare it. Now she was hungrier than she would have expected under the circumstances. Everything was delicious, better than gourmet fare. Olive loaf and cheese on white bread, with mustard, recalled for her the appetites of childhood, the intense flavors and forgotten innocent sensuality of youth.

They did not talk much as they ate. Silences did not make either of them feel awkward, and they were taking such primal pleasure from the meal that no conversation, regardless of how witty, could have improved the moment. But that was only part of the reason for their mutual reticence. Holly, at least, was also unable to think *what* to say under these bizarre circumstances, sitting in the high room of a crumbling old mill, waiting for an encounter with something supernatural. No small talk of any kind felt adequate to the moment, and a serious discussion of just about anything would seem ludicrous.

"I feel sort of foolish," she said eventually.

"Me, too," he admitted. "Just a little."

At seven o'clock, when she was opening the box of chocolate-covered doughnuts, she suddenly realized the mill had no lavatory. "What about a bathroom?"

He picked up his ring of keys from the floor and handed them to her. "Go on over to the house. The plumbing works. There's a half-bath right off the kitchen."

She realized the room was filling with shadows, and when she glanced at the window, she saw that twilight had arrived. Putting the doughnuts aside, she said, "I want to zip over there and get back before dark."

"Go ahead." Jim raised one hand as if pledging allegiance to the flag. "I swear on all that I hold sacred, I'll leave you at least one doughnut."

"Half the box better be there when I get back," she said, "or I'll kick your butt all the way into Svenborg to buy more."

"You take your doughnuts seriously."

"Damn right."

He smiled. "I like that in a woman."

Taking a flashlight to negotiate the mill below, she rose and went to the door. "Better start up the Coleman."

"Sure thing. When you get back, it'll be a right cozy little campsite."

Descending the narrow stairs, Holly began to worry about being separated from Jim, and step by step her anxiety increased. She was not afraid of being alone. What bothered her was leaving him by himself. Which was ridiculous. He was a grown man and far more capable of effective self-defense than was the average person.

The lower floor of the mill was much darker than when she had first seen it. Curtained with cobwebs, the dirty windows admitted almost none of the weak light of dusk.

As she crossed toward the arched opening to the antechamber, she was overcome by a creepy sense of being watched. She knew they were alone in the mill, and she chided herself for being such a ninny. But by the time she reached the archway, her apprehension had swelled until she could not resist the urge to turn and shine the flashlight into the chamber behind her. Shadows were draped across the old machinery as copiously as black crepe in an amusement-park haunted house; they slid aside when the flashlight beam touched them, fell softly back into place as the beam moved on. Each corner, undraped, revealed no spy. Someone could be sheltering behind one part of the millworks or another, and she considered prowling through the ruins in search of an intruder.

But abruptly she felt foolish, too easily spooked. Wondering what had happened to the intrepid reporter she had once been, Holly left the mill.

The sun was beyond the mountains. The sky was purple and that deep iridescent blue seen in old Maxfield Parrish paintings. A few toads were croaking from their shadowy niches along the banks of the pond.

All the way around the water, past the barn, to the back door of the house, Holly continued to feel watched. However, though it was possible that someone might be lurking in the mill, it was not too likely that a virtual platoon of spies had taken up positions in the barn, the surrounding fields, and the distant hills, ·intent on observing her every move.

"Idiot," she said self-mockingly as she used one of Jim's keys to open the back door.

Though she had the flashlight, she tried the wall switch unthinkingly. She was surprised to discover that the electrical service was still connected.

She was more surprised, however, by what the light revealed: a fully furnished kitchen. A breakfast table and four chairs stood by the window. Copper pots and pans dangled from a ceiling fixture, and twin racks of knives and other utensils hung on the wall near the cooktop. A toaster, toaster oven, and blender stood on the counters. A shopping list of about fifteen items was affixed to the refrigerator with a magnet in the shape of a can of Budweiser.

Hadn't Jim gotten rid of his grandparents' belongings when they had died five years ago?

Holly ran a finger along one of the counters, drawing a line through the thin coat of dust. But it was, at most, a three-month accumulation, not five years' worth of dirt.

After she used the bathroom adjacent to the kitchen, she wandered along the hallway, through the dining room and living room, where a full complement of furniture also stood under a light shroud of dust. Some of the paintings hung aslant. Crocheted antimacassars protected the backs and arms of the chairs and sofas. Long unwound, the tall grandfather clock was not ticking. In the living room, the magazine rack beside the La-Z-Boy recliner was crammed full of publications, and inside a mahogany display case, bibelots gleamed dully beneath their own skin of dust.

Her first thought was that Jim had left the house furnished in order to be able to rent it out while searching for a buyer. But on one wall of the living room were framed 8 × 10 photographs that would not have been left to the mercy of a tenant: Jim's father as a young man of about twenty-one; Jim's father and mother in their wedding finery; Jim at the age of five or six, with both parents.

The fourth and final picture was a two-shot, head and shoulders, of a pleasant-looking couple in their early fifties. The man was on the burly side, with bold square features, yet recognizably an Ironheart; the woman was more handsome, in a female way, than pretty, and elements of her face could also be seen in Jim and his father. Holly had no doubt that they were Jim's paternal grandparents, Lena and Henry Ironheart.

Lena Ironheart was the woman in whose body Holly

had ridden like a spirit during last night's dream. Broad, clear face. Wide-set eyes. Full mouth. Curly hair. A natural beauty spot, just a little round dot of skin discoloration, marked the high curve of her right cheek.

Though Holly had described this woman accurately to Jim, he had not recognized her. Maybe he didn't think of her eyes as being wide-set or her mouth as being full. Maybe her hair had been curly only during part of her life, due to the attentions of a beautician. But the beauty spot had to have clicked a switch in his memory, even five years after his grandmother's death.

The sense of being watched had not entirely left Holly even after she had entered the house. Now, as she stared at Lena Ironheart's face in the photograph, the feeling of being under observation grew so acute that she abruptly wheeled around and looked back across the living room.

She was alone.

She stepped quickly to the archway and through it into the front hall. Deserted.

A dark mahogany staircase led up to the second floor. The dust on the newel post and bannister was undisturbed: no palm marks, no fingerprints.

Looking up the first flight, she said, "Hello?" Her voice sounded queerly flat in the empty house.

No one responded to her.

Hesitantly, she started to climb the stairs.

"Who's there?" she called.

Only silence answered her.

Frowning, she stopped on the third step. She glanced down into the front hall, then up toward the landing again.

The silence was too deep, unnatural. Even a deserted house had some noise in it, occasional creaks and ticks and pops from old wood swelling or contracting, a rattle from a loose windowpane tapped by a finger of wind. But the Ironheart house was so hushed, Holly might have thought that she'd gone deaf, except that she could hear the sounds she made herself.

She climbed two more steps. Stopped again.

She *still* felt she was under observation. It was as if the old house itself watched her with malevolent interest, alive and sentient, possessed of a thousand eyes hidden in the wood moldings and in the pattern of the wallpaper.

Dust motes drifted in the rays of the landing light above. Twilight pressed its purple face to the windows.

Standing just four steps below the landing, partly under the second flight that led into the unseen upstairs hallway, she became convinced that something was waiting for her on the second floor. It was not necessarily The Enemy up there, not even anything alive and hostile—but something horrible, the discovery of which would shatter her.

Her heart was hammering. When she swallowed, she found a lump in her throat. She drew breath with a startling, ragged sound.

The feeling of being watched and of trembling on the brink of a monstrous revelation became so overpowering that she turned and hurried down the steps. She did not flee pell-mell out of the house; she retraced her path and turned off all the lights as she went; but she did not dally, either.

Outside, the sky was purple-black where it met the mountains in the east, purplish-red where it touched the mountains in the west, and sapphire-blue between. The golden fields and hills had changed to pale gray, fading to charcoal, as if a fire had swept them while she was in the house.

As she crossed the yard and moved past the barn, the conviction that she was under observation only grew more intense. She glanced apprehensively at the open black square of the hay loft, the windows on either side of the big red double doors. It was a gut-clenching sensation of such primitive power that it transcended mere instinct. She felt as if she were a guinea pig in a laboratory experiment, with wires hooked into her brain, while scientists sent pulses of current directly into the raw cerebral tissues that controlled the fear reflex and generated paranoid delusions. She had never experienced anything like it, knew that she was teetering on the thin edge of panic, and struggled to get a grip on herself.

By the time she reached the graveled drive that curved

around the pond, she was running. She held the extinguished flashlight like a club, prepared to swing it hard at anything that darted toward her.

The bells rang. Even above her frantic breathing, she heard the pure, silvery trilling of clappers rapidly striking the inner curves of perfectly tuned bells.

For an instant she was amazed that the phenomenon was audible outside the windmill and at a distance, as the building was halfway around the pond from her. Then something flickered in her peripheral vision even before the first spell of ringing ended, and she looked away from the mill, toward the water.

Pulses of blood-red light, originating at the center of the pond, spread outward toward the banks in tight concentric circles, like the measured ripples that radiated from the point at which a dropped stone struck deep water. That sight brought Holly to a stumbling halt; she almost went to her knees as gravel rolled under her feet.

When the bells fell silent, the crimson light in the pond was immediately snuffed out. The water was much darker now than when she had first seen it in mid-afternoon. It no longer had all the somber hues of slate, but was as black as a polished slab of obsidian.

The bells rang again, and the crimson light pulsed from the heart of the pond, radiating outward. She could see that each new bright blossom was not born on the surface of the water but in its depths, dim at first but swiftly rising, almost bursting like an overheated incandescent bulb when it neared the surface, casting waves of light toward the shore.

The ringing ceased.

The water darkened.

The toads along the shoreline were not croaking any more. The ever-murmuring world of nature had fallen as silent as the interior of the Ironheart farmhouse. No coyote howl, no insect cry, no owl hoot, no bat shriek or flap of wing, no rustling in the grass.

The bells sounded again, and the light returned, but this time it was not as red as gore, more of an orange-red, though it was brighter than before. At the water's edge, the feathery white panicles of the pampas grass caught the curious radiance and glowed like plumes of iridescent gas.

Something was rising from the bottom of the pond.

As the throbbing luminescence faded with the next cessation of the bells, Holly stood in the grip of awe and fear, knowing she should run but unable to move.

Ringing.

Light. Muddy-orange this time. No red tint at all. Brighter than ever.

Holly broke the chains of fear and sprinted toward the windmill.

On all sides, the palpitant light enlivened the dreary dusk. Shadows leapt rhythmically like Apaches dancing around a war fire. Beyond the fence, dead cornstalks bristled as repulsively as the spiny legs and plated torsos of praying mantises. The windmill appeared to be in the process of changing magically from stone to copper or even to gold.

The ringing stopped and the light went out as she reached the open door of the mill.

She raced across the threshold, then skidded to a stop in the darkness, on the brink of the lower chamber. No light at all came through the windows now. The blackness was tarry, cloying. As she fumbled for the switch on the flashlight, she found it hard to draw breath, as if the darkness itself had begun flowing into her lungs, suffocating her.

The flashlight came on just as the bells began to ring again. She slashed the beam across the room and back, to be sure nothing was there in the gloom, reaching for her. Then she found the stairs to her left and hurried toward the high room.

When she reached the window at the halfway point, she put her face to the pane of glass that she had wiped clean with her hand earlier in the day. In the pond below, the rippling bull's-eye of light was brighter still, now amber instead of orange.

Calling for Jim, Holly ran up the remaining stairs.

As she went, lines of Edgar Allan Poe's poetry, studied

an age ago in junior high school and thought forgotten, rang crazily through her mind:

Keeping time, time, time,
In a sort of Runic rhyme,
To the tintinnabulation that so musically wells
From the bells, bells, bells, bells,
Bells, bells, bells—

She burst into the high room, where Jim stood in the soft winter-white glow of the Coleman gas lantern. He was smiling, turning in a circle and looking expectantly at the walls around him.

As the bells died away, she said, "Jim, come look, come quick, something's in the lake."

She dashed to the nearest window, but it was just far enough around the wall from the pond to prevent her seeing the water. The other two windows were even more out of line with the desired view, so she did not even try them.

"The ringing in the stone," Jim said dreamily.

Holly returned to the head of the stairs as the bells began to ring again. She paused and looked back just long enough to be sure that Jim was following her, for he seemed in something of a daze.

Hurrying down the stairs, she heard more lines of Poe's poem reverberating in her mind:

Hear the loud alarum bells—
Brazen bells!
What a tale of terror, now, their turbulency tells!

She had never been the kind of woman to whom sprang lines of verse appropriate to the moment. She couldn't recall quoting a line of poetry or even reading any—other than Louise Tarvohl's treacle!—since college.

When she reached the window, she scrubbed frantically at another pane with the palm of her hand, to give them a better view of the spectacle below. She saw that the light was blood-red again and dimmer, as if whatever had been rising through the water was now sinking again.

Oh, the bells, bells, bells!
What a tale their terror tells—

It seemed crazy to be mentally reciting poetry in the midst of these wondrous and frightening events, but she had never been under such stress before. Maybe this was the way the mind worked—giddily dredging up long-forgotten knowledge—when you were about to meet a higher power. Because that's just what she felt was about to happen, an encounter with a higher power, perhaps God but most likely not. She didn't really think God lived in a pond, although any minister or priest would probably tell her that God lived everywhere, in all things. God was like the eight-hundred-pound gorilla who could live anywhere he wanted.

Just as Jim reached her, the ringing stopped, and the crimson light in the pond quickly faded. He squeezed in beside her and put his face to the glass.

They waited.

Two seconds ticked by. Two more.

"No," she said. "Damn it, I wanted you to see."

But the ringing did not resume, and the pond remained dark out there in the steadily dimming twilight. Night would be upon them within a few minutes.

"What was it?" Jim asked, leaning back from the window.

"Like something in a Spielberg film," she said excitedly, "rising up out of the water, from deep under the pond, light throbbing in time with the bells. I think that's where the ringing originates, from the thing in the pond, and somehow it's transmitted through the walls of the mill."

"Spielberg film?" He looked puzzled.

She tried to explain: "Wonderful and terrifying, awesome and strange, scary and damned exciting all at once."

"You mean like in *Close Encounters*? Are you talking a starship or something?"

"Yes. No. I'm not sure. I don't know. Maybe something weirder than that."

"Weirder than a starship?"

Her wonder, and even her fear, subsided in favor of frustration. She was not accustomed to finding herself at a complete loss for words to describe things that she had felt or seen. But with this man and the incomparable experiences in which he became entangled, even her sophisticated vocabulary and talent for supple phrase-making failed her miserably.

"Shit, yes!" she said at last. "Weirder than a starship. At least weirder than the way they show them in the movies."

"Come on," he said, ascending the stairs again, "let's get back up there." When she lingered at the window, he returned to her and took her hand. "It isn't over yet. I think it's just beginning. And the place for us to be is the upper room. I *know* it's the place. Come on, Holly."

5

They sat on the inflatable-mattress sleeping bags again.

The lantern cast a pearly-silver glow, whitewashing the yellow-beige blocks of limestone. In the baglike wicks inside the glass chimney of the lamp, the gas burned with a faint hiss, so it seemed as if whispering voices were rising through the floorboards of that high room.

Jim was poised at the apex of his emotional roller coaster, full of childlike delight and anticipation, and this time Holly was right there with him. The light in the pond had terrified her, but it had also touched her in other ways, sparking deep psychological responses on a primitive sub-subconscious level, igniting fuses of wonder and hope which were fizzing-burning unquenchably toward some much-desired explosion of faith, emotional catharsis.

She had accepted that Jim was not the only troubled person in the room. His heart might contain more turmoil than hers, but she was as empty, in her own way, as he was in his. When they'd met in Portland, she had been a burnt-out cynic, going through the motions of a life, not even trying to identify and fill the empty spaces in her heart. She had not experienced the tragedy and grief that he had known, but now she realized that leading a life equally devoid of tragedy *and* joy could breed despair. Passing days and weeks and years in the pursuit of goals that had not really mattered to her, driven by a purpose she had not truly embraced, with no one to whom she was profoundly committed, she had been eaten by a dry-rot of the soul. She and Jim were the two pieces of a yin-yang puzzle, each shaped to fill the hollowness in the other, healing each other merely by their contact. They fit together astonishingly well, and the match seemed inevitable; but the puzzle might never have been solved if the halves of it had not been brought together in the same place at the same time.

Now she waited with nervous excitement for contact with the power that had led Jim to her. She was ready for God or for something quite different but equally benign. She could not believe that what she had seen in the pond was The Enemy. That creature was apart from this, connected somehow but different. Even if Jim had not told her that something fine and good was coming, she eventually would have sensed, on her own, that the light in the water and the ringing in the stone heralded not blood and death but rapture.

They spoke tersely at first, afraid that voluble conversation would inhibit that higher power from initiating the next stage of contact.

"How long has the pond been here?" she asked.

"A long time."

"Before the Ironhearts?"

"Yeah."

"Before the farm itself?"

"I'm sure it was."

"Possibly forever?"

"Possibly."

"Any local legends about it?"

"What do you mean?"

"Ghost stories, Loch Ness, that kind of stuff."

"No. Not that I've ever heard."

They were silent. Waiting.

Finally Holly said, "What's your theory?"

"Huh?"

"Earlier today you said you had a theory, something strange and wonderful, but you didn't want to talk about it till you'd thought it through."

"Oh, right. Now maybe it's more than a theory. When you said you'd seen something under the pond in your dream . . . well, I don't know why, but I started thinking about an encounter. . . ."

"Encounter?"

"Yeah. Like what you said. Something . . . alien."

"Not of this world," Holly said, remembering the sound of the bells and the light in the pond.

"They're out there in the universe somewhere," he said with quiet enthusiasm. "It's too big for them not to be out there. And someday they'll be coming. Someone will encounter them. So why not me, why not you?"

"But it must've been there under the pond when you were ten."

"Maybe."

"Why would it be there all this time?"

"I don't know. Maybe it's been there a lot longer. Hundreds of years. Thousands."

"But why a starship at the bottom of a pond?"

"Maybe it's an observation station, a place where they monitor human civilization, like an outpost we might set up in Antarctica to study things there."

Holly realized they sounded like kids sitting under the stars on a summer night, drawn like all kids to the contemplation of the unknown and to fantasies of exotic adventure. On one level she found their musings absurd, even laughable, and she was unable to believe that recent events could have such a neat yet fanciful explanation. But on another level, where she was still a child and always would be, she desperately wanted the fantasy to be made real.

Twenty minutes passed without a new development, and gradually Holly began to settle down from the heights of excitement and nervous agitation to which the lights in the pond had catapulted her. Still filled with wonder but no longer mentally numbed by it, she remembered what had happened to her just prior to the appearance of the radiant presence in the millpond: the overwhelming, preternatural, almost panic-inducing awareness of being watched. She was about to mention it to Jim when she recalled the *other* strange things she had found at the farmhouse.

"It's completely furnished," she said. "You never cleaned the house out after your grandfather died."

"I left it furnished in case I was able to rent it while waiting for a buyer."

Those were virtually the same words she had used, standing in the house, to explain the curious situation to herself. "But you left all their personal belongings there, too."

He did not look at her but at the walls, waiting for some sign of a superhuman presence. "I'd have taken that stuff away if I'd ever found a renter."

"You've left it there for almost five years?"

He shrugged.

She said, "It's been cleaned more or less regularly since then, though not recently."

"A renter might always show up."

"It's sort of creepy, Jim."

Finally he looked at her. "How so?"

"It's like a mausoleum."

His blue eyes were utterly unreadable, but Holly had the feeling she was annoying him, perhaps because this mundane talk of renters and house cleaning and real estate was pulling him away from the more pleasurable contemplation of alien encounters.

He sighed and said, "Yeah, it is creepy, a little."

"Then why . . . ?"

He slowly twisted the lantern control, reducing the flow of gas to the wicks. The hard white light softened to a moon-pale glow, and the shadows eased closer. "To tell you the truth, I couldn't bear to pack up my granddad's things. Together, we'd sorted through grandma's belongings only eight months earlier, when she'd died, and that had been hard enough. When he . . . passed away so soon after her, it was too much for me. For so long, they'd been all I had. Then suddenly I didn't even have them."

A tortured expression darkened the blue of his eyes.

As a flood of sympathy washed through Holly, she reached across the ice chest and took his hand.

He said, "I procrastinated, kept procrastinating, and the longer I delayed sorting through his things, the harder it became to *ever* do it." He sighed again. "If I'd have found a renter or a buyer, that would have forced me to put things in order, no matter how unpleasant the job. But this old farm is about as marketable as a truckload of sand in the middle of the Mojave."

Closing the house upon the death of his grandfather, touching nothing in it for four years and four months, except to clean it once in a while—that was eccentric. Holly couldn't see it any other way. At the same time, however, it was an eccentricity that touched her, moved her. As she had sensed from the start, he was a gentle man beneath his rage, beneath his steely superhero identity, and she liked the soft-hearted part of him, too.

"We'll do it together," Holly said. "When we've figured out what the hell is happening to us, wherever and however we go on from here, there'll be time for us to sort through your grandfather's things. It won't be so difficult if we do it together."

He smiled at her and squeezed her hand.

She remembered something else. "Jim, you recall the description I gave you of the woman in my dream last night, the woman who came up the mill stairs?"

"Sort of."

"You said you didn't recognize her."

"So?"

"But there's a photo of her in the house."

"There is?"

"In the living room, that photograph of a couple in their early fifties—are they your grandparents, Lena and Henry?"

"Yeah. That's right."

"Lena was the woman in my dream."

He frowned. "Isn't that odd . . . ?"

"Well, maybe. But what's odder is, you didn't recognize her."

"I guess your description wasn't that good."

"But didn't you hear me say she had a beauty mark—"

His eyes narrowed, and his hand tightened around hers. "Quick, the tablets."

Confused, she said, "What?"

"Something's about to happen, I feel it, and we need the tablets we bought at The Center."

He let go of her hand, and she withdrew the two yellow, lined tablets and felt-tip pen from the plastic bag at her side. He took them from her, hesitated, looking around at the walls and at the shadows above them, as if waiting to be told what to do next.

The bells rang.

▼ ▲ ▼

That musical tintinnabulation sent a thrill through Jim. He knew that he was on the verge of discovering the meaning not merely of the events of the past year but of the last two and a half decades. And not just that, either. More. Much more. The ringing heralded the revelation of even greater understanding, transcendental truths, an explanation of the fundamental meaning of his entire life, past and future, origins and destiny, and of the meaning of existence itself. Grandiose as such a notion might be, he sensed that the secrets of creation would be revealed to him before he left the windmill, and that he would reach the state of enlightenment he had sought—and failed to find—in a score of religions.

As the second spell of ringing began, Holly started to get up.

Jim figured she intended to descend to the window on the stairs and look into the pond. He said, "No, wait. It's going to happen *here* this time."

She hesitated, then sat down.

As the ringing stopped again, Jim felt compelled to push the ice chest out of the way and put one of the yellow, lined tablets on the floor between him and Holly. He was not sure what he was expected to do with the other tablet and the pen, but after a brief moment of indecision, he held on to them.

When the melodic ringing began a third time, it was accompanied by an impossible pulse of light within the limestone walls. The red glow seemed to well up from inside the stone at a point directly in front of them, then suddenly raced around the room, encircling them with a throbbing band of luminescence.

Even as the strange flare whipped around them, Holly issued a wordless sound of fear, and Jim remembered what she had told him of her dream last night. The woman— whether it had been his grandmother or not—had climbed the stairs into the high room, had seen an amber emanation within the walls, as if the mill was made of colored glass, and had witnessed something unimaginably hostile being born out of those mortared blocks.

"It's okay." He was eager to reassure her. "This isn't The Enemy. It's something else. There's no danger here. This is a different light."

He was only sharing with her the reassurances that were flooding into him from a higher power. He hoped to God that he was correct, that no threat was imminent, for he remembered too well the hideous biological transformation of his own bedroom ceiling in Laguna Niguel little more than twelve hours ago. Light had pulsed within the oily, insectile birth sac that had blistered out of ordinary drywall, and the shadowy form within, writhing and twitching, had been nothing he would ever want to see more directly.

During two more bursts of melodic ringing, the color of the light changed to amber. But otherwise it in no way resembled the menacing radiance in his bedroom ceiling, which had been a different shade of amber altogether—the vile yellow of putrescent matter or of rich dark pus—and which had throbbed in sympathy with an ominous tripartite heartbeat that was not audible now.

Holly looked scared nonetheless.

He wished he could pull her close, put his arm around

her. But he needed to give his undivided attention to the higher power that was striving to reach him.

The ringing stopped, but the light did not fade. It quivered, shimmered, dimmed, and brightened. It moved through the otherwise dark wall in scores of separate amoeba-like forms that constantly flowed together and separated into new shapes; it was like a one-dimensional representation of the kaleidoscopic display in one of those old Lava lamps. The ever-changing patterns evolved on all sides of them, from the base of the wall to the apex of the domed ceiling.

"I feel like we're in a bathysphere, all glass, suspended far, far down in the ocean," Holly said. "And great schools of luminescent fish are diving and soaring and swirling past us on all sides, through the deep black water."

He loved her for putting the experience into better words than he could summon, words that would not let him forget the images they described, even if he lived a hundred years.

Unquestionably, the ghostly luminosity lay within the stone, not merely on the surface of it. He could see *into* that now-translucent substance, as if it had been alchemized into a dark but well-clarified quartz. The amber radiance brightened the room more than did the lantern, which he had turned low. His trembling hands looked golden, as did Holly's face.

But pockets of darkness remained, and the constantly moving light enlivened the shadows as well.

"What now?" Holly asked softly.

Jim noticed that something had happened to the yellow tablet on the floor between them. "Look."

Words had appeared on the top third of the first page. They looked as if they had been formed by a finger dipped in ink:

I AM WITH YOU.

6

Holly had been distracted—to say the least!—by the light-show, but she did not think that Jim could have leaned to the tablet and printed the words with the felt-tip pen or any other instrument without drawing her attention. Yet she found it hard to believe that some disembodied presence had conveyed the message.

"I think we're being encouraged to ask questions," Jim said.

"Then ask it what it is," she said at once.

He wrote a question on the second tablet, which he was holding, and showed it to her:

Who are you?

As they watched, the answer appeared on the first tablet, which lay between and slightly in front of them at such an angle that they could both read it. The words were not burnt onto the paper and were not formed by ink that dripped magically from the air. Instead, the irregular, wavery letters appeared as dim gray shapes and grew darker as they seemed to float up out of the paper, as though a page of the tablet were not one-five-hundredth of an inch thick but a pool of liquid many feet deep. She recognized immediately that this was similar to the effect she had seen earlier when the balls of light had risen to the center of the pond before bursting and casting concentric rings of illumination outward through the water; this was, as well, how the light had first welled up in the limestone walls before the blocks had become thoroughly translucent.

THE FRIEND.

Who are you? The Friend.

It seemed to be an odd self-description. Not "your friend" or "a friend" but *The* Friend.

For an alien intelligence, if indeed that's all it was, the name had curious spiritual implications, connotations of divinity. Men had given God many names—Jehovah, Allah, Brahma, Zeus, Aesir—but even more titles. God was The Almighty, The Eternal Being, The Infinite, The Father, The Savior, The Creator, The Light. The Friend seemed to fit right into that list.

Jim quickly wrote another question and showed it to Holly: *Where do you come from?*

ANOTHER WORLD.

Which could mean anything from heaven to Mars.

Do you mean another planet?

YES.

"My God," Holly said, awed in spite of herself.

So much for the great hereafter.

She looked up from the tablet and met Jim's eyes. They seemed to shine brighter than ever, although the chrome-yellow light had imparted to them an exceptional green tint.

Restless with excitement, she rose onto her knees, then eased back again, sitting on her calves. The top tablet page was filled with the entity's responses. Holly equivocated only briefly, then tore it off and set it aside, so they could see the second page. She glanced back and forth between Jim's questions and the rapidly appearing answers.

From another solar system?

YES.

From another galaxy?

YES.

Is it your vessel we've seen in the pond?

YES.

How long have you been here?

10,000 YEARS.

As she stared at that figure, it seemed to Holly that this moment was more like a dream than some of the actual dreams she'd been having lately. After so much mystery, there were answers—but they seemed to be coming too easily. She did not know what she had expected, but she had not imagined that the murkiness in which they had been operating would clear as quickly as if a drop of a magical universal detergent had been dropped into it.

"Ask her why she's here," Holly said, tearing off the second sheet and putting it with the first.

Jim was surprised. *"She?"*

"Why not?"

He brightened. "Why not?" he agreed.

He turned to a new page in his own tablet and wrote her question: *Why are you here?*

Floating up through the paper to the surface: TO OBSERVE, TO STUDY, TO HELP MANKIND.

"You know what this is like?" Holly said.

"What's it like?"

"An episode of *Outer Limits.*"

"The old TV show?"

"Yeah."

"Wasn't that before your time?"

"It's on cable."

"But what do you mean it's like an episode of *Outer Limits?*"

She frowned at TO OBSERVE, TO STUDY, TO HELP MANKIND and said, "Don't you think it's a little . . . trite?"

"Trite?" He was irritated. "No, I don't. Because I haven't any idea what alien contact *should* be like. I haven't had a whole lot of experience with it, certainly not enough to have expectations or be jaded."

"I'm sorry. I don't know . . . it's just . . . okay, let's see where this leads."

She had to admit that she was no less awed than she had been when the light had first appeared in the walls. Her heart continued to thud hard and fast, and she was still unable to draw a really deep breath. She still felt that they were in the presence of something superhuman, maybe even a higher power by one definition or another, and she was humbled by it. Considering what she had seen in the pond, the pulsing luminescence even now swimming through the wall, and the words that kept shimmering into view on the tablet, she would have been hopelessly stupid if she had *not* been awed.

Undeniably, however, her sense of wonder was dulled by the feeling that this entity was structuring the encounter like an old movie or TV script. With a sarcastic note in his voice, Jim had said that he had too little experience with alien contact to have developed any expectations that could be disappointed. But that was not true. Having grown up in the sixties and seventies, he had been as media-saturated as she had been. They'd been exposed to the same TV shows and movies, magazines and books; science fiction had been a major influence in popular culture all their lives. He had acquired plenty of detailed expectations about what alien contact would be like—and the entity in the wall was playing to all of them. Holly's only conscious expectation had been that a *real* close encounter of the third kind would be like nothing the novelists and screenwriters imagined in all their wildest flights of fantasy, because when referring to life from another world, alien *meant* alien, different, beyond easy comparison or comprehension.

"Okay," she said, "maybe familiarity is the point. I mean, maybe it's using our modern myths as a convenient way to present itself to us, a way to make itself comprehensible to us. Because it's probably so radically different from us that we could never understand its true nature or appearance."

"Exactly," Jim said. He wrote another question: *What is the light we see in the walls?*

THE LIGHT IS ME.

Holly didn't wait for Jim to write the next question. She addressed the entity directly: "How can you move through a wall?"

Because the alien seemed such a stickler about form, she

was somewhat surprised when it did not insist on hewing to the written question-reply format. It answered her at once: I CAN BECOME PART OF ANYTHING, MOVE WITHIN IT, TAKE SHAPE FROM IT WHENEVER I CHOOSE.

"Sounds a little like bragging," she said.

"I can't believe you can be sarcastic at a time like this," Jim said impatiently.

"I'm not being sarcastic," she explained. "I'm just trying to understand."

He looked doubtful.

To the alien presence, she said, "You understand the problems I'm having with this, don't you?"

On the tablet: YES.

She ripped away that page, revealing a fresh one. Increasingly restless and nervous, but not entirely sure why, Holly got to her feet and turned in a circle, looking at the play of light in the walls as she formulated her next question. "Why is your approach marked by the sound of bells?"

No answer appeared on the tablet.

She repeated the question.

The tablet remained blank.

Holly said, "Trade secret, I guess."

She felt a bead of cold sweat trickle out of her right armpit and down her side, under her blouse. A childlike wonder still worked in her, but fear was on the rise again. Something was wrong. Something more than the clichéd nature of the story the entity was giving them. She couldn't quite put her finger on what spooked her.

On his own tablet, Jim quickly wrote another question, and Holly leaned down to read it: *Did you appear to me in this room when I was ten years old?*

YES. OFTEN.

Did you make me forget it?

YES.

"Don't bother writing your questions," Holly said. "Just ask them like I do."

Jim was clearly startled by her suggestion, and she was

surprised that he had persisted with his pen and tablet even after seeing that the questions she asked aloud were answered. He seemed reluctant to put aside the felt-tip and the paper, but at last he did. "Why did you make me forget?"

Even standing, Holly could easily read the bold words that appeared on the yellow tablet:

YOU WERE NOT READY TO REMEMBER.

"Unnecessarily cryptic," she muttered. "You're right. It must be male."

Jim tore off the used page, put it with the others, and paused, chewing his lip, evidently not sure what to ask next. Finally he said, "Are you male or female?"

I AM MALE.

"More likely," Holly said, "it's neither. It's *alien,* after all, and it's as likely to reproduce by parthenogenesis."

I AM MALE, it repeated.

Jim remained seated, legs folded, an undiminished look of wonder on his face, more boylike now than ever.

Holly did not understand why her anxiety level was soaring while Jim continued to bounce up and down— well, virtually—with enthusiasm and delight.

He said, "What do you look like?"

WHATEVER I CHOOSE TO LOOK LIKE.

"Could you appear to us as a man or woman?" Jim asked.

YES.

"As a dog?"

YES.

"As a cat?"

YES.

"As a beetle?"

YES.

Without the security of his pen and tablet, Jim seemed to have been reduced to inane questions. Holly half expected him to ask the entity what its favorite color was, whether it preferred Coke or Pepsi, and if it liked Barry Manilow music.

But he said, "How old are you?"

I AM A CHILD.

"A child?" Jim responded. "But you told us you've been on our world for ten thousand years."

I AM STILL A CHILD.

Jim said, "Then is your species very long-lived?"

WE ARE IMMORTAL.

"Wow."

"It's lying," Holly told him.

Appalled by her effrontery, he said, "Jesus, Holly!"

"Well, it is."

And *that* was the source of her renewed fear—the fact that it was not being straight with them, was playing games, deceiving. She had a sense that it regarded them with enormous contempt. In which case, she probably should have shut up, been meekly adoring before its power, and tried not to anger it.

Instead she said, "If it were really immortal, it wouldn't think of itself as a child. It *couldn't* think that way about itself. Infancy, childhood, adolescence, adulthood—those are age categories a species concerns itself with if it has a finite lifespan. If you're immortal, you might be born innocent, ignorant, uneducated, but you aren't born young because you're never really going to get old."

"Aren't you splitting hairs?" Jim asked almost petulantly.

"I don't think so. It's lying to us."

"Maybe its use of the word 'child' was just another way it was trying to make its alien nature more understandable."

YES.

"Bullshit," Holly said.

"Damn it, Holly!"

As Jim removed another page from the tablet, detaching it neatly along its edge, Holly moved to the wall and studied the patterns of light churning through it. Seen close up, they were quite beautiful and strange, not like a smooth-flowing phosphorescent fluid or fiery streams of lava, but like scintillant swarms of fireflies, millions of spangled points not unlike her analogy of luminous, schooling fish.

Holly half expected the wall in front of her to bulge suddenly. Split open. Give birth to a monstrous form.

She wanted to step back. Instead she moved closer. Her nose was only an inch from the transmuted stone. Viewed this intimately, the surge and flux and whirl of the millions of bright cells was dizzying. There was no heat from it, but she imagined she could feel the flicker of light and shadow across her face.

"Why is your approach marked by the sound of bells?" she asked.

After a few seconds, Jim spoke from behind her: "No answer."

The question seemed innocent enough, and one that they should logically be expected to ask. The entity's unwillingness to answer alerted her that the ringing must be somehow vitally important. Understanding the bells might be the first step toward learning something real and true about this creature.

"Why is your approach marked by the sound of bells?"

Jim reported: "No answer. I don't think you should ask that question again, Holly. It obviously doesn't want to answer, and there's nothing to be gained by aggravating it. This isn't The Enemy, this is—"

"Yeah, I know. It's The Friend."

She remained at the wall and felt herself to be face-to-face with an alien presence, though it had nothing that corresponded to a face. It was focused on her now. It was right *there*.

Again she said, "Why is your approach marked by the sound of bells?"

Instinctively she knew that her innocent question and her not-so-innocent repetition of it had put her in great danger. Her heart was thudding so loud that she wondered if Jim could hear it. She figured The Friend, with all its powers, could not only hear her hammering heart but see it jumping like a panicked rabbit within the cage of her chest. It knew she was afraid, all right. Hell, it might even be able to read her mind. She had to show it that she would not allow fear to deter her.

She put one hand on the light-filled stone. If those luminous clouds were not merely a projection of the creature's consciousness, not just an illusion or representation for their benefit, if the thing was, as it claimed, actually alive in the wall, then the stone was now its flesh. Her hand was upon its body.

Faint vibrations passed across the wall in distinctive, whirling vortexes. That was all she felt. No heat. The fire within the stone was evidently cold.

"Why is your approach marked by the sound of bells?"

"Holly, don't," Jim said. Worry tainted his voice for the first time. Perhaps he, too, had begun to sense that The Friend was not entirely a friend.

But she was driven by a suspicion that willpower mattered in this confrontation, and that a demonstration of unflinching will would set a new tone in their relationship with The Friend. She could not have explained why she felt so strongly about it. Just instinct—not a woman's but an ex-reporter's.

"Why is your approach marked by the sound of bells?"

She thought she detected a slight change in the vibrations that tingled across her palm, but she might have imagined it, for they were barely perceptible in the first place. Through her mind flickered an image of the stone cracking open in a jagged mouth and biting off her hand, blood spurting, white bone bristling from the ragged stump of her wrist.

Though she was shaking uncontrollably, she did not step back or lift her hand off the wall.

She wondered if The Friend had sent her that horrifying image.

"Why is your approach marked by the sound of bells?"

"Holly, for Christ's sake—" Jim broke off, then said, "Wait, an answer's coming."

Willpower *did* matter. But for God's sake, why? Why should an all-powerful alien force from another galaxy be intimidated by her unwavering resolution?

Jim reported the response: "It says . . . 'For drama?' "

"For drama?" she repeated.

"Yeah. F-O-R, then D-R-A-M-A, then a question mark."

To the thing in the wall, she said, "Are you telling me the bells are just a bit of theater to dramatize your apparitions?"

After a few seconds, Jim said, "No answer."

"And why the question mark?" she asked The Friend. "Don't you know what the bells mean yourself, where the sound comes from, what makes it, why? Are you only guessing when you say 'for drama'? How can you not know what it is if it always accompanies you?"

"Nothing," Jim told her.

She stared into the wall. The churning, schooling cells of light were increasingly disorienting her, but she did not close her eyes.

"A new message," Jim said. " 'I am going.' "

"Chicken," Holly said softly into the amorphous face of the thing in the wall. But she was sheathed in cold sweat now.

The amber light began to darken, turn orange.

Stepping away from the wall at last, Holly swayed and almost fell. She moved back to her bedroll and dropped to her knees.

New words appeared on the tablet: I WILL BE BACK.

"When?" Jim asked.

WHEN THE TIDE IS MINE.

"What tide?"

THERE IS A TIDE IN THE VESSEL, AN EBB AND FLOW, DARKNESS AND LIGHT. I RISE WITH THE LIGHT TIDE, BUT HE RISES WITH THE DARK.

"He?" Holly asked.

THE ENEMY.

The light in the walls was red-orange now, dimmer, but still ceaselessly changing patterns around them.

Jim said, "Two of you share the starship?"

YES. TWO FORCES. TWO ENTITIES.

It's lying, Holly thought. This, like all the rest of its story, is just like the bells: good theater.

WAIT FOR MY RETURN.

"We'll wait," Jim said.

DO NOT SLEEP.

"Why can't we sleep?" Holly asked, playing along.

YOU MIGHT DREAM.

The page was full. Jim ripped it off and stacked it with the others.

The light in the walls was blood-red now, steadily fading.

DREAMS ARE DOORWAYS.

"What are you telling us?"

The same three words again: DREAMS ARE DOORWAYS.

"It's a warning," Jim said.

DREAMS ARE DOORWAYS.

No, Holly thought, it's a threat.

7

The windmill was just a windmill again. Stones and timbers. Mortar and nails. Dust sifting, wood rotting, iron rusting, spiders spinning in secret lairs.

Holly sat directly in front of Jim, in powwow position, their knees touching. She held both his hands, partly because she drew strength from his touch, and partly because she wanted to reassure him and take the sting out of what she was about to say.

"Listen, babe, you're the most interesting man I've ever known, the sexiest, for sure, and I think, at heart, the kindest. But you do a lousy interview. For the most part, your questions aren't well-thought-out, you don't get at the meat of an issue, you follow up on irrelevancies but generally fail to follow up on the really important answers. And you're a naive enough reporter to think that the subject is always being straight with you, when they're almost never straight with an interviewer, so you don't *probe* the way you should."

He did not seem offended. He smiled and said, "I didn't think of myself as a reporter doing an interview."

"Well, kiddo, that's exactly what the situation was. The Friend, as he calls himself, has information, and we need information to know where we stand, to do our job."

"I thought of it more as . . . I don't know . . . as an epiphany. When God came to Moses with the Ten Commandments, I figure He just told Moses what they were, and if Moses had other questions he didn't feel he had to grill the Big Guy."

"This wasn't God in the walls."

"I know that. I'm past that idea now. But it was an alien intelligence so superior to us that it almost might as well *be* God."

"We don't know that," she said patiently.

"Sure we do. When you consider the high degree of intelligence and the millennia needed to build a civilization capable of traveling across galaxies—good heavens, we're only monkeys by comparison!"

"There, you see, that's what I'm talking about. How do you know it's from another galaxy? Because you believe what it told you. How do you know there's a spaceship under the pond? Because you believe what it told you."

Jim was getting impatient now. "Why would it lie to us, what would it have to gain from lies?"

"I don't know. But we can't be sure that it isn't manipulating us. And when it comes back, like it promised, I want to be ready for it. I want to spend the next hour or two or three—however long we've got—making a list of questions, so we can put it through a carefully planned inquisition. We've got to have a strategy for squeezing *real* information from it, facts not fantasies, and our questions have to support that strategy." When he frowned, she hastened on before he could interrupt. "Okay, all right, maybe it's incapable of lying, maybe it's noble and pure, maybe everything it's told us is the gospel truth. But listen, Jim, this is not an epiphany. The Friend set the rules by influencing you to buy the tablets and pen. It established the question-and-answer format. If it didn't want us to make the best of that format, it would've just told you to shut up and would've blabbered at you from a burning bush!"

He stared at her. He chewed his lip thoughtfully.

He shifted his gaze to the walls where the creature of light had swum in the stone.

Pressing her point, Holly said, "You never even asked it

why it wants you to save people's lives, or why some people and not others."

He looked at her again, obviously surprised to realize that he had not pursued the answer to the most important question of all. In the lactescent glow of the softly hissing gas lantern, his eyes were blue again, not green as the amber light had temporarily made them. And troubled.

"Okay," he said. "You're right. I guess I was just swept away by it all. I mean, Holly, whatever the hell it is—it's astounding."

"It's astounding," she acknowledged.

"We'll do what you want, make up a list of carefully thought-out questions. And when it comes back, you should be the one to ask all of them, 'cause you'll be better at ad-libbing other questions if it says anything that needs follow-up."

"I agree," she said, relieved that he had suggested it without being pressured.

She was better schooled at interviewing than he was, but she was also more trustworthy in this particular situation than Jim could ever be. The Friend had a long past relationship with him and had, admittedly, already messed with his memory by making him forget about the encounters they'd had twenty-five years ago. Holly had to assume that Jim was co-opted, to one degree or another corrupted, though he could not realize it. The Friend had been *in his mind,* perhaps on scores or hundreds of occasions, when he had been at a formative age, and when he had been particularly vulnerable due to the loss of his parents, therefore even more susceptible to manipulation and control than most ten-year-old boys. On a subconscious level, Jim Iron-heart might be programmed to protect The Friend's secrets rather than help to reveal them.

Holly knew she was walking a thread-thin line between judicious precaution and paranoia, might even be treading more on the side of the latter than the former. Under the circumstances, a little paranoia was a prescription for survival.

When he said he was going outside to relieve himself,

however, she much preferred to be with him than alone in the high room. She followed him downstairs and stood by the Ford with her back to him while he peed against the split-rail fence beside the cornfield.

She stared out at the deep black pond.

She listened to the toads, which were singing again. So were the cicadas. The events of the day had rattled her. Now even the sounds of nature seemed malevolent.

She wondered if they had come up against something too strange and too powerful to be dealt with by just a failed reporter and an ex-schoolteacher. She wondered if they ought to leave the farm right away. She wondered if they would be allowed to leave.

Since the departure of The Friend, Holly's fear had not abated. If anything, it had increased. She felt as if they were living under a thousand-ton weight that was magically suspended by a single human hair, but the magic was weakening and the hair was stretched as taut and brittle as a filament of glass.

▼ ▲ ▼

By midnight, they had eaten six chocolate doughnuts and composed seven pages of questions for The Friend. Sugar was an energizer and a consolation in times of trouble, but it was no help to already-frayed nerves. Holly's anxiety had a sharp refined-sugar edge to it now, like a well-stropped razor.

Pacing with the tablet in her hand, Holly said, "And we're not going to let it get away with written answers this time. That just slows down the give and take between interviewer and interviewee. We're going to insist that it talk to us."

Jim was lying on his back, his hands folded behind his head. "It can't talk."

"How do you know that?"

"Well, I'm assuming it can't, or otherwise it would've talked right from the start."

"Don't assume anything," she said. "If it can mix its molecules with the wall, swim through stone—through *anything,* if it's to be believed—and if it can assume any form it wishes, then it can sure as hell form a mouth and vocal cords and talk like any self-respecting higher power."

"I guess you're right," he said uneasily.

"It already said that it could appear to us as a man or woman if it wanted, didn't it?"

"Well, yeah."

"I'm not even asking for a flashy materialization. Just a voice, a disembodied voice, a little sound with the old lightshow."

Listening to herself as she talked, Holly realized that she was using her edginess to pump herself, to establish an aggressive tone that would serve her well when The Friend returned. It was an old trick she had learned when she had interviewed people whom she found imposing or intimidating.

Jim sat up. "Okay, it could talk if it wanted to, but maybe it doesn't want to."

"We already decided we can't let it set all the rules, Jim."

"But I don't understand why we have to antagonize it."

"I'm not antagonizing it."

"I think we should be at least a little respectful."

"Oh, I respect the hell out of it."

"You don't seem to."

"I'm convinced it could squash us like bugs if it wanted to, and that gives me tremendous respect for it."

"That's not the kind of respect I mean."

"That's the only kind of respect it's earned from me so far," she said, pacing around him now instead of back and forth. "When it stops trying to manipulate me, stops trying to scare the crap out of me, starts giving me answers that ring true, then maybe I'll respect it for other reasons."

"You're getting a little spooky," he said.

"Me?"

"You're so hostile."

"I am not."

He was frowning at her. "Looks like blind hostility to me."

"It's adversarial journalism. It's the modern reporter's

tone and theme. You don't question your subject and later explain him to readers, you *attack* him. You have an agenda, a version of the truth you want to report regardless of the full truth, and you fulfill it. I never approved of it, never indulged in it, which is why I was always losing out on stories and promotions to other reporters. Now, here, tonight, I'm all for the attack part. The big difference is, I *do* care about getting to the truth, not shaping it, and I just want to twist and yank some real facts out of this alien of ours."

"Maybe he won't show up."

"He said he would."

Jim shook his head. "But why should he if you're going to be like this?"

"You're saying he might be *afraid* of me? What kind of higher power is that?"

The bells rang, and she jumped in alarm.

Jim got to his feet. "Just take it easy."

The bells fell silent, rang again, fell silent. When they rang a third time, a sullen red light appeared at one point in the wall. It grew more intense, assumed a brighter shade, then suddenly burst across the domed room like a blazing fireworks display, after which the bells stopped ringing and the multitude of sparks coalesced into the pulsing, constantly moving amoeba-like forms that they had seen before.

"Very dramatic," Holly said. As the light swiftly progressed from red through orange to amber, she seized the initiative. "We would like you to dispense with the cumbersome way you answered our questions previously and simply speak to us directly."

The Friend did not reply.

"Will you speak to us directly?"

No response.

Consulting the tablet that she held in one hand, she read the first question. "Are you the higher power that has been sending Jim on life-saving missions?"

She waited.

Silence.

She tried again.

Silence.

Stubbornly, she repeated the question.

The Friend did not speak, but Jim said, "Holly, look at this."

She turned and saw him examining the other tablet. He held it toward her, flipping through the first ten or twelve pages. The eerie and inconstant light from the stone was bright enough to show her that the pages were filled with The Friend's familiar printing.

Taking the tablet from him, she looked at the first line on the top page: YES. I AM THAT POWER.

Jim said, "He's already answered every one of the questions we've prepared."

Holly threw the tablet across the room. It hit the far window without breaking the glass, and clattered to the floor.

"Holly, you can't—"

She cut him off with a sharp look.

The light moved through the transmuted limestone with greater agitation than before.

To The Friend, Holly said, "God gave Moses the Ten Commandments on tablets of stone, yeah, but He also had the courtesy to talk to him. If God can humble Himself to speak directly with human beings, then so can you."

She did not look to see how Jim was reacting to her adversarial tack. All she cared about was that he not interrupt her.

When The Friend remained silent, she repeated the first question on her list. "Are you the higher power that has been sending Jim on life-saving missions?"

"Yes. I am that power." The voice was a soft, mellifluous baritone. Like the ringing of the bells, it seemed to come from all sides of them. The Friend did not materialize out of the wall in human form, did not sculpt a face from the limestone, but merely produced its voice out of thin air.

She asked the second question on her list. "How can you know these people are about to die?"

"I am an entity that lives in all aspects of time."

"What do you mean by that?"

"Past, present, and future."

"You can foresee the future?"

"I live in the future as well as in the past and present."

The light was coruscating through the walls with less agitation now, as if the alien presence had accepted her conditions and was mellow again.

Jim moved to her side. He put a hand on her arm and squeezed gently, as if to say "good work."

She decided not to ask for any more clarification on the issue of its ability to see the future, for fear they would be off on a tangent and never get back on track before the creature next announced that it was departing. She returned to the prepared questions. "Why do you want these particular people saved?"

"To help mankind," it said sonorously. There might have been a note of pomposity in it, too, but that was hard to tell because the voice was so evenly modulated, almost machinelike.

"But when so many people are dying every day—and *most* of them are innocents—why have you singled out these particular people to be rescued?"

"They are special people."

"In what way are they special?"

"If allowed to live, each of them will make a major contribution to the betterment of mankind."

Jim said, "I'll be damned."

Holly had not been expecting that answer. It had the virtue of being fresh. But she was not sure she believed it. For one thing, she was bothered that The Friend's voice was increasingly familiar to her. She was sure she had heard it before, and in a context that undermined its credibility now, in spite of its deep and authoritative tone. "Are you saying you not only see the future as it will be but as it *might* have been?"

"Yes."

"Aren't we back to your being God now?"

"No. I do not see as clearly as God. But I see."

In his boyish best humor again, Jim smiled at the

kaleidoscopic patterns of light, obviously excited and pleased by all that he was hearing.

Holly turned away from the wall, crossed the room, squatted beside her suitcase, and opened it.

Jim loomed over her. "What're you doing?"

"Looking for this," she said, producing the notebook in which she had chronicled the discoveries she'd made while researching him. She got up, opened the notebook, and paged to the list of people whose lives he had saved prior to Flight 246. Addressing the entity throbbing through the limestone, she said, "May fifteenth. Atlanta, Georgia. Sam Newsome and his five-year-old daughter Emily. What are they going to contribute to humanity that makes them more important than all the other people who died that day?"

No answer was forthcoming.

"Well?" she demanded.

"Emily will become a great scientist and discover a cure for a major disease." Definitely a note of pomposity this time.

"What disease?"

"Why do you not believe me, Miss Thorne?" The Friend spoke as formally as an English butler on duty, yet in that response, Holly felt she heard the subtle pouting tone of a child under the dignified, reserved surface.

She said, "Tell me what disease, and maybe I'll believe you."

"Cancer."

"Which cancer? There are all types of cancer."

"All cancers."

She referred to her notebook again. "June seventh. Corona, California. Louis Andretti."

"He will father a child who will grow up to become a great diplomat."

Better than dying of multiple rattlesnake bites, she thought.

She said, "June twenty-first. New York City. Thaddeus—"

"He will become a great artist whose work will give millions of people hope."

"He seemed like a nice kid," Jim said happily, buying into the whole thing. "I liked him."

Ignoring him, Holly said, "June thirtieth. San Francisco—"

"Rachael Steinberg will give birth to a child who will become a great spiritual leader."

That voice was bugging her. She knew she had heard it before. But where?

"July fifth—"

"Miami, Florida. Carmen Diaz. She will give birth to a child who will become president of the United States."

Holly fanned herself with the notebook and said, "Why not president of the world?"

"July fourteenth. Houston, Texas. Amanda Cutter. She will give birth to a child who will be a great peacemaker."

"Why not the Second Coming?" Holly asked.

Jim had moved away from her. He was leaning against the wall between two windows, the display of light quietly exploding around him. "What's the matter with you?" he asked.

"It's all too much," she said.

"What is?"

"Okay, it says it wants you to save special people."

"To help mankind."

"Sure, sure," Holly said to the wall.

To Jim she said, "But these people are all just too special, don't you think? Maybe it's me, but it all seems overblown, it's gotten trite again. Nobody's growing up to be just a damned good doctor, or a businessman who creates a new industry and maybe ten thousand jobs, or an honest and courageous cop, or a terrific nurse. No, they're great diplomats, great scientists, great politicians, great peacemakers. Great, great, great!"

"Is this adversarial journalism?"

"Damn right."

He pushed away from the wall, used both hands to smooth his thick hair back from his forehead, and cocked his head at her. "I see your point, why it's starting to sound like another episode of *Outer Limits* to you, but let's think about this. It's a crazy, extravagant situation. A being from another world, with powers that seem godlike to us, decides to use me to better the chances of the human race. Isn't it logical that he'd send me out to save special, *really* special people instead of your theoretical business tycoon?"

"Oh, it's logical," she said. "It just doesn't ring true to me, and I've got a fairly well-developed nose for deception."

"Is that why you were a great success as a reporter?"

She might have laughed at the image of an alien, vastly superior to human beings, stooping to engage in a bickering match. But the impatience and poutiness she'd thought she detected as an undercurrent in some of its previous answers was now unmistakable, and the concept of a hypersensitive, resentful creature with godlike power was too unnerving to be funny at the moment.

"How's that for a higher power?" she asked Jim. "Any second now, he's going to call me a bitch."

The Friend said nothing.

Consulting her notebook again, she said, "July twentieth. Steven Aimes. Birmingham, Alabama."

Schools of light swam through the walls. The patterns were less graceful and less sensuous than before; if the lightshow had been the visual equivalent of one of Brahms's most pacific symphonies, it was now more like the discordant wailing of bad progressive jazz.

"What about Steven Aimes?" she demanded, scared but remembering how an exertion of will had been met with respect before.

"I am going now."

"That was a short tide," she said.

The amber light began to darken.

"The tides in the vessel are not regular or of equal duration. But I will return."

"What about Steven Aimes? He was fifty-seven, still capable of siring a great something-or-other, though maybe a little long in the tooth. Why did you save Steve?"

The voice grew somewhat deeper, slipping from baritone toward bass, and it hardened. *"It would not be wise for you to attempt to leave."*

She had been waiting for that. As soon as she heard the words, she knew she had been tensed in expectation of them.

Jim, however, was stunned. He turned, looking around at the dark-amber forms swirling and melding and splitting apart again, as if trying to figure out the biological geography of the thing, so he could look it in the eyes. "What do you mean by that? We'll leave any time we want."

"You must wait for my return. You will die if you attempt to leave."

"Don't you want to help mankind anymore?" Holly asked sharply.

"Do not sleep."

Jim moved to Holly's side. Whatever estrangement she had caused between her and Jim, by taking an aggressive stance with The Friend, was apparently behind them. He put an arm around her protectively.

"You dare not sleep."

The limestone was mottled with a deep red glow.

"Dreams are doorways."

The bloody light went out.

The lantern provided the only illumination. And in the deeper darkness that followed The Friend's departure, the quiet hiss of the burning gas was the only sound.

8

Holly stood at the head of the stairs, shining a flashlight into the gloom below. Jim supposed she was trying to make up her mind whether they really would be prevented from leaving the mill—and if so, how violently.

Watching her from where he sat on his sleeping bag, he could not understand why it was all turning sour.

He had come to the windmill because the bizarre and frightening events in his bedroom in Laguna Niguel, over eighteen hours ago, had made it impossible to continue ignoring the dark side to the mystery in which he had become enwrapped. Prior to that, he had been willing to drift along, doing what he was compelled to do, pulling people out of the fire at the last minute, a bemused but game superhero who had to rely on airplanes when he wanted to fly and who had to do his own laundry. But the increasing intrusion of The Enemy—whatever the hell it was—its undeniable evil and fierce hostility, no longer allowed Jim the luxury of ignorance. The Enemy was struggling to break through from some other place, another dimension perhaps, and it seemed to be getting closer on each attempt. Learning the truth about the higher power behind his activities had not been at the top of his agenda, because he had felt that enlightenment would be granted to him in time, but learning about The Enemy had come to seem urgently necessary for his survival—and Holly's.

Nevertheless, he had traveled to the farm with the expectation that he would encounter good as well as evil, experience joy as well as fear. Whatever he learned by plunging into the unknown should at least leave him with a greater understanding of his sacred life-saving mission and the supernatural forces behind it. But now he was more confused than before he'd come. Some developments *had* filled him with the wonder and joy for which he longed: the ringing in the stone, for one; and the beautiful, almost divine, light that was the essence of The Friend. He had been moved to rapture by the revelation that he was not merely saving lives but saving people so special that their survival would improve the fate of the entire human race. But that spiritual bliss had been snatched away from him by the growing realization that The Friend was either not telling them the whole truth or, worst case, was not telling them anything true at all. The childish petulance of the creature was unnerving in the extreme, and now Jim was not sure that *anything* he had done since saving the Newsomes last May was in the service of good rather than evil.

Yet his fear was still tempered by hope. Though a splinter of despair had lodged in his heart and begun to fester, that spiritual infection was held in check by the core of optimism, however fragile, that had always been at the center of him.

Holly switched off the flashlight, returned from the open door, and sat down on her mattress. "I don't know, maybe it was an empty threat, but there's no way of telling till we try to leave."

"You want to?"

She shook her head. "What's the point in getting off the farm anyway? From everything we know, it can reach out to us anywhere we go. Right? I mean it reached you in Laguna Niguel, sent you on these missions, reached you out there in Nevada and sent you on to Boston to rescue Nicholas O'Conner."

"I've felt it with me, at times, no matter where I've gone. In Houston, in Florida, in France, in England—it guided

me, let me know what was coming, so I could do the job
it wanted done."

Holly looked exhausted. She was drawn and paler than
the eerie glow of the gas lantern could account for, and her
eyes were shadowed with rings of weariness. She closed her
eyes for a moment and pinched the bridge of her nose with
thumb and forefinger, a strained look on her face, as if she
was trying to suppress a headache.

With all his heart, Jim regretted that she had been drawn
into this. But like his fear and despair, his regret was im-
pure, tempered by the deep pleasure he took in her very
presence. Though it was a selfish attitude, he was glad that
she was with him, no matter where this strange night led
them. He was no longer alone.

Still pinching the bridge of her nose, the lines in her
forehead carved deep by her scowl, Holly said, "This creature isn't restricted to the area near the pond, or just to
psychic contact across great distances. It can manifest itself
anywhere, judging by the scratches it left in my sides and
the way it entered the ceiling of your bedroom this morning."

"Well, now wait," he said, "we know The Enemy can
materialize over considerable distance, yes, but we don't
know that The Friend has that ability. It was The Enemy
that came out of your dream and The Enemy that tried to
reach us this morning."

Holly opened her eyes and lowered her hand from her
face. Her expression was bleak. "I think they're one and
the same."

"What?"

"The Enemy and The Friend. I don't believe two entities
are living under the pond, in that starship, if there *is* a
starship, which I guess there is. I think there's only a single
entity. The Friend and The Enemy are nothing more than
different aspects of it."

Holly's implication was clear, but it was too frightening
for Jim to accept immediately. He said, "You can't be
serious? You might as well be saying . . . it's insane."

"That *is* what I'm saying. It's suffering the alien equivalent of a split personality. It's acting out both personalities, but isn't consciously aware of what it's doing." Jim's almost desperate need to believe in The Friend as a separate and purely benign creature must have been evident in his face, for Holly took his right hand, held it in both hers, and hurried on before he could interrupt: "The childish petulance, the grandiosity of its claim to be reshaping the entire destiny of our species, the flamboyance of its apparitions, its sudden fluctuations between an attitude of syrupy goodwill and sullen anger, the way it lies so damned transparently yet deludes itself into believing it's clever, its secretiveness about some issues when there is no apparent reason to be secretive—all of that makes sense if you figure we're dealing with an unbalanced mind."

He looked for flaws in her reasoning, and found one. "But you can't believe an insane person, an insane alien individual, could pilot an unimaginably complex spacecraft across lightyears through countless dangers, while completely out of its mind."

"It doesn't have to be like that. Maybe the insanity set in *after* it got here. Or maybe it didn't have to pilot the ship, maybe the ship is essentially automatic, an entirely robotic mechanism. Or maybe there were others of its kind aboard who piloted it, and maybe they're all dead now. Jim, it's never mentioned a crew, only The Enemy. And assuming you buy its extraterrestrial origins, does it really ring true that only two individuals would set out on an intergalactic exploration? Maybe it killed the others."

Everything she was theorizing could be true, but then *anything* she theorized could be true. They were dealing with the Unknown, capital "U," and the possibilities in an infinite universe were infinite in number. He remembered reading somewhere—even many scientists believed that anything the human imagination conceived, regardless of how fanciful, could conceivably exist somewhere in the universe, because the infinite nature of creation meant that it was no less fluid, no less fertile than any man's or woman's dreams.

Jim expressed that thought to Holly, then said, "But

what bothers me is that you're doing now what you rejected earlier. You're trying hard to explain it in human terms, when it may be too alien for us to understand it at all. How can you assume that an alien species can even suffer insanity the way we can, or that it's capable of multiple personalities? These are all strictly human concepts."

She nodded. "You're right, of course. But at the moment, this theory's the only one that makes sense to me. Until something happens to disprove it, I've got to operate on the assumption that we're not dealing with a rational being."

With his free hand, he reached out and increased the gas flow to the wicks in the Coleman lantern, providing more light. "Jesus, I've got a bad case of the creeps," he said, shivering.

"Join the club."

"If it is schizo, and if it slips into the identity of The Enemy and can't get back out . . . what might it do to us?"

"I don't even want to think about that," Holly said. "If it's as intellectually superior to us as it seems to be, if it's from a long-lived race with experience and knowledge that makes the whole of the human experience seem like a short story compared to the Great Books of the Western World, then it sure as hell knows some tortures and cruelties that would make Hitler and Stalin and Pol Pot look like Sunday-school teachers."

He thought about that for a moment, even though he tried not to. The chocolate doughnuts he had eaten lay in an undigested, burning wad in his stomach.

Holly said, "When it comes back—"

"For God's sake," he interrupted, "no more adversarial tactics!"

"I screwed up," she admitted. "But the adversarial approach was the correct one, I just carried it too far. I pushed too hard. When it comes back, I'll modify my technique."

He supposed he had more fully accepted her insanity theory than he was willing to acknowledge. He was now in a cold sweat about what The Friend might do if their behavior tipped it into its other, darker identity. "Why don't we jettison confrontation altogether, play along with it, stroke its ego, keep it as happy as we—"

"That's no good. You can't control madness by indulging it. That only creates more and deeper madness. I suspect any nurse in a mental institution would tell you the best way to deal with a potentially violent paranoid is to be nice, respectful, but *firm.*"

He withdrew his hand from hers because his palms were clammy. He blotted them on his shirt.

The mill seemed unnaturally silent, as if it were in a vacuum where sound could not travel, sealed in an immense bell jar, on display in a museum in a land of giants. At another time Jim might have found the silence disturbing, but now he embraced it because it probably meant The Friend was sleeping or at least preoccupied with concerns other than them.

"It *wants* to do good," he said. "It might be insane, and it might be violent and even evil in its second identity, a regular Dr. Jekyll and Mr. Hyde. But like Dr. Jekyll it really wants to do good. At least we've got that going for us."

She thought about it a moment. "Okay, I'll give you that one. And when it comes back, I'll try to pry some truth out of it."

"What scares me most—is there really anything we can learn from it that could help us? Even if it tells us the whole truth about everything, if it's insane it's going to turn to irrational violence sooner or later."

She nodded. "But we gotta try."

They settled into an uneasy silence.

When he looked at his watch, Jim saw that it was ten minutes past one in the morning. He was not sleepy. He didn't have to worry about drifting off and dreaming and thereby opening a doorway, but he was physically drained. Though he had not done anything but sit in a car and drive, then sit or stand in the high room waiting for revelations, his muscles ached as if he had put in ten hours of heavy manual labor. His face felt slack with weariness, and his eyes were hot and grainy. Extreme stress could be every bit as debilitating as strenuous physical activity.

He found himself wishing The Friend would never return, wishing not in an idle way but with the wholehearted commitment of a young boy wishing that an upcoming visit to the dentist would not transpire. He put every fiber of his being into the wish, as if convinced, the way a kid sometimes could be, that wishes really did now and then come true.

He remembered a quote from Chazal, which he had used when teaching a literature unit on the supernatural fiction of Poe and Hawthorne: *Extreme terror gives us back the gestures of our childhood.* If he ever went back into the classroom, he would be able to teach that unit a hell of a lot better, thanks to what had happened to him in the old windmill.

At 1:25 The Friend disproved the value of wishing by putting in a sudden appearance. This time no bells heralded its approach. Red light blossomed in the wall, like a burst of crimson paint in clear water.

Holly scrambled to her feet.

So did Jim. He could no longer sit relaxed in the presence of this mysterious being, because he was now more than half-convinced that at any moment it might strike at them with merciless brutality.

The light separated into many swarms, surged all the way around the room, then began to change from red to amber.

The Friend spoke without waiting for a question: *"August first. Seattle, Washington. Laura Lenaskian, saved from drowning. She will give birth to a child who will become a great composer and whose music will give solace to many people in times of trouble. August eighth. Peoria, Illinois. Doogie Burkette. He will grow up to be a paramedic in Chicago, where he will do much good and save many lives. August twelfth. Portland, Oregon. Billy Jenkins. He will grow up to be a brilliant medical technologist whose inventions will revolutionize medical care—"*

Jim met Holly's eyes and did not even have to wonder what she was thinking: the same thing he was thinking. The Friend was in its testy, I'll-show-you mode, and it was providing details which it expected would lend credibility to its extravagant claim to be altering human destiny. But it was impossible to know if what it said was true—or merely fantasies that it had worked up to support its story. The important thing, perhaps, was that it seemed to care deeply that they believe it. Jim had no idea why his or Holly's opinion should matter at all to a being as intellectually superior to them as they were to a field mouse, but the fact that it *did* evidently matter seemed to be to their advantage.

"—August twentieth. The Mojave Desert, Nevada. Lisa and Susan Jawolski. Lisa will provide her daughter with the love, affection, and counseling that will make it possible for the girl eventually to overcome the severe psychological trauma of her father's murder and grow up to be the greatest woman statesman in the entire history of the world, a force for enlightenment and compassionate government policies. August twenty-third. Boston, Massachusetts. Nicholas O'Conner, saved from an electrical-vault explosion. He will grow up to become a priest who will dedicate his life to caring for the poor in the slums of India—"

The Friend's attempt to answer Holly's criticism and present a less grandiose version of its work was childishly transparent. The Burkette boy was not going to save the world, just be a damned good paramedic, and Nicholas O'Conner was going to be a humble man leading a self-effacing existence among the needy—but the rest of them were still great or brilliant or staggeringly talented in one way or another. The entity now recognized the need for credibility in its tale of grandeur, but it could not bring itself to significantly water down its professed accomplishments.

And something else was bothering Jim: that voice. The longer he listened to it, the more he became convinced that he had heard it before, not in this room twenty-five years ago, not within its current context at all. The voice had to be appropriated, of course, because in its natural condition the alien almost certainly did not possess anything similar to human vocal cords; its biology would be inhuman. The voice it was imitating, as if it were an impersonator performing in a cosmic cocktail lounge, was that of a person Jim had once known. He could not quite identify it.

"—August twenty-sixth. Dubuque, Iowa. Christine and Casey Dubrovek. Christine will give birth to another child who will grow up to be the greatest geneticist of the next century. Casey will become an exceptional schoolteacher who will tremendously influence the lives of her students, and who will never fail one of them to the extent that a suicide results."

Jim felt as if he had been hit in the chest with a hammer. That insulting accusation, directed at him and referring to Larry Kakonis, shook his remaining faith in The Friend's basic desire to do good.

Holly said, "Shit, that was low."

The entity's pettiness sickened Jim, because he wanted so badly to believe in its stated purpose and goodness.

The scintillant amber light swooped and swirled through the walls, as if The Friend was delighted by the effect of the blow it had struck.

Despair welled so high in Jim that for a moment he even dared to consider that the entity under the pond was not good at all but purely evil. Maybe the people he had saved since May fifteenth were not destined to elevate the human condition but debase it. Maybe Nicholas O'Conner was really going to grow up to be a serial killer. Maybe Billy Jenkins was going to be a bomber pilot who went rogue and found a way to override all the safeguards in the system in order to drop a few nuclear weapons on a major metropolitan area; and maybe instead of being the greatest woman statesman in the history of the world, Susie Jawolski was going to be a radical activist who planted bombs in corporate boardrooms and machine-gunned those with whom she disagreed.

But as he swayed precariously on the rim of that black chasm, Jim saw in memory the face of young Susie Jawolski, which had seemed to be the essence of innocence. He could not believe that she would be anything less than a positive force in the lives of her family and neighbors. He *had* done good works; therefore The Friend had done good works, whether or not it was insane, and even though it had the capacity to be cruel.

Holly addressed the entity within the wall: "We have more questions."

"Ask them, ask them."

Holly glanced at her tablet, and Jim hoped she would remember to be less aggressive. He sensed that The Friend was more unstable than at any previous point during the night.

She said, "Why did you choose Jim to be your instrument?"

"He was convenient."

"You mean because he lived on the farm?"

"Yes."

"Have you ever worked through anyone else the way you've been working through Jim?"

"No."

"Not in all these ten thousand years?"

"Is this a trick question? Do you think you can trick me? Do you still not believe me when I tell you the truth?"

Holly looked at Jim, and he shook his head, meaning that this was no time to be argumentative, that discretion was not only the better part of valor but their best hope of survival.

Then he wondered if this entity could read his mind as well as intrude into it and implant directives. Probably not. If it could do that, it would flare into anger now, incensed that they still thought it insane and were patronizing it.

"I'm sorry," Holly said. "It wasn't a trick question, not at all. We just want to know about you. We're fascinated by you. If we ask questions that you find offensive, please understand that we do so unintentionally, out of ignorance."

The Friend did not reply.

The light pulsed more slowly through the limestone, and

though Jim knew the danger of interpreting alien actions in human terms, he felt that the changed patterns and tempo of the radiance indicated The Friend was in a contemplative mood. It was chewing over what Holly had just said, deciding whether or not she was sincere.

Finally the voice came again, more mellow than it had been in a while: *"Ask your questions."*

Consulting her tablet again, Holly said, "Will you ever release Jim from this work?"

"Does he want to be released?"

Holly looked at Jim inquiringly.

Considering what he had been through in the past few months, Jim was a bit surprised by his answer: "Not if I'm actually doing good."

"You are. How can you doubt it? But regardless of whether you believe my intentions to be good or evil, I would never release you."

The ominous tone of that last statement mitigated the relief Jim felt at the reassurance that he had not saved the lives of future murderers and thieves.

Holly said, "Why have you—"

The Friend interrupted. *"There is one other reason that I chose Jim Ironheart for this work."*

"What's that?" Jim asked.

"You needed it."

"I did?"

"Purpose."

Jim understood. His fear of The Friend was as great as ever, but he was moved by the implication that it had wanted to salvage him. By giving meaning to his broken and empty life, it had redeemed him just as surely as it had saved Billy Jenkins, Susie Jawolski, and all the others, though they had been rescued from more immediate deaths than the death of the soul that had threatened Jim. The Friend's statement seemed to reveal a capacity for pity. And Jim knew he'd deserved pity after the suicide of Larry Kakonis, when he had spiraled into an unreasonable depression. This compassion, even if it was another lie, affected Jim more strongly than he would have expected, and a shimmer of tears came to his eyes.

Holly said, "Why have you waited ten thousand years to decide to use someone like Jim to shape human destinies?"

"I had to study the situation first, collect data, analyze it, and then decide if my intervention was wise."

"It took ten thousand years to make that decision? Why? That's longer than recorded history."

No reply.

She tried the question again.

At last The Friend said, *"I am going now."* Then, as if it did not want them to interpret its recent display of compassion as a sign of weakness, it added: *"If you attempt to leave, you will die."*

"When will you be back?" Holly asked.

"Do not sleep."

"We're going to have to sleep sooner or later," Holly said as the amber light turned red and the room seemed to be washed in blood.

"Do not sleep."

"It's two in the morning," she said.

"Dreams are doorways."

Holly flared up: "We can't stay awake forever, damn it!"

The light in the limestone was snuffed out.

The Friend was gone.

▼ ▲ ▼

Somewhere people laughed. Somewhere music played and dancers danced, and somewhere lovers strained toward ecstasy.

But in the high room of the mill, designed for storage and now stacked to the ceiling with an anticipation of violence, the mood was decidedly grim.

Holly loathed being so helpless. Throughout her life she had been a woman of action, even if the actions she took were usually destructive rather than constructive. When a job turned out to be less satisfying than she had hoped, she never hesitated to resign, move on. When a relationship soured or just proved uninteresting, she was always quick to terminate it. If she had often retreated from problems—from the responsibilities of being a conscientious journalist when she had seen that journalism was as corrupt as anything else, from the prospect of love, from putting down roots and committing to one place—well, at least retreat was a form of action. Now she was denied even that.

The Friend had that one good effect on her. It was not going to let her retreat from *this* problem.

For a while she and Jim discussed the latest visitation and went over the remaining questions on her list, to which they made changes and additions. The most recent portion of her ongoing interview with The Friend had resulted in some interesting and potentially useful information. It was only *potentially* useful, however, because they both still felt that nothing The Friend said could be relied upon to be true.

By 3:15 in the morning, they were too weary to stand and too bottom-sore to continue sitting. They pulled their sleeping bags together and stretched out side by side, on their backs, staring at the domed ceiling.

To help guard against sleep, they left the gas lantern at its brightest setting. As they waited for The Friend to return, they kept talking, not about anything of importance, small talk of every kind, anything to keep their minds occupied. It was difficult to doze off in the middle of a conversation; and if one did slip away, the other would know it by the lack of a response. They also held hands, her right in his left—the logic being that even during a brief pause in the conversation, if one of them started to take a nap, the other would be warned by the sudden relaxation of the sleeper's grip.

Holly did not expect to have difficulty staying awake. In her university days she had pulled all-nighters before exams or when papers were due, and had stayed awake for thirty-six hours without much of a struggle. During her early years as a reporter, when she'd still believed that journalism mattered to her, she had labored away all night on a story, poring over research or listening yet again to interview tapes or sweating over the wording of a paragraph. She had missed nights of sleep in recent years, as well, if only because she was occasionally plagued by insomnia. She was a night owl by nature anyway. Piece of cake.

But though she had not yet been awake twenty-four hours since bolting out of bed in Laguna Niguel yesterday morning, she felt the sandman sliding up against her, whispering his subliminal message of sleep, sleep, sleep. The past few days had been a blur of activity and personal change, both of which could be expected to take a toll of her resources. And some nights she had gotten too little rest, only in part because of the dreams. *Dreams are doorways.* Sleep was dangerous, she had to stay awake. Damn it, she shouldn't need sleep this badly yet, no matter how much stress she had been under lately. She struggled to keep up her end of the conversation with Jim, even though at times she realized that she was not sure what they were talking about and did not fully understand the words that came out of her own mouth. *Dreams are doorways.* It was almost as if she had been drugged, or as if The Friend, after warning them against sleep, was secretly exerting pressure on a narcoleptic button in her brain. *Dreams are doorways.* She fought against the descending oblivion, but she found that she did not possess the strength or will to sit up . . . or to open her eyes. Her eyes were closed. She had not realized that her eyes were closed. *Dreams are doorways.* Panic could not arouse her. She continued to drift deeper under the sandman's spell even as she heard her heart pound harder and faster. She felt her hand loosening its grip on Jim's hand, and she knew he would respond to that warning, would keep her awake, but she felt *his* grip loosening on her hand, and she realized they were succumbing to the sandman simultaneously.

She drifted in darkness.

She felt that she was being watched.

It was both a reassuring and a frightening feeling.

Something was going to happen. She sensed it.

For a while, however, nothing happened. Except darkness.

Then she became aware that she had a mission to perform.

But that couldn't be right. Jim was the one who was sent on missions, not her.

A mission. *Her* mission. She would be sent on a mission of her own. It was vitally important. Her life depended on how well she performed. Jim's life depended on it as well. The whole world's continued existence depended on it.

But the darkness remained.

She just drifted. It felt nice.

She slept and slept.

At some point during the night, she dreamed. As nightmares went, this one was a lulu, all the stops pulled out, but it was nothing like her recent dreams of the mill and The Enemy. It was worse than those because it was painted in excruciating detail and because throughout the experience she was in the grip of anguish and terror so intense that nothing in her experience prepared her for it, not even the crash of Flight 246.

Lying on a tile floor, under a table. On her side. Peering out at floor level. Directly ahead is a chair, tubular metal and orange plastic, under the chair a scattering of golden french fries and a cheeseburger, the meat having slid halfway out of the bun on a skid of ketchup-greased lettuce. Then a woman, an old lady, also lying on the floor, head turned toward Holly. Looking through the tubular legs of the chair, across the fries and disarranged burger, the lady stares at her, a look of surprise, stares and stares, never blinking, and then Holly sees that the lady's eye nearest the floor isn't there anymore, an empty hole, blood leaking out. Oh, lady. Oh, lady, I'm sorry, I'm so sorry. Holly hears a terrible sound, *chuda-chuda-chuda-chuda-chuda-chuda-chuda,* doesn't recognize it, hears people screaming, a lot of people, *chuda-chuda-chuda-chuda,* still screaming but not as much as before, glass shattering, wood breaking, a man shouting like a bear, roaring, very angry and roaring, *chuda-chuda-chuda-chuda-chuda-chuda-chuda-chuda.* She knows now that its gunfire, the heavy rhythmic pounding of an automatic weapon, and she wants to get out of there. So she turns in the opposite direction from which she's been facing because she doesn't want to—can't, just can't!—crawl by the old lady whose eye has been shot out. But behind her is a little girl, about eight, lying on the floor in a pink dress with black patent-leather shoes and white socks, a little girl with white-blond hair, a little girl with, a little girl with, a little girl with patent-leather shoes, a little girl with, a little girl with, a little girl with white socks, a little girl with, a little girl with with with with *with half her face shot off!* A red smile. Broken white teeth in a red, lopsided smile. Sobbing, screaming, and still more *chuda-chuda-chuda-chuda,* it's never going to stop, it's going to go on forever, that terrible sound, *chuda-chuda-chuda.* Then Holly's moving, scrambling on her hands and knees, away from both the old lady and the little girl with half a face. Unavoidably her hands slap-skip-skid-slide through warm french fries, a hot fish sandwich, a puddle of mustard, as she moves, moves, staying under the tables, between the chairs, then she puts her hand down in the icy slush of a spilled Coke, and when she sees the image of Dixie Duck on the large paper cup from which the soda has spilled, she knows where she is, she's in a Dixie Duck Burger Palace, one of her favorite places in the world. Nobody's screaming now, maybe they realize that a Dixie Duck is not a place you should scream, but somebody is sobbing and groaning, and somebody else is saying please-please-please-please over and over again. Holly starts to crawl out from under another table, and she sees a man in a costume standing a few feet from her, turned half away from her, and she thinks maybe this is all just a trick, trick-or-treat, a Halloween performance. But it isn't Halloween. Yet the man is in a *costume,* he's wearing combat boots like G.I. Joe and camouflage pants and a black T-shirt and a beret, like the Green Berets wear, only this one is black, and it must be a costume because he isn't really a soldier, can't be a soldier with that big sloppy belly overhanging his pants, and he hasn't shaved in maybe a week, soldiers have to shave, so he's only wearing soldier stuff. This girl is kneeling on the floor in front of him, one of the teenagers who works at Dixie Duck, the pretty one with the red hair, she winked at Holly when she took her order, now she's kneeling in front of the guy in the soldier costume, with her head bowed like she's praying, except what she's saying is please-please-please-please. The guy is shouting at her about the CIA and mind control and secret spy networks operated out of the Dixie Duck storeroom. Then the guy stops shouting and he looks at the red-haired girl awhile, just looks down at her, and then he says look-at-me, and she says please-please-don't, and he says look-at-me again, so she raises her head and looks at him, and he says what-do-you-think-I-am-stupid? The girl is so scared, she is just so scared, and she says no-please-I-don't-know-anything-about-this, and he says like-shit-you-don't, and he lowers the big gun, he puts the big gun right there in her face, just maybe an inch or two from her face. She says oh-my-god-oh-my-god, and he says you're-one-of-the-rat-people, and Holly is sure the guy will now throw the gun aside and laugh, and everyone playing dead people will get up and laugh, too, and the manager will come out and take bows for the Halloween performance, except it isn't Halloween. Then the guy pulls the trigger, *chuda-chuda-chuda-chuda-chuda,* and the red-haired girl dissolves. Holly eels around and heads back the way she came, moving so fast, trying to get away from him before he sees her, because he's crazy, that's what he is, he's a crazyman. Holly is splashing through the same spilled food and drinks that she splashed through before, past the little girl in the pink dress and right through the girl's blood, praying the crazyman can't hear her scuttling away from him. *CHUDA-CHUDA-CHUDA-CHUDA-CHUDA-CHUDA!* But he must be shooting the other direction, because no bullets are smashing into anything around her, so she keeps going, right across a dead man with his insides coming out, hearing sirens now, sirens wailing outside, the cops'll get this crazyman. Then she hears a crash behind her, a table being overturned, and it sounds so close, she looks back, she sees him, the crazyman, he's coming straight toward her, pushing tables out of his way, kicking aside chairs, he sees her. She clambers over another dead woman and then she's in a corner, on top of a dead man who's slumped in the corner, she's in the lap of the dead man, in the arms of the dead man, and no way to get out of there because the crazyman is coming. The crazyman looks so scary, so bad and scary, that she can't watch him coming, doesn't want to see the gun in her face the way the red-haired girl saw it, so she turns her head away, turns her face to the dead man—

She woke from the dream as she had never awakened from another, not screaming, not even with an unvoiced cry caught in her throat, but gagging. She was curled into a tight ball, hugging herself, dry-heaving, choking not on anything she had eaten but on sheer throat-clogging repulsion.

Jim was turned away from her, lying on his side. His knees were drawn up slightly in a modified fetal position. He was still sound asleep.

When she could get her breath, she sat up. She was not merely shaking, she was rattling. She was convinced she could hear her bones clattering against one another.

She was glad that she had not eaten anything after the doughnuts last evening. They had passed through her stomach hours ago. If she had eaten anything else, she'd be wearing it now.

She hunched forward and put her face in her hands. She sat like that until the rattling quieted to a shudder and the shudder faded to spasms of shivering.

When she raised her face from her hands, the first thing she noticed was daylight at the narrow windows of the high room. It was opalescent gray-pink, a weak glow rather than a sunny-blue glare, but daylight nonetheless. Seeing it, she realized that she had not been convinced she would ever see daylight again.

She looked at her wristwatch. 6:10. Dawn must have broken only a short while ago. She could have been asleep only two to two and a half hours. It had been worse than no sleep at all; she did not feel in the least rested.

The dream. She suspected that The Friend had used its

telepathic power to push her down into sleep against her will. And because of the unusually intense nature of the nightmare, she was convinced it had sent her that gruesome reel of mind-film.

But why?

Jim murmured and stirred, then grew still again, breathing deeply but quietly. His dream must not be the same one she'd had; if it was, he would be writhing and crying out like a man on the rack.

She sat for a while, considering the dream, wondering if she had been shown a prophetic vision. Was The Friend warning her that she was going to wind up in a Dixie Duck Burger Palace scrambling for her life through food and blood, stalked by a raving maniac with an automatic carbine? She had never even heard of Dixie Duck, and she couldn't imagine a more ludicrous place to die.

She was living in a society where the streets were crawling with casualties of the drug wars, some of them so brain-blasted that they might well pick up a gun and go looking for the rat people who were working with the CIA, running spy networks out of burger restaurants. She had worked on newspapers all her adult life. She had seen stories no less tragic, no more strange.

After about fifteen minutes, she couldn't bear to think about the nightmare any more, not for a while. Instead of getting a handle on it through analysis, she became more confused and distressed the longer she dwelt on it. In memory, the images of slaughter did not fade, as was usually the case with a dream, but became more vivid. She didn't need to puzzle it out right now.

Jim was sleeping, and she considered waking him. But he needed his rest as much as she did. There was no sign of The Enemy making use of a dream doorway, no change in the limestone walls or the oak-plank floor, so she let Jim sleep.

As she had looked around the room, studying the walls, she had noticed the yellow tablet lying on the floor under the far window. She had pitched it aside last evening when The Friend had resisted vocalizing its answers and had tried, instead, to present her with responses to all her written questions at once, before she was able to read them aloud. She'd never had a chance to ask it all of the questions on her list, and now she wondered what might be on that answer-tablet.

She eased off her bedding as quietly as possible, rose, and walked carefully across the room. She tested the floorboards as she went to make sure they weren't going to squeak when she put her full weight on them.

As she stooped to pick up the tablet, she heard a sound that froze her. Like a heartbeat with an extra thump in it.

She looked around at the walls, up at the dome. The light from the high-burning lantern and the windows was sufficient to be certain that the limestone was only limestone, the wood only wood.

Lub-dub-DUB, lub-dub-DUB . . .

It was faint, as if someone was tapping the rhythm out on a drum far away, outside the mill, somewhere up in the dry brown hills.

But she knew what it was. No drum. It was the tripartite beat that always preceded the materialization of The Enemy. Just as the bells had, until its final visit, preceded the arrival of The Friend.

As she listened, it faded away.

She strained to hear it.

Gone.

Relieved but still trembling, she picked up the tablet. The pages were rumpled, and they made some noise falling into place.

Jim's steady breathing continued to echo softly around the room, with no change of rhythm or pitch.

Holly read the answers on the first page, then the second. She saw that they were the same responses The Friend had vocalized—although without the spur-of-the-moment questions that she had not written down on the question-tablet. She skimmed down the third and fourth pages, on which it had listed the people Jim had saved—Carmen Diaz, Amanda Cutter, Steven Aimes, Laura Lenaskian—

explaining what great things each of them was destined to achieve.

Lub-dub-DUB, lub-dub-DUB, lub-dub-DUB . . .

She snapped her head up.

The sound was still distant, no louder than before.

Jim groaned in his sleep.

Holly took a step away from the window, intending to wake him, but the dreaded sound faded away again. Evidently The Enemy was in the neighborhood, but it had not found a doorway in Jim's dream. He *had* to get his sleep, he couldn't function without it. She decided to let him alone.

Easing back to the window again, Holly held the answer-tablet up to the light. She turned to the fifth page—and felt the flesh on the nape of her neck go as cold and nubbly as frozen turkey skin.

Peeling the pages back with great delicacy, so as not to rustle them more than absolutely necessary, she checked the sixth page, the seventh, the eighth. They were all the same. Messages were printed on them in the wavery hand that The Friend had used when pulling its little words-rising-as-if-through-water trick. But they were not answers to her questions. They were two alternating statements, unpunctuated, each repeated three times per page:

HE LOVES YOU HOLLY
HE WILL KILL YOU HOLLY
HE LOVES YOU HOLLY
HE WILL KILL YOU HOLLY
HE LOVES YOU HOLLY
HE WILL KILL YOU HOLLY

Staring at those obsessively repeated statements, she knew that "he" could be no one but Jim. She focused only on the five hateful words, trying to understand.

And suddenly she thought that she did. The Friend was warning her that in its madness it would act against her, perhaps because it hated her for bringing Jim to the mill, for making him seek answers, and for being a distraction from his mission. If The Friend, which was the sane half of the alien consciousness, could reach into Jim's mind and compel him to undertake life-saving missions, was it possible that The Enemy, the dark half, could reach into his mind and compel him to kill? Instead of the insane personality materializing in monstrous form as it had done for an instant at the motel Friday night and as it attempted to do in Jim's bedroom yesterday, might it choose to use Jim against her, take command of him to a greater extent than The Friend had ever done, and turn him into a killing machine? That might perversely delight the mad-child aspect of the entity.

She shook herself as if casting off a pestering wasp.

No. It was impossible. All right, Jim could kill in the defense of innocent people. But he was incapable of killing someone innocent. No alien consciousness, no matter how powerful, could override his true nature. In his heart he was good and kind and caring. His love for her could not be subverted by this alien force, no matter how strong it was.

But how did she know that? She was engaging in wishful thinking. For all she knew, The Enemy's powers of mental control were so awesome that it could reach into her brain right now and tell her to drown herself in the pond, and she would do as told.

She remembered Norman Rink. The Atlanta convenience store. Jim had pumped eight rounds from a shotgun into the guy, blasting at him again and again, long after he was dead.

Lub-dub-DUB, lub-dub-DUB . . .

Still far away.

Jim groaned softly.

She moved away from the window again, intent on waking him, and almost called out his name, before she realized that The Enemy might be in him already. Dreams are doorways. She didn't have a clue as to what The Friend meant by that, or if it was anything more than stage dressing like the bells. But maybe what it had meant was that The Enemy could enter the dreamer's dream and thus the dreamer's mind. Maybe this time The Enemy did not intend to materialize from the wall but from Jim, in the person of Jim, in total control of Jim, just for a murderous little lark.

Lub-dub-DUB, lub-dub-DUB, lub-dub-DUB . . .

A little louder, a little closer?

Holly felt that she was losing her mind. Paranoid, schizoid, flat-out crazy. No better than The Friend and his other half. She was frantically trying to understand a totally alien consciousness, and the more she pondered the possibilities, the stranger and more varied the possibilities became. In an infinite universe, anything can happen, any nightmare can be made flesh. In an infinite universe, life was therefore essentially the same as a dream. Contemplation of *that*, under the stress of a life-or-death situation, was guaranteed to drive you bugshit.

Lub-dub-DUB, lub-dub-DUB . . .

She could not move.

She could only wait.

The tripartite beat faded again.

Letting her breath out in a rush, she backed up against the wall beside the window, less afraid of the limestone now than she was of Jim Ironheart. She wondered if it was all right to wake him when the three-note heartbeat was not audible. Maybe The Enemy was only in his dream—and therefore in him—when that triple thud could be heard.

Afraid to act and afraid not to act, she glanced down at the tablet in her hand. Some of the pages had fallen shut, and she was no longer looking at the HE LOVES YOU HOLLY/HE WILL KILL YOU HOLLY litany. Before her eyes, instead, was the list of people who had been saved by Jim, along with The Friend's grandiose explanations of their importance.

She saw "Steven Aimes" and realized at once that he was the only one on the list whose fate The Friend had not vocalized during one or another of their conversations last night. She remembered him because he was the only older person on the list, fifty-seven. She read the words under his name, and the chill that had touched her nape earlier was nothing compared to the spike of ice that drove through it now and pierced her spine.

Steven Aimes had not been saved because he would father a child who would be a great diplomat or a great artist or a great healer. He had not been saved because he would make an enduring contribution to the welfare of mankind. The reason for his salvation was expressed in just eleven words, the most horrifying eleven words that Holly had ever read or hoped to read: BECAUSE HE LOOKS LIKE MY FATHER WHOM I FAILED TO SAVE. Not "like *Jim's* father" which The Friend would have said. Not "whom *he* failed to save," as the alien would surely have put it. MY FATHER. I FAILED. MY. I.

The infinite universe just kept expanding, and now an entirely new possibility presented itself to her, revealed in the telling words about Steven Aimes. No starship rested under the pond. No alien had been in hiding on the farm for ten thousand years, ten years, or ten days. The Friend and The Enemy were real enough: they were thirds, not halves, of the same personality, three in one entity, an entity with enormous and wonderful and terrifying powers, an entity both godlike and yet as human as Holly was. Jim Ironheart. Who had been shattered by tragedy when he was ten years old. Who had painstakingly put himself together again with the help of a complex fantasy about star-traveling gods. Who was as insane and dangerous as he was sane and loving.

She did not understand where he had gotten the power that he so obviously possessed, or why he was not aware whatsoever that the power was within him rather than coming from some imaginary alien presence. The realization that he was everything, that the end and beginning of this mystery lay solely in him and not beneath the pond, raised more questions than it answered. She didn't understand how such a thing could be true, but she knew it was, at last, the truth. Later, if she survived, she might have the time to seek a better understanding.

Lub-dub-DUB, lub-dub-DUB . . .

Closer but not close.

Holly held her breath, waiting for the sound to get louder.

Lub-dub-DUB, lub-dub-DUB . . .

Jim shifted in his sleep. He snorted softly and smacked his lips, just like any ordinary dreamer.

But he was three personalities in one, and at least two of them possessed incredible power, and at least one of them was deadly. And it was coming.

Lub-dub-DUB . . .

Holly pressed back against the limestone. Her heart was pounding so hard that it seemed to have hammered her throat half shut; she had trouble swallowing.

The tripartite beat faded.

Silence.

She moved along the curved wall. Easy little steps. Sideways. Toward the timbered, ironbound door. She eased away from the wall just far enough to reach out and snare her purse by its straps.

The closer she got to the head of the stairs, the more certain she became that the door was going to slam shut before she reached it, that Jim was going to sit up and turn to her. His blue eyes would not be beautiful but cold, as she had twice glimpsed them, filled with rage but cold.

She reached the door, eased through it backward onto the first step, not wanting to take her eyes off Jim. But if she tried to back down those narrow stairs without a handrail, she would fall, break an arm or leg. So she turned away from the high room and hurried toward the bottom as quickly as she dared, as quietly as she could.

Though the velvety-gray morning light outlined the windows, the lower chamber was treacherously dark. She had no flashlight, only the extra edge of an adrenaline rush. Unable to remember if any rubble was stacked along the wall that might set up a clatter when she knocked it over, she moved slowly along that limestone curve, her back to it, edging sideways again. The antechamber archway was somewhere ahead on her right. When she looked to her left, she could barely see the foot of the stairs down which she had just descended.

Feeling the wall ahead of her with her right hand, she discovered the corner. She stepped through the archway and into the antechamber. Though that space had been blind-dark last night, it was dimly lit now by the pale post-dawn glow that lay beyond the open outside door.

The morning was overcast. Pleasantly cool for August. The pond was still and gray.

Morning insects issued a thin, almost inaudible background buzz, like faint static on a radio with the volume turned nearly off.

She hurried to the Ford and stealthily opened the door.

Another panic hit her as she thought of the keys. Then she felt them in a pocket of her jeans, where she had slipped them last night after using the bathroom at the farmhouse. One key for the farmhouse, one key for his house in Laguna Niguel, two keys for the car, all on a simple brass-bead chain.

She threw the purse and tablet into the back seat and got behind the wheel, but didn't close the door for fear the sound would wake him. She was not home free yet. He might burst out of the windmill, The Enemy in charge of him, leap across the short expanse of gravel, and drag her from the car.

Her hands shook as she fumbled with the keys. She had trouble inserting the right one in the ignition. But then she got it in, twisted it, put her foot on the accelerator, and almost sobbed with relief when the engine turned over with a roar.

She yanked the door shut, threw the Ford in reverse, and backed along the gravel path that circled the pond. The wheels spun up a hail of gravel, which rattled against the back of the car as she reversed into it.

When she reached the area between the barn and the house, where she could turn around and head out of the driveway front-first, she jammed on the brakes instead. She stared at the windmill, which was now on the far side of the water.

She had nowhere to run. Wherever she went, he would find her. He could see the future, at least to some extent, if not as vividly or in as much detail as The Friend had claimed. He could transform drywall into a monstrous living organism, change limestone into a transparent substance filled with whirling light, project a beast of hideous design into her dreams and into the doorway of her motel, track her, find her, trap her. He had drawn her into his mad fantasy and most likely still wanted her to play out her role in it. The Friend in Jim—and Jim himself—might let her go. But the third personality—the murderous part of him, The Enemy—would want her blood. Maybe she would be fortunate, and maybe the two benign thirds of him would prevent the other third from taking control and coming after her. But she doubted it. Besides, she could not spend the rest of her life waiting for a wall to bulge outward unexpectedly, form into a mouth, and bite her hand off.

And there was one other problem.

She could not abandon him. He needed her.

Part Three

THE ENEMY

From childhood's hour
I have not been
As others were—
I have not seen
As others saw.

—*Alone,* EDGAR ALLAN POE

▲

Vibrations in a wire.
Ice crystals
in a beating heart.
Cold fire.

A mind's frigidity:
frozen steel,
dark rage, morbidity.
Cold fire.

Defense against
a cruel life
death and strife:
Cold fire.

—THE BOOK OF COUNTED SORROWS

THE REST OF AUGUST 29

1

Holly sat in the Ford, staring at the old windmill, scared and exhilarated. The exhilaration surprised her. Maybe she felt upbeat because for the first time in her life she had found something to which she was willing to commit herself. Not a casual commitment, either. Not an until-I-get-bored commitment. She was willing to put her life on the line for this, for Jim and what he could become if he could be healed, for what they could become together.

Even if he had told her she could go, and even if she had felt that his release of her was sincere, she would not have abandoned him. He was her salvation. And she was his.

The mill stood sentinel against the ashen sky. Jim had not appeared at the door. Perhaps he had not yet awakened.

There were still many mysteries within this mystery, but so much was painfully obvious now. He sometimes failed to save people—like Susie Jawolski's father—because he was not really operating on behalf of an infallible god or a prescient alien; he was acting on his own phenomenal but imperfect visions; he was just a man, special but only a man, and even the best of men had limits. He evidently felt that he had failed his parents somehow. Their deaths weighed heavily on his conscience, and he was trying to redeem himself by saving the lives of others: HE LOOKED LIKE MY FATHER, WHOM I FAILED TO SAVE.

It was now obvious, as well, why The Enemy broke through only when Jim was asleep: he was terrified of that dark aspect of himself, that embodiment of his rage, and he strenuously repressed it when he was awake. At his place in Laguna, The Enemy had materialized in the bedroom while Jim was sleeping and actually had been sustained for a while after Jim had awakened, but when it had crashed through the bathroom ceiling, it had simply evaporated like the lingering dream it was. Dreams are doorways, The Friend had warned, which had been a warning from Jim himself. Dreams were doorways, yes, but not for evil, mind-invading alien monsters; dreams were doorways to the subconscious, and what came out of them was all too human.

She had other pieces of the puzzle, too. She just didn't know how they fit together.

Holly was angry with herself for not having asked the correct questions on Monday, when Jim had finally opened his patio door and let her into his life. He'd insisted that he was only an instrument, that he had no powers of his own. She'd bought it too quickly. She should have probed harder, asked tougher questions. She was as guilty of amateurish interviewing technique as Jim had been when The Friend had first appeared to them.

She had been annoyed by his willingness to accept what The Friend said at face value. Now she understood that he had created The Friend for the same reason that other victims of multiple-personality syndrome generated splinter personalities: to cope in a world that confused and frightened them. Alone and afraid at the age of ten, he had taken refuge in fantasy. He created The Friend, a magical being, as a source of solace and hope. When Holly pressed The Friend to explain itself logically, Jim resisted her because her probing threatened a fantasy which he desperately needed to sustain himself.

For similar reasons of her own, she had not questioned him as toughly as she should have on Monday evening. *He* was *her* sustaining dream. He had come into her life like a heroic figure in a dream, saving Billy Jenkins with dreamlike grace and panache. Until she had seen him, she had not realized how much she needed someone like him. And instead of probing deeply at him as any good reporter would have done, she had let him be what he wanted to pretend to be, for she had been reluctant to lose him.

Now their only hope was to press hard for the whole truth. He could not be healed until they understood why this particular and bizarre fantasy of his had evolved and how in the name of God he had developed the superhuman powers to support it.

She sat with her hands on the steering wheel, prepared to act but with no idea what to do. There seemed to be no one to whom she could turn for help. She needed answers that were to be found only in the past or in Jim's subconscious mind, two terrains that at the moment were equally inaccessible.

Then, hit by a thunderbolt of insight, she realized Jim already had given her a set of keys to unlock his remaining mysteries. When they had driven into New Svenborg, he had taken her on a tour of the town which, at the time, seemed like a tactic to delay their arrival at the farm. But she realized now that the tour had contained the most important revelations he had made to her. Each nostalgic landmark was a key to the past and to the remaining mysteries that, once unlocked, would make it possible for her to help him.

He wanted help. A part of him understood that he was sick, trapped in a schizophrenic fantasy, and he wanted out. She just hoped that he would suppress The Enemy until they had time to learn what they needed to know. That darkest splinter of his mind did not want her to succeed; her success would be its death, and to save itself, it would destroy her if it got the chance.

If she and Jim were to have a life together, or any life at all, their future lay in the past, and the past lay in New Svenborg.

She swung the wheel hard right, began to turn around to head out of the driveway to the county road—then stopped. She looked at the windmill again.

Jim had to be part of his own cure. She could not track down the truth and *make* him believe it. He had to see it himself.

She loved him.

She was afraid of him.

She couldn't do anything about the love; that was just part of her now, like blood or bone or sinew. But almost any fear could be overcome by confronting the cause of it.

Wondering at her own courage, she drove back along the graveled path to the foot of the windmill. She pumped three long blasts from the horn, then three more, waited a few seconds and hit it again, again.

Jim appeared in the doorway. He came out into the gray morning light, squinting at her.

Holly opened her door and stepped out of the car. "You awake?"

"Do I look like I'm sleepwalking?" he asked as he approached her. "What's going on?"

"I want to be damn sure you're awake, *fully* awake."

He stopped a few feet away. "Why don't we open the hood, I'll put my head under it, then you can let out maybe a two-minute blast, just to be sure. Holly, what's going on?"

"We have to talk. Get in."

Frowning, he went around to the passenger's side and got into the Ford with her.

When he settled into the passenger's seat, he said, "This isn't going to be pleasant, is it?"

"No. Not especially."

In front of them, the sails of the windmill stuttered. They began to turn slowly, with much clattering and creaking, shedding chunks and splinters of rotten vanes.

"Stop it," she said to Jim, afraid that the turning sails were only a prelude to a manifestation of The Enemy. "I know you don't want to hear what I have to say, but don't try to distract me, don't try to stop me."

He did not respond. He stared with fascination at the mill, as if he had not heard her.

The speed of the sails increased.

"Jim, damn it!"

At last he looked at her, genuinely baffled by the anger underlying her fear. "What?"

Around, around, around-around-around, around-aroundaround. It turned like a haunted Ferris wheel in a carnival of the damned.

"Shit!" she said, her fear accelerating with the pace of the windmill sails. She put the car in reverse, looked over her shoulder, and backed at high speed around the pond.

"Where are we going?" he asked.

"Not far."

Since the windmill lay at the center of Jim's delusion, Holly thought it was a good idea to put it out of sight while they talked. She swung the car around, drove to the end of the driveway, and parked facing out toward the county road.

She cranked down her window, and he followed suit.

Switching off the engine, she turned more directly toward him. In spite of everything she now knew—or suspected—about him, she wanted to touch his face, smooth his hair, hold him. He elicited a mothering urge from her of which she hadn't even known she'd been capable—just as he engendered in her an erotic response and passion that were beyond anything she had experienced before.

Yeah, she thought, and evidently he engenders in you a suicidal tendency. Jesus, Thorne, the guy as much as said he'll kill you!

But he also had said he loved her.

Why wasn't *anything* easy?

She said, "Before I get into it . . . I want you to understand that I love you, Jim." It was the dumbest line in the world. It sounded so insincere. Words were inadequate to describe the real thing, partly because the feeling ran deeper than she had ever imagined it would, and partly because it was not a single emotion but was mixed up with other things like anxiety and hope. She said it again anyway: "I really do love you."

He reached for her hand, smiling at her with obvious pleasure. "You're wonderful, Holly."

Which was not exactly I-love-you-too-Holly, but that was okay. She didn't harbor romance-novel expectations. It was not going to be that simple. Being in love with Jim Ironheart was like being in love simultaneously with the tortured Max de Winter from *Rebecca,* Superman, and Jack Nicholson in any role he'd ever played. Though it wasn't easy, it wasn't dull either.

"The thing is, when I was paying my motel bill yesterday morning and you were sitting in the car watching me, I realized you hadn't said you loved me. I was going off with you, putting myself in your hands, and you hadn't said the words. But then I realized I hadn't said them either, I was playing it just as cool, holding back and protecting myself. Well, I'm not holding back any more, I'm walking out on that highwire with no net below—and largely because you told me you loved me last night. So you better have meant it."

A quizzical expression overtook him.

She said, "I know you don't remember saying it, but you did. You have problems with the 'L' word. Maybe because you lost your folks when you were so young, you're afraid to get close to anyone for fear of losing them, too. Instant analysis. Holly Freud. Anyway, you did tell me you loved me, and I'll prove it in a little while, but right now, before I get into this mess, I want you to know I never imagined I could feel about anyone the way I feel about you. So if whatever I say to you in the next few minutes is hard to take, even *impossible* to take, just know where it comes from, only from love, from nothing else."

He stared at her. "Yeah, all right. But Holly, this—"

"You'll get your turn." She leaned across the seat, kissed him, then pulled back. "Right now, you've got to listen."

She told him everything she had theorized, why she had crept out of the mill while he'd been asleep—and why she had returned. He listened with growing disbelief, and she repeatedly cut off his protests by lightly squeezing his hand, putting a hand to his lips, or giving him a quick kiss. The answer-tablet, which she produced from the back seat, stunned him and rendered his objections less vehement.

BECAUSE HE LOOKS LIKE MY FATHER WHOM I FAILED TO SAVE. His hands shook as he held the tablet and stared at that incredible line. He turned back to the other surprising messages, repeated page after page—HE LOVES YOU HOLLY/HE WILL KILL YOU HOLLY—and the tremors in his hands became even more severe.

"I would never harm you," he said shakily, staring down at the tablet. "Never."

"I know you'd never want to."

Dr. Jekyll had never wanted to be the murderous Mr. Hyde.

"But you think I sent you this, not The Friend."

"I know you did, Jim. It feels right."

"So if The Friend sent it but the The Friend is me, a part of me, then you believe it really says 'I love you Holly.' "

"Yes," she said softly.

He looked up from the tablet, met her eyes. "If you believe the I-love-you part, why don't you believe the I-will-kill-you part?"

"Well, that's the thing. I do believe a small, dark part of you wants to kill me, yes."

He flinched as if she had struck him.

She said, "The Enemy wants me dead, it wants me dead real bad, because I've made you face up to what's behind these recent events, brought you back here, forced you to confront the source of your fantasy."

He started to shake his head in denial.

But she went on: "Which is what you *wanted* me to do. It's why you drew me to you in the first place."

"No. I didn't—"

"Yes, you did." Pushing him toward enlightenment was extremely dangerous. But that was her only hope of saving him. "Jim, if you can just understand what's happened, accept the existence of two other personalities, even the possibility of their existence, maybe that'll be the beginning of the end of The Friend and The Enemy."

Still shaking his head, he said, "The Enemy won't go peacefully," and immediately blinked in surprise at the words he had spoken and the implication that they conveyed.

"Damn," Holly said, and a thrill coursed through her, not merely because he had just confirmed her entire theory, whether he could admit it or not, but because the five words he had spoken were proof that he wanted out of the Byzantine fantasy in which he had taken refuge.

He was as pale as a man who had just been told that a cancer was growing in him. In fact a malignancy *did* reside within him, but it was mental rather than physical.

A breeze wafted through the open car windows, and it seemed to wash new hope into Holly.

That buoyant feeling was short-lived, however, because new words suddenly appeared on the tablet in Jim's hands: YOU DIE.

"This isn't me," he told her earnestly, in spite of the subtle admission he had made a moment ago. "Holly, this can't be me."

On the tablet, more words appeared: I AM COMING. YOU DIE.

Holly felt as if the world had become a carnival funhouse, full of ghouls and ghosts. Every turn, any moment, without warning, something might spring at her from out of a shadow—or from broad daylight, for that matter. But unlike a carnival monster, this one would inflict real pain, draw blood, kill her if it could.

In hopes that The Enemy, like The Friend, would respond well to firmness, Holly grabbed the tablet from Jim's hand and threw it out the window. "To hell with that. I won't read that crap. Listen to me, Jim. If I'm right, The Enemy is the embodiment of your rage over the deaths of your parents. Your fury was so great, at ten, it terrified you, so you pushed it outside yourself, into this other identity. But you're a unique victim of multiple-personality syndrome because your power allows you to create physical existences for your other identities."

Though acceptance had a toehold in him, he was still struggling to deny the truth. "What're we saying here?

That I'm insane, that I'm some sort of socially functional lunatic, for Christ's sake?"

"Not insane," she said quickly. "Let's say disturbed, troubled. You're locked in a psychological box that you built for yourself, and you want out, but you can't find the key to the lock."

He shook his head. Fine beads of sweat had broken out along his hairline, and he was into whiter shades of pale. "No, that's putting too good a face on it. If what you think is true, then I'm all the way off the deep end, Holly, I should be in some damned rubber room, pumped full of Thorazine."

She took both of his hands again, held them tight. "No. Stop that. You can find your way out of this, you can do it, you can make yourself whole again, I know you can."

"How can you know? Jesus, Holly, I—"

"Because you're not an ordinary man, you're special," she said sharply. "You have this power, this incredible force inside you, and you can do such good with it if you want. The power is something you can draw on that ordinary people don't have, it can be a *healing* power. Don't you see? If you can cause ringing bells and alien heartbeats and voices to come out of thin air, if you can turn walls into flesh, project images into my dreams, see into the future to save lives, then you can make yourself whole and right again."

Determined disbelief lined his face. "How could any man have the power you're talking about?"

"I don't know, but you've got it."

"It has to come from a higher being. For God's sake, I'm not Superman."

Holly pounded a fist against the horn ring and said, "You're telepathic, telekinetic, tele-fucking-everything! All right, you can't fly, you don't have X-ray vision, you can't bend steel with your bare hands, and you can't race faster than a speeding bullet. But you're as close to Superman as any man's likely to get. In fact, in some ways you've got him beat because you can see into the future. Maybe you see only bits and pieces of it, and only random visions when you aren't trying for them, but you *can* see the future."

He was shaken by her conviction. "So where'd I get all this magic?"

"I don't know."

"That's where it falls apart."

"It doesn't fall apart just because I don't know," she said frustratedly. "Yellow doesn't stop being yellow just because I don't know anything about why the eye sees different colors. You *have* the power. You *are* the power, not God or some alien under the millpond."

He pulled his hands from hers and looked out the windshield toward the county road and the dry fields beyond. He seemed afraid to face up to the tremendous power he possessed—maybe because it carried with it responsibilities that he was not sure he could shoulder.

She sensed that he was also shamed by the prospect of his own mental illness, and unable to meet her eyes any longer. He was so stoic, so strong, so proud of his strength that he could not accept this suggested weakness in himself. He had built a life that placed a high value on self-control and self-reliance, that made a singular virtue out of self-imposed solitude, in the manner of a monk who needed no one but himself and God. Now she was telling him that his decision to become an iron man and a loner was not a well-considered choice, that it was a desperate attempt to deal with emotional turmoil that had threatened to destroy him, and that his need for self-control had carried him over the line of rational behavior.

She thought of the words on the tablet: I AM COMING. YOU DIE.

She switched on the engine.

He said, "Where are we going?"

As she put the car in gear, pulled out onto the county road, and turned right toward New Svenborg, she did not answer him. Instead, "Was there anything special about you as a boy?"

"No," he said a little too quickly, too sharply.

"Never any indication that you were gifted or—"

"No, hell, nothing like that."

Jim's sudden nervous agitation, betrayed by his restless movement and his trembling hands, convinced Holly that she had touched on a truth. He *had* been special in some way, a gifted child. Now that she had reminded him of it, he saw in that early gift the seeds of the powers that had grown in him. But he didn't want to face it. Denial was his shield.

"What have you just remembered?"

"Nothing."

"Come on, Jim."

"Nothing, really."

She didn't know where to go with that line of questioning, so she could only say, "It's true. You're gifted. No aliens, only you."

Because of whatever he had just remembered and was not willing to share with her, his adamancy had begun to dissolve. "I don't know."

"It's true."

"Maybe."

"It's true. Remember last night when The Friend told us it was a child by the standards of its species? Well, that's because it *is* a child, a perpetual child, forever the age at which you created it—ten years old. Which explains its childlike behavior, its need to brag, its poutiness. Jim, The Friend didn't behave like a ten-thousand-year-old alien child, it just behaved like a ten-year-old human being."

He closed his eyes and leaned back, as if it was exhausting to consider what she was telling him. But his inner tension remained at a peak, revealed by his hands, which were fisted in his lap.

"Where are we going, Holly?"

"For a little ride." As they passed through the golden fields and hills, she kept up a gentle attack: "That's why the manifestation of The Enemy is like a combination of every movie monster that ever frightened a ten-year-old boy. The thing I caught a glimpse of in my motel-room doorway wasn't a *real* creature, I see that now. It didn't have a biological structure that made sense, it wasn't even alien. It was too familiar, a ten-year-old boy's hodgepodge of boogeymen."

He did not respond.

She glanced at him. "Jim?"

His eyes were still closed.

Her heart began to pound. "Jim!"

At the note of alarm in her voice, he sat up straighter and opened his eyes. "What?"

"For God's sake, don't close your eyes that long. You might've been asleep, and I wouldn't have realized it until—"

"You think I can sleep with *this* on my mind?"

"I don't know. I don't want to take the chance. Keep your eyes open, okay? You obviously suppress The Enemy when you're awake, it only comes through all the way when you're asleep."

In the windshield glass, like a computer readout in a fighter-plane cockpit, words began to appear from left to right, in letters about one inch high: DEAD DEAD DEAD DEAD DEAD DEAD.

Scared but unwilling to show it, she said, "To hell with that," and switched on the windshield wipers, as if the threat was dirt that could be scrubbed away. But the words remained, and Jim stared at them with evident dread.

As they passed a small ranch, the scent of new-mown hay entered with the wind through the windows.

"Where are we going?" he asked again.

"Exploring."

"Exploring what?"

"The past."

Distressed, he said, "I haven't bought this scenario yet. I can't. How the hell can I? And how can we ever prove it's true or isn't?"

"We go to town," she said. "We take that tour again, the one you took me on yesterday. Svenborg—port of mystery and romance. What a dump. But it's got *something*. You wanted me to see those places, your subconscious was telling me answers can be found in Svenborg. So let's go find them together."

New words appeared under the first six: DEAD DEAD DEAD DEAD DEAD DEAD.

Holly knew that time was running out. The Enemy wanted through, wanted to gut her, dismember her, leave her in a steaming heap of her own entrails before she had a chance to convince Jim of her theory—and it did not want to wait until Jim was asleep. She was not certain that he could repress that dark aspect of himself as she pushed him closer to a confrontation with the truth. His self-control might crack, and his benign personalities might sink under the rising dark force.

"Holly, if I had this bizarre multiple personality, wouldn't I be cured as soon as you explained it to me, wouldn't the scales immediately fall off my eyes?"

"No. You have to *believe* it before you can hope to deal with it. Believing that you suffer an abnormal mental condition is the first step toward an understanding of it, and understanding is only the first painful step toward a cure."

"Don't talk at me like a psychiatrist, you're no psychiatrist."

He was taking refuge in anger, in that arctic glare, trying to intimidate her as he had tried on previous occasions when he'd not wanted her to get any closer. Hadn't worked then, wouldn't work now. Sometimes men could be so dense.

She said, "I interviewed a psychiatrist once."

"Oh, terrific, that makes you a qualified therapist."

"Maybe it does. The psychiatrist I interviewed was crazy as a loon himself, so what does a university degree matter?"

He took a deep breath and let it out with a shudder. "Okay, suppose you're right and somehow we do turn up undeniable proof that *I'm* crazy as a loon—"

"You aren't crazy, you're—"

"Yeah, yeah, I'm disturbed, troubled, in a psychological box. Call it whatever you want. If we find proof somehow—and I can't imagine how—then what happens to me? Maybe I just smile and say, 'Oh, yes, of course, I made it all up, I was living in a delusion, I'm ever so much better now, let's have lunch.' But I don't think so. I think what happens is . . . I blow apart, into a million pieces."

"I can't promise you that the truth, if we find it, will be any sort of salvation, because so far I think you've found your salvation in fantasy not in truth. But we can't go on like this because The Enemy resents me, and sooner or later it'll kill me. You warned me yourself."

He looked at the words on the windshield, and said nothing. He was running out of arguments, if not resistance.

The words quickly faded, then vanished.

Maybe that was a good sign, an indication of his subconscious accommodation to her theory. Or maybe The Enemy had decided that she could not be intimidated with threats—and was struggling to burst through and savage her.

She said, "When it's killed me, you'll realize it *is* part of you. And if you love me, like you told me you did through The Friend last night, then what's that going to do to you? Isn't that going to destroy the Jim I love? Isn't that going to leave you with just one personality—the dark one, The Enemy? I think it's a damned good bet. So we're talking your survival here as well as mine. If you want to have a future, then let's dig to the bottom of this."

"Maybe we dig and dig—but there is no bottom. Then what?"

"Then we dig a little deeper."

▼ ▲ ▼

As they were entering town, making the abrupt transition from dead-brown land to tightly grouped pioneer settlement, Holly suddenly said aloud: "Robert Vaughn."

Jim twitched with surprise, not because she had said something mystifying but because that name made an immediate connection for him.

"My God," he said, "that was the voice."

"The voice of The Friend," she said, glancing at him. "So you realized it was familiar, too."

Robert Vaughn, the wonderful actor, had been the hero

of television's *The Man from U.N.C.L.E.* and exquisitely oily villain of countless films. He possessed one of those voices with such a rich timbre and range that it could be as threatening, or as fatherly and reassuring, as he chose to make it.

"Robert Vaughn," Holly said. "But why? Why not Orson Welles or Paul Newman or Sean Connery or Fred Flintstone? It's too quirky a choice not to be meaningful."

"I don't know," Jim said thoughtfully, but he had the unnerving feeling he *should* know. The explanation was within his grasp.

Holly said, "Do you still think it's an alien? Wouldn't an alien just manufacture a nondescript voice? Why would it imitate any one particular actor?"

"I saw Robert Vaughn once," Jim said, surprised by a dim memory stirring within him. "I mean, not on TV or in the movies, but for real, up close. A long time ago."

"Where, when?"

"I can't . . . it won't . . . won't come to me."

Jim felt as if he were standing on a narrow spine of land between two precipices, with safety to neither side. On the one hand was the life he had been living, filled with torment and despair that he had tried to deny but that had over-whelmed him at times, as when he had taken his spiritual journey on the Harley into the Mojave Desert, looking for a way out even if the way was death. On the other hand lay an uncertain future that Holly was trying to paint in for him, a future that she insisted was one of hope but which looked to him like chaos and madness. And the narrow spine on which he stood was crumbling by the minute.

He remembered an exchange they'd had as they lay side by side in his bed two nights ago, before they had made love for the first time. He'd said, *People are always more . . . complex than you figure.*

Is that just an observation . . . or a warning?

Warning?

Maybe you're warning me that you're not what you seem to be.

After a long pause, he had said, *Maybe.*

And after her own long pause, she had said, *I guess I don't care.*

He was sure, now, that he had been warning her. A small voice within told him that she was right in her analysis, that the entities at the mill had only been different aspects of him. But if he was a victim of multiple-personality syndrome, he did not believe that his condition could be casually described as a mere mental disturbance or a troubled state of mind, as she had tried to portray it. Madness was the only word that did it justice.

They entered Main Street. The town looked strangely dark and threatening—perhaps because it held the truth that would force him to step off his narrow mental perch into one world of chaos or another.

He remembered reading somewhere that only mad people were dead-certain of their sanity. He was dead-certain of nothing, but he took no comfort from that. Madness was, he suspected, the very essence of uncertainty, a frantic but fruitless search for answers, for solid ground. Sanity was that place of certainty above the whirling chaos.

Holly pulled to the curb in front of Handahl's Pharmacy at the east end of Main Street. "Let's start here."

"Why?"

"Because it's the first stop we made when you were pointing out places that had meant something to you as a kid."

He stepped out of the Ford under the canopy of a Wilson magnolia, one of several interspersed with other trees along both sides of the street. That landscaping softened the hard edges but contributed to the unnatural look and discordant feeling of the town.

When Holly pushed open the front door of the Danish-style building, its glass panes glimmered like jewels along their beveled edges, and a bell tinkled overhead. They went inside together.

Jim's heart was hammering. Not because the pharmacy seemed likely to be a place where anything significant had happened to him in his childhood, but because he sensed it was the first stone on a path to the truth.

The cafe and soda fountain were to the left, and through the archway Jim saw a few people at breakfast. Immediately inside the door was the small newsstand, where morning papers were stacked high, mostly the Santa Barbara daily; there were also magazines, and to one side a revolving wire rack filled with paperback books.

"I used to buy paperbacks here," he said. "I loved books even back then, couldn't get enough of them."

The pharmacy was through another archway to the right. It resembled any modern American pharmacy in that it stocked more cosmetics, beauty aids, and hair-care products than patent medicines. Otherwise, it was pleasantly quaint: wood shelves instead of metal or fiberboard; polished-granite counters; an appealing aroma composed of bayberry candles, nickel candy, cigar-tobacco effluvium filtering from the humidified case behind the cash register, faint traces of ethyl alcohol, and sundry pharmaceuticals.

Though the hour was early, the pharmacist was on duty, serving as his own checkout clerk. It was Corbett Handahl himself, a heavy wide-shouldered man with a white mustache and white hair, wearing a crisp blue shirt under his starched white lab jacket.

He looked up and said, "Jim Ironheart, bless my soul. How long's it been—at least three, four years?"

They shook hands.

"Four years and four months," Jim said. He almost added, *since grandpa died,* but checked himself without quite knowing why.

Spritzing the granite prescription-service counter with Windex, Corbett wiped it with paper towels. He smiled at Holly. "And *whoever* you are, I am eternally grateful to you for bringing beauty into this gray morning."

Corbett was the perfect smalltown pharmacist: just jovial enough to seem like ordinary folks in spite of being placed in the town's upper social class by virtue of his occupation, enough of a tease to be something of a local character, but with an unmistakable air of competence and probity that made you feel the medicines he compounded would always be safe. Townfolk stopped in just to say hello, not only when they needed something, and his genuine interest in people serve l his commerce. He had been working at the pharmacy for thirty-three years and had been the owner since his father's death twenty-seven years ago.

Handahl was the least threatening of men, yet Jim suddenly felt threatened by him. He wanted to get out of the pharmacy before . . .

Before what?

Before Handahl said the wrong thing, revealed too much.

But what could he reveal?

"I'm Jim's fiancée," Holly said, somewhat to Jim's surprise.

"Congratulations, Jim," Handahl said. "You're a lucky man. Young lady, I just hope you know, the family changed its name from Ironhead, which was more descriptive. Stubborn group." He winked and laughed.

Holly said, "Jim's taking me around town, showing me favorite places. Sentimental journey, I suppose you'd call it."

Frowning at Jim, Handahl said, "Didn't think you ever liked this town well enough to feel sentimental about it."

Jim shrugged. "Attitudes change."

"Glad to hear it." Handahl turned to Holly again. "He started coming in here soon after he moved in with his grandfolks, every Tuesday and Friday when new books and magazines arrived from the distributor in Santa Barbara." He had put aside the Windex. He was arranging counter displays of chewing gum, breath mints, disposable lighters, and pocket combs. "Jim was a real reader then. You still a real reader?"

"Still am," Jim said with growing uneasiness, terrified of what Handahl might say next. Yet for the life of him, he did not know what the man could say that would matter so much.

"Your tastes were kinda narrow, I remember." To Holly: "Used to spend his allowance buying most every science fiction or spook-'em paperback that came in the door. Course, in those days, a two-dollar-a-week allowance went pretty far, if you remember that a book was about forty-five or fifty cents."

Claustrophobia settled over Jim, thick as a heavy shroud. The pharmacy began to seem frighteningly small, crowded with merchandise, and he wanted to get out of there.

It's coming, he thought, with a sudden quickening of anxiety. It's coming.

Handahl said, "I suppose maybe he got his interest in weird fiction from his mom and dad."

Frowning, Holly said, "How's that?"

"I didn't know Jamie, Jim's dad, all that well, but I was only one year behind him at county high school. No offense, Jim, but your dad had some exotic interests— though the way the world's changed, they probably wouldn't seem as exotic now as back in the early fifties."

"Exotic interests?" Holly prodded.

Jim looked around the pharmacy, wondering where it would come from, which route of escape might be blocked and which might remain open. He was swinging between tentative acceptance of Holly's theory and rejection of it, and right now, he was sure she had to be wrong. It wasn't a force inside him. It was entirely a separate being, just as The Friend was. It was an evil alien, just as The Friend was good, and it could go anywhere, come out of anything, at any second, and it *was* coming, he knew it was coming, it wanted to kill them all.

"Well," Handahl said, "when he was a kid, Jamie used to come in here—it was my dad's store then—and buy those old pulp magazines with robots, monsters, and scanty-clad women on the covers. He used to talk a lot about how we'd put men on the moon someday, and everyone thought he was a little strange for that, but I guess he was right after all. Didn't surprise me when I heard he'd given up being an accountant, found a showbiz wife, and was making his living doing a mentalist act."

"Mentalist act?" Holly said, glancing at Jim. "I thought your dad was an accountant, your mom was an actress."

"They were," he said thinly. "That's what they were—before they put together the act."

He had almost forgotten about the act, which surprised him. How could he have forgotten the act? He had all the photographs from the tours, so many of them on his walls; he looked at them every day, yet he'd pretty much forgotten that they had been taken during travels between performances.

It was coming very fast now.

Close. It was very close.

He wanted to warn Holly. He couldn't speak.

Something seemed to have stolen his tongue, locked his jaws.

It was coming.

It didn't want him to warn her. It wanted to take her by surprise.

Arranging the last of the counter displays, Handahl said, "It was a tragedy, what happened to them, all right. Jim, when you first came to town to stay with your grandfolks, you were so withdrawn, nobody could get two words out of you."

Holly was watching Jim rather than Handahl. She seemed to sense that he was in grave distress.

"Second year, after Lena died," Handahl said, "Jim pretty much clammed up altogether, totally mute, like he was never going to talk another word as long as he lived. You remember that, Jim?"

In astonishment, Holly turned to Jim and said, "Your grandmother died the second year you were here, when you were only eleven?"

I told her five years ago, Jim thought. Why did I tell her five years ago when the truth is twenty-four?

It was coming.

He sensed it.

Coming.

The Enemy.

He said, "Excuse me, gotta get some fresh air." He hurried outside and stood by the car, gasping for breath.

Looking back, he discovered that Holly had not followed him. He could see her through a pharmacy window, talking to Handahl.

It was coming.

Holly, don't talk to him, Jim thought. Don't listen to him, get out of there.

It was coming.

Leaning against the car, he thought: the only reason I fear Corbett Handahl is because he knows more about my life in Svenborg than I remember myself.

Lub-dub-DUB.

It was here.

▼ ▲ ▼

Handahl stared curiously after Jim.

Holly said, "I think he's never gotten over what happened to his parents . . . or to Lena."

Handahl nodded. "Who could get over a horrible thing like that? He was such a nice little kid, it broke your heart." Before Holly could ask anything more about Lena, Handahl said, "Are you two moving into the farmhouse?"

"No. Just staying for a couple of days."

"None of my business, really, but it's a shame that land isn't being farmed."

"Well, Jim's not a farmer himself," she said, "and with nobody willing to buy the place—"

"Nobody willing to buy it? Why, young lady, they'd stand twenty deep to buy it if Jim would put it on the market."

She blinked at him.

He went on: "You have a real good artesian well on that property, which means you always have water in a county that's usually short of it." He leaned against the granite counter and folded his arms across his chest. "The way it works—when that big old pond is full up, the weight of all that water puts pressure on the natural wellhead and slows the inflow of new water. But you start pumping it out of there to irrigate crops, and the flow picks up, and the pond is pretty much always full, like the magic pitcher in that old fairytale." He tilted his head and squinted at her. "Jim tell you he couldn't sell it?"

"Well, I assumed—"

"Tell you what," Handahl said, "maybe that man of yours *is* more sentimental than I'd thought. Maybe he doesn't want to sell the farm because it has too many memories for him."

"Maybe," she said. "But there're bad as well as good memories out there."

"You're right about that."

"Like his grandmother dying," she noodged, trying to get him back on that subject. "That was—"

A rattling sound interrupted her. She turned and saw bottles of shampoo, hairspray, vitamins, and cold medicines jiggling on their shelves.

"Earthquake," Handahl said, looking up worriedly at the ceiling, as if he thought it might tumble in on them.

The containers rattled more violently than ever, and Holly knew they were disturbed by something worse than an earthquake. She was being warned not to ask Handahl any more questions.

Lub-dub-DUB, lub-dub-DUB.

The cozy world of the quaint pharmacy started coming apart. The bottles exploded off the shelves, straight at her. She swung away, drew her arms over her head. The containers hammered her, flew past her and pelted Handahl. The humidor, which stood behind the counter, was vibrating. Instinctively Holly dropped to the floor. Even as she went down, the glass door of that case blew outward. Glass shrapnel cut the air where she had been standing. She scrambled toward the exit as glittering shards rained to the floor. Behind her the heavy cash register crashed off the granite counter, missing her by inches, barely sparing her a broken spine. Before the walls could begin to blister and pulse and bring forth an alien form, she reached the door, fled through the newsstand, and went into the street, leaving Handahl in what he no doubt assumed was earthquake rubble.

The tripartite beat was throbbing up from the brick walkway beneath her feet.

She found Jim leaning against the car, shuddering and wheyfaced, with the expression of a man standing on a precipice, peering into a gulf—longing to jump. He did not respond to her when she said his name. He seemed on the verge of surrendering to the dark force that he'd held within—and nurtured—all these years and that now wanted its freedom.

She jerked him away from the car, put her arms around him, held him tight, tighter, repeating his name, expecting the sidewalk to erupt in geysers of brick, expecting to be seized by serrated pincers, tentacles, or cold damp hands of inhuman design. But the triple-thud heartbeat faded, and after a while Jim raised his arms and put them around her.

The Enemy had passed.

But it was only a temporary reprieve.

▼▲▼

Svenborg Memorial Park was adjacent to Tivoli Gardens. The cemetery was separated from the park by a spearpoint wrought-iron fence and a mix of trees—mostly white cedars and spreading California Peppers.

Jim drove slowly along the service road that looped through the graveyard. "Here." He pulled to the side and stopped.

When he got out of the Ford, he felt almost as claustrophobic as he had in the pharmacy, even though he was standing in the open air. The slate-dark sky seemed to press down toward the gray granite monuments, while those rectangles and squares and spires strained up like the knobs of ancient time-stained bones half buried in the earth. In that dreary light, the grass looked gray-green. The trees were gray-green, too, and seemed to loom precariously, as if about to topple on him.

Going around the car to Holly's side, he pointed north. "There."

She took his hand. He was grateful to her for that.

Together they walked to his grandparents' gravesite. It

was on a slight rise in the generally flat cemetery. A single rectangular granite marker served both plots.

Jim's heart was beating hard, and he had difficulty swallowing.

Her name was chiseled into the right-hand side of the monument. LENA LOUISE IRONHEART.

Reluctantly he looked at the dates of her birth and death. She had been fifty-three when she died. And she had been dead twenty-four years.

This must be what it felt like to have been brainwashed, to have had one's memory painted over, false memories air-brushed into the blanks. His past seemed like a fog-bound landscape revealed only by the eerie and inconstant luminescent face of a cloud-shrouded moon. He suddenly could not see back through the years with the same clarity he had enjoyed an hour ago, and he could not trust the reality of what he still did see; clear recollections might prove to be nothing more than tricks of fog and shadow when he was forced to confront them closely.

Disoriented and afraid, he held fast to Holly's hand.

"Why did you lie to me about this, why did you say five years?" she asked gently.

"I didn't lie. At least . . . I didn't realize I was lying." He stared at the granite as if its polished surface was a window into the past, and he struggled to remember. "I can recall waking up one morning and knowing that my grandmother was dead. Five years ago. I was living in the apartment then, down in Irvine." He listened to his own voice as if it belonged to someone else, and the haunted tone of it gave him a chill. "I dressed . . . drove north . . . bought flowers in town . . . then came here. . . ."

After a while, when he did not continue, Holly said, "Do you remember a funeral that day?"

"No."

"Other mourners?"

"No."

"Other flowers on the grave?"

"No. All I remember is . . . kneeling at the headstone

with the flowers I'd brought for her . . . crying . . . I cried
for a long time, couldn't stop crying."

Passing him on the way to other graves, people had
looked at him with sympathy, then with embarrassment as
they had realized the extent of his emotional collapse, then
with uneasiness as they had seen a grief in him so wild that
it made him seem unbalanced. He could even now remember how wild he had felt that day, glaring back at those
who stared at him, wanting nothing more than to claw his
way down into the earth and pull it over him as if it were
a blanket, taking rest in the same hole as his grandmother.
But he could not remember *why* he had felt that way or
why he was beginning to feel that way again.

He looked at the date of her death once more—September 25—and he was too frightened now to cry.

"What is it? Tell me," Holly urged.

"That's when I came with the flowers, the only other
time I've ever come, the day I remember as the day she
died. September twenty-fifth . . . but five years ago, not
twenty-four. It was the nineteenth anniversary of her death
. . . but at the time it seemed to me, and always has, that
she'd only just then died."

They were both silent.

Two large blackbirds wheeled across the somber sky,
shrieking, and disappeared over the treetops.

Finally Holly said, "Could it be, you denied her death,
refused to accept it when it really happened, twenty-four
years ago? Maybe you were only able to accept it nineteen
years later . . . the day you came here with the flowers.
That's why you remember her dying so much more recently than she did. You date her death from the day you
finally accepted it."

He knew at once that she had hit upon the truth, but the
answer did not make him feel better. "But Holly, my God,
that *is* madness."

"No," she said calmly. "It's self-defense, part of the
same defenses you erected to hide so much of that year
when you were ten." She paused, took a deep breath, and
said, "Jim, how did your grandma die?"

"She . . ." He was surprised to realize that he could not recall the cause of Lena Ironheart's death. One more fog-filled blank. "I don't know."

"I think she died in the mill."

He looked away from the tombstone, at Holly. He tensed with alarm, although he did not know why. "In the windmill? How? What happened? How can you know?"

"The dream I told you about. Climbing the mill stairs, looking through the window at the pond below, and seeing another woman's face reflected in the glass, your grand-mother's face."

"It was only a dream."

Holly shook her head. "No, I think it was a memory, your memory, which you projected from your sleep into mine."

His heart fluttered with panic for reasons he could not quite discern. "How can it have been my memory if I don't have it now?"

"You have it."

He frowned. "No. Nothing like that."

"It's locked down in your subconscious, where you can access it only when you're dreaming, but it's there, all right."

If she had told him that the entire cemetery was mounted on a carousel, and that they were slowly spinning around under the bleak gun-metal sky, he would have accepted what she said more easily than he could accept the memory toward which she was leading him. He felt as if he were spinning through light and darkness, light and darkness, fear and rage. . . .

With great effort, he said, "But in your dream . . . I was in the high room when grandma got there."

"Yes."

"And if she died there . . ."

"You witnessed her death."

He shooked his head adamantly. "No. My God, I'd remember that, don't you think?"

"No. I think that's why you needed nineteen years even to admit to yourself that she died. I think you saw her die, and it was such a shock that it threw you into long-term amnesia, which you overlaid with fantasies, always more fantasies."

A breeze stirred, and something crackled around his feet. He was sure it was the bony hands of his grandmother clawing out of the earth to seize him, but when he looked down he saw only withered leaves rattling against one another as they blew across the grass.

With each heartbeat now like a fist slamming into a punching bag, Jim turned away from the grave, eager to get back to the car.

Holly put a hand on his arm. "Wait."

He tore loose of her, almost shoved her away. He glared at her and said, "I want to get out of here."

Undeterred, she grabbed and halted him again. "Jim, where is your grandfather? Where is he buried?"

Jim pointed to the plot beside his grandmother's. "He's there, of course, with her."

Then he saw the left half of the granite monument. He had been so intently focused on the right half, on the impossible date of his grandmother's death, that he had not noticed what was missing from the left side. His grandfather's name was there, as it should be, engraved at the same time that Lena's had been: HENRY JAMES IRONHEART. And the date of his birth. But that was all. The date of his death had never been chiseled into the stone.

The iron sky was pressing lower.

The trees seemed to be leaning closer, arching over him.

Holly said, "Didn't you say he died eight months after Lena?"

His mouth was dry. He could hardly work up enough spit to speak, and the words came out in dry whispers like susurrant bursts of sand blown against desert stone. "What the hell do you want from me? I told you . . . eight months . . . May twenty-fourth of the next year. . . ."

"How did he die?"

"I . . . I don't . . . I don't remember."

"Illness?"

Shut up, shut up!

"I don't know."

"An accident?"

"I . . . just . . . I think . . . I think it was a stroke."

Large parts of the past were mists within a mist. He realized now that he rarely thought about the past. He lived totally in the present. He had never realized there were huge holes in his memories simply because there were so many things he had never before *tried* to remember.

"Weren't you your grandfather's nearest relative?" Holly asked.

"Yes."

"Didn't you attend to the details of his funeral?"

He hesitated, frowning. "I think . . . yes . . ."

"Then did you just forget to have the date of his death added to the headstone?"

He stared at the blank spot in the granite, frantically searching an equally blank spot in his memory, unable to answer her. He felt sick. He wanted to curl up and close his eyes and sleep and never wake up, let something else wake up in his place. . . .

She said, "Or did you bury him somewhere else?"

Across the ashes of the burnt-out sky, the shrieking blackbirds swooped again, slashing calligraphic messages with their wings, their meaning no more decipherable than the elusive memories darting through the deeper grayness of Jim's mind.

▼ ▲ ▼

Holly drove them around the corner to Tivoli Gardens.

When they had left the pharmacy, Jim had wanted to drive to the cemetery, worried about what he would find there but at the same time eager to confront his misremembered past and wrench his recollections into line with the truth. The experience at the gravesite had shaken him, however, and now he was no longer in a rush to find out what additional surprises awaited him. He was content to let Holly drive, and she suspected that he would be happier if she just drove out of town, turned south, and never spoke to him of New Svenborg again.

The park was too small to have a service road. They left the car at the street and walked in.

Holly decided that Tivoli Gardens was even less inviting close up than it had been when glimpsed from a moving car yesterday. The dreary impression it made could not be blamed solely on the overcast sky. The grass was half parched from weeks of summer sun, which could be quite intense in any central California valley. Leggy runners had sprouted unchecked from the rose bushes; the few remaining blooms were faded and dropping petals in the thorny sprawl. The other flowers looked wilted, and the two benches needed painting.

Only the windmill was well maintained. It was a bigger, more imposing mill than the one at the farm, twenty feet higher, with an encircling deck about a third of the way up.

"Why are we here?" she asked.

"Don't ask me. You're the one who wanted to come."

"Don't be thick, babe," she said.

She knew that pushing him was like kicking a package of unstable dynamite, but she had no choice. He was going to blow anyway, sooner or later. Her only hope of survival was to force him to acknowledge that he was The Enemy before that personality seized control of him permanently. She sensed that she was running out of time.

She said, "You're the one who put it on the itinerary yesterday. You said they'd made a movie here once." She was jolted by what she had just said. "Wait a sec—is *this* where you saw Robert Vaughn? Was he in the movie they made here?"

With a bewildered expression that slowly gave way to a frown, Jim turned in place, surveying the small park. At last he headed toward the windmill, and she followed him.

Two historical-marker lecterns flanked the flagstone path in front of the mill door. They were all-weather stone stands. The reading material on the slanted tops was protected behind sheets of Plexiglas in watertight frames. The lectern on the left, to which they stepped first, provided background information about the use of windmills for grain milling, water pumping, and electricity production in the Santa Ynez Valley from the 1800s until well into the twentieth century, followed by a history of the preserved mill in front of them, which was called, rather aptly, the New Svenborg Mill.

That material was as dull as dirt, and Holly turned to the second lectern only because she still had some of the doggedness and appetite for facts that had made her a passable journalist. Her interest was instantly piqued by the title at the top of the second plaque—THE BLACK WIND-MILL: BOOK AND MOVIE.

"Jim, look at this."

He joined her by the second marker.

There was a photograph of the jacket of a young-adult novel—*The Black Windmill* by Arthur J. Willott, and the illustration on it was obviously based on the New Svenborg Mill. Holly read the lectern text with growing astonishment. Willott, a resident of the Santa Ynez Valley—Solvang, not Svenborg—had been a successful author of novels for young adults, turning out fifty-two titles before his death in 1982, at the age of eighty. His most popular and enduring book, by far, had been a fantasy-adventure about a haunted old mill and a boy who discovered that the ghosts were actually aliens from another world and that under the millpond was a spaceship which had been there for ten thousand years.

"No," Jim said softly but with some anger, "no, this makes no sense, this can't be right."

Holly recalled a moment from the dream in which she had been in Lena Ironheart's body, climbing the mill stairs. When she had reached the top, she had found ten-year-old Jim standing with his hands fisted at his sides, and he had turned to her and said, "I'm scared, help me, the walls, the *walls!*" At his feet had been a yellow candle in a blue dish. Until now she'd forgotten that beside the dish lay a hard-cover book in a colorful dustjacket. It was the same dustjacket reproduced on the lectern: *The Black Windmill.*

"No," Jim said again, and he turned away from the plaque. He stared around worriedly at the breeze-ruffled trees.

Holly read on and discovered that twenty-five years ago, the very year that ten-year-old Jim Ironheart had come to town, *The Black Windmill* had been made into a motion picture. The New Svenborg Mill had served as the primary location. The motion-picture company had created a shallow but convincing millpond around it, then paid to restore the land after filming and to establish the current pocket park.

Still turning slowly around, frowning at the trees and shrubs, at the gloom beneath them that the overcast day could not dispel, Jim said, "Something's coming."

Holly could see nothing coming, and she believed that he was just trying to distract her from the plaque. He did not want to accept the implications of the information on it, so he was trying to make her turn away from it with him.

The movie must have been a dog, because Holly had never heard of it. It appeared to have been the kind of production that was big news nowhere but in New Svenborg and, even there, only because it was based on a book by a valley resident. On the historical marker, the last paragraph of copy listed, among other details of the production, the names of the five most important members of the cast. No big box-office draws had appeared in the flick. Of the first four names, she recognized only M. Emmet Walsh, who was a personal favorite of hers. The fifth cast member was a young and then-unknown Robert Vaughn.

She looked up at the looming mill.

"What is happening here?" she said aloud. She lifted her gaze to the dismal sky, then lowered it to the photo of the dustjacket for Willott's book. "What the *hell* is happening here?"

In a voice quaking with fear but also with an eerie note of desire, Jim said, "It's coming!"

She looked where he was staring, and saw a disturbance in the earth at the far end of the small park, as if something was burrowing toward them, pushing up a yard-wide hump of dirt and sod to mark its tunnel, moving fast, straight at them.

She whirled on Jim, grabbed him. "Stop it!"

"It's coming," he said, wide-eyed.

"Jim, it's you, it's only you."

"No . . . not me . . . The Enemy." He sounded half in a trance.

Holly glanced back and saw the thing passing under the concrete walkway, which cracked and heaved up in its wake.

"Jim, damn it!"

He was staring at the approaching killer with horror but also with, she thought, a sort of longing.

One of the park benches was knocked over as the earth bulged then sank under it.

The Enemy was only forty feet from them, coming fast.

She grabbed Jim by the shirt, shook him, tried to make him look at her. "I saw this movie when I was a kid. What was it called, huh? Wasn't it *Invaders from Mars,* something like that, where the aliens open doors in the sand and suck you down?"

She glanced back. It was thirty feet from them.

"Is that what's going to kill us, Jim? Something that opens a door in the sand, sucks us down, something from a movie to give ten-year-old boys nightmares?"

Twenty feet away.

Jim was sweating, shuddering. He seemed to be beyond hearing anything Holly said.

She shouted in his face anyway: "Are you going to kill me *and* yourself, suicide like Larry Kakonis, just stop being strong and put an end to it, let one of your own nightmares pull you in the ground?"

Ten feet.

Eight.

"Jim!"

Six.

Four.

Hearing a monstrous grinding of jaws in the ground under them, she raised her foot, rammed the heel of her shoe down across the front of his shin, as hard as she could, to make him feel it through his sock. Jim cried out in pain as the ground shifted under them, and Holly looked down in horror at the rupturing earth. But the burrowing stopped simultaneously with his sharp cry. The ground didn't open. Nothing erupted from it or sucked them down.

Shaking, Holly stepped back from the ripped sod and cracked earth on which she had been standing.

Jim looked at her, aghast. "It wasn't me. It can't have been."

▼▲▼

Back in the car, Jim slumped in his seat.

Holly folded her arms on the steering wheel, put her forehead on her arms.

He looked out the side window at the park. The giant mole trail was still there. The sidewalk was cracked and tumbled. The bench lay on its side.

He just couldn't believe that the thing beneath the park had been only a figment of his imagination, empowered only by his mind. He had been in control of himself all his life, living a Spartan existence of books and work, with no vices or indulgences. (Except a frighteningly convenient forgetfulness, he thought sourly.) Nothing about Holly's theory was harder for him to accept than that a wild and savage part of him, beyond his conscious control, was the only real danger that they faced.

He was beyond ordinary fear now. He was no longer perspiring or shivering. He was in the grip of a primal terror that left him rigid and Dry-Ice dry.

"It wasn't me," he repeated.

"Yes, it was." Considering that she believed he'd almost killed her, Holly was surprisingly gentle with him. She did not raise her voice; it was softened by a note of great tenderness.

He said, "You're still on this split-personality kick."

"Yes."

"So it was my dark side."

"Yes."

"Embodied in a giant worm or something," he said, trying to hone a sharp edge on his sarcasm, failing. "But you said The Enemy only broke through when I was sleeping, and I wasn't sleeping, so even if I *am* The Enemy, how could I have been that thing in the park?"

"New rules. Subconsciously, you're getting desperate. You're not able to control that personality as easily as before. The closer you're forced to the truth, the more aggressive The Enemy's going to become in order to defend itself."

"If it was me, why wasn't there an alien heartbeat like before?"

"That's always just been a dramatic effect, like the bells ringing before The Friend put in an appearance." She raised her head from her arms and looked at him. "You dropped it because there wasn't time for it. I was reading that plaque, and you wanted to stop me as fast as you could. You needed a distraction. Let me tell you, babe, it was a lulu."

He looked out the window again, toward the windmill and the lectern that held the information about *The Black Windmill.*

Holly put a hand on his shoulder. "You were in a black despair after your parents died. You needed to escape. Evidently a writer named Arthur Willott provided you with a fantasy that fit your needs perfectly. To one extent or another, you've been living in it ever since."

Though he could not admit it to her, he had to admit to himself that he *was* groping toward understanding, that he was on the brink of seeing his past from a new perspective that would make all of the mysterious lines and angles fall into a new and comprehensible shape. If selective amnesia, carefully constructed false memories, and even multiple personalities were not indications of madness but only the hooks he had used to hold on to sanity—as Holly insisted—then what would happen to him if he let go of those hooks? If he dug up the truth about his past, faced the things he had refused to face when he had turned to fantasy as a child, would the truth drive him mad *this* time? What was he hiding from?

"Listen," she said, "the important thing is that you shut it down before it reached us, before it did any harm."

"My shin hurts like hell," he said, wincing.

"Good," she said brightly.

She started the engine.

"Where are we going now?" he asked.

"Where else? The library."

▼ ▲ ▼

Holly parked on Copenhagen Lane in front of the small Victorian house that served as the New Svenborg library.

She was pleased that her hands were not shaking, that her voice was level and calm, and that she had been able to drive from Tivoli Gardens without weaving all over the road. After the incident in the park, she was amazed that her pants were still clean. She had been reduced to raw terror—a pure, intense emotion untainted by any other. Diluted now, it was still with her, and she knew it would remain with her until they were out of these spooky old woods—or dead. But she was determined not to reveal the depth of her fear to Jim, because he had to be worse off than she was. After all, it was *his* life that was turning out to be a collage of flimsy lies. He needed to lean on her.

As she and Jim went up the front walk to the porch (Jim limping), Holly noticed he was studying the lawn around him, as if he thought something might start burrowing toward them.

Better not, she thought, or you'll have *two* bleeding shins.

But as she went through the front door, she wondered if a jolt of pain would work a second time.

In the paneled foyer, a sign announced NONFICTION SECOND FLOOR. An arrow pointed to a staircase on her right.

The foyer funneled into a first-floor hallway off which lay two large rooms. Both were filled with bookshelves. The chamber on the left also contained reading tables with chairs and a large oak desk.

The woman at the desk was a good advertisement for country living: flawless complexion, lustrous chestnut hair, clear hazel eyes. She looked thirty-five but was probably twelve years older.

The nameplate in front of her said ELOISE GLYNN.

Yesterday, when Holly had wanted to come into the library to see if the much-admired Mrs. Glynn was there, Jim had insisted that she would be retired, that she had been "quite old" twenty-five years ago, when in fact she obviously had been fresh out of college and starting her first job.

By comparison with previous discoveries, this was only a minor surprise. Jim hadn't wanted Holly to come into the library yesterday, so he'd simply lied. And from the look on his face now, it was clear that Eloise Glynn's youth was no surprise to him either; he had known, yesterday, that he was not telling the truth, though perhaps he had not understood *why* he was lying.

The librarian did not recognize Jim. Either he had been one of those kids who left little impression or, more likely, he had been telling the truth when he'd said he had not been to the library since he'd left for college eighteen years ago.

Eloise Glynn had the bouncy manner and attitude of a girls' sports coach that Holly remembered from high school. "Willott?" she said in answer to Holly's question. "Oh, yes, we've got a truckload of Willott." She bounced up from her chair. "I can show you right where he's at." She came around her desk, stepping briskly, and led Holly and Jim across the hall to the other large room. "He was local, as I'm sure you know. Died a decade ago, but two-thirds of his books are still in print." She stopped in front of the young-adult section and made a sweeping gesture with one hand to indicate two three-foot shelves of Willott titles. "He was a productive man, Artie Willott, so busy that beavers hung their heads in shame when he walked by."

She grinned at Holly, and it was infectious. Holly grinned back at her. "We're looking for *The Black Windmill.*"

"That's one of his most popular titles, never met a kid

didn't love it." Mrs. Glynn plucked the book off the shelf
almost without looking to see where it was, handed it to
Holly. "This for your kid?"

"Actually for me. I read about it on the plaque over in
Tivoli Gardens."

"I've read the book," Jim said. "But she's curious."

With Jim, Holly returned to the main room and sat at
the table farthest from the desk. With the book between
them, they read the first two chapters.

She kept touching him—his hand, shoulder, knee—gen-
tling him. Somehow she had to hold him together long
enough for him to learn the truth and be healed by it, and
the only glue she could think of was love. She had convinced herself that each small expression of love—each
touch, smile, affectionate look or word—was a bonding
agent that prevented him from shattering completely.

The novel was well and engagingly written. But what it
revealed about Jim Ironheart's life was so astonishing that
Holly began to skim and spot read, whispering passages to
him, urgently seeking the next startling revelation.

The lead character was named Jim, not Ironheart but
Jamison. Jim Jamison lived on a farm that had a pond and
an old windmill. The mill was supposedly haunted, but
after witnessing a number of spooky incidents, Jim discovered that an alien presence, not a spirit, was quartered in
a spacecraft under the pond and was manifesting itself in
the mill. It revealed itself to Jim as a soft light that glowed
within the mill walls. Communication between Jim and the
alien was achieved with the use of two lined, yellow tablets—one for Jim's questions, and one for the alien's answers, which appeared as if by magic. According to the
extraterrestrial, it was a being of pure energy and was on
earth "TO OBSERVE, TO STUDY, TO HELP MAN-
KIND." It referred to itself as THE FRIEND.

Marking her place with a finger, Holly flipped through
the rest of the book to see if The Friend continued to use
the awkward tablets for communication all the way to the
end. It did. In the story on which Jim Ironheart had based
his fantasy, the alien never vocalized.

"Which is why you doubted that *your* alien could vocalize and why you resisted my suggestion that we refuse to play along with the tablet system."

Jim was beyond denial now. He stared at the book with wonder.

His response gave Holly hope for him. In the cemetery, he had been in such distress, his eyes so cold and bleak, that she had begun to doubt if, indeed, he could turn his phenomenal power inward to heal himself. And in the park, for one terrible moment, she had thought that his fragile shell of sanity would crack and spill the yolk of madness. But he had held together, and now his curiosity seemed to be overcoming his fear.

Mrs. Glynn had gone off to work in the stacks. No other patrons had come in to browse.

Holly returned to the story, skim-reading. At the midpoint of the tale, just after Jim Jamison and the alien had their second encounter, the ET explained that it was an entity that lived "IN ALL ASPECTS OF TIME," could perceive the future, and wanted to save the life of a man who was fated to die.

"I'll be damned," Jim said softly.

Without warning, a vision burst in Holly's mind with such force and brilliance that the library vanished for a moment and her inner world became the only reality: she saw herself naked and nailed to a wall in an obscene parody of a crucifix, blood streaming from her hands and feet (a voice whispering: *die, die, die*), and she opened her mouth to scream but, instead of sound, swarms of cockroaches poured out between her lips, and she realized she was already dead *(die, die, die)*, her putrid innards crawling with pests and vermin—

The hateful phantasm flickered off the screen of her mind as suddenly as it had appeared, and she snapped back into the library with a jolt.

"Holly?" Jim was looking at her worriedly.

A part of him had sent the vision to her, no question about that. But the Jim she was looking at now was not the Jim who had done it. The dark child within him, The

Enemy, hate-filled and murderous, was striking at her with a new weapon.

She said, "It's okay. It's all right."

But she didn't feel all right. The vision had left her nauseous and somewhat disoriented.

She had to struggle to refocus on *The Black Windmill*:

The man Jim Jamison had to save, The Friend explained, was a candidate for the United States Presidency, soon to pass through Jim's hometown, where he was going to be assassinated. The alien wanted him to live, instead, because "HE IS GOING TO BE A GREAT STATESMAN AND PEACEMAKER WHO WILL SAVE THE WORLD FROM A GREAT WAR." Because it had to keep its presence on earth a secret, The Friend wanted to work through Jim Jamison to thwart the assassins: "YOU WILL THROW HIM A LIFE LINE, JIM."

The novel did not include an evil alien. The Enemy had been entirely Jim Ironheart's embellishment, an embodiment of his own rage and self-hatred, which he had needed to separate from himself and control.

With a crackle of inner static, another vision burst across her mind-screen, so intense that it blotted out the real world: she was in a coffin, dead but somehow still in possession of all her senses; she could feel worms churning in her *(die, die, die, die)*, could smell the vile stench of her own decaying body, could see her rotted face reflected on the inside of the coffin lid as if it was lit and mirrored. She raised skeletal fists and beat on the lid, heard the blows reverberating into the yards of compacted earth above her—

The library again.

"Holly, for God's sake, what's happening?"

"Nothing."

"Holly?"

"Nothing," she said, sensing that it would be a mistake to admit that The Enemy was rattling her.

She finished skimming *The Black Windmill*:

At the end of the novel, when Jim Jamison had saved the future president, The Friend had subsided into quiescence under the pond, instructing Jim to forget that their encounter had ever taken place, and to remember only that he had saved the politician on his own initiative. If a repressed memory of the alien ever surfaced in Jim's mind, he was told that he would "REMEMBER ME ONLY AS A DREAM, AN ENTITY IN A DREAM YOU ONCE HAD." When the alien light faded out of the wall for the last time, the messages on the tablet vanished, leaving no trace of the contact.

Holly closed the book.

She and Jim sat for a while, staring at the dustjacket.

Around her, thousands of times and places, people and worlds, from Mars to Egypt to Yoknapatawpha County, were closed up in the bindings of books like the shine trapped under the tarnished veneer of a brass lamp. She could almost feel them waiting to dazzle with the first turn of a page, come alive with brilliant colors and pungent odors and delicious aromas, with laughter and sobbing and cries and whispers. Books were packaged dreams.

"Dreams are doorways," she told Jim, "and the story in any novel is a kind of dream. Through Arthur Willott's dream of alien contact and adventure, you found a doorway out of your despair, an escape from a crushing sense of having failed your mother and father."

He had been unrelievedly pale since she had shown him the tablet with The Friend's answers. HE LOVES YOU HOLLY/HE WILL KILL YOU HOLLY. Now some color had returned to his face. His eyes were still ghost-ridden, and worry clung to him like shadows to the night, but he seemed to be feeling his way toward an accommodation with all the lies that were his life.

Which was what frightened The Enemy in him. And made it desperate.

Mrs. Glynn had returned from the stacks. She was working at her desk.

Lowering her voice even further, Holly said to Jim, "But why would you hold yourself to blame for the traffic accident that killed them? And how could any kid that age have such a tremendously heavy sense of responsibility?"

He shook his head. "I don't know."

Remembering what Corbett Handahl had told her, Holly put a hand on Jim's knee and said, "Think, honey. Did the accident happen when they were on the road with this mentalist act of theirs?"

He hesitated, frowned. "Yes . . . on the road."

"You traveled with them, didn't you?"

He nodded.

Recalling the photograph of his mother in a glittery gown, Jim and his father in tuxedos, Holly said, "You were part of the act."

Some of his memories apparently were rising like the rings of light had risen in the pond. The play of emotions in his face could not have been faked; he was genuinely astonished to be moving out of a life of darkness.

Holly felt her own excitement growing with his. She said, "What did you do in the act?"

"It was . . . a form of stage magic. My mom would take objects from people in the audience. My dad would work with me, and we would . . . I would hold the objects and pretend to have psychic impressions, tell the people things about themselves that I couldn't know."

"Pretend?" she asked.

He blinked. "Maybe not. It's so strange . . . how little I remember even when I try."

"It wasn't a trick. You could really do it. That's why your folks put together the act in the first place. You *were* a gifted child."

He ran his fingers down the Bro Dart–protected jacket of *The Black Windmill*. "But . . ."

"But?"

"There's so much I still don't understand. . . ."

"Oh, me too, kiddo. But we're getting closer, and I have to believe that's a good thing."

A shadow, cast from within, stole across his face again.

Not wanting to see him slip back into a darker mood, Holly said, "Come on." She picked up the book and took it to the librarian's desk. Jim followed her.

The energetic Mrs. Glynn was drawing on posterboard

with a rainbow of colored pencils and magic markers. The colorful images were of well-rendered boys and girls dressed as spacemen, spelunkers, sailors, acrobats, and jungle explorers. She had penciled in but not yet colored the message: THIS IS A LIBRARY. KIDS AND ADVENTURERS WELCOME. ALL OTHERS STAY OUT!

"Nice," Holly said sincerely, indicating the poster. "You really put yourself into this job."

"Keeps me out of barrooms," Mrs. Glynn said, with a grin that made it clear why any kid would like her.

Holly said, "My fiancée here has spoken so highly of you. Maybe you don't remember him after twenty-five years."

Mrs. Glynn looked speculatively at Jim.

He said, "I'm Jim Ironheart, Mrs. Glynn."

"Of course I remember you! You were the most special little boy." She got up, leaned across the desk, and insisted on getting a hug from Jim. Releasing him, turning to Holly, she said, "So you're going to be marrying my Jimmy. That's wonderful! A lot of kids have passed through here since I've been running the place, even for a town this small, and I can't pretend I'd remember all of them. But Jimmy was special. He was a very special boy."

Holly heard, again, how Jim had had an insatiable appetite for fantasy fiction, how he'd been so terribly quiet his first year in town, and how he'd been totally mute during his second year, after the sudden death of his grandmother.

Holly seized that opening: "You know, Mrs. Glynn, one of the reasons Jim brought me back here was to see if we might like to live in the farmhouse, at least for a while—"

"It's a nicer town than it looks," Mrs. Glynn said. "You'd be happy here, I'll guarantee it. In fact, let me issue you a couple of library cards!" She sat down and pulled open a desk drawer.

As the librarian withdrew two cards from the drawer and picked up a pen, Holly said, "Well, the thing is . . . there're as many bad memories for him as good, and Lena's death is one of the worst."

COLD FIRE ▲ 385

"And the thing is," Jim picked up, "I was only ten when she died—well, almost eleven—and I guess maybe I made myself forget some of what happened. I'm not too clear on how she died, the details, and I was wondering if you remember . . ."

Holly decided that he might make a decent interviewer after all.

Mrs. Glynn said, "I can't say I recall the details of it. And I guess nobody'll ever know what on earth she was doing out in that old mill in the middle of the night. Henry, your grandpa, said she sometimes went there just to get away from things. It was peaceful and cool, a place she could do a little knitting and sort of meditate. And, of course, in those days it wasn't quite the ruin it's become. Still . . . it seemed odd she'd be out there knitting at two o'clock in the morning."

As the librarian recounted what she could recall of Lena's death, confirming that Holly's dream had really been Jim's memory, Holly was touched by both dread and nausea. What Eloise Glynn did not seem to know, what perhaps no one knew, was that Lena had not been in that mill alone.

Jim had been there, too.

And only Jim had come out of it alive.

Holly glanced at him and saw that he had lost all color in his face again. He was not merely pale now. He was as gray as the sky outside.

Mrs. Glynn asked Holly for her driver's license, to complete the library card, and even though Holly didn't want the card, she produced the license.

The librarian said, "Jim, I think what got you through all that pain and loss, more than anything, was books. You pulled way into yourself, read *all* the time, and I think you used fantasy as sort of a painkiller." She handed Holly the license and library card, and said to her: "Jim was an awfully bright boy. He could get totally *into* a book, it became real for him."

Yeah, Holly thought, did it ever.

"When he first came to town and I heard he'd never been

to a real school before, been educated by his parents, I thought that was just terrible, even if they did have to travel all the time with that nightclub act of theirs—"

Holly recalled the gallery of photographs on Jim's study walls in Laguna Niguel: Miami, Atlantic City, New York, London, Chicago, Las Vegas . . .

"—but they'd actually done a pretty fine job. At least they'd turned him into a booklover, and that served him well later." She turned to Jim. "I suppose you haven't asked your grandpa about Lena's death because you figure it might upset him to talk about it. But I think he's not as fragile as you imagine, and he'd know more about it than anyone, of course." Mrs. Glynn addressed Holly again: "Is something wrong, dear?"

Holly realized she was standing with the blue library card in her hand, statue-still, like one of those waiting-to-be-reanimated people in the worlds within the books upon the shelves within these rooms. For a moment she could not respond to the woman's question.

Jim looked too stunned to pick up the ball this time. His grandfather was alive somewhere. But where?

"No," Holly said, "nothing's wrong. I just realized how late it's getting—"

A shatter of static, a vision: her severed head screaming, her severed hands crawling like spiders across a floor, her decapitated body writhing and twisting in agony; she was dismembered but not dead, impossibly alive, in a thrall of horror beyond endurance—

Holly cleared her throat, blinked at Mrs. Glynn, who was staring at her curiously. "Uh, yeah, quite late. And we're supposed to go see Henry before lunch. It's already ten. I've never met him." She was babbling now, couldn't stop. "I'm really looking forward to it."

Unless he really *did* die over four years ago, like Jim had told her, in which case she wasn't looking forward to it at all. But Mrs. Glynn did not appear to be a spiritualist who would blithely suggest conjuring up the dead for a little chat.

"He's a nice man," Eloise Glynn said. "I know he

must've hated having to move off the farm after his stroke, but he can be thankful it didn't leave him worse than he is. My mother, God rest her soul, had a stroke, left her unable to walk, talk, blind in one eye, and so confused she couldn't always recognize her own children. At least poor Henry has his wits about him, as I understand it. He can talk, and I hear he's the leader of the wheelchair pack over there at Fair Haven."

"Yes," Jim said, sounding as wooden as a talking post, "that's what I hear."

"Fair Haven's such a nice place," Mrs. Glynn said, "it's good of you to keep him there, Jim. It's not a snakepit like so many nursing homes these days."

▼▲▼

The Yellow Pages at a public phone booth provided an address for Fair Haven on the edge of Solvang. Holly drove south and west across the valley.

"I remember he had a stroke," Jim said. "I was in the hospital with him, came up from Orange County, he was in the intensive-care unit. I hadn't . . . hadn't seen him in thirteen years or more."

Holly was surprised by that, and her look generated a hot wave of shame that withered Jim. "You hadn't seen your own grandfather in thirteen years?"

"There was a reason. . . ."

"What?"

He stared at the road ahead for a while, then let out a guttural sound of frustration and disgust. "I don't know. There was a reason, but I can't remember it. Anyway, I came back when he had his stroke, when he was dying in the hospital. And I remember him dead, damn it."

"Clearly remember it?"

"Yes."

She said, "You remember the sight of him dead in the hospital bed, all his monitor lines flat?"

He frowned. "No."

"Remember a doctor telling you he'd passed away?"

"No."

"Remember making arrangements for his burial?"

"No."

"Then what's so clear about this memory of him being dead?"

Jim brooded about that awhile as she whipped the Ford around the curving roads, between gentle hills on which scattered houses stood, past white-fenced horse pastures green as pictures of Kentucky. This part of the valley was lusher than the area around New Svenborg. But the sky had become a more somber gray, with a hint of blue-black in the clouds—bruised.

At last he said, "It isn't clear at all, now that I look close at it. Just a muddy impression . . . not a real memory."

"Are you paying to keep Henry at Fair Haven?"

"No."

"Did you inherit his property?"

"How could I inherit if he's alive?"

"A conservatorship then?"

He was about to deny that, as well, when he suddenly remembered a hearing room, a judge. The testimony of a doctor. His granddad's counsel, appearing on the old man's behalf to testify that Henry was of sound mind and wanted his grandson to manage his property.

"Good heavens, yes," Jim said, shocked that he was capable not only of forgetting events from the distant past but from as recently as four years ago. As Holly swung around a slow-moving farm truck and accelerated along a straight stretch of road, Jim told her what he had just remembered, dim as the recollection was. "How can I do this, live this way? How can I totally rewrite my past when it suits me?"

"Self-defense," she said, as she had said before. She swung in front of the truck. "I'd bet that you remember a tremendous amount of precise detail about your work as a teacher, about your students over the years, colleagues you've taught with—"

It was true. As she spoke, he could flash back, at will, through his years in the classroom, which seemed so vivid that those thousands of days might have occurred concurrently only yesterday.

"—because that life held no threat for you, it was filled with purpose and peace. The only things you forget, push relentlessly down into the deepest wells of memory, are those things having to do with the death of your parents, the death of Lena Ironheart, and your years in New Svenborg. Henry Ironheart is part of that, so you continue to wipe him from your mind."

The sky was contusive.

He saw blackbirds wheeling across the clouds, more of them now than he had seen in the cemetery. Four, six, eight. They seemed to be paralleling the car, following it to Solvang.

Strangely, he recalled the dream with which he had awakened on the morning that he had gone to Portland, saved Billy Jenkins, and met Holly. In the nightmare, a flock of large blackbirds shrieked around him in a turbulent flapping of wings and tore at him with hooked beaks as precision-honed as surgical instruments.

"The worst is yet to come," he said.

"What do you mean?"

"I don't know."

"You mean what we learn at Fair Haven?"

Above, the blackbirds swam through the high, cold currents.

Without having a clue as to what he meant, Jim said, "Something very dark is coming."

COLD FIRE

2

Fair Haven was housed in a large, U-shaped, single-story building outside the town limits of Solvang, with no trace of Danish influence in its architecture. It was strictly off-the-rack design, functional and no prettier than it had to be: cream-tinted stucco, concrete-tile roof, boxy, flat-walled, without detail. But it was freshly painted and in good repair; the hedges were neatly trimmed, the lawn recently mown, and the sidewalks swept clean.

Holly liked the place. She almost wished she lived there, was maybe eighty, watching some TV every day, playing some checkers, with no worry bigger than trying to figure out where she had put her false teeth when she'd taken them out last night.

Inside, the hallways were wide and airy, with yellow vinyl-tile floors. Unlike in many nursing homes, the air was neither tainted with the stench of incontinent patients left unclean by inattentive staff nor with a heavy aerosol deodorant meant to eliminate or mask that stench. The rooms she and Jim passed looked attractive, with big windows opening to valley views or a garden courtyard. Some of the patients lay in their beds or slumped in their wheelchairs with vacant or mournful expressions on their faces, but they were the unfortunate victims of major strokes or late-stage Alzheimer's disease, locked away in memories or torment, largely unconnected to the world around them.

Everyone else appeared happy; and patients' laughter actually could be heard, a rarity in such places.

According to the supervisor on duty at the nurses' station, Henry Ironheart had been a resident of Fair Haven for over four years.

Mrs. Danforth, the administrator into whose office they were shown, was new since Henry Ironheart had been checked in. She had the slightly plump, well-groomed, and inoffensively self-satisfied look of a minister's wife in a prosperous parish. Though she could not understand why they needed her to verify something that Jim knew already, she checked her records and showed them that, indeed, Henry Ironheart's monthly bill was always promptly paid by James Ironheart, of Laguna Niguel, by check.

"I'm glad you've come to visit at last, and I hope you'll have a pleasant time," Mrs. Danforth said, with genteel reproach meant to make him feel guilty for not visiting his grandfather more often while at the same time not directly offending him.

After they left Mrs. Danforth, they stood in a corner of the main hallway, out of the bustle of nurses and wheelchair-bound patients.

"I can't just walk in on him," Jim said adamantly. "Not after all this time. I feel . . . my stomach's clutched up, cramped. Holly, I'm afraid of him."

"Why?"

"I'm not sure." Desperation, bordering on panic, made his eyes so disquieting that she did not want to look into them.

"When you were little, did he ever harm you?"

"I don't think so." He strained to see back through the clouds of memory, then shook his head. "I don't know."

Largely because she was afraid to leave Jim alone, Holly tried to convince him that it would be better for them to meet the old man together.

But he insisted she go first. "Ask him most of what we need to know, so when I come into it, we won't have to stay much longer if we don't want to . . . in case it goes bad, gets awkward, unpleasant. Prepare him for seeing me, Holly. Please."

Because he appeared ready to bolt if she did not play things his way, Holly finally agreed. But watching Jim walk into the courtyard to wait there, she already regretted letting him move out of her sight. If he started to lose control again, if The Enemy began to break through, nobody would be with him to encourage him to resist the onslaught.

A friendly nurse helped Holly find Henry Ironheart when he proved not to be in his room. She pointed him out at a card table in the cheery recreation center, at the other end of which a half-dozen residents were watching a game show on television.

Henry was playing poker with his cronies. Four of them were at a table designed to accommodate wheelchairs, and none wore the standard nursing-home attire of pajamas or sweatsuits. Besides Henry, there were two fragile-looking elderly men—one in slacks and a red polo shirt; the other in slacks, white shirt, and bow tie—and a birdlike woman with snow-white hair, who was in a bright-pink pantsuit. They were halfway through a hotly contested hand, with a substantial pile of blue plastic chips in the pot, and Holly waited to one side, reluctant to interrupt them. Then one by one, exhibiting a flair for drama, they revealed their cards, and with a whoop of delight the woman—Thelma, her name was—raked in her winnings, theatrically gloating as the men goodnaturedly questioned her honesty.

Finally intruding into their banter, Holly introduced herself to Henry Ironheart, though without identifying herself as Jim's fiancée. "I'd like to have a few minutes to talk with you about something if I could."

"Jesus, Henry," the man in the polo shirt said, "she's less than half your age!"

"He always was an old pervert," said the guy in the bow tie.

"Oh, get a life, Stewart," Thelma said, speaking to Mr. Bow Tie. "Henry's a gentleman, and he's never been anything else."

"Jesus, Henry, you're gonna be married for sure before you get out of this room today!"

"Which *you* certainly won't be, George," Thelma continued. "And as far as I'm concerned"—she winked—"if it's Henry, marriage doesn't have to be part of it."

They all roared at that, and Holly said, "I can see I'm going to be aced out of this one."

George said, "Thelma gets what she's after more often than not."

Noticing that Stewart had gathered the cards up and was shuffling the deck, Holly said, "I don't mean to interrupt your game."

"Oh, don't worry yourself," Henry said. His words were slightly slurred as a result of his stroke, but he was quite intelligible. "We'll just take a bathroom break."

"At our age," George said, "if we didn't coordinate our bathroom breaks, there'd never be more than two of us at the card table at any one time!"

The others wheeled away, and Holly pulled up a chair to sit near Henry Ironheart.

He was not the vital-looking, square-faced man she had seen in the photograph on the living-room wall of the farmhouse last evening, and without help Holly might not have recognized him. His stroke had left his right side weak, though not paralyzed, and a lot of the time he held that arm curled against his chest, the way an injured animal might favor a paw. He had lost a lot of weight and was no longer a burly man. His face was not gaunt but nearly so, though his skin had good color; the facial muscles on the right side were unnaturally relaxed, allowing his features to droop a little.

His appearance, combined with the slur that thickened every word he spoke, might have sent Holly into a depression over the inevitable direction of every human life—if not for his eyes, which revealed an unbowed soul. And his conversation, though slowed somewhat by his impediment, was that of a bright and humorous man who would not give the fates the satisfaction of his despair; his treacherous body was to be cursed, if at all, in private.

"I'm a friend of Jim's," she told him.

He made a lopsided "O" of his mouth, which she decided was an expression of surprise. At first he did not seem to know what to say, but then he asked, "How is Jim?"

Deciding to opt for the truth, she said, "Not so good, Henry. He's a very troubled man."

He looked away from her, at the pile of poker chips on the table. "Yes," he said softly.

Holly had half expected him to be a child-abusing monster who had been at least in part responsible for Jim's withdrawal from reality. He seemed anything but that.

"Henry, I wanted to meet you, talk to you, because Jim and I are more than friends. I love him, and he's said that he loves me, and it's my hope that we're going to be together a long, long time."

To her surprise, tears brimmed up and slipped from Henry's eyes, forming bright beads in the soft folds of his aged face.

She said, "I'm sorry, have I upset you?"

"No, no, good lord, no," he said, wiping at his eyes with his left hand. "Excuse me for being an old fool."

"I can tell you're anything but that."

"It's just, I never thought . . . Well, I figured Jim was going to spend his life alone."

"Why did you think that?"

"Well . . ."

He seemed distressed at having to say anything negative about his grandson, completely dispelling her lingering expectations that he would be a tyrant of some kind.

Holly helped him. "He does have a way of keeping people at arm's length. Is that what you mean?"

Nodding, he said, "Even me. I've loved him with all my heart, all these years, and I know he loves me in his way, though he's always had real trouble showing it, and he could *never* say it." As Holly was about to ask him a question, he suddenly shook his head violently and wrenched his distorted face into an expression of anguish so severe that for an instant she thought he was having another stroke. "It's not all him. God knows, it's not." The slur in his voice thickened when he grew more emotional. "I've got to face it—part of the distance between us is me, my fault, the blame I put on him that I never should've."

"Blame?"

"For Lena."

A shadow of fear passed across her heart and induced a quiver of angina-like pain.

She glanced at the window that looked out on a corner of the courtyard. It was not the corner to which Jim had gone. She wondered where he was, how he was . . . *who* he was.

"For Lena? I don't understand," she said, though she was afraid that she did.

"It seems unforgivable to me now, what I did, what I allowed myself to think." He paused, looking not at her but through her now, toward a distant time and place. "But he was just so strange in those days, not the child he had been. Before you can even hope to understand what I did, you have to know that, after Atlanta, he was so very strange, all locked up inside."

Immediately Holly thought of Sam and Emily Newsome, whose lives Jim had saved in an Atlanta convenience store—and Norman Rink, into whom he had pumped eight rounds from a shotgun in a blind rage. But Henry obviously was not talking about a recent event in Atlanta; he was referring to some previous incident, much further in the past.

"You don't know about Atlanta?" he asked, reacting to her evident mystification.

A queer sound chittered through the room, alarming Holly. For an instant she could not identify the noise, then realized it was several birds shrieking the way they did when protecting their nests. No birds were in the room, and she supposed their cries were echoing down the fireplace chimney from the roof. Just birds. Their chatter faded.

She turned to Henry Ironheart again. "Atlanta? No, I guess I don't know about that."

"I didn't think you did. I'd be surprised if he talked

about it, even to you, even if he loves you. He just doesn't talk about it."

"What happened in Atlanta?"

"It was a place called the Dixie Duck—"

"Oh, my God," she whispered. She had *been* there in the dream.

"Then you do know some of it," he said. His eyes were pools of sorrow.

She felt her face crumple in grief, not for Jim's parents, whom she had never known, and not even for Henry, who presumably had loved them, but for Jim. "Oh, my God." And then she couldn't say any more because her words backed up behind her own tears.

Henry reached out to her with one liver-spotted hand, and she took it, held it, waiting until she could speak again.

At the other end of the room, bells were ringing, horns blaring, on the TV game show.

No traffic accident had killed Jim's parents. That story was his way of avoiding a recounting of the terrible truth.

She had known. She had known, and refused to know.

Her latest dream had not been a warning prophecy but another memory that Jim had projected into her mind as they had both slept. She had not been herself in the dream. She had been Jim. Just as she had been Lena in a dream two nights ago. If a mirror had given her a look at her face, she would have seen Jim's countenance instead of her own, as she had seen Lena's in the windmill window. The horror of the blood-drenched restaurant returned to her now in vivid images that she could not block from memory, and she shuddered violently.

She looked toward the window, the courtyard, frightened for him.

"They were performing for a week at a club in Atlanta," Henry said. "They went out for lunch to Jimmy's favorite place, which he remembered from the last time they'd played Atlanta."

Voice trembling, Holly said, "Who was the gunman?"

"Just a nut. That's what made it so hard. No meaning to it. Just a crazy man."

"How many people died?"

"A lot."

"How many, Henry?"

"Twenty-four."

She thought of young Jim Ironheart in that holocaust, scrambling for his life through the shattered bodies of the other customers, the room filled with cries of pain and terror, reeking with the stench of blood and vomit, bile and urine from the slaughtered corpses. She heard the heavy sound of the automatic weapon again, *chuda-chuda-chuda-chuda-chuda-chuda*, and the please-please-please-please of the terrified young waitress. Even as a dream, it had been almost beyond endurance, all the random horror of existence and all the cruelty of humankind boiled down to one devastating experience, a savage ordeal from which full psychological recovery, even for an adult, would take a lifetime of struggle. For a ten-year-old boy, recovery might seem impossible, reality intolerable, denial necessary, and fantasy the only tool with which to hold on to a shred of sanity.

"Jimmy was the only survivor," Henry said. "If the police had gotten there a few seconds later, Jimmy wouldn't have made it either. They shot the man down." Henry's grip tightened slightly on Holly's hand. "They found Jim in a corner, in Jamie's lap, in his daddy's lap, his daddy's arms, all covered with . . . with his daddy's blood."

Holly remembered the end of the dream—

—the crazyman is coming straight at her, knocking tables and chairs aside, so she scrambles away and into a corner, on top of a dead body, and the crazyman is coming closer, closer, raising his gun, she can't bear to look at him the way the waitress looked at him and then died, so she turns her face to the corpse—

—and she remembered awakening with a jolt, gagging in revulsion.

If she'd had time to look into the face of the corpse, she would have seen Jim's father.

The avian shriek shrilled through the recreation room again. It was louder this time. A couple of the ambulatory residents went to the fireplace to see if any birds were caught behind the damper in the chimney.

"In his daddy's blood," Henry repeated softly. It was clear that, even after all these years, the consideration of that moment was intolerably painful to him.

The boy had not only been in his dead father's arms but surely had known that his mother lay dead among the ruins, and that he was orphaned, alone.

▼▲▼

Jim sat on a redwood bench in the Fair Haven courtyard. He was alone.

For a day late in August, when the seasonal drought should have been at its peak, the sky was unusually heavy with unshed moisture, yet it looked like an inverted bowl of ashes. Mixes of late-summer flowers, cascading from planting beds onto the wide concrete walkways, were missing half their color without the enhancement of sunshine. The trees shivered as if chilled by the mild August breeze.

Something was coming. Something bad was coming.

He clung to Holly's theory, told himself that nothing would come unless he caused it to appear. He only had to control himself, and they would all survive.

But he still felt it coming.

Something.

He heard the screaky cries of birds.

▼▲▼

The birds had fallen silent.

After a while Holly let go of Henry Ironheart's hand, took some Kleenex from her purse, blew her nose, and blotted her eyes. When she could speak, she said, "He blames himself for what happened to his mom and dad."

"I know. He always did. He'd never talk about it, but there were ways it showed, how he blamed himself, how he thought he should have saved them."

"But why? He was only ten years old, a small boy. He couldn't have done anything about a grown man with a submachine gun. For God's sake, how could he feel responsible?"

For the moment, the brightness had gone out of Henry's eyes. His poor lopsided face, already pulled down to the right, was pulled down farther by an inexpressible sadness.

At last he said, "I talked to him about it lots of times, took him on my lap and held him and talked about it, like Lena did, too, but he was so much locked in himself, wouldn't open up, wouldn't say why he blamed himself—hated himself."

Holly looked at her watch.

She had left Jim alone too long.

But she could not interrupt Henry Ironheart in the middle of the revelations that she had come to hear.

"I've thought about it all these long years," Henry continued, "and maybe I figured it out a little. But by the time I started to understand, Jim was grown up, and we'd stopped talking about Atlanta so many years ago. To be completely honest, we'd stopped talking about everything by then."

"So what is it you figured out?"

Henry put his weak right hand in his strong left and stared down at the gnarled lumps that his knuckles made within his time-thinned skin. From the old man's attitude, Holly sensed that he was not sure he should reveal what he needed and wanted to reveal.

"I love him, Henry."

He looked up and met her eyes.

She said, "Earlier you said I'd come here to learn about Atlanta because Jim wouldn't talk about it, and in a way you were right. I came to find out a number of things, because he's frozen me out of some areas of his life. He really loves me, Henry, I've no doubt of that, but he's clenched up like a fist, he can't let loose of certain things. If I'm going to marry him, if it's going to come to that, then I've got to know all about him—or we'll never have a chance to be happy. You can't build a life together on mysteries."

"Of course, you're right."

"Tell me why Jim blames himself. It's killing him, Henry. If I have any hope of helping him, I've got to know what you know."

He sighed and made up his mind. "What I've got to say will sound like superstitious nonsense, but it isn't. I'll make it simple and short, 'cause it sounds even screwier if I dress it up at all. My wife, Lena, had a power. Presentiment, you'd call it, I guess. Not that she could see the future, tell you who would win a horserace or where you'd be a year from now or anything like that. But sometimes . . . well, you might invite her to a picnic Sunday a week, and without thinking, she'd say it was going to rain like-for-Noah come Sunday a week. And by God it would. Or some neighbor would be pregnant, and Lena would start referring to the baby as either a 'he' or a 'she,' when there was no way for her to know which it would be—and she was always right."

Holly sensed some of the last pieces of the puzzle falling into place. When Henry gave her a maybe-you-think-I'm-an-old-fool look, she took his bad hand and held it reassuringly.

After studying her a moment, he said, "You've seen something special Jim did, haven't you, something like magic?"

"Yes."

"So you maybe know where this is going."

"Maybe."

The unseen birds began to screech again. The residents at the television set turned the sound off and looked around, trying to identify the source of the squealing.

Holly looked toward the courtyard window. No birds there. But she knew why their cries made the hair stand up on the back of her neck: they were somehow connected with Jim. She remembered the way he had looked up at them in the graveyard and how he had studied them in the sky during the drive to Solvang.

"Jamie, our son, was like his mother," Henry said, as if he did not even hear the birds. "He just sometimes *knew* things. Fact is, he was a little more gifted than Lena. And after Jamie had been married to Cara for a while, when she got pregnant, Lena just one day up and said, 'The baby's going to be special, he's going to be a real mage.' "

"Mage?"

"Country talk for someone with a power, with something special about him the way Lena had something special and Jamie, too. Only she meant *real* special. So Jim was born, and by the time he was four . . . well, he was doing things. Like once he touched my pocket comb, which I'd bought at the local barbershop here, and he started talking about things that were in the shop, though he'd never been in there in his life 'cause he lived with Jamie and Cara down in Los Angeles."

He paused and took a few deep breaths. The slur in his voice had begun to thicken. His right eyelid drooped. Talking seemed to tire him as if it were a physical labor.

A male nurse with a flashlight was at the fireplace. He was squinting up into the flue, past the cracks around the damper, trying to see if any birds were trapped up in there.

The shrieking was now overlaid by the frenzied flapping of wings.

"Jimmy would touch an item and *know* where it'd been, bits and pieces about who owned it. Not everything about them, mind you. He just knew whatever he knew, that was it. Maybe he'd touch a personal item of yours and know the names of your parents, what you did for a living. Then he'd touch a personal item from someone else and only know where they'd gone to school, names of their children. Always different things, he couldn't control it. But he always came up with *something* when he tried."

The nurse, trailed by three patients offering advice, had moved away from the fireplace and was frowning up at the air-conditioning vents. The quarrelsome sound of birds still echoed through the room.

"Let's go out to the courtyard," Holly said, getting up.

"Wait," Henry said with some distress, "let me finish this, let me tell you."

Jim, for God's sake, Holly thought, hold on another minute, just another minute or two.

Reluctantly she sat down.

Henry said, "Jim's specialness was a family secret, like Lena's and Jamie's. We didn't want the world to know, come snooping around, call us freaks and God knows what. But Cara, she always wanted so bad to be in show business. Jamie worked down there at Warner Brothers, which was where'd he'd met her, and he wanted what Cara wanted. They decided they could form an act with Jimmy, call him the boy-wonder mentalist, but nobody would ever suspect he really had a power. They played it as a trick, lots of winking at the audience, daring them to figure out just how it was all done—when all the time it was *real.* They made a good living at it, too, and it was good for them as a family, kept them together every day. They'd been so close before the act, but they were closer than ever after they went on the road. No parents ever loved their child more than they loved Jim—or ever got more love given back to them. They were so close . . . it was impossible to think of them ever being apart."

▼ ▼
▲

Blackbirds streaked across the bleak sky.

Sitting on the redwood bench, Jim stared up at them.

They almost vanished into the eastern clouds, then turned sharply and came back.

For a while they kited overhead.

Those dark, jagged forms against the sere sky composed an image that might have come from some poem by Edgar Allan Poe. As a kid he'd had a passion for Poe and had memorized all of the more macabre pieces of his poetry. Morbidity had its fascination.

▼ ▼
▲

The bird shrieks suddenly stopped. The resulting quiet was a blessing, but Holly was, oddly, more frightened by the cessation of the cries than she had been by the eerie sound of them.

"And the power grew," Henry Ironheart said softly, thickly. He shifted in his wheelchair, and his right side resisted settling into a new position. For the first time he showed some frustration at the limitations of his stroke-altered body. "By the time Jim was six, you could put a penny on the table, and he could move it just by *wanting* it to move, slide it back and forth, make it stand on end. By the time he was eight, he could pitch it in the air, float it there. By the time he was ten, he could do the same with a quarter, a phonograph record, a cake tin. It was the most amazing thing you ever saw."

You should see what he can do at thirty-five, Holly thought.

"They never used any of that in their act," Henry said, "they just stuck to the mentalism, taking personal items from members of the audience, so Jim could tell them things about themselves that just, you know, astonished them. Jamie and Cara figured to include some of his levitations eventually, but they just hadn't figured out how to do it yet without giving the truth away. Then they went to the Dixie Duck down in Atlanta . . . and that was the end of everything."

Not the end of everything. It was the end of one thing, the dark beginning of another.

She realized why the absence of the birds' screams was more disturbing than the sound itself. The cries had been like the hiss of a sparking fuse as it burned down toward an explosive charge. As long as she could hear the sound, the explosion was still preventable.

"And *that's* why I figure Jim thought he should've been able to save them," Henry said. "Because he could do those little things with his mind, float and move things, he thought he should've been able maybe to jam the bullets in that crazy man's gun, freeze the trigger, lock the safety in place, something, something . . ."

"Could he have done that?"

"Yeah, maybe. But he was just a scared little boy. To do those things with pennies and records and cake tins, he had to concentrate. No time to concentrate when the bullets started flying that day."

Holly remembered the murderous sound: *chuda-chuda-chuda-chuda* . . .

"So when we brought him back from Atlanta, he would hardly talk, just a word or two now and then. Wouldn't meet your eyes. Something died in him when Jamie and Cara died, and we could never bring it back again, no matter how much we loved him and how hard we tried. His power died, too. Or seemed to. He never did one of his tricks again, and after a lot of years it was sometimes hard to believe he'd ever done those strange things when he was little."

In spite of his good spirits, Henry Ironheart had looked every one of his eighty years. Now he appeared to be far older, ancient.

He said, "Jimmy was so strange after Atlanta, so unreachable and full of rage . . . sometimes it was possible to love him and still be a little afraid of him. Later, God forgive me, I suspected him of . . ."

"I know," Holly said.

His slack features tightened, and he looked sharply at her.

"Your wife," she said. "Lena. The way she died."

More thickly than usual, he said, "You know so much."

"Too much," she said. "Which is funny. Because all my life I've known too little."

Henry looked down at his culpable hands again. "How could I believe that a boy of ten, even a disturbed boy, could've shoved her down the mill stairs when he loved her so much? Too many years later, I saw that I'd been so damned cruel to him, so unfeeling, so damned stupid. By then, he wouldn't give me the chance to apologize for what I'd done . . . what I'd thought. After he left for college, he never came back. Not once in more than thirteen years, until I had my stroke."

He came back once, Holly thought, nineteen years after Lena's death, to face up to it and put flowers on her grave.

Henry said, "If there was some way I could explain to him, if he'd just give me one chance. . . ."

"He's here now," Holly said, getting up again.

The weight of fear that pulled on the old man's face made him appear even more gaunt than he had been. "Here?"

"He's come to give you that chance," was all that Holly could say. "Do you want me to take you to him?"

▼▲▼

The blackbirds were flocking. Eight of them had gathered now in the sky above, circling.

> *Once upon a midnight dreary,*
> *while I pondered, weak and weary*
> *Over many a quaint and curious volume*
> *of forgotten lore—*
> *While I nodded, nearly napping,*
> *suddenly there came a tapping,*
> *As of some one gently rapping,*
> *rapping at my chamber door.*

To the real birds above, Jim whispered, " 'Quoth the Raven, *Nevermore.*' "

He heard a soft rhythmic creaking, as of a wheel going around and around, and footsteps. When he looked up, he saw Holly pushing his wheelchair-bound grandfather along the walkway toward the bench.

Eighteen years had passed since he had gone away to school, and he had seen Henry only once before in all this time. Initially, there had been a few telephone calls, but soon Jim stopped making those and, eventually, stopped accepting them as well. When letters came, he threw them away unopened. He remembered all of that now—and he was beginning to remember why.

He began to rise. His legs would not support him. He remained on the bench.

▼▲▼

Holly parked the wheelchair facing Jim, then sat beside him. "How you doing?"

Nodding dumbly, he glanced up at the birds circling

against the ashen clouds, rather than face his grandfather.
The old man could not look at Jim, either. He studied
the beds of flowers intently, as if he had been in a great rush
to get outside and have a look at those blooms and nothing
else.

Holly knew this was not going to be easy. She was
sympathetic toward each of the men and wanted to do her
best to bring them together at last.

First, she had to burn away the tangled weeds of one last
lie that Jim had told her and that, consciously if not subconsciously, he had successfully told himself. "There was
no traffic accident, honey," she said, putting a hand on his
knee. "That isn't how it happened."

Jim lowered his eyes from the blackbirds and regarded
her with nervous expectation. She could see that he longed
to know the truth and dreaded hearing it.

"It happened in a restaurant—"

Jim slowly shook his head in denial.

"—down in Atlanta, Georgia—"

He was still shaking his head, but his eyes were widen-
ing.

"—you were with them—"

He stopped denying, and a terrible expression stained
his face.

"—it was called the Dixie Duck," she said.

When the memory exploded back to him with pile-driver
force, he hunched forward on the bench as if he might
vomit, but he did not. He curled his hands into fists on his
knees, and his face tightened into a clench of pain, and he
made small inarticulate sounds that were beyond grief and
horror.

She put an arm around his bent shoulders.

Henry Ironheart looked at her and said, "Oh, my God,"
as he began to realize the extremity of denial to which his
grandson had been driven. "Oh, my God." As Jim's stran-
gled gasps of pain changed into quiet sobs, Henry Ironheart looked at the flowers again, then at his aged hands,
then at his feet on the tilted braces of the wheelchair,
everywhere he could think to look to avoid Jim and Holly,

but at last he met Holly's eyes again. "He had therapy," he said, trying hard to expiate his guilt. "We knew he might need therapy. We took him to a psychiatrist in Santa Barbara. Took him there several times. We did what we could. But the psychiatrist—Hemphill, his name was—he said Jim was all right, he said there was no reason to bring him any more, just after six visits, he said Jim was all right."

Holly said, "What do they ever know? What could Hemphill have done when he didn't really know the boy, didn't love him?"

Henry Ironheart flinched as if she had struck him, though she had not meant her comment to be a condemnation of him.

"No," she said quickly, hoping he would believe her, "what I meant was, there's no mystery why I've gotten farther than Hemphill ever could. It's just because I love him. It's the only thing that ever leads to healing." Stroking Jim's hair, she said, "You couldn't have saved them, baby. You didn't have the power then, not like you have it now. You were lucky to get out alive. Believe me, honey, listen and believe me."

For a moment they sat unspeaking, all of them in pain.

Holly noticed more blackbirds had gathered in the sky. Maybe a dozen of them now. She didn't know how Jim was drawing them there—or why—but she knew that he was, and regarded them with growing dread.

She put a hand over one of Jim's hands, encouraging him to relax it. Though he slowly stopped crying, he kept his fist as tight as a fist of sculpted stone.

To Henry, she said, "Now. This is your chance. Explain why you turned away from him, why you did . . . whatever you did to him."

Clearing his throat, wiping nervously at his mouth with his weak right hand, Henry spoke at first without looking at either of them. "Well . . . you have to know . . . how it was. A few months after he came back from Atlanta, there was this film company in town, shooting a movie—"

"The Black Windmill," Holly said.

"Yeah. He was reading all the time. . . ." Henry stopped,

closed his eyes as if to gather strength. When he opened them, he stared at Jim's bowed head and seemed prepared to meet his eyes if he looked up. "You was reading all the time, going through the library shelf by shelf, and because of the film you read the Willott book. For a while it became . . . hell, I don't know . . . I guess maybe you'd have to say it was an obsession with you, Jim. It was the only thing that brought you out of your shell, talking about that book, so we encouraged you to go watch them shoot the picture. Remember? After a while, you started telling us an alien was in our pond and windmill, just like in the book and movie. At first we thought you was just play-acting."

He paused.

The silence lengthened.

About twenty birds in the sky above.

Circling. Silent.

To Henry, Holly said, "Then it began to worry you."

Henry wiped one shaky hand down his deeply lined face, not so much as if he was trying to scrub away his weariness but as if he was trying to slough off the years and bring that lost time closer. "You spent more and more hours in the mill, Jim. Sometimes you'd be out there all day. And evenings, too. Sometimes we'd get up in the middle of the night to use the john, and we'd see a light out there in the mill, two or three or four o'clock in the morning. And you wouldn't be in your room."

Henry paused more often. He wasn't tired. He just didn't want to dig into this part of the long-buried past.

"If it was the middle of the night, we'd go out there to the mill and bring you in, either me or Lena. And you'd be telling us about The Friend in the mill. You started spooking us, we didn't know what to do . . . so I guess . . . we didn't do anything. Anyway, that night . . . the night she died . . . a storm was coming up—"

Holly recalled the dream:

. . . a fresh wind blows as she hurries along the gravel path . . .

"—and Lena didn't wake me. She went out there by herself and up to the high room—"

. . . she climbs the limestone stairs . . .

"—pretty good thunderstorm, but I used to be able to sleep through anything—"

. . . the heavens flash as she passes the stairwell window, and through the glass she sees an object in the pond below . . .

"—I guess, Jim, you was just doing what we always found you doing out there at night, reading that book by candlelight—"

. . . inhuman sounds from above quicken her heart, and she climbs to the high room, afraid, but also curious and concerned for Jim . . .

"—a crash of thunder finally woke me—"

. . . she reaches the top of the stairs and sees him standing, hands fisted at his sides, a yellow candle in a blue dish on the floor, a book beside the candle . . .

"—I realized Lena was gone, looked out the bedroom window, and saw that dim light in the mill—"

. . . the boy turns to her and cries out, *I'm scared, help me, the walls, the walls!* . . .

"—and I couldn't believe my eyes because the sails of the mill were turning, and even in those days the sails hadn't turned in ten or fifteen years, been frozen up—"

. . . she sees an amber light within the walls, the sour shades of pus and bile; the limestone bulges, and she realizes something is impossibly *alive* in the stone . . .

"—but they were spinning like airplane propellers, so I pulled on my pants, and hurried downstairs—"

. . . with fear but also with perverse excitement, the boy says, *It's coming, and nobody can stop it!* . . .

"—I grabbed a flashlight and ran out into the rain—"

. . . the curve of mortared blocks splits like the spongy membrane of an insect's egg; taking shape from a core of foul muck, where limestone should have been, is the embodiment of the boy's black rage at the world and its injustice, his self-hatred made flesh, his own death-wish given a vicious and brutal form so solid that it is an entity itself, quite separate from him . . .

"—I reached the mill, couldn't believe how those old sails were spinning, whoosh, whoosh, whoosh!—"

Holly's dream had ended there, but her imagination too easily supplied a version of what might have happened thereafter. Horrified at the materialization of The Enemy, stunned that the boy's wild tales of aliens in the mill were true, Lena had stumbled backward and fallen down the winding stone stairs, unable to arrest her fall because there was no handrail at which to grab. Somewhere along the way she broke her neck.

"—went inside the mill . . . found her at the bottom of the stairs all busted up, neck twisted . . . dead."

Henry paused for the first time in a while and swallowed hard. He had not looked at Holly once throughout his account of that stormy night, only at Jim's bowed head. With less of a slur in his voice, as if it were vitally important to him to tell the rest of it as clearly as he could, he said:

"I went up the steps and found you in the high room, Jimmy. Do you remember that? Sitting by the candle, holding the book in your hands so tight it couldn't be taken from you till hours later. You wouldn't speak." The old man's voice quavered now. "God forgive me, but all I could think about was Lena being dead, my dear Lena gone, and you being such a strange child all year, and still strange even at that moment, with your book, refusing to talk to me. I guess . . . I guess I went a little mad right then, for a while. I thought you might've pushed her, Jimmy. I thought you might've been in one of your . . . upsets . . . and maybe you pushed her."

As if it had become too much for him to address himself to his grandson any longer, Henry shifted his gaze to Holly. "That year after Atlanta, he'd been a strange boy . . . almost like a boy we didn't know. He was quiet, like I said, but there was rage in him, too, a fury like no child should ever have. It sometimes scared us. The only time he ever showed it was in his sleep . . . dreaming . . . we'd hear him screeching, and we'd go down the hall to his room . . . and he'd be kicking and punching at the mattress, the pillows, clawing at the sheets, furious, taking it all out on something in his dreams, and we'd have to wake him."

Henry paused and looked away from Holly, down at his bent right hand, which lay half useless in his lap.

Jim's fist, under Holly's hand, remained vise-tight.

"You never struck out at Lena or me, Jimmy, you was a good boy, never gave us that kind of trouble. But in the mill that night, I grabbed you and shook you, Jimmy, tried to make you admit how you'd pushed her down the stairs. There was no excuse for what I did, how I behaved . . . except I was grief-crazy over Jamie and Cara, and now over Lena, everyone dying around me, and there was only you, and you were so strange, so strange and locked up in yourself that you scared me, so I turned on you when I should have been taking you in my arms. Turned on you that night . . . and didn't realize what I'd done until a lot of years later . . . too late."

The birds were in a tighter circle now. Directly overhead.

"Don't," she said softly to Jim. "Please don't."

Until Jim responded, Holly could not know if these revelations were for better or worse. If he had blamed himself for his grandma's death merely because Henry had instilled the guilt in him, then he would get past this. If he blamed himself because Lena had come into the high room, had seen The Enemy materializing from the wall, and had stumbled backward down the stairs in terror, he might still overcome the past. But if The Enemy had torn itself free of the wall and *pushed* her . . .

"I treated you like a murderer for the next six years, until you went away to school," Henry said. "When you was gone . . . well, in time, I started to think about it with a clearer head, and I knew what I'd done. You'd had nowhere to turn for comfort. Your mom and dad were gone, your grandma. You went into town to get books, but you couldn't join in with other kids because that little Zacca bastard, Ned Zacca, he was twice your size and wouldn't ever let you alone. You had no peace except in books. I tried to call you, but you wouldn't take the calls. I wrote but I think you never read the letters."

Jim sat unmoving.

Henry Ironheart shifted his attention to Holly. "He came back at last when I had my stroke. He sat beside me when I was in intensive care. I couldn't speak right, couldn't say what I tried to say, the wrong words kept coming out, making no sense—"

"Aphasia," Holly said. "A result of the stroke."

Henry nodded. "Once, hooked up to all those machines, I tried to tell him what I'd known for almost thirteen years—that he wasn't a killer and that I'd been cruel to him." New tears flooded his eyes. "But when it came out, it wasn't right at all, not what I meant, and he misunderstood it, thought I'd *called* him a murderer and was afraid of him. He left, and now's the first I've seen him since. More than four years."

Jim sat with his head bowed.

Hands fisted.

What had he remembered of that night in the mill, the part that no one but him could know?

Holly got up from the bench, unable to endure the wait for Jim's reaction. She stood there, with no idea where to go. At last she sat down again. She put her hand over his fist, as before.

She looked up.

More birds. Maybe thirty of them now.

"I'm afraid," Jim said, but that was all.

"After that night," Henry said, "he never went into the mill again, never mentioned The Friend or the Willott book. And at first I thought it was good he turned away from that obsession . . . . he seemed less strange. But later I've wondered . . . maybe he lost the one comfort he had."

"I'm afraid to remember," Jim said.

She knew what he meant: only one last long-hidden memory waited to be revealed. Whether his grandmother had died by accident. Or whether The Enemy had killed her. Whether *he*, as The Enemy, had killed her.

Unable to stare at Jim's bowed head a moment longer, unable to bear Henry Ironheart's wretched look of guilt and fragile hope, Holly glanced up at the birds again—and

saw them coming. More than thirty of them now, dark
knives slicing down through the somber sky, still high up
but coming straight toward the courtyard.

"Jim, no!"

Henry looked up.

Jim lifted his face, too, but not to see what was coming.
He *knew* what was coming. He raised his face as if to offer
his eyes to their sharp beaks and frenzied claws.

Holly leaped to her feet, making herself a more promi-
nent target than he was. "Jim, face it, remember it, for
Christ's sake!"

She could hear the shrieks of the swift-descending birds.

"Even if The Enemy did it," she said, pulling Jim's
upturned face to her breast, shielding him, "you can get
past that somehow, you can go on."

Henry Ironheart cried out in shock, and the birds burst
over Holly, flapping and squirming against her, swooping
away, then more of them fluttering and scraping, trying to
get past her and at Jim's face, at his eyes.

They didn't tear at her with either their beaks or talons,
but she did not know how long they would spare her. They
were The Enemy, after all, manifesting itself in a whole
new way, and The Enemy hated her as much as it hated
Jim.

The birds swirled out of the courtyard, back into the sky,
gone like so many leaves in a violent updraft.

Henry Ironheart was frightened but unhurt. "Move
away," she told him.

"No," he said. He reached helplessly for Jim, who would
not reach for him.

When Holly dared look up, she knew that the birds were
not finished. They had only soared to the fringe of the
bearded gray clouds, where another score of them had
collected. Fifty or sixty now, churning and dark, hungry
and quick.

She was aware of people at the windows and sliding
glass doors that opened onto the courtyard. Two nurses
came through the same slider that she had used when
wheeling Henry out to meet Jim.

"Stay back!" she shouted at them, not sure how much danger they might be in.

Jim's rage, while directed at himself and perhaps at God for the very fact of death's existence, might nevertheless spill over and spend itself on the innocent. Her shouted warning must have frightened the nurses, for they retreated and stood in the doorway.

She raised her eyes again. The larger flock was coming.

"Jim," she said urgently, holding his face in both hands, peering into his beautiful blue eyes, icy now with a cold fire of self-hatred, "only one more step, only one more thing to remember." Though their eyes were only a few inches apart, she did not believe that he saw her; he seemed to be looking through her as he had earlier in Tivoli Gardens when the burrowing creature had been racing at them.

The descending flock squealed demonically.

"Jim, damn you, what happened to Lena might not be *worth* suicide!"

The rustle-roar of wings filled the day. She pulled Jim's face against her body, and as before he did not struggle when she shielded him, which gave her hope. She bent her head and closed her eyes as tightly as she could.

They came: silken feathers; smooth cold beaks ticking, prying, searching; claws scrabbling gently, then not so gently, but still not drawing blood; swarming around her almost as if they were hungry rats, swirling, darting, fluttering, squirming along her back and legs, between her thighs, up along her torso, trying to get between his face and her bosom, where they could tear and gouge; batting against her head; and always the shrieking, as shrill as the cries of madwomen in a psychopathic fury, screaming in her ears, wordless demands for blood, blood, blood, and then she felt a sharp pain in her arm as one of the flock ripped open her sleeve and pinched skin with it.

"No!"

They rose and departed again. Holly did not realize they were gone, because her own beating heart and fluttering breath continued to sound like thunderous wings to her. Then she raised her head, opened her eyes, and saw they were spiraling back into the leaden sky to join a storm cloud of other birds, a mass of dark bodies and wings, perhaps two hundred of them high overhead.

She glanced at Henry Ironheart. The birds had drawn blood from one of his hands. Having huddled back into his chair during the attack, he now leaned forward again, reached out with one hand, and called Jim's name pleadingly.

Holly looked down into Jim's eyes as he sat on the bench in front of her, and still he was not there. He was in the mill, most likely, on the night of the storm, looking at his grandmother just one second before the fall, frozen at that moment in time, unable to advance the memory-film one more frame.

The birds were coming.

They were still far away, just under the cloud cover, but there were so many of them now that the thunder of their wings carried a greater distance. Their shrieks were like the voices of the damned.

"Jim, you can take the path that Larry Kakonis took, you can kill yourself. I can't stop you. But if The Enemy doesn't want me anymore, if it wants only you, don't think I'm spared. If you die, Jim, I'm dead, too, as good as dead, I'll do what Larry Kakonis did, I'll kill myself, and I'll rot in hell with you if I can't have you anywhere else!"

The Enemy of countless parts fell upon her as she pulled Jim's face against her a third time. She didn't hide her own face or close her eyes as before, but stood in that maelstrom of wings and beaks and talons. She looked back into scores of small, glistening, pure-black eyes that circled her unblinking, each as wet and deep as the night reflected on the face of the sea, each as merciless and cruel as the universe itself and as anything in the heart of humankind. She knew that, staring into those eyes, she was staring into a part of Jim, his most secret and darkest part, which she could not reach otherwise, and she said his name. She did not shout, did not scream, did not beg or plead, did not vent her anger or fear, but said his name softly, again and again, with all the tenderness that she felt for him, with all the love she had. They battered against her so hard that pinions snapped, opened their hooked beaks and shrieked in her face, plucked threateningly at her clothes and hair, tugging but not ripping, giving her one last chance to flee. They tried to intimidate her with their eyes, the cold and uncaring eyes of beasts of prey, but she was not intimidated, she just kept repeating his name, then the promise that she loved him, over and over until—

—they were gone.

They didn't whirl up into the sky, as before. They vanished. One moment the air was filled with them and their fierce cries—but the next moment they were gone as if they had never been.

Holly held Jim against her for a moment then let him go. He still looked through her more than at her and seemed to be in a trance.

"Jim," Henry Ironheart said beseechingly, still reaching out toward his grandson.

After a hesitation, Jim slid off the bench, onto his knees in front of the old man. He took the withered hand and kissed it.

Without looking up at either Holly or Henry, Jim said, "Grandma saw The Enemy coming out of the wall. First time it happened, first time I saw it, too." His voice sounded far away, as if a part of him were still back in the past, reliving that dreaded moment, grateful that there had not been as much reason to dread it as he had thought. "She saw it, and it frightened her, and she stumbled back into the stairs, tripped, fell . . . ." He pressed his grandfather's hand to his cheek and said, "I didn't kill her."

"I know you didn't, Jim," Henry Ironheart said. "My God, I know you didn't."

The old man looked up at Holly with a thousand questions about birds and enemies and things in walls. But she knew he would have to wait for answers until another day, as she had waited—as Jim had waited, too.

3

During the drive over the mountains and down into Santa Barbara, Jim slumped in his seat, eyes closed. He seemed to have fallen into a deep sleep. She supposed he needed sleep as desperately as any man could need it, for he'd enjoyed almost no real rest in twenty-five years.

She was no longer afraid to let him sleep. She was certain that The Enemy was gone, with The Friend, and that only one personality inhabited his body now. Dreams were no longer doorways.

For the time being, she did not want to return to the mill, even though they had left some gear there. She'd had enough of Svenborg, too, and all it represented in Jim's life. She wanted to hole up in a new place, where neither of them had been, where new beginnings might be forged with no taint of the past.

As she drove through that parched land under the ashen sky, she put the pieces together and studied the resulting picture:

. . . an enormously gifted boy, far more gifted than even he knows, lives through the slaughter in the Dixie Duck, but comes out of the holocaust with a shattered soul. In his desperation to feel good about himself again, he borrows Arthur Willott's fantasy, using his special power to create

The Friend, an embodiment of his most noble aspirations, and The Friend tells him he has a mission in life.

But the boy is so full of despair and rage that The Friend alone is not enough to heal him. He needs a third personality, something into which he can shove all his negative feelings, all the darkness in himself that frightens him. So he creates The Enemy, embellishing Willott's story structure. Alone in the windmill, he has exhilarating conversations with The Friend—and works out his rage through the materialization of The Enemy.

Until, one night, Lena Ironheart walks in at the wrong moment. Frightened, she falls backward. . . .

In shock because of what The Enemy has done, merely by its presence, Jim forces himself to forget the fantasy, both The Friend and Enemy, just as Jim Jamison forgot his alien encounter after saving the life of the future president of the United States. For twenty-five years, he struggles to keep a lid firmly on those fragmented personalities, suppressing both his very best and his very worst qualities, leading a relatively quiet and colorless life because he dares not tap his stronger feelings.

He finds purpose in teaching, which to some extent redeems him—until Larry Kakonis commits suicide. Without purpose anymore, feeling that he has failed Kakonis as he failed his parents and, even more profoundly, his grandmother, he subconsciously longs to live out Jim Jamison's courageous and redeeming adventure, which means freeing The Friend.

But when he frees The Friend, he frees The Enemy as well. And after all these years of being bottled inside him, his rage has only intensified, become blacker and more bitter, utterly inhuman in its intensity. The Enemy is something even more evil now than it was twenty-five years ago, a creature of singularly murderous appearance and temperament. . . .

▼▲▼

So Jim was like any victim of multiple-personality syndrome. Except for one thing. One little thing. He created

nonhuman entities to embody aspects of himself, not other
human identities—and had the power to give them flesh of
their own. He hadn't been like Sally Field playing Sybil,
sixteen people in one body. He had been three beings in
three bodies, and one of them had been a killer.

Holly turned on the car heater. Though it must have
been seventy degrees outside, she was chilled. The heat
from the dashboard vents did nothing to warm her.

▼ ▲ ▼

The clock behind the registration desk showed 1:11 P.M.
when Holly checked them into a Quality motor lodge in
Santa Barbara. While she filled out the form and provided
her credit card to the clerk, Jim continued to sleep in the
Ford.

When she returned with their key, she was able to rouse
him enough to get him out of the car and into their room.
He was in a stupor and went directly to the bed, where he
curled up and once more fell instantly into a deep sleep.

She got diet sodas, ice, and candy bars from the vending-
machine center near the pool.

In the room again, she closed the drapes. She switched
on one lamp and arranged a towel over the shade to soften
the light.

She pulled a chair near the bed and sat down. She drank
diet soda and ate candy while she watched him sleep.

The worst was over. The fantasy had been burned away,
and he had plunged completely into cold reality.

But she did not know what the aftermath would bring.
She had never known him without his delusions, and she
didn't know what he would be like when he had none. She
didn't know if he would be a more optimistic man—or a
darker one. She didn't know if he would still have the same
degree of superhuman powers that he'd had before. He had
summoned those powers from within himself only because
he had needed them to sustain his fantasy and cling to his
precarious sanity; perhaps, now, he would be only as gifted
as he had been before his parents had died—able to levitate

a pie pan, flip a coin with his mind, nothing more. Worst of all, she didn't know if he would still love her.

By dinnertime he was still asleep.

She went out and got more candy bars. Another binge. She *would* end up as plump as her mother if she didn't get control of herself.

He was still asleep at ten o'clock. Eleven. Midnight.

She considered waking him. But she realized that he was in a chrysalis, waiting to be born from his old life into a new one. A caterpillar needed time to turn itself into a butterfly. That was her hope, anyway.

Sometime between midnight and one o'clock in the morning, Holly fell asleep in her chair. She did not dream.

He woke her.

She looked up into his beautiful eyes, which were not cold in the dim light of the towel-draped lamp, but which were still mysterious.

He was leaning over her chair, shaking her gently. "Holly, come on. We've got to go."

Instantly casting off sleep, she sat up. "Go where?"

"Scranton, Pennsylvania."

"Why?"

Grabbing up one of her uneaten candy bars, peeling off the wrapper, biting into it, he said, "Tomorrow afternoon, three-thirty, a reckless schoolbus driver is going to try to beat a train at a crossing. Twenty-six kids are going to die if we're not there first."

Rising from her chair, she said, "You know all that, the whole thing, not just a part of it?"

"Of course," he said around a mouthful of candy bar. He grinned. "I know these things, Holly. I'm psychic, for God's sake."

She grinned right back at him.

"We're going to be something, Holly," he said enthusiastically. "Superman? Why the hell did he waste so much time holding down a job on a newspaper when he could've been doing good?"

In a voice that cracked with relief and with love for him, Holly said, "I always wondered about that."

Jim gave her a chocolaty kiss. "The world hasn't seen anything like us, kid. Of course, you're going to have to learn martial arts, how to handle a gun, a few other things. But you're gonna be good at it, I know you are."

She threw her arms around him and hugged him fiercely, with unadulterated joy.

Purpose.